LOVE IN JAPAN
COMING CLEAN AND FOUR MORE WAYS OF F**KING UP

a collection of novellas

Rule number one for hostesses in Tokyo: Never give a customer your phone number. Rule number two: Never fall in love ...

A collection of novellas about women on the wrong side of the world, by turns bleak and incisively funny. Felicity Savage's *Love in Japan* draws on the author's experience as an expat to paint devastating portraits of five women grappling with a foreign culture and their own desires. From a grotty Tokyo hostess club to the hinterlands of China, *Love in Japan* lays bare the seamy underbelly of the Far East.

Also by Felicity Savage

Novels

Music to Die By
Humility Garden (A Garden of Salt 1)
Delta City (A Garden of Salt 2)
The War in the Waste (EVER Part One)
The Daemon in the Machine (EVER Part Two)
A Trickster in the Ashes (EVER Part Three)

Collections

Black Wedding and Five More Funerals

Ebook Singles

The Immortals
Good Money
Coming Clean
Going Under
The Forest of Sincerity
Walking All the Way
Black Wedding
A Natural Phenomenon
The Kingdom of Darkness
In the Black Desert

Writing as Rose Nanashima

Vampire Democracy

Felicity Savage

LOVE IN JAPAN
COMING CLEAN AND FOUR
MORE WAYS OF F**KING UP

a collection of novellas

KNIGHTS
HILL

FIRST KNIGHTS HILL PUBLISHING EDITION, JUNE 2011

Knights Hill Publishing ISBN: 978-1-937396-04-6

www.knightshillpublishing.com

Printed in the United States of America

CONTENTS

GOOD MONEY

I had psoriasis on my arms, recurrent stomach pain, and occasional trouble focusing my eyes on things in the distance. I was also a heavy smoker. When I lay down to sleep, usually at seven or eight o'clock in the morning, my heartbeat would speed up and random parts of my body would go numb. I had a permanent collection of pimples on my forehead. Sometimes I thought my symptoms were those of a fatal disease. Sometimes I thought they were psychosomatic symptoms of moral decay. At these times I would fantasize about quitting my job in Tokyo. I'd have been giving up the best money I'd ever made – more money than I ever *could* have made at journalism, my first career, or teaching – but all you can do with money is buy stuff, anyway.

Besides, my conscience wasn't the only thing that had its limits. I was twenty-eight. Soon I wouldn't look nineteen even in the dark. Rather than deceive myself, I'd worked the aging process into my agenda. On the day I found my first grey hair I meant to apply for a Lay Missioner position with my favorite charity, the Salesians. For years I'd been sending them the money I didn't spend on other stuff and getting back newsletters filled with photos of happy poor children. These had affected me deeply, and now I was anxious to make a bigger contribution. I wanted to work in the field, preferably in Southeast Asia, teaching school or helping to run a health clinic. In case the Salesians had no use for a Comparative Literature major with a censored resume, I'd also researched several other organizations that seemed to fit the bill: Heal The Nations, the Maryknoll Mission Family, VICS, and VOICA. If worst came to worst I meant to apply to the Peace Corps.

I didn't talk much about my plans to anyone except Dorothy, my coworker and best friend. She sympathized, but that was all, and that was all I expected from her. She was completely different from me, which was why I loved her.

With my twenty-ninth birthday approaching, I used a hand mirror to examine my scalp under the fluorescent light in the bathroom of my tiny apartment in Ikebukuro. On the day I finally found a strand that glittered suspiciously, someone jumped in front of a train somewhere on the Yamanote line, causing half an hour's delay throughout the system. I got to work with six minutes to spare, sweating in the cool September night.

The club was on the seventh floor of a grimy commercial block at the déclassé end of Roppongi. Jimmy the bartender, a handsome Filipino, was running the vacuum cleaner among the low tables and sofas. I went through the velvet curtains in the corner behind the karaoke stage. A fog of deodorant, hairspray, perfume, and cigarette smoke filled the dressing-room. Elena, Irina, Anastasia, and Tania were all talking at once and doing each other's eyebrows. Dorothy had the only chair. A Marlboro was growing ash between her fingers. "Hey girl," she said without moving a muscle.

I started to tell her about my discovery and then interrupted myself to ask, "Where's Natalia?"

Dorothy shrugged. "Halfway to Moscow, I expect." In her accent it was *Ha'fway d' Mawsco, Ah speck,* but that wasn't what

I consciously heard. I'd gotten used to filling out her sentences in my head. "They say she went to the convenience store and never came back."

I laughed. It actually would have been funny if it hadn't been Natalia, who I'd gotten along with to the extent that her Japanese and mine permitted. Sad to say, it was funny, anyway. I tried and failed to find an appropriate tone in which to say, "She told me she wanted to die. I hope she hasn't…"

"Don't be stupid, Ruth. She is not enough brave to kill herself," said Elena irritably. Elena was the only one of our coworkers who spoke English, and she always spat out the words as if they tasted bad. "She want to go home, sure. But she can't escape Japan. She has overstayed visa. It's big trouble if she go to airport. Anyway she has no money."

"I think she run away with boyfriend," said Anastasia in Japanese.

Irina, wriggling into a silver boob tube, said in the same language, "I think she run away with *your* boyfriend." All of us burst into laughter. Outside the curtains, Jimmy turned off the vacuum cleaner, which made our voices sound fragile.

"Good morning, girls!" Mrs Kikuchi parted the curtains, her wig in place, her lipstick just a bit wonky.

"Good morning, Mama-san!"

Dorothy's and my voices added an ironic note to the chorus. Mrs Kikuchi didn't notice. Her greeting wasn't ironic; it was merely an acknowledgement that our day started after dark. She was immune to all forms of humor except slapstick, and Dorothy and I got a good deal of fun out of being sarcastic to her. In many ways, working at Pub Club Paradise was like being back in fourth grade. In other ways, it wasn't like it at all. Mrs Kikuchi's little eyes clocked Natalia's absence, but maybe she'd already dealt with it, because she uttered nothing more except her standard exhortation: "Let's do our very best today, too, girls!"

I whipped off my jeans and sweatshirt and threw on a plain blue shift that was sexy only by virtue of stopping about two inches below my crotch. Clothes shopping in Japan is an exercise in frustration if you're not Japanese. On the rare occasions I found something that fitted right, I bought five of it, so I owned this shift in every color they made, and I wore the same strappy white sandals with all of them. Elena, Irina, Anastasia, and Tania solved the problem by dressing exclusively in Lycra. Dorothy solved it by wearing what she would have worn anyway – vampire slut gear from the gothic boutiques in Harajuku: heavy flounces and frills held together with zips, her long legs always on display in fishnets. She'd changed into her stilettos before I got in, and now she began taking off the denim jacket she wore in the street to hide her cleavage. Her skin was the color of peanut butter where it wasn't covered with black freckles and moles. She had a heavy jaw and a big nose. Her hair was frizzing out of a French braid, currently on its third day, that ended in a silver barrette the shape of a spider. This was a unique accessory made for her by one of her more viable friends. I coveted it, but I could never have worn it, because the spider was Dorothy's trademark. She had one tattooed between her shoulderblades and another on her upper thigh which she would show to customers when she was feeling provocative, first warning them that it was ¥1000 a look, and afterwards making them pay up.

She'd lived in Tokyo for six years, mixing with artists and socking away her salary. She spoke better Japanese than the rest of us put together, and she was the best of us at milking Pub Club Paradise for fun and profit.

"What gets me mad," she said as we filed out of the dressing-room, "is she owed me money."

"Natalia?"

"The same. And I'm not talking peanuts."

We had no customers. We seldom did until nine or ten o'clock on a weeknight. But we opened at eight o'clock and that was that. The plastic candelabra on the walls glowed pink, the disco ball showered sparkles over the karaoke stage, and to a soundtrack of lite rock (if Mrs Kikuchi was in a better mood it would have been country and western) we arrayed ourselves on the sofas to the left of the door. Dorothy unwrapped a chunk of Bubblicious. I pinched one of her Marlboros and lit up. Mrs Kikuchi nailed us with a look of loathing and took it out on Jimmy behind the bar. Jimmy owed Dorothy the price of the digital camera he'd recently sent his mother for her birthday.

"Is there anyone who isn't in debt to you, Dorothy?" I said, meaning: Apart from me. "How much did you lend Natalia?"

"Enough for her to run away on, obviously. All I'm going to say right now is, she'd better not come back. Not without my money, anyway. Fool me once, shame on you; fool me twice, it gonna be the *worse* for you."

"That's not how it goes, Dorothy. Fool me twice, shame on *me*."

"You think I give a fuck how it goes?" Dorothy rolled her eyes to heaven. We both screeched with mirth. Elena, Irina, Anastasia, and Tania regarded us contemptuously. All of them were more or less blonde, with blue eyes and high cheekbones mantled in blusher. Even after you got to know them individually, they could give the impression of being sisters. All of them had grown up in the countryside, which explained why they were so cynical.

The door chimed and in came Mr Himemiya, their manager. He was the Japanese representative of the talent agency that had recruited them in Russia, flown them to Tokyo, and installed them in a shitty little apartment a few stops from Pub Club Paradise on the Oedo line. He'd charged each of them a hefty introduction fee that they had to pay off in full before they started earning their own money. That was the spiel, anyway. The reality was that he banked their salaries and gave them just enough pocketmoney to keep them hanging around for more. That was the theory, anyway. The reality was that they were getting fucked over. No wonder they resented Dorothy and me. Mrs Kikuchi had hired us locally to break up the Hotpants Barbie wallpaper effect. She paid us generously and regularly, and we could quit any time we felt like it. We had the luxury of objectivity where Mr Himemiya was concerned. Dorothy saw him as a funny little pimp. I saw him as symptomatic of a diseased society. But our coworkers saw him as a monster. At every opportunity they frustrated and annoyed him with a glee that suggested the outlines of a Soviet paradigm.

How much Mr Himemiya knew about Soviet paradigms was a good question. He was small and pudgy with a beard that looked glued on, dressed tonight in navy slacks and a tweed blazer with cuffs short enough to flash his Rolex. Mrs Kikuchi seated him at his usual table. A stack of manila envelopes came out of his briefcase and scattered their contents over the oak-look veneer. Without having to be told, Jimmy poured drinks at the bar: noname whiskey on the rocks for Mr Himemiya and oolong tea for Mrs Kikuchi. She was an alcoholic but had most people fooled, including herself. Without waiting to be told no, Dorothy hopped up and seized the tray. While serving Mr Himemiya she spoke to him with a dimply smile.

"Portfolios," she said, sitting down beside me again. "If Natalia's coming back she'd better make it snappy."

"Are they girls from Lithuania?" asked Tania. Her Japanese was heavily accented. "My friend is coming to Tokyo, very soon, she say to me."

"Honey, I can't tell a Lithuanian from a Siberian," said Dorothy. "I *can* tell you none of them were worth taking pictures of. They're probably working their asses off at some grimy old roadhouse in the boondocks, waiting for their chance to get a piece of Tokyo. But they're going to be waiting some time yet. I told him he might as well put those snaps away, 'cause we're not interested."

She probably *had* said it, too. Being Mrs Kikuchi's righthand girl, if only by default, she could get away with that kind of thing.

"This would appear to be where I come in," she whispered to me. One corner of her mouth was twitching with excitement. "I've got a friend who's looking for a job this minute. I'm gonna call her and tell her to haul her ass down here."

I mentally riffled through the roster of Dorothy's friends, who were also my friends to some extent. I couldn't think of anyone who would fit in at Pub Club Paradise, or even want to give it a go.

"You haven't met her. Her name's Kathy. No, wait up, Kirsty? Carly? Something like that. She just got here a couple of months ago. From New York. Speaks Japanese; studied it at school. She's crazy."

"The whole procedure strikes me as unnecessarily complicated," I said. "Why don't you just set Himemiya-san's beard on fire and steal his wallet?"

"Fuck him. He's nothing but a smalltimer. And that Russian guy that hangs around him sometimes? That Vladimir?"

"Vasily."

"He acts like he's a badass, but he's nothing."

The door jangled again and five men came in at once, evidently for no other reason than that they'd ridden up together in the elevator. Three of them were salarymen with inflated expectations written all over their faces. "Welcome to Pub Club Paradise!" we chorused, tailing off as we recognized the other two. Elena and Anastasia jumped up, cooing in Japanese, and steered the salarymen clear of them. They both had all their fingers, they wore double-breasted suits and carried oversized snakeskin wallets instead of briefcases, and they seemed to be in excellent spirits. But that's what you've got to look out for these days. Mrs Kikuchi greeted them with the bonhomie of resignation. This was the first time I'd ever seen Mr Himemiya in a position of having to interact with them. As they bore down on him, he leapt to his feet and started bowing. Barely acknowledging this servile display, they made themselves as comfortable as was possible on the squidgy velour sofas. They spoke to Mrs Kikuchi without turning their heads.

"Now you're looking at a couple of *real* badasses," said Dorothy, languishing against me cozily.

I went downstairs at ten o'clock to stand in front of the convenience store on the first floor of the building. One of the

Chinese girls from Club Mirabelle on the sixth floor was already there, importuning pedestrians. So was Kaito, who worked for Club Vector on the fifth floor. The girls at Vector were all Japanese and they never came outside, probably because it would have been too much trouble for them to get dressed. Nineteen, tanned darker than Dorothy, Kaito was rocking the regulation hustler look: baggy black suit over a white shirt, pale purple hair, and diamond studs in his ears that weren't. He squatted in front of the convenience store talking on his cellphone and talking to his friends when they passed by. Every so often a group of men said hello to him and went upstairs. "Best job in Tokyo," he said to me with the smirk of a high school dropout who'd beat the system, and you could see where he was coming from. But it wasn't always September. Kaito was out here on sticky summer nights, too, and in wet winter weather, manfully defending his two square meters of sidewalk against crazy Chinese girls, drunken salarymen, U.S. servicemen looking for beef, Iranians with territory issues, and men in double-breasted suits who said they wanted everyone to enjoy themselves and acted as if they thought everyone would be better off dead. If Kaito didn't find a different job in the next twelve months or so, I calculated his chances were better than even of winding up – not dead maybe, but just as gone: in hospital or on the run.

The same calculation applied to me, of course. I'd worked at Pub Club Paradise for eight months and at another club called Sweetheart's for nine months before that. While this was a mere fraction of Dorothy's career, it made me a Roppongi veteran. The talent agency girls seldom hung around as long as I already had. In Russian, as Dorothy said, *salvation* was spelled "spouse visa." I was on a three-year working visa courtesy of Howdy English Center, the company I'd quit a year and a half ago. I examined the ends of my hair, trying to find the grey strand again. Could I go back to teaching English? Why not? Well, in the first place I didn't think I could readjust to dealing with people so naïve they thought Roppongi was dangerous. And in the second place, I'd hated teaching English. I'd hated it slightly more, if anything, than I'd hated writing up press releases into articles for the *Concord Bugle-Tribune* of Concord, MA, pop. 18,000 and change.

Dorothy's visa arrangements had been opaque to me for so long that I'd wondered if she was an overstayer. In fact she was married to a Japanese Rasta who lived in Kichijoji producing avant garde CDs. I'd met him once when we came on him playing his bongos in Yoyogi Park. Their marriage had been a nonstarter for obvious reasons: apart from being black, Dorothy couldn't have been further out of step with the Rasta way of life. One of the reasons she'd come to Japan in the first place was because she'd heard this country was free of drugs.

Our local hash dealer, Hassan from Tehran, stopped to talk to Kaito. A claque of white girls passed by and stared at me. Not quite able to bring myself to stare back, I lit a cigarette and gazed at the giant fiberglass ape scrambling up the façade of the building across the street. I made no attempt to hand out flyers, which was what I was supposed to be doing. If anyone wanted to stop and ask for one he was more than welcome.

"Hi. God, aren't you cold?"

The girl who'd spoken was wearing a witchy black dress over black leggings and clodhoppers.

I said, "I'm so damn sexy I don't feel the cold. Besides, smoking warms you up. It's an empirically proven fact."

She wasn't sure whether to laugh or not. She was tall and shapely, with long ragged hair dyed the shade of blonde that's supposed to look dyed. She said, "You must be Ruth. I'm Casey."

This went some way towards alleviating my insecurities. "Go on up," I said. "Seventh floor. No, hang on. Kaito! Can you hold the fort for a few minutes?"

"Sure. My pleasure." Kaito straightened his back and looked capable. He regularly touted for us when we girls were all busy. He got an insignificant kickback for each punter he brought up to Paradise.

"Your Japanese is very good," said Casey in that language, smiling widely enough to make it a backhanded compliment.

"It's my hobby. When I run out of things to say to customers, I ask them to teach me some slang. I doubt I'll ever be as fluent as Dorothy, but she says she learned everything she knows in Roppongi, so maybe there's hope." What was I saying? I didn't give a damn about improving my Japanese any more. "I hear you studied it at college?"

"Yeah, well, I'm still studying it." We stepped into the elevator. Casey added modestly, "I'm at NYU now, but I went to Columbia for undergrad, and they make you take a foreign language. So I got started earlier than most people. I think it's a good policy, actually."

"I think it's a *fabulous* policy," I enthused. "I might even write and suggest it to my old adviser at Harvard." The closest I'd ever been to Harvard was waitressing at a bar in Somerville, but Casey believed me. She looked dumbfounded for an instant before she managed to reboot her smile.

"So what's a nice Ivy League girl like you doing here?" she demanded playfully.

"Researching my autobiography. It's been a long slog, but I've almost decided on the title. What about you, Casey? What brought you here?"

"Well, I've always been fascinated by the culture. I..."

"Really? Any aspect of it in particular? Ikebana? Kendo? Anime? Haiku? Pachinko? Rice production? Robotics research? Automobile manufacturing?"

"It's kind of a long story," she said rapidly, "but I'm working towards my master's in Comparative Literature." I made a note to myself not to say anything more about my own college days. "I'm doing my thesis on Yukio Mishima, so I'm here to research his literary and cultural legacy. I've done interviews with some pretty big names, and now I want to check out the underground scene and listen to the voices of the next generation. I'm also doing some work for this professor my supervisor knows at Waseda University, but that's only a few hours a week, so..." she followed me out of the elevator. I could hear Ricky Martin's *She Bangs* pumping at showtime volume beyond the club door. Casey finished, "I've been partying my brains out, basically. I met Dorothy at Mortuary a couple of weeks ago. Didn't she say? She's been a huge help with my research."

I looked at her again. In addition to multiply pierced ears, etc., etc., she had black fingernails and an ornate crucifix dangling on the bodice of her black dress. This, I thought, was a woman lying to herself in a big way.

"You should tag along with us next time we go out," she said. "It's a hoot."

"So many parties, so little motivation," I said, and pushed the door open a crack, letting the music out. Floodlit on the stage, Irina removed her bra and twirled it. Her breasts didn't jiggle because she'd had them done in Seoul a couple of months ago: she'd gone from B to DD for less than $2000, and so far as she knew none of her internal organs were missing. A small bald man crawled out of the darkness and tried to insert a bill in her G-string. She snatched it, turned around, and wiggled her bottom in his face. He made a desperate attempt to throw his arms around her. She pranced out of reach.

"Go girl!" whooped Casey, startling me. "Yeeeaah! *Shaking* that bootay!"

Irina danced around for another thirty seconds and then darted offstage with her G-string still in place. Mrs Kikuchi believed that girls should preserve an aura of mystery. The clapping died into a buzz of conversation, the music sank to its normal volume, and the darkness reverted to pink dusk, revealing Tania and Anastasia snuggling with a regular in one corner, Elena in another corner speaking English loudly to those first three salarymen, and Dorothy doing her best to entertain a corporate party that took up four tables pushed together. They must have walked past me while I was daydreaming in front of the convenience store. I counted heads and multiplied by ¥700. Mrs Kikuchi caught my eye and rose.

"Do *you* strip?" demanded Casey as I hustled her into the tiny, cluttered office behind the bar. "Not that I'd mind trying it, but Dorothy said…"

11

"She? Stripper?" tittered Mrs Kikuchi, whisking in after us. She spoke in English, a sign that Jimmy had begun serving her out of the jug of oolong tea that was half rice liquor. He pre-mixed this evil stuff for her every night and colluded in her charade of concealing it from us girls. At a loss to know why, we'd speculated that they were sleeping together. I thought Jimmy was probably just trying to help her kill herself faster, but I found it helpful to visualize the other possibility when Mrs Kikuchi came out with things such as, "She can't stripper. She is small body and skinny like Japanese girl. Ugly! Guests don't want see! You can stripper, maybe. You have beautiful chest, elegant like Russian. You native English speaker? You name?" Casey looked flattered. Mrs Kikuchi pushed me with a veiny claw. "Go! Table five! And six, seven, eight!"

"Don't worry," I said over my shoulder. "They don't really expect it of us."

"The stereotype is that we're uptight and headstrong," Dorothy was lecturing her party in Japanese. "You hear people saying this shit, right? American girls! They think the world owes them a living. You set them straight and they smack you upside the head… you've heard this shit, right? Well, let me tell you, it's mostly true."

She let the laughter die down.

"Funny thing is, in America we've got our own stereotypes. For instance, girls from Texas, they're dumb bimbos. *Black* girls from Texas, they're dumb ho's."

The man on her left asked her if she would do it with him.

"You wish," said Dorothy. "But you're out of luck, big guy, 'cause I am an educated woman. Yeah. I got a degree in Japanese male psychology."

This killed them. I sat down and introduced myself to as many of them as I could reach. Some of them just stared cross-eyed at my hand; others shook it. The mirthful silverhaired guy on Dorothy's right lunged across the tables, seized my hand, and planted a wet kiss on it. A roar of laughter proved my initial guess that he was the boss. He had a face like a

12

crumpled paper bag and he was egging on the spotty guy who kept propositioning Dorothy.

"Now this is my girl Ruth from Massachussetts! You all know where Massachussetts is?"

"America," hazarded the spotty one.

"That's right. New England. And you know what we say in America about girls from New England? They're frigid." She used the English word and winked at me. "Means they don't like doing it. But that's not true, is it, Ruth? She's just waiting for the right guy to come along. Aren't you, Ruth?"

"I'm saving myself for marriage," I said. "But here at Pub Club Paradise we're one big happy family. And I consider Dorothy my older sister." That was all I needed to say, given that younger sisters traditionally couldn't get married until their older sisters cleared the way. The men yukked it up, loving me for teasing them about their own culture. They weren't to know that I'd learned everything I knew about Japan while researching my senior thesis, *Independent of the World: Bourgeois Values in 19th Century British Poetry.* "'Others, I am not the first,'" I muttered, scratching my arms, "'Have willed more mischief than they durst.'"

"No one gets married anymore!" the silver-haired boss told me. "And they wonder why the birthrate is declining. Look at these boys. Half of them over thirty and none of them anywhere near settling down. No plans, no dreams, no savings. Why?"

"Could it be because you don't pay them shit?" said Dorothy.

They were the entire staff of a commercial cleaning company, which explained why only the boss and his spotty sidekick were in suits and the others were dressed as if they ought to have been wearing coveralls. One of these was quitting his job in two days' time. They'd come here to give him a rousing sendoff. When I learned this, I felt a surge of pity for them and resolved to put my heart into it for a change.

"What are you doing here?" asked the guy who was quitting in two days' time. His name was Shinji, and he was lying on one of the sofas with his head in my lap. He reached up and fingered my hair. "You're an angel. My angel."

"You're going to have a massive hangover," I said. "Stop fighting it. Pass out. I won't take it personally."

"You're American. You don't have to be doing this."

"The money's pretty good."

"Better than scrubbing bathrooms?"

"Much."

"Better than painting pictures?"

"I should think so."

"Better than teaching English?"

"Yes, unless you teach college or cram school classes, and I hate lecturing people. I don't think it's fair when they can't lecture me back. I don't have a TEFL certificate, anyway."

"Will you teach *me* English?"

"No."

"I want to paint your portrait. I'd pose you at a piano with your head turned... yes, turn your head... like that. Do you play the piano?"

"No."

"I have a piano in my studio. Well, actually, it's not *my* piano, but there was no place else to put it. It's not my studio, either. But I had to have a place of my own. Do you have a place of your own?"

"Yes."

"Good." He blinked up at me and grew almost coherent. "Japan is overcrowded. That's the root of all our problems. No one should have to deal with other people on a daily basis. It's just too confusing."

"Now that you're quitting your job," I said, "you'll be able to paint all day, every day. You won't have to deal with other people if you don't want to. Except for your mom, I guess."

He took my hand and pressed it over his eyes. His eyelashes tickled my fingers. "I shouldn't have quit. It was a mistake. I knew it was a mistake, too, but I went ahead and quit...

that's me all over. It's stupid, but I can't explain it. Not in words, anyway... I have a few good pictures at home. I'd like to show them to you sometime."

"I don't know anything about art."

"All the better. I want you to see... I want you to understand..."

Thinking he'd passed out, I raised my head and caught Dorothy looking at us strangely. At first I thought she was looking at me. Then I realized she was looking at Shinji. I slid my arm under his head, meaning to shift him off my lap, then changed my mind and left my arm there. Dorothy dragged on her Marlboro. At her side, Shinji's boss sprawled with his tie off and his face more crumpled than ever, talking about the company's financial problems. The spotty one lay askew on a spare sofa, out cold. The rest of the company had croawled off home. In the corner of the club most remote from us, Elena and Casey were struggling to keep up a conversation with a couple of salarymen who'd reeled in at midnight, dead set on groping some ass. Elena would probably have worked out a deal with them if Casey had cooperated. Casey was glaring piteously at Dorothy, hoping to be rescued.

"Why don't you just declare personal bankruptcy?" said Dorothy with a yawn. "Put your assets in your wife's or your son's name first, and your creditors will be shit out of luck."

"But it's my son I'm really disappointed in," mumbled the boss, his head dipping towards her shoulder.

Shinji awoke with a convulsion, saying, "Help me." He closed his eyes again, retrieved my hand, and pressed it to his mouth like a child with a teddybear. "I love you. Teach me English."

"Oh, get off me," I said.

"Help me."

I lifted him into a sitting position and steadied him.

"I want to go home." He put his head in his hands. "I *ought* to go home. But I can't."

"Why not?"

"The trains have stopped running for the night."

"I should have fired your worthless ass instead of letting you quit on me," exclaimed his boss. "Off with you. Go whine at someone else."

Dorothy and I laughed mechanically. Shinji fumbled among the glasses on the table, found one that had some melting ice in it, and drank from it. Then he slid his arms around me. His mouth found mine for an instant, cold and lemon-flavored. I punched him in the belly.

"Aren't we all having a lovely time!" Mrs Kikuchi sat down and patted the boss's knee. She'd just finished checking the cash register's roll against its contents. Elena and Casey were giving their salarymen their cellphone numbers. Jimmy was clattering glasses in the sink behind the bar. I kicked the legs of the nearest table with my sandalled toes. Mrs Kikuchi said, "We should do this more often!"

"I'm drunk," said Shinji, falling against the wall as we waited with them for the elevator. He tried to smile at me, then grimaced in horror and made a dash for the stairwell.

"I know I've seen that guy somewhere before. I was thinking it from the minute they came in: yo, I have seen you around the way, brother."

"Recently?" I hopped into my jeans and put on my sneakers.

"No, it can't have been that recent or I'd remember. It was probably at a party or a show or something, like he was there but I didn't actually talk to him. Damn. Well, maybe it'll come to me."

"He's an artist. He said his thing is superrealism, whatever that is. He's quitting his job so he'll have more time to paint."

"Oh yeah? He was cute, wasn't he?"

"If you like the pale and scrawny type."

"Stop lying!" crowed Dorothy. "I've never seen you let a guy kiss you before."

"I didn't *let* him."

"Did too!"

"He wasn't my type! Besides, he was totally wasted."

There was a moment's silence. Dorothy blotted her face with an oil control sheet, examining it in between applications. "So let me get this straight," she said in a distorted voice. "You won't let me fix you up with anyone, you're picky, and that's your decision even though I think you're *too* picky, and then you let a customer stick his tongue in your mouth. And he didn't tip you, either. Did he? I didn't think so. And now you say he wasn't even cute? *Okayyyy*. So what were you acting all sweet to him for? Sometimes I really don't understand you, Ruth."

"Excuse me, guys, is this the, you know, the *meeting?*" Casey edged her head around the door. "My name is Casey and I'm a hostess." She pirouetted into the dressing-room.

"Don't hassle me, girl. We're going for a drink right now." Dorothy tossed her stilettos into her bag. "Ruth," she added as if it were an afterthought, "you want to come?"

I swallowed a lump in my throat. "Sure."

It was three o'clock in the morning. We went down the street to a bar filled with howling expats. We usually went to Den, where Dorothy's countercultural friends congregated, but Den was a basement bar and Dorothy couldn't risk losing her cellphone signal tonight. She was expecting a call from someone who needed a loan yesterday. Casey let her pint sit sweating in front of her while she sang along with the Red Hot Chili Peppers. It turned out that every time a customer offered to buy her a drink she'd been ordering a G&T, so she was already plastered. "You stupid bitch!" Dorothy screeched. "I guess Mama didn't explain the system real well, did she?"

There was no rule against drinking on the job, but there was no profit in it, either. You got paid for as many drinks as you could induce the punters to buy for you, but only if they were oolong tea, which cost nothing.

"Oh hell!" exclaimed Casey. "I hate that shit."

"You get used to it. You might even get to like it. I've been drinking the damn stuff so long I be getting high on it." Dorothy hung Casey's arm around her shoulders. "How high? So high that I could kiss the sky. Up, up…"

"Sounds like Jimmy got the jugs mixed up in the fridge," I muttered.

Casey laughed. Dorothy threw me a smile as genuine as a rubber chicken. I fought my way to the vending machine for a pack of cigarettes. When I came back, Dorothy was scolding Casey for giving her cellphone number to her last customer. I sat on the last three inches of our bench and pretended I wasn't listening.

"Do I look crazy?"

"No, but girl, I *know* you're crazy. That's why I'm telling you for your own good…"

"It wasn't my real number!"

"She did not say that. She *did* say that. OK. Lesson one. No, lesson one was the drink back system. Lesson two. You don't give out your number. And you *definitely* don't give out no fake numbers! What's that guy going to think when he tries to call you and gets some stranger that has that number you wrote down for him? He's going to think, 'Them girls at Paradise ain't nothing but chickenheads. Fuck that shit.' And he's never going to come back."

"Well, exactly! It was the only way he was ever going to leave!" Casey was still laughing. I couldn't help admiring her nerve. She had to know Dorothy and I had both seen her losing her cool less than an hour ago. "Anyway, Elena gave her guy *her* number."

"And Elena's going to go on a date with him, and they're most likely going to end up at a love hotel."

"Doesn't she have a boyfriend? She said…"

"She's got five or six," I said, exaggerating.

"That so-called manager of theirs, he doesn't give them enough money to buy lunch, never mind shit like them Gucci mules she had on tonight. He's an asshole. A *successful* asshole."

"Oh my God, that's terrible," said Casey judiciously.

"It's Russian roulette for girls. But not limited or confined to Russians only. There are three hundred thousand foreigners in sexual slavery in this country," said Dorothy, exaggerating in her turn. "Most of them are Filipinas and Thais. Stuck in the countryside so they can't run away, in debt to their pimps, fucking anyone they're told to fuck. Now you're a Westerner, so you don't have to worry about the pimps, but you do have to worry about the psychos. There was a British girl that got dumped into Tokyo Bay in eighteen pieces last year. Remember her? *That's* why you don't give out your fucking phone number."

I wished I'd given Shinji my number.

Dorothy went to the bathroom. Casey drank some of her wine and said, "I didn't think I was going to have to work tonight. I thought I was just coming down for an interview. I wasn't even planning to take the job. But now I think… I mean, I could use the money, and it's not really difficult, is it? And it's interesting."

"I honestly can't recommend it as a career choice," I said. "In fact, I decided today that I…"

"I'd only be working four nights a week. Mrs Kikuchi said that would be fine. Oh, Mama, Mama, Mama, Mama-san," sang Casey to the tune of the old Clash song, and screwed herself around to face me. I was about to resume my confession when I was distracted by the sight of Dorothy standing near the bar with a finger stuck into her ear, screaming into her phone. Casey touched my arm. "I don't know if I should ask you this, Ruth, but is Dorothy… would she get a fee for recruiting me? It's not like that would influence my decision, of course. But I think I have a right to know."

I tried to influence her decision. "Are you kidding? She'd get a cut of your wages. At least for a couple of months, while you're still only earning four thousand an hour. That's why it would work out to Mrs Kikuchi's advantage to hire you, because Mr Himemiya's girls start at five thousand an hour."

"She said I'd be starting at *three* thousand an hour." Casey frowned. "I thought that seemed like plenty of money."

"Well, actually," I felt compelled to say, "it's pretty much standard for beginners. Dorothy told her you had six months of experience."

"No way! Oh my God, I hope I didn't give myself away!"

"Don't worry. You've got big boobs; much will be forgiven you."

Casey glanced involuntarily at my breasts, what there was of them. "Did Dorothy recruit you, too?"

"No, I just lost my way one night. But I think that's when she thought of it. She's been waiting for another opportunity ever since."

"Well," laughed Casey, "in that case I'll definitely have to take the job! I can't flake out on her after all she's done for me."

I had a sense of failure.

Dorothy came bouncing back to us. "I just made ten thousand yen in two minutes!"

"Every little helps," I said.

"Ten G, baby! Oooh, we're flossin' now!"

She pulled Casey to her feet, waltzed her around, and dipped her, knocking a chair over. People stepped aside and carried on screaming at each other.

"Sure, it's not the Lotto jackpot," she admitted a few minutes later. "But it really does mean a lot to me. You see, Casey, I am a one woman charity organization. I help out anyone that needs it, and if they feel motivated to show me a sign of their gratitude... well, I'm going to say thank you very much. So I make a bit of money for myself now and then. But the problem is I'm softhearted. Spin me a hard luck story and I'm there for you. Sometimes people take advantage of me, you know? That's why I'm not rich yet."

Casey looked amused. I tried unsuccessfully to send Dorothy a telepathic command to shut up. All this nonsense about charity and philanthropy was ruining her image in Casey's eyes. It was my fault she felt compelled to justify herself like this; it was also my fault that Casey wasn't taking her seriously. I seethed with pity for her and hatred of Casey. It seemed like mere justice when I realized that I couldn't possibly make my confession now.

I'd only read one of Yukio Mishima's novels, and I knew about him only what I remembered from its introduction: he'd committed seppuku in 1970 after an attempt to take over the Japanese army that was more of a PR coup than a military coup. Casey believed this had been the inevitable climax of his career. His novels, she said, outlined a program for the regeneration of Japanese society by purging it of Western influences. His legacy would seem to have been nil. I was unsurprised to learn that there existed a Mishima Society *and* a Mishima Club. He was just the kind of figure to have two posthumous cult followings in competition for marginally illustrious members. The ones who lived in Tokyo met up on the first and third Sundays of the month respectively and read things aloud to each other, and on other Sundays there were meetings of other literary societies. Like so many things in life these seemed to be dominated by tyrannical old experts, but they tolerated a sprinkling of lonely young geeks and goths, for whom Casey had lots of questions. Most weeks Dorothy went with her in the role of interpreter. They would call me in the evening from someplace noisy, and I would listen to them passing the phone back and forth until they told me where to come find them.

The second Sunday in October was my birthday. I went to six o'clock Mass at St Ignatio's and then met up with Dorothy and Casey to go to the launch of the winter collection at Virtuesse, a jewellery boutique tucked away behind the Harajuku branch of The Gap. A holdout in this artsy, edgy neighborhood, Virtuesse displayed handmade pieces by an everchanging roster of young designers. Sometimes it even sold something.

People had been drawn to the launch party by the rumor that there would be a more exclusive afterparty. Outside the storefront, which was got up with mouldering logs to look rustic, kids in black clothes stained with white paint and fake blood sat smoking. Bossa nova trickled out into the spookily warm grey afternoon. Inside we located Yoshi, Dorothy's pet silversmith, and some of his newest creations – including a pair of spider earrings with garnet eyes. "He thinks he's got a guaranteed sale there," muttered Dorothy. "But would you look at that? They're hooks. I can't wear those." She turned on him. "Haven't you ever noticed I don't have pierced ears?"

Not bothering to deny that he'd made the earrings for her, Yoshi apologized and started describing how he could rework them into clasps. Dorothy listened with a sphinx's smile. I knew she would end up getting them for free. I spotted some bottles of chardonnay beside the cash register and fetched paper cups of it for myself and Casey. I felt strangely cheerful. Having missed my self-imposed deadline to get out of Tokyo, I felt free to waste as much more time here as I wanted to. Sooner or later something would give me the fresh impetus I needed to complete my application to the Salesian Missioners and email it; or if nothing happened except that more time passed, my decision would be made for me that way. My grey hair had been joined by another one. I was twenty-nine today. My window of opportunity was closing, and soon it would close completely. Time had been dribbling past in enlightening instalments as I waited to see whether anything would happen to make my life unbearable first. I felt pretty confident that nothing *would*, because my life should already have been unbearable – and it wasn't. Under the very conditions I'd postulated as fatal to my emotional equilibrium, I'd found myself becoming more objective about things. My skin had cleared up, too.

"Look at the lovely pictures," I said to Casey, indicating the paintings on the walls. Virtuesse doubled as an art gallery, which gave people another excuse to come and sit outside on the steps. This month's canvases were of monkeys and apes on primary colored backgrounds. "That's what I want for my birthday: an anatomically incorrect orangutan. It's a steal at fifty thousand yen, too. I wonder if shipping and handling is extra?"

"Do you like them? I think they're gross." Casey drifted from showcase to showcase with me trailing after her. She glanced over her shoulder and shuddered theatrically. "I keep thinking I'm going to see that asshole Ivan."

"Vasily."

"He was outside my building again this morning. I waved at him, like 'Hi,' but it was like he didn't hear me. He walked off before I got close enough to talk to him. I just wish I knew what he wanted from me," she sighed disingenuously.

"A green card," I said.

"Ugh!" She laughed. "Dorothy said I should just go ahead and corrupt him."

"Better you than me."

"Well, exactly! That's what I said to her. And I said if he keeps it up I'm going to report him to the police, but she vetoed that right away. She said if I really couldn't handle it she'd talk to Mr Himemiya about him. Of course I can handle it, but it's all right for her; he's not stalking *her!*"

Casey's confidential manner was making me nervous. I glanced between people's heads at Dorothy and Yoshi. An older woman joined them as I watched, causing them both to break into smiles of rapturous happiness. It was impossible for me to tell nowadays by Dorothy's behavior what was on her mind. "Do you know who that is?" I said.

"No. Should I?"

"I think she's the owner. I was introduced to her once. Her name's Chitose Kato." She was in her fifties, swathed in black and laden with jewelry, her hair in an angular bob streaked with purple. Her features gave an impression of supercilious rapacity. I giggled. "Look how Yoshi's sucking up to her."

"He's such a little creep," said Casey. I looked at her. She broke eye contact. "Are you coming with us tonight?"

"Probably not."

"Oh, but you have to! It's your birthday! Dorothy would be absolutely broken up if you didn't come!"

Sometimes I just didn't know whether to take her seriously or not. At these times the only thing to do was to turn away. I turned away and bumped into Shinji.

I looked at the monkeys and apes on the walls and back at him with an appalled surmise.

"I had an exhibition here about six months ago," he said. "I sold a couple of canvases, too. It's a great venue. Amano-san's on track to sell most of these pieces. Have you met her? I'll introduce you to her, shall I? Yes, why not?"

He plunged into the crowd and resurfaced with a thin girl in a stripy sweater.

"This is Noriko Amano. This is my friend Ruth."

"Congratulations. I love your work. I was just saying I'd buy the orangutan if I could afford it."

"It is not orangutan," said Noriko Amano in English. "It is man putting on orangutan clothings. Or it is orangutan, maybe. When he putting on orangutan clothings he become same like orangutan for persons watching him. Therefore the title of exhibition is *Tsukutta Sarutachi,* this mean in English *I Created Monkeys,* or maybe…"

Casey clapped her hands. "Of course! I knew the proportions weren't right for real monkeys. That's a fascinating thesis, Noriko; I'd love to talk with you about it at greater length. I'm sorry, nice to meet you. I'm Casey and this is Ruth. We're not English teachers," she added with a little laugh, having wised up to a few Japanese stereotypes in her months here. "And in case you were wondering, we're not in the army, either!"

I cringed in anticipation of the inevitable sequel. It was all right for Casey, who had an ironclad reason to be in Japan, and would admit without a blush to hostessing, too.

"Come see my pictures?" said Shinji diffidently.

"Oh yes, please," I said, envisaging a train ride to some outflung suburb, a journey of an hour or so that would feel like a journey of a thousand miles.

We went around the back of the boutique, climbed over some recycling bins, squeezed past a BMW, and emerged into an alley between the backs of big shops and the fronts of pocketsized ones. It debouched onto a street that had some of the characteristics of an oldfangled Main Street: a mom 'n' pop electronics store, a bawling fishmonger, grannies toddling along behind shopping trolleys, tempura and sushi takeout joints, and coin-operated kiddie rides outside a pharmacy. After just five minutes Shinji led me around the corner of a greengrocery and down another alley that doglegged between overhanging camellias and deadended in a metal gate. "Well, this is it. I'm pretty sure no one's home."

The tiny yard beyond the gate boasted some scruffy bushes and a planksided sandpit littered with shit. The wooden house had upcurled eaves and iron railings cupping the frosted second floor windows. If the street outside was a relic of bygone days, this was an anachronism. I hadn't known there was any such thing in Harajuku nowadays as a *house,* and I said so.

Shinji entered a code into the electronic burglar alarm. "You wouldn't believe the property taxes. I keep telling her to sell up, but she won't hear of it. I suppose I understand how she feels: after all, she's lived her whole life in this neighborhood."

"What does your father think?"

Shinji hesitated. At last he said, "He doesn't live here."

We entered a genkan that was ankle deep in mostly feminine shoes. A polyphony of yelps shattered the silence. Groaning theatrically, Shinji kicked off his sneakers and yanked open the sliding doors on our right. Three longhaired dachshunds barreled into my legs. I scooped one of them up and hugged it. Untrimmed toenails scratched my wrist. I squeaked in pain and let it slither down. It tumbled out the door after the other two.

"Poor little wretches," Shinji said. "I wish she'd take them with her when she goes out."

"At least you've got a yard. I don't believe in keeping dogs unless you've got a yard."

"I don't believe in keeping dogs. Not while there are people in the world going hungry... including *me.* I'm not joking, Ruth. Unemployment isn't as much fun as I expected it would be. Many's the night I've thought about trying dogfood as a change from instant noodles."

"I expect it's equally rich in essential carcinogens," I said, my eyes filling.

"Oh, shit. You're bleeding."

He hustled me up a wooden staircase to another set of sliding doors. The second floor turned out to be a self-contained apartment. I washed the scratch on my wrist at the sink in the chaotic little kitchen. Shinji insisted on treating it with iodine and a Bandaid out of the rusty medicine cabinet in a bathroom that looked as if it hadn't been scrubbed in years. Although there was a trashcan, he dropped the wrapper of the Bandaid on the floor where it joined a disgusting ring of debris around the drain. I refused his offer of tea or coffee.

We went into the front room. There was a reek of chemicals. Halogen lights glared from skeleton stands. At the far end of the room stood an upright piano surrounded by old furniture. The floorboards in the forepart of the room were splattered with all the colors of the spectrum. Paintings in various stages of incompletion leaned against the walls. A table held artistic paraphernalia: overflowing ashtrays, wine bottles, corkscrews, and empty beer cans. Shinji propelled me towards a stack of unframed canvases with their faces to the wall. "These are the ones I want you to see."

There was no getting out of it. I sat crosslegged on the floor and looked at the pictures. They were all small enough to hold easily. Shinji crouched beside me telling me their titles, and I was so busy trying to translate these into English that I almost forgot to look at the paintings themselves: *R.I.P.*, *Grow Old Along With Me*, *A Little Evolution Theory*, *There's No There Up There*, *Grrr!*, *Everyone's Missing You*, and more. The cumulative effect of the images caught up with me around the fifth canvas, and I started puzzling over them more carefully. In vivid realistic settings, cavorting together with animals or all piled up like clumsy acrobats, appeared what seemed to be a new species of humanoid: pale, unclothed, vulnerably pudgy creatures with moon faces that expressed exuberant happiness. Eyes squeezed shut, they looked almost autistic in their transports. I felt compassion being drawn out of me irresistibly. I also had the feeling that I was missing some piece of information vital to a proper understanding of the paintings. It was like looking at scenes from a lost world. I didn't want to pass judgement on them, but there was no getting out of it. I said, "You're crazy, aren't you? You're completely cracked."

"Some people think they're too cute."

"They're adorable. I'd be concerned, if anything, that you're relying too heavily on manga techniques."

"I think so, too. So I've been experimenting with some more conceptual stuff. This one's called *Friends Everywhere*." He dragged me over to one of the big canvases leaning face out against the wall. "It's different, isn't it?"

I was glad I hadn't asked him when it was going to be finished. What I had thought a patterned background waiting for a picture was a mosaic in shades of red. The motif was a blobby creature that looked vaguely like the humanoids from his other paintings. I said, "Frankly, it looks like a tank full of acid. All your little pudgy guys have fallen in and they're melting."

"I know." He grinned. "It's shit, isn't it? But I got a deal on a lot of red and I had to use it up somehow."

He was no taller than me, looselimbed and angular in his jeans and ragged black sweatshirt. The bones in his thin wrists looked like bits of machinery. When he lay on top of me I felt comfortable and safe. He kissed my nose and said, "You might want to reconsider this. I'm broke. I'm unemployed – albeit by choice – and I'm living here on sufferance. I haven't contributed to the housekeeping in two months. I can't even afford new canvases. I'm not a good prospect."

I said, "I haven't considered you as a prospect for anything. I thought I was never going to see you again, so I've been trying not to think about you."

"I've been thinking about *you*."

"You could have come back to the club."

"No, I couldn't. What if I'd run into my… my old boss?"

"He hasn't been back, either."

"Oh."

"Oh, I see," I exclaimed. "You think that because I'm a hostess I'm going to expect you to give me money or buy me things. Don't worry. Money bores me stiff." I was about to tell him it bored me so much nowadays that I gave as much as possible of mine away, but thought better of it.

"Money bores me, too," Shinji said earnestly. "I hate thinking about it, and I have to think about it all the time. Or rather I have to think about getting it, and that's even more boring. In fact, I think poverty might be the most boring thing in the world. Apart from being rich, that is," he added, straining for a lighter note.

"I think you might be right." But his poverty was interesting to *me*. "Is your mother angry with you for quitting your job? Is that why she doesn't give you any money? Or are you too proud to ask for any?"

"I hardly ever talk to her these days. I thought I had it all worked out and then it all went wrong. I guess that teaches me to go against my better instincts." He looked so distraught that I kissed him. Both of us were still wearing all our clothes. His bed was a nest of futons, quilts, and blankets so soft and deep as to deter much movement. He played with my hair, arranging it around my face, and kissed the bits of my shoulders that my sweater left exposed. I nuzzled his neck and kneaded his ribs. I'd never had an experience remotely like this before. In some ways it was like being a child again. In other ways it was even better. Several years of broken nights catching up with me, I nestled my head in the crook of his shoulder and was actually drifting off when I felt my right nipple being teased between his fingers. I yawned. He rolled on his back, laughing. "It's OK, Ruth. Go to sleep. This is only what I've been dreaming about for the last month and a half. Go to sleep."

"Oh God," I giggled.

"No, really; you go to sleep and I'll draw you. I've been wanting to do that, too. I'd rather not make love to you here, anyway, come to think of it."

"Actually," I said, "I probably ought to tell you…"

My cellphone rang. Relieved to be interrupted, I wrangled it out of my back pocket, but by the time my thumb reached the connect button it had gone to voicemail. Dorothy. I remembered that it was my birthday, and was about to call her back when the front door downstairs opened. Shinji put his hand on my thigh.

"Shinji? Are you home? The dogs are outside. Did you let them out?"

"Oh, shit. Yeah! I let them out! Sorry!" He rolled to his feet. "Stay where you are, Ruth, *please*. I'll be back in a minute."

"As a matter of fact, I'd better get my skates on." I explained about the afterparty. "It's at Den. Do you want to come?"

"I'm broke," he reminded me.

"Oh, what a bore. Oh, it *is* boring, isn't it? Listen, I'll stand you a drink or two. You can pay me back when you're famous."

"I can't take your money."

"You'll lose your creative edge if you just stay home every night."

"I wish you'd stay here with me. I know what kind of party it's going to be. I know who's going to be there."

"All my friends, for starters."

"And all mine."

A horrible possibility occurred to me. I stared at him, wondering if I was being stupid, and saw the same possibility entering his mind on the provocation of my gaze.

"OK, I've changed my mind," he said. "I'm going to take you up on that offer. I accept free drinks on principle, actually. I…" He pulled me into his arms. We shared a hug so tender I almost changed my mind about going. Then we went down the stairs without any pretence of stealth. The sliding doors on the first floor stood open. I saw, framed as if in a snapshot, the figures of Chitose Kato – black robe pushed up to her elbows, a dachshund clasped to her bosom – and a stocky young man with bright orange hair, magisterially asprawl on the sofa, glaring at Shinji like a crab in a tank.

We put on our shoes in a resounding silence.

My brain started working again when we reached the street. It seemed bizarre to me that Shinji's mother should be the owner of Virtuesse. On the other hand, why shouldn't she be? Everyone's mother is something. Why hadn't he mentioned it? Well, he might think I'd already known it. He might even think I'd come to Virtuesse today *because* I'd known it. I didn't think I should let him get away with a misconception like that… but how could I blame him for it if it existed, as it probably did exist, only in my mind? And what did it really matter, anyway? I scratched my arms distractedly. Shinji shook the last cigarette out of his pack of Salems. I whipped out my lighter and lit it for him, which made him smile – it was a hostess thing to do. "Who was that guy?" I said.

"Her new boyfriend."

"Seems like a big fan of yours."

"He hates my guts. I think he's actually jealous of me. I don't give a damn about him either way, and that bugs him." Shinji walked with his head down, smoking furiously. "Why *should* I give a damn? It's her house; she has the right to bring home whoever she likes. I'm up on the second floor. I'm not even costing her… well, I'm not costing her much. So why do the two of them glare at me like that? What have I done?"

"Maybe they were just surprised to see me."

"I guess they were."

"Is she coming to the afterparty, do you think?"

"Of course. She'd never disappoint her fans." He grabbed my hand and swung it. "Tell you what. Let's show our faces, do the networking thing, and then take off and go for a walk or something. There's some stuff I have to say to you that I couldn't say back there."

I squeezed his fingers understandingly, since I hadn't a clue what he was talking about.

We took a taxi to West Azabu, the expensive end of Roppongi. I paid. On the corner of the block was a trattoria; halfway down the street was a chichi florist's shop; 伝, said a tiny blue sign on the forecourt wall of an apartment building. We went downstairs between collages of posters for gothic bands. Kaz, who ran the place with his schizophrenic wife Shinobu, stood at the promotions desk talking to a girl in whiteface. His smile revealed neat little fangs. "Long time no see, Ruth. How're you doing, man?" He looked from Shinji to me and back again.

"I'm going to model for him," I explained brightly. Kaz intimidated me. He had a skull and crossbones floating in the center of each pupil.

"Where's Kato-san, then? I've got the honorable guest's seat reserved for her."

"Traditionally in Japan, you see," said Shinji, "the honorable guest is given the seat farthest from the door, so they can't escape."

Kaz laughed, exposing a tongue as blue as a hyacinth.

Carpeted in black pile and furnished with black sofas on which most of the crowd from Virtuesse had already reassembled, the basement had a homey feel. We stashed our shoes in the freestanding cubbyholes in front of the door. There were turntables at the far end of the room, but no one was manning them. The ambient noise came from something in Kaz's CD collection. Dorothy would know what it was; so would the regulars gathered around her at the bar. Their outfits ranged from the mildly gothic to the terrifying. As well as being walking encyclopedias of punk, industrial, trance, and darkwave, they were all brimful of wacky occult lore and romantic notions about the infinitude of human potential. I felt tenderly protective of them. Reminding Shinji that I'd promised to buy him a drink, I inserted myself into their midst.

"There she is! Where'd you fucking go to back there?" squealed Dorothy, shooting her arm around my waist. "And why haven't you been answering your phone? I've been worrying, you know that? I can't but worry about this girl," she addressed the others. "She doesn't drink, she doesn't have sex, she doesn't even eat chocolate. All she does do is smoke cigarettes."

"I do so drink," I laughed, leaning across her to the bar. "Could I have a glass of white wine and a Corona, please?"

Shinobu smiled at me and cut a lime into eighths. She looked anaemically pretty in skintight black lace with a plunging neckline. Arabesques of gold and silver paint framed her eyes. She believed she was the reincarnation of an Egyptian princess, and everyone gave her the benefit of the doubt. When I tried to pay her, she pushed the notes back into my hand. "It's on the house."

"Happy birthday to you," everyone started singing. "Happy birthday to you! Happy birthday, dear Ruth…"

Dorothy wound her arms around my neck and planted a kiss on my mouth. "Bet you thought I forgot."

"*I'd* forgotten."

"Been having your mind took off it?"

"Dorothy, I know you don't like him, but…"

"I never said that, girl! It's against my principles to date customers, that's all. But as long as he's not some kind of axe murderer, I want you to be happy with him." She held me off by the shoulders. If I hadn't known better I would have thought her eyes were shiny. "Seeing the two of you together, it makes me feel all warm and gooshy inside. Like love *do* exist, that kind of feeling."

I clinked my glass of wine against the glasses and bottles crowding towards me. Shinji drank off half of his Corona at a gulp. Dorothy locked her arms around me from behind and went on talking to a producer who went by the pseudonym of Ryohaku. He was short and jolly with tattoos covering his upper body and little red horns on his shaved skull. Dorothy rested her chin on my shoulder and giggled into my hair at things he said. With a certain sense of relief I saw Casey coming across the room and wriggled free. We met in the shadow of the metal grapevine that climbed up the end of the bar to the ceiling.

"So what's the deal with that guy?" she gushed. "Are you *together?* You'd make such a cute couple!"

"Well…"

"OK, let me rephrase that. Have you slept with him?"

"No."

"Are you going to?"

"I don't know."

Casey laughed with me. "It's impossible to tell with Japanese guys, isn't it? You think they like you, so you start liking them, and then they flip the script and start acting all weird on you. It's like they're attracted to us but they're afraid of us."

"Casey, how many stalkers do you *have?*"

"I'm talking about my regulars," she said with a roll of her eyes. "Oh my God, would you look what just walked in. Can you say *revealing?*"

I looked. It was Chitose Kato with her boyfriend at heel. They must have left the house in Harajuku soon after we did. The boyfriend's hair flamed in the murky lighting. Chitose was talking to Shinji. All I could see of her outfit was the straps crisscrossing her naked back.

"Call the fashion police," said Casey. "You'd think she'd be embarrassed at her age."

"I think it's vintage Gaultier," I said, but my attention was on Shinji, who was hunched over his crossed knees, his hands squeezed into his armpits. I didn't think it was normal for anyone to be that intimidated by his mother. When he tried to catch my eye I looked away, embarrassed for him. Kaz was talking into a mic at the far end of the basement. I dragged Casey in among the people who were drifting towards him. We sat down on the floor just as Kaz ceded the mic to a sweet-faced tyke who cleared his throat and introduced himself as the author of *To Wake The Wind*, the slender hardback he was holding up.

"It's a poet," I whispered, shaking with suppressed laughter. "How classic, how archetypal, how goddamn quixotic. I love this country."

"What a yummy morsel," said Casey intensely. "I'd like to put him in my pocket and take him home."

"To Fuji House?" This was the gaijin house where Casey was staying among transient English teachers and Chinese vocational school students. "He'd die of culture shock."

Casey made a face as if pleased with my remark. "My neighbors are such a hoot! I get home from work at four in the morning and they're playing mahjongg with the door wide open and the TV on. Like it's a fucking undergrad dorm or something."

"Like wounded wildflowers," declaimed the poet.

"When dusk comes calling
We must stand
In a field
And repent like wounded wildflowers.
Even if our hearts are cold
And our limbs frozen stiff
We must fold our hands at our breasts
And repent everything."

After five minutes or so, when I realized the poem wasn't going to end any time soon, I turned to Casey with a comment on my lips. It died there. She had her fists pressed to her mouth and her eyes squeezed shut. Tears were trickling over her knuckles.

A patter of applause broke my paralysis. I picked my way out of the audience. Shinji moved towards me and pushed my cardigan into my hands.

"I honestly didn't think she'd come before midnight. Let's go before the situation deteriorates any further."

"I'm worried about Casey," I said.

"Why, doesn't she like poetry?"

"I don't know. She never says what she really thinks about anything," I blurted.

A tall Japanese man in black was tiptoeing through the audience towards Casey. She looked up, then covered her face with her hands. He squatted in the place I'd vacated, put his arm around her, and patted her shoulder.

"Looks like she's going to be all right," Shinji said. "Come on, *please*."

"But who's that guy?"

"Riku," said Dorothy, appearing at my side.

"Riku? Who's Riku?" He had a heavy build and a curtain of black hair to his shoulders. His prominent nose and chin gave him a knightly appearance. "I'd remember if I'd ever seen *him* before."

"You probably haven't. That girl's deep. She keeps her business to herself. You ain't noticed? All I know is that's her friend that she got to know on the Internet before she came here. He turned her onto those Mishima meetings. She was crazy about him to start with; then she cooled off, but now it's on again, seemingly. He doesn't go out much. Spends most of his time at home writing poems about death. You tell *me* what she sees in him," said Dorothy, and proceeded to tell me. "She thinks that that melancholy voodoo is the authentic shit."

"I kind of figured," I said, swallowing.

"Did you?" Dorothy cocked her head and then pinched my cheek affectionately. "Well, it *shouldn't* come as a surprise, should it? Everyone wants love, and most of us have to sell our souls to get even just a little piece of it. You ain't no exception, honey," she added inexplicably, smiling at Shinji. "You got nothing to be ashamed of."

"I was going to tell her, anyway," Shinji said. "Shit, how I hate being broke!"

"What does that have to do with anything?" I said.

"Oh, it's got everything to do with it," said Dorothy. "Everything."

Shinji took my arm and tugged me aside, ducking his head to Dorothy.

"I'm living with Kato-san," he began, glancing down the length of the bar. I glanced, too, and saw her watching us over her flute of champagne. Her boyfriend was talking to Ryohaku and his gothic sidekicks as if they were old friends. I felt cold inside: a mountainous, insuperable coldness that cleared my head. "I've been living with her for about a year. I mean... I always do things the wrong way around. I..."

"Can I look in your wallet?"

"All I have is yours," he said, hooking a battered billfold out of his pocket.

"Ugh. Your hair," I said, giggling at his driver's license. "You look like a Beatle."

"Lennon, not Harrison, I hope."

"How do you read this?"

"Endo. If you read the kanji separately you get 'distant wisteria.' A lot of Japanese names have embedded meanings that have nothing to do with anything."

"You ought to sign your paintings more legibly," I said, handing the wallet back.

"Just for your information, I thought you knew. By the time I figured out you *didn't* know, it was too late to tell you without... it was too late to tell you." Looking away from me, he said, "Happy birthday, anyway."

I completed my application to the Salesians and emailed it. With the coming of November the weather got cold and dry. My psoriasis spread to my neck. I started wearing turtlenecks to work, and Mrs Kikuchi chewed me out for dressing too casually. I told her to fuck off. Further undermining her authority, Vasily came to the club the next night to see me. He was a balding young bodybuilder in name brand athletic gear and a gold pinky ring. He implied that since I was American I could walk into a better job than this any day of the week. Dorothy left the customers she was entertaining and sat down with us. "You're just pissed because Elena quit, aren't you?" she said, punching him in the Fila logo.

Ten days ago Elena had accused a customer of making fun of her, walked out of the club, and vanished into thin air. She hadn't been replaced yet. Mrs Kikuchi said the Japanese economy was in a bad way. Dorothy said she was still looking for the right girl. While Tokyo sometimes seemed to be teeming with broke foreigners, there was a dearth of pretty English speakers willing to work for ¥2000 an hour.

"It's not my fault you and Himemiya-san don't pay your girls like you should be paying them," Dorothy said to Vasily. "It's not Ruth's fault, either, so why are you taking it out on her?"

"She don't earn her keep."

"Nor do you, bigmouth."

I rolled my eyes and lit a cigarette.

"By the way," said Dorothy, standing up again, "I was real glad to hear you've given up following Casey home, following her on the train and shit. She doesn't scare that easily, as I guess you realized *now;* so it was a waste of your time. And I don't like to see you wasting your time, Vladimir Ivanovich, because time is money, as we say in America."

"We have this same saying in Russian. I think we invent it," snapped Vasily to her back. "She's some bitch, eh? Why you hang with a bitch like that?"

"You can tell Mr Himemiya I'll be quitting soon enough," I said, picturing a village schoolhouse in Cambodia shaded by banyan trees. "In the meantime, there's no reason we have to see any more of each other, is there?"

"Casey tell me she and Dorothy are lesbians. She say they are fucking together."

"I'll have to try that one next time a customer asks me for my phone number."

"It is a man's fantasy. Unfortunately, I don't believe," said Vasily bitterly, glancing across the club at Casey. "What I want with her, anyway? She is a nice girl and very beautiful, but she sleep with a knife under her pillow and everything she say is lies."

I retreated into the dressing-room to spray my hands with the antibiotic cleansing stuff I kept in my bag. Presently Dorothy came in and said, "Smile, for fuck's sake. The wind's gonna change and you'll be stuck that way."

"I love you, Dorothy," I said, throwing my arms around her. It was impossible for me to repeat Vasily's words, which was probably just as well, as they proved nothing.

"I love you, too, girl." She patted my back and then squatted to get her foundation compact out of her bag. "Them motherfuckers are testing me. They've been going on too long with their sheisty ways; they forgot that if it don't come from the heart it don't mean shit. But they'll learn. Have you heard from Shinji recently?"

"No."

"Why don't you call him yourself?"

"Oh, I know where you're coming from," I said, "but what's the point unless his situation has changed? And if it does change and he doesn't get in touch with *me,* I'll know he wasn't really interested in the first place."

"I told you what he said to me that night."

"Yes. But if he really wanted to be with me, he'd be trying to make some changes, wouldn't he?"

"It's not like they're still sleeping together, Ruth. She might still have a soft spot for him, but she's doing the nasty with that low-IQ clown, what's he called."

"Kimura-kun."

"I've seen them together a few times since. She can't keep her hands off him. I heard she's paying *his* rent, too. He lives in Okubo."

"That doesn't change the fact that Shinji's living off her."

"She's supporting him because she thinks he's a genius. And speaking for myself, I admire that. When I'm her age I want to be using my money in the same way. But hell, I also hear what you're saying, girl. You wanna get with me, you gotta have money," sang Dorothy softly, putting her makeup away. "No scrubs, no scrubs. Come on, back to work. Keep your head up."

On Monday, which was our day off, Shinji called me and told me he'd sold a painting – *There's No There Up There,* which had been one of my favorites – for ¥200,000.

In a state of euphoria mingled with distress, I called Dorothy and reported the news. "It seems like persistence *does* pay off! It's such an affirmation of his talent, Dorothy! I can hardly believe it."

"Well, well," said Dorothy amusedly. "Maybe Kato-san isn't the only person that thinks he's a genius. There's people that decide to invest in an unknown artist, you know. It's like investing in cheap stocks. Some people made a fortune buying what's he called, that guy that painted soup cans, in 1960, just like that guy who made a fortune buying Microsoft in 1980."

"Andy Warhol."

"Uh uh, I think it was Warren. Warren something. Anyway, art is a good investment as long as you're not looking for overnight returns."

"Dorothy, have you ever tried playing the stock market? I bet you'd be a natural."

"I wish I could," she said sombrely. "The fact is, I'm hurting a little bit right now. There's people asking me for money and I don't have shit to give them."

I sat down on my bed. "Is there anything I can do?"

"You can come with me tonight to meet this girl that lives at Casey's place. Bring Shinji, too. Make him spread that windfall around some before he spends it all on canvases and shit."

"Well," I said. "That's what I wanted to talk to you about, actually. I'm not sure… He did imply he wanted to see me, but I'm not sure I can… I'm not sure I *should*."

Dorothy was silent. I could hear the crowd roaring on the Malice Mizer concert video that she'd adopted as sonic wallpaper for her apartment. "You're kidding me," she said at last.

"It's an impossible situation," I tried to explain. "I couldn't go out with him because he was living with Kato-san, not because he was broke. If I go out with him now, it'll look as if all it took to make me sacrifice my principles was a little bit of money."

"You think two hundred thousand yen is a little bit of money?"

"All right, *some* money. He said he wanted to celebrate at a nice restaurant or something. I know he'd want to treat me, and if I didn't let him he'd be offended, but how can I let him…"

"I do *not* understand you, Ruth. What's the poor guy got to do? Win the fucking lottery? He sold one of his pictures for you, and the way artists are, as you very well know, that must have felt to him like selling a baby, and that still isn't good enough?" Dorothy blew out an exasperated breath. "God-damn! OK. Fuck. Well, how about this. Next Sunday me and Casey are going to Mortuary. DJ Darker's coming from Osaka: you know, the guy who does the Netherworld events. That friend of hers, Riku, is supposed to be coming, too. Ask Shinji to *that*. If it's in a crowd of people you won't feel any pressure to do anything you don't want to do."

Kneeling on my bed, I looked out across the alleyway I lived on. A man in a chef's hat was splashing water on the as-phalt among the parked bicycles. While the western sky still glowed pink, the neon signs towering over Ikebukuro station had come on: Aiful, Promise, Tower, Seibu, Visa, Kirin. I re-flected wretchedly that I was complying with my own degra-dation, and not just my own, either. Since I started working in Roppongi I'd become better aware of this inertial tendency in myself, and better able to resist it, up to a point. I agreed to Dorothy's proposal.

Within two minutes of our reunion I'd come down to earth, like Wile E. Coyote, plummetting off a cliff. Shinji's hair had grown until it was in his eyes, he was wearing a green nylon motocross jacket with corrugated yellow sleeves, and he was talking to Dorothy about the art market. Not only had my pu-erile yearnings betrayed me, but they had the vicious effect of preventing me from interacting with him as naturally and easily as I had on my birthday. He bought me a drink, and instead of thanking him I made an ungrateful joke about how I would return the favor when he ran out of money again.

He said, "I'm having a show in December. I wish I'd brought the flyers. It's at this tiny gallery in Kichijōji that only costs twenty thousand yen to rent."

"Next stop the National Museum of Fine Arts," I said.

"Nice kimono, by the way," he said.

"It's Dorothy's."

"Did you know that the nape of the neck is traditionally considered an erogenous zone?"

"Oh yes, the bit that shows at the back of the collar. Except I've got psoriasis, which isn't very erogenous."

"It's funny. I've dated Japanese girls before, but none of them ever wore a kimono. At least not when I was around."

Dorothy laughed into her tequila sunrise. Wishing for the umpteenth time that I hadn't let her talk me into it, I pushed my dangling sleeves out of the way and extracted my cigarettes from the drawstring handbag that went with the kimono. Shinji was still waiting for me to say something. I said, "Have you sold any more paintings recently?"

Instead of answering, he glanced at Dorothy as if he suspected her of putting me up to it.

"Funnily enough," she said, "I was just asking him the same thing."

"Well, it's not as if sales have anything to do with anything, of course," I drawled. "Look at the trash that goes for a million dollars nowadays."

"She doesn't know anything," said Dorothy with a smile. "She's as innocent as a newborn chick."

"I am not!"

"That's why I love her," said Shinji.

These words, which I'd been hearing in my dreams for months, fell curiously flat, like a stone falling on the moon. Shinji pretended to be interested in the other people at the bar. There was plenty to pretend about. You had your vampires, your princesses (Egyptian and other), your sadomasochistic couples joined by leashes, a sprinkling of hyperfashionable ravers, and one alien with a rubber head so big it had to duck to go through doors. While Mortuary lay smack in the middle of Roppongi, deep beneath five floors of snack bars and cabarets, most clubbers had never heard of it and would have been turned away, had they tried to come in, for looking too normal. This exclusivity was more than a commercial calculation: it was what kept Mortuary something of a conservatory, where tender delusions could blossom.

Dorothy pretended to wipe away a tear. "Man, this is too heavy for me. I always wanted to feel like that about someone.

I guess I did feel like that about Yukio for a while, but it didn't last. You have to know what the other person's like and love them not because they're that way; love them *anyway*. But he quit loving me when he found out I got all kinds of sides to my character."

She stood up and swayed to the industrial beats piped into the bar. She had on a floorlength dress with ruched black satin and chartreuse lace panels over a black hoop petticoat. Her spider tattoo showed between her shoulderblades. She'd combed her hair into a soft mass and pinned it into a twisted confection redolent of the 17th century with little luminous flowers fastened in it.

"I'll leave you two lovebirds to yourselves," she said, setting her empty glass down.

A while later I saw her on the dancefloor. Apart from the ravers, who bopped madly with their multicolored dreadlocks flying, most people's notion of dancing to DJ Darker's brand of dark electronica was to strike a succession of poses and then fake a swoon. Dorothy was waltzing. Her partner, a tall man in a red tuxedo, swirled her around with athletic grace. They threaded among the posers in figure eights as if they could hear Chopin in their heads.

"She took ballroom dancing lessons when she was little!" I shouted enviously.

"I took the violin!" shouted Shinji. "But I had to give it up when my father's first business went bankrupt."

"I always wanted to date a musician," I said.

The kimono may have been a beautiful and practical garment, making a virtue of a flat chest and supporting an obsolescent textile industry, but it wasn't designed for dancing in, and nor were the geta sandals I was wearing with it. Shinji and I soon gave up our exertions and stood embracing in the noisy darkness. People navigated around us as if we were inanimate objects. He asked me about my family and I told him some funny anecdotes about growing up with three brilliant brothers, a mother who died of breast cancer when I was twenty-three, and a father who regretted not becoming a priest. He told me that his father was an entrepreneur who worked too much, his mother lived in a world of her own, and his younger brother had moved to Niigata to be a ski instructor. These facts seemed to put his relationship with Chitose Kato into perspective. I stuffed her into the deepest closet in my mind, slammed the door, and kissed Shinji ardently.

Aviva was there, too, bouncing up and down in front of the DJ booth in an orange vinyl minidress and matching moonboots, waving a glowstick in either hand. Aviva was our new coworker at Pub Club Paradise, a twenty-one-year-old Israeli who thought ¥2000 an hour was plenty of money. She lived at Fuji House, where Casey had met her. Until then she'd been manning a jewelry stall in Kabukicho, which was what most Israelis in Tokyo did. The pay, she'd told us, was terrible, reflecting the high price of renting sidewalk space from the men in the double-breasted suits. She was dodging the draft. I would have liked to talk to her about the Middle East and the planetary crisis of faith, but I had nothing to say to her. She was Casey's friend, not mine.

Casey was there, too, snuggling in a corner with Riku.

"The elephant in the living-room," I said in English, and had to explain to Shinji what I meant. It had been some time since my dislike of Casey metamorphosed into plain old dread, yet the dread in its turn showed no signs of subsiding. I took care never to be alone with her at work, and not for the world would I have asked her how her thesis was going. I wanted to ask her about Riku, but I was afraid of the cost of gratifying my curiosity. "'O the mind, mind has mountains; cliffs of fall frightful, sheer, no-man-fathomed!'" I said in English, trying to laugh at myself.

Shinji didn't laugh. He said, "Isn't there any other kind of job you could do? Couldn't you be a translator or something?"

"My Japanese isn't that good. I don't understand everything you say to me."

"That's amazing. Most people don't understand *anything* I say to them."

"You should try living overseas for a while."

"Do you ever get homesick?"

"No."

"You can't mean you like it here," he said.

"I love this country," I insisted, laughing at the look on his face.

At three o'clock I went outside by myself for some fresh air. The night sparkled with advertisements. People reeled along in high heels and expensive coats, bouncing off the parked cars, shrieking and teasing each other the way you can only do at three in the morning when Monday is a holiday. Vomit splattered the stairs leading up from the unmarked entrance to the club. I stepped into the street. The wind cooled the sweat on my neck. There was a Family Mart on the corner where this street joined Gaien Avenue East. I set off to buy a bottle of hot tea or something. Maybe a dose of the real world of fluorescent lights and cash registers would restore me to my senses.

"You don't have to be unreasonable. We can cut a deal. Just wait until I get back some of the money I've loaned out."

The familiar timbre of Dorothy's voice penetrated my trance before the words themselves did. Replaying and re-translating them in my head, deciding that that *was* what she'd said, I slowed down and tuned into my surroundings. About fifteen metres ahead of me a white Mercedes Benz blocked the street, its wing mirrors practically scraping the paintwork of the parked cars on either side. Dorothy stood at its driver's side window with her back to me, her arms folded over her décolletage, her skirt billowing up alongside the Benz's hood. The window was rolled down, but I could see nothing of the driver. The interior of that car was darker than the night sky. I shuffled backwards. The ambient clamor drowned out Dorothy's voice. I perceived that the man standing a few paces from her, whom I'd thought a mere bystander, was Kaito from our block. I kept on moving backwards. I'd achieved my purpose in coming outside, which had been to remind myself that Mortuary was only a few blocks from Pub Club Paradise.

Shinji found me sitting on the stairs from the dancefloor to the bar. "I've had it," he said. "Let's go."

"Where to?" I said, knuckling my eyes. "The trains aren't running yet. We could go sit in a café; yes, let's do that."

If we went the other way we could get back to Gaien Avenue East without having to squeeze past Dorothy and the Benz, I calculated, on the off chance they hadn't wound it up by now.

"We could take a taxi," countered Shinji.

"Where to?"

"Well, to your place, if you don't want to come back to Harajuku with me."

"Shinji, I don't know how to tell you this, but…"

"I know," he said immediately. "It's *your* place. I'm an idiot. How about a hotel? There are plenty of them in Akasaka, right down the hill. Don't worry; I'll pay."

"Shinji, I'm a Catholic."

He laughed, pretending to get it, so that I knew he didn't.

"Let me put it this way," I said, and stumbled into an explanation of the church's teachings on chastity.

He sat down on the stairs and asked me questions that proved he didn't know the first thing about Christianity. I went back to the beginning and started again. I'd never tried to explain my faith in Japanese before, and I knew I was doing a poor job of it.

"I've never felt like this about anyone before," he said slowly. "It stands to reason that there are going to be obstacles I've never encountered before. I'd like to work around this one. I'd like to learn more about Catholicism, and I'd like you to learn about Buddhism. For that matter, I could stand to learn some more about Buddhism myself. It's supposedly my religion, but I don't know much about it." He stubbed out his cigarette on the stairs and rubbed the smear of ash into a pattern that gradually came to look like a mandala. "You have faith and I don't, but that doesn't mean you're the only one with ideas of what a relationship should be. We're both going to have to compromise a bit. Do you think you can do that?"

"I guess," I muttered.

He looked at his watch. "What do you know? The trains are running."

So we took the Oedo line and the Yamanote line to Ikebukuro and spent the entire day together in my bed. Fully clothed.

"I keep wanting to tear your clothes off," I confessed, "but all I have to do is think about Kato-san and I'm OK. It's better than a cold shower."

"I keep wanting to tear your clothes off, too, so I'm pretending this is ascetic training. You'll make a proper Buddhist of me yet."

We watched television, took baths, and snacked on toasted cheese sandwiches. My apartment was very small – there was barely enough space in the bedroom for my bed and desk, and barely enough space in the kitchen for two people – which forced us to be polite to each other. We talked about philosophy, art, war, and the afterlife instead of about ourselves; and that was the form our relationship took for the next month. I started to have delusions of normality.

Under The Clouds, at the Sawamura Gallery, which was the basement of a café in Kichijōji, opened in the middle of December. Shinji included in his exhibition at the last minute a picture called *The Virgin*. It depicted a girl kneeling, hands folded in prayer, with her back to a highway where cars were piled up in a gory traffic accident. It sold on the second day of the exhibition for ¥60,000. I was glad. It was me but it wasn't me, being beautified and holified in a way that told me more than I really wanted to know about Shinji's relationship to his work.

It was the only picture that did sell, apart from one he'd done five years back of an elderly man in kimono writing a scroll with the bleeding stump of his index finger.

His Pudgies series provoked technical debates among his friends, most of whom were artists themselves; they bewildered the punters who idled into the gallery after finishing their coffee; they inspired no one to fork out. Dorothy was disgusted. I worried that Shinji would despair of his future. I should have known him better than that. "This way I get to keep all of them," he said happily. "I know they're the only worthwhile things I've done, even if no one else likes them; and I've already started on another one. It's called *Nativity*. By the time I finish it, Christmas will be over, but I can exhibit it next year. It's of a Pudgie with nipples all over her body, and she has about thirty babies hanging off her like decorations on a Christmas tree."

I was clearly influencing him to some extent.

On the last day of the exhibition Chitose Kato dropped by, toting a dachshund in her handbag. I threw down my book (*Buddhism For Dummies* in a brown paper wrapper) and served her a plastic cup of wine with trembling hands. The dachshund looked at the pictures. Chitose Kato praised me lavishly for my helpfulness, joked with Shinji about the title of the exhibition, and condescended to him about the sales situation.

What would Siddhartha do? I thought.

"Of course," she said, "no one with money to spend comes to an out-of-the-way venue like this. You can say what you like about Kichijōji, but it's not Harajuku, is it?"

"Om," I muttered.

"It's a pity Kimura-kun couldn't make it," Shinji said. "I guess they keep him busy at the construction site."

I went to the toilet and hid there, chainsmoking, until I was sure Chitose had gone.

When the exhibition closed, Shinji admitted he was broke again. I'd been hanging out at the house in Harajuku on weekdays, but now I felt unable to go back, no matter how persuasively he argued that it would be all right. On the Thursday before Christmas, in the middle of the night, he turned up at my apartment with the first two fingers of his left hand splinted and bandaged. "It's no big deal. If it was my right hand, I'd be mad," was all he would say. I nagged him into inventing a tale about an accident with a kitchen knife, then said that I didn't believe a word of it.

He said, "There's more than one kind of lie. There are white lies and then there are lies of omission. Dorothy tells me you're going to leave Japan after Christmas."

And why shouldn't she have? I'd told her only a few days ago that the Salesians had invited me to take part in an orientation program to be held in America in January. I'd told her I had no idea what I ought to do.

I slept with him. His injured hand made it an awkward operation. I'd never had sex with anyone before, and it wasn't like I had expected. He sprawled across my body afterwards to grab his cigarettes. His skin glistened and his shoulder-blades stuck out like amputated wings. "I guess I'd better tell you what happened," he said, exhaling smoke. "My fingers got crushed in a car door."

I saw the trap I'd set for myself. It was like someone had hit me on the top of the head. I covered his mouth. "Not another word. If you couldn't tell me before, you definitely can't tell me now. I know we said we were both going to have to compromise, but this isn't what I meant!" Furious with myself, I jumped up and dragged my clothes on.

"Then I guess there's no point asking you," he said.

"Asking me what?"

"Whether I can stay here tomorrow while you're at work," he said softly.

My stomach started to hurt. "Sure you can. Do you want my spare key?"

"I guess I'd better have it."

Crushed in a car door?

That day, for the first time ever, Mrs Kikuchi failed to show up at work.

"She caught cold," said Jimmy the bartender. "She in hospital."

Arriving in a little red suit that made her look startlingly normal, Dorothy said she'd spoken to her and that we were to open for business as usual. Still queasy from my fight with Shinji, I felt obscurely comforted to know that Mrs Kikuchi trusted Dorothy with the cash register and the accounts.

"I got a treat for you all," she said, and distributed Santa Claus bobble hats. "I want to get some Christmas spirit up in here. And don't start crying to me that you're Jewish, Vivi, because I know you haven't stepped foot in a synagogue since you were baptized, or whatever it is you all do."

"I love Christmas," insisted Aviva, dancing around with her bobble hat on. "Jingle bells, jingle bells, I hope Mama-san dies."

Irina, Anastasia, and Tania started giggling. "We take her Christmas present! One big bottle vodka, souvenir from Russia, she finish!"

They were in a better mood than usual. Dorothy had negotiated, in open defiance of Mr Himemiya, a cash bonus for them that brought their actual wages almost to a par with Aviva's.

Going into hospital beat every measure that our poor Mama-san had ever tried to improve the ambience of the club. We put on a CD of Christmas carols and I went down the street to buy tinsel garlands and some plastic holly. Our sense of emancipation infected the customers to the point of making them acknowledge each other. Towards the end of the night Dorothy organized a grand karaoke contest with a lap dance as first prize. A fat sales manager performed "Santa Claus Is Coming To Town" in a wonderful bass voice, bringing the house down by wiggling his hips like a battery-operated Santa figurine, and chose Dorothy herself. I dived past Jimmy to get to the stereo behind the bar and cranked up Diana King's "Black Roses," the song Dorothy used on the rare occasions when she stripped. Writhing over the sales manager's lap, she slithered out of her clothes without missing a beat, removed her bra at the end of the song, and leapt back before he could grab her breasts. Everyone roared.

"This is how it must have been in the days of the bubble economy," I said to Casey.

"Mutual exploitation and faux camaraderie," she nodded wryly. "Well, that's what Christmas is all about! No wonder the Japanese are so big on it."

I looked at her in wonder. She'd actually said something I agreed with. She was dressed in trailing black garments, as usual, and she'd taken off her Santa hat. She didn't fit in.

"The end of the year is supposed to be a time of purification," she informed me, and I got the impression that it was something she'd been planning to say as soon as she got an opening. "You're supposed to apologize to anyone you've treated badly during the year. So I guess I have to apologize to you, Ruth. Sorry."

"What for?" I said.

She shrugged. "Oh, you know, everything."

"It's OK," I muttered, scratching my neck. The next day was Christmas Eve, and I was going to Midnight Mass. I had an impulse to invite her, but it would be difficult for both of us to take the night off. Besides, Shinji had said he wanted to come. I could just imagine the small talk. I said nothing.

So the two of us went by ourselves and stood at the back of St Ignacio's, which was designed like an auditorium and packed to capacity, and I had one of those moments of certainty you only get a few times in your life. Back at my apartment, I called my father in Concord. Two of my brothers had come home for Christmas, one with his girlfriend in tow, the other with the small son he was raising alone. I exhorted them all to go to Mass when midnight came in America, and they laughed at me affectionately. They knew better than to ask me whether I was spending the holidays alone. My father, however, never lost hope. "Who's that in the background, love?" he said. "Your local wassailers?"

It was Shinji humming the catchiest bits of the *Gloria* as he washed up our cocoa cups. I swung around, holding out my cellphone. "Shinji! Say Happy Christmas to my dad."

At five in the morning I got up and turned on my computer. Hunched over the screen, teeth chattering, I emailed the Salesians to the effect that I regretted wasting their time. I'd found my own mission. I hit send and climbed back into bed beside Shinji, praying that I'd done the right thing.

His voice woke me what felt like minutes later. It was broad day. He was spinning around in my desk chair, talking on his cellphone. Seeing me move, he locked himself in the bathroom. Listening unwillingly, with winter sunshine sliding through the gap in the curtains onto my face, I heard, although I couldn't hear *what* he was saying, that he was saying it with anger in his voice. He came out of the bathroom, pointlessly flushing the toilet behind him.

"I'll tell you everything," he said, "sooner or later. Right now I just can't."

I remembered that I'd forfeited the right to ask him to tell me anything. I rolled over and pulled the futon over my head.

"It was Kato-san. She wants me to come collect my pictures."

He'd taken the unsold ones back there after his exhibition.

"It doesn't have to be today, though. She knows," he said, "that I don't have anywhere else to put my stuff. She knows I can't bring everything here."

While I didn't understand Chitose Kato, I knew that she was pure social polish most of the way down. No way would she have called Shinji at nine o'clock in the morning to demand that he come pick up his pictures *sometime*. I felt as if my insides had been scooped out, leaving me empty and floppy in the middle like a poorly made stuffed animal. I said, "You can bring as much stuff here as you think makes sense. Just remember we have to be able to get in and out at the door."

"Thanks. I'll go see what's what this evening."

"Do you think that's soon enough?"

"Yes." He hesitated. "I don't want to leave you here alone."

"I thought I was the one looking after you."

"We have to look after each other. And besides, it's Christmas. Your father said he was glad you had company. I can't leave you alone after *that*. Which reminds me! You might not like it, but…" He started digging in the rucksack he was living out of.

"Oh no," I wailed. "I didn't get you anything."

I trailed into Pub Club Paradise at seven thirty, yawning my head off. Only the lights behind the bar and in the office were on. Dorothy and Aviva sat in the jaggedly falling shadows of the cash register and the bottles of European liquors that served as bar ornaments. They were both dressed for work: Dorothy in her red suit, Aviva in one of her cheap evening dresses, forest green with a bow under the bust. The stereo was silent. So were they. "Happy Christmas," I said. I went into the dressing-room, changed into my now-standard outfit of a black turtleneck and black tights under a lavender shift, and rejoined them. "Where's Jimmy?"

"I gave him the night off," said Dorothy. "He's a Catholic, too."

"I knew that." I scratched my neck. Why had it never occurred to me to try a few believers' catchphrases out on Jimmy? "I wonder which church he goes to? I've never seen him at St Ignacio's."

"I ain't asked him. Girl, what's that on your finger?"

"It doesn't mean anything," I laughed. "Shinji did give it to me, but just as jewelry, and I'm sure it's only glass."

"Let me look." Aviva took the ring and held it up to what light there was. "I think it's a diamond! You can tell from the cut."

"A diamond. Well, well. Round about how much would that go for, Vivi?"

"We didn't sell anything like this at the stall. I don't know, but maybe ninety thousand or one hundred thousand yen."

"Oh no," I said.

"Now that's strange. That's real strange, because the last thing I heard, Shinji was so short of money he'd have been ass out on the street if you didn't let him stay at your house. Now I come to find out he had a hundred grand to buy you a rock."

"He might have bought it ages ago. He might not even have *bought* it." I admitted the possibility I hadn't let myself think of yet: "He might have whipped it from somewhere."

"You don't know him that well if you're saying that. He's not that type. His priorities are fucked up, for sure, but not that way. Anyway, you better take it off."

"I don't care how much it cost," I said mutinously. "I think it's pretty."

"For fuck's sake, Ruth! You're supposed to be smart and all! The same thing that me and Vivi thought straight off is what the customers are going to think. You ain't gonna get one single tip all night."

We put on the lights and the CD of Christmas carols. Eight o'clock came and went. There was no sign of Anastasia, Irina, Tania, or Casey. Dorothy got out her cellphone and punched in numbers. Whoever she was calling, they didn't pick up. She lit a Marlboro and suggested that we all have a drink, which incited us temporarily to a spirit of fun. We took it in turns to fix cocktails and drink them standing up behind the bar, so that if some customers came in we could pretend to be busy. No customers came in – unusually, for a Saturday night – nor did any of the other girls. Aviva and I voiced silly speculations. Dorothy picked at the fraying seams of the sofa that she was sitting on. Her long legs looked slimmer than ever in translucent hose, and her hair glowed like ridges of polished teak.

Eight thirty.

Eight forty-five.

"Fuck this shit," said Dorothy, rising. "I expect Casey's slept through her alarm, the lazy bitch. Somebody's got to go pick her up."

"I'll go," volunteered Aviva. It made sense as she lived in Fuji House, too, on a different floor. But Dorothy shook her head.

"I want Ruth to go. You stay here with me, Vivi."

I agreed with alacrity. I didn't even stop to change back into my jeans. I just swapped my sandals for my sneakers and threw on my coat. Dorothy came with me as far as the elevator.

"If you can't wake her up, or whatever happens, call me. I don't want you coming back here by yourself."

"That sounds like an ultimatum," I said.

"You're taking me wrong, as usual. It's just that I might have to step out, and if I do, I'm gonna send Vivi over to those Israelis on the corner of Roppongi Avenue. They'll look after her. So there wouldn't be anyone here, and it wouldn't make any sense for you to be up in here by yourself. Besides, this door would be locked, so you couldn't get in."

I didn't like the sound of that, but it would have been fruitless to press her for more. Shivering in the winter wind, I hurried to Roppongi station, took the Hibiya line to Ebisu, took the Yamanote line one stop south, and changed to the Tokyu Meguro line that runs overground towards the wealthy outlying parts of Meguro ward and the Tama River. Before it got there, I got off at Musashi-Koyama, one of the old neighborhoods that fringe the city. Cheap merchandise spilled onto the sidewalks of the main street; old ladies barrelled along on bicycles. I got lost, returned to the station to get my bearings, and drove myself at last successfully through the intricate sequence of turnings that led to Fuji House, a block of concrete with garbage bags piled in its forecourt. A tabby cat ran away from me. The front door was unlocked. I climbed draughty stairs to the third floor.

I could smell curry, and hear rap coming from somewhere, but all the doors on the corridor were closed. I knocked on #303. "Casey?" Nothing happened. I tried the knob. It turned in my hand. The door breathed out an evil odor.

I felt along the jamb for the light switch, unwilling to put a toe over the threshhold until I found it.

The room was knee deep in clothes, shoes, books, printouts, old newspapers, and plastic bags with empty food containers in them. The last time I came here it had been mildly messy, like anyone's room. I'd never seen anything like this.

54

I scanned every corner before picking my way through the chaos towards Casey's desk. I perched on her chair, above the tide of garbage, and stared at the bed. The futon and blanket weren't rucked up high enough to hide anything. I knelt on the chair, pushed aside a pile of black clothes, and peered under the bed. Nothing except dust.

She might have gone to the bathroom down the hall; she might be downstairs in the communal kitchen. But if she was here at all, why wasn't she at work? The dingy curtains billowed in the breeze from the open window. It felt colder in here than it was outdoors. There were a couple of towels crumpled up on the bed. I felt them. Dry; stiff, in fact, and stained with something dark that looked purple on the blue stripes and brown on the yellow ones. A picture came into my mind: Casey with one towel over her shoulders and another turbanning her hair, which she was dyeing black. I lifted the towels to my nose and sniffed. They had an acrid smell which I couldn't positively identify. I dropped them and started shuffling through the papers on the desk (which were mostly in Japanese), looking for something addressed to someone.

My hand knocked against the mouse of the computer. The screen lit up, displaying a document comprised of words all different sizes, from minuscule up to an inch high.

*I'm dying for blood. Blood is the purest source of pranic energy. Life kills. If I don't get out of this trap I will die. **I need him.** When we're together we fill the holes in each other's auras and I feel WHOLE for the first time in my life.*

There were pages and pages of it. The file was called "Voices." Some of it had the flavor of Japanese translated into English. Some of it even made sense, as far as karma and psychic energies make sense in the first place. It was the typography that got to me. It made me think of echoes bouncing around in a dark theater. My face went hot as I read it, while my hands had gone so cold they were stiff. I glanced through the other documents on the computer. There were a few old essays on writers such as Junichiro Tanizaki and Kenzaburo Oe, but nothing related to Yukio Mishima apart from a file of depressing quotations from his novels. It looked like Casey had done no work at all on her thesis (unless "Voices" counted), or unless she'd done it in longhand – a possibility: I could imagine her hunched over a notebook, scribbling with the intense concentration she was capable of. *If I don't get out of this trap I will die.*

I jumped to my feet. "She's gone home," I said aloud. "She wasn't crazy. She knew she was in danger. Didn't even stop to pack."

"You OK?"

The door had been open all this time, and now a Chinese girl was sticking her ponytailed head around it.

"You don't clean in here, cockroaches arriving," she added in Japanese.

"I'm not Casey," I said, and she looked at me as if I was out of my mind.

I fled the building and called Dorothy. She didn't pick up. I didn't have Aviva's number. I called Shinji. He didn't pick up, either. I should have made him wait to go to Harajuku until I could go with him, I reproached myself as I hurried back towards Musashi-Koyama station. Just because I was in the wrong didn't mean that I'd had to decline to get involved. Maybe I couldn't have been any use, but at least I would now have known what was going on. The same criticism, of course, applied in spades to my attitude towards Casey. When I tried to estimate the cost of my cowardice, my imagination crumpled under its weight. But I didn't trust myself to make reliable inferences: I'd already missed too much, and I didn't know what I'd missed. I needed a second opinion, and that meant I needed Shinji, because second opinions weren't Dorothy's style.

All the way back to Meguro, and then on the Yamanote line, I stood facing the doors of the train, dialing Dorothy and Shinji in vain. It was Riku I should have been calling. But I didn't have his number. Did anyone?

In Harajuku, every one of the trees marching up Omotesando Boulevard sparkled with fairy lights, very

Christmassy. It was past ten o'clock so most of the boutiques had closed, including Virtuesse. I cut through the back alleys and hurried along the street that I'd often loitered along with Shinji. All the mom 'n' pop stores were shuttered and the yellow chinks in the second-floor windows gave the impression of a town locked down against invasion. At Chitose Kato's, however, every window blazed with light. It was bright enough in the yard for me to navigate with confidence between the dog turds. Kimura-kun answered the door, his orange hair standing up in tufts. "He's not here."

"Do you know where he is?" It was the first time we'd exchanged more than nods. I stumbled over my Japanese, which got me a stare of exaggerated incomprehension. I tried the same sentence in honorific language. Kimura-kun smiled, appreciating my sense of humor.

"He *was* here. He's gone out with her." He referred to Chitose Kato the way Shinji had when I first met him: *her*. "You can come in and wait for them to get back, if you want."

I followed his flowered slippers up the stairs.

"Make yourself at home."

I went into the studio.

"Let me know if you need anything," added Kimura-kun, cracking up at his own pretense of hospitality, and retreated.

I circled the studio. The dust in the corners showed up under the halogen lights. All Shinji's pictures were gone.

His paints and brushes and stuff were still there on the table. So was the ashtray. I sat down on his folding chair and smoked a cigarette. Now and then a snort of laughter escaped me. I went back downstairs and rattled my knuckles on the front room door. Kimura-kun reappeared with a can of beer in his hand, the dachshunds at his feet. "Did Shinji take his pictures with him?" I asked.

"Take them? He went to look for the guys that took them."

I crouched and petted the dachshunds. Kimura-kun grinned.

"I guess no one's filled you in! Well, they showed up here around lunchtime. Two of them, and there must have been another one that stayed in the truck."

"Yeah?"

"What do I know about Endo-san's life? I figured he'd paid them to move his shit for him. I said sure, get on with the job. So they cleaned the place out and took off. Next thing, I guess it was a couple of hours ago, he shows up here and goes crazy. She gets home from the shop about the same time. Can't accuse him of being shy: first thing he does is ask her for a loan. Two hundred grand he wants. Says if he can't pay them off he'll never get his pictures back. She says she's not in the consumer finance business; call one of those shark agencies, they've got twenty-four hour toll free numbers. But I figure he's already in pretty deep with some sharks of the unlisted variety. Who else would take him on?"

I didn't believe it. Shinji was the last person to resort to illegal borrowing. He'd hardly known what to do with the money he made from the sale of *There's No There Up There*. The proof was on my finger. I'd begun to think he *preferred* being broke.

Yet there'd been that phone call this morning. And there were his injured fingers.

Relishing my confusion, Kimura-kun alleged that Shinji and Chitose Kato had gone out in hopes of locating the loan sharks and recovering at least a few of Shinji's pictures. He was still here himself, he said, because Chitose Kato thought that the sharks, having had a chance to case the house, might come back for a spot of freelance burgling. I pretended to swallow the story whole. He went back to the television and I went back upstairs. The minutes limped past. I called Dorothy again. She didn't pick up. Deciding to pack up what few possessions Shinji had, because I had plenty of money in the bank and as soon as he got back we were both getting out of here forever, I went into the bedroom and opened the closet. I recalled that he kept a battered hardshell suitcase in here. He did; and inside the suitcase was *There's No There Up There*.

I sat down on the floor with the painting in my hands. It depicted a yak or buffalo standing on a crag contemplating a void. Balanced on the animal's back, one of Shinji's pudgy humanoids was reaching up to clasp forearms with another humanoid standing upside down on another crag that grew out of the top of the painting, this one made of bright green crystal. I still couldn't put my finger on whatever it was that gave the picture its hermetic fairytale quality. Six weeks ago I'd been astonished to hear that someone had paid ¥200,000 for it. I'd reminded myself that the contemporary art market didn't make any sense, and let it go at that. But now I saw that it wasn't worth ¥200,000. It was worth nothing at all, or more. Teetering on the edge of meaninglessness, it promised to reveal, if you could only crack its code, a message that might be beautiful or horrifying but would anyway change your way of looking at the world forever.

As I puzzled over it with fractured concentration, Casey came floating back into my head, ethereal in her black garments, floating or dancing or swimming in some medium other than air – the medium, perhaps, of Shinji's paintings.

As soon as I started thinking about her again I couldn't help it.

I just couldn't make myself believe she'd gone home to New York. I kept running up against the same problems: not *why* she would have done such a thing, but that a) all the Christmas Day flights had probably been booked up for weeks, and b) she hadn't stopped to pack. Don't we have packing in our bones? And paying our rent, and giving notice at our jobs?

Maybe she'd been as desperate as I'd been when I first came to Japan, when it hit me that I'd fucked my life up and I wanted to die. I hadn't had a boyfriend at that stage. But Casey had Riku (while *boyfriend* didn't seem the right description for him, nothing else fitted, either).

So maybe they'd taken off on a trip together.

The front door of the apartment rattled along its grooves. I scrambled up off the floor as Shinji came in. His gaze flickered to the painting in my hands. "What are you doing here?" he said, and I realized he had a point.

I held up *There's No There Up There.* "It's a funny thing, isn't it, the artist's relationship to his work? A bond that even money can't break."

"You're wrong there. I have to get my hands on two hundred thousand yen by tomorrow or I'll never see any of my stuff again. Five years' work! Shit!" He took *There's No There Up There* from me and turned on his heel. I followed him into the studio, where he cut a length of bubble wrap from the roll that stood amidst Chitose Kato's old furniture. He flung the shears casually to the floor when he was done with them. I followed him back into the bedroom, where he placed the wrapped painting in the suitcase and started throwing his clothes in on top of it. "She said she'd lend me a hundred grand," he explained, his back to me. "But when we got as far as the ATM she changed her mind. We called them, and she didn't like the sound of their voices. She has these intuitions about people."

Chitose Kato was *she* again.

"I'll lend you the money," I said. "I've got it. But I don't think I can withdraw that much from an ATM all at once. Can it wait until the banks open tomorrow?"

He froze. He had a shirt in his hands. Still with his back to me, he folded it deliberately. "I can't take your money."

"Why not, if the alternative is losing all your pictures? You were staying with me. What's the difference? That's taking my money, too, isn't it?"

"I never meant to go on staying with you forever."

We proceeded back to the studio, where he laid the suitcase on the floor and started packing his paints and equipment.

"I need a place of my own," he said. "I think I told you that before. Your place is too small for two. And sooner or later you'd have got angry with me for not helping with the rent."

"I wouldn't."

"Money fucks up relationships. Don't you know that?"

"I haven't had many relationships before."

"I never had a chunk of money before. I thought it would make you like me better, and look at us now."

I stood there with my toes turned in, my coat open over my ridiculously short dress, and watched him fitting paint-brushes into their cases. He'd become adept at using his bandaged hand like pincers. "I didn't come here to get angry with you," I said. "I came because Casey's missing. Her room's unlocked and all her stuff is there, and I found a weird document on her computer."

I described "Voices" as best I could.

"She's probably topped herself along with that gloomy boyfriend of hers," Shinji said. "I always thought that story about her working at Waseda was suspect. In fact, if you want to know, I don't think she was a graduate student at all. Dorothy said to me that *she* didn't think she was; and as soon as she said it, it was obvious. I didn't say anything to you, since Casey was your friend and it was none of my business, but I think she and the gloomy one probably had a suicide pact. They got to know each other on the Internet, didn't they? Well, there you are. That kind of thing happens all the time."

"And… and she came to Japan to go through with it?"

"Something like that. Different strokes for different folks. If I was going to commit suicide I'd do it at home."

One of the dachshunds started barking under our feet. Chitose Kato stood on the threshhold. She was all in black except for a ruby-red shawl fastened around her shoulders with a cluster of silver flowers. "I told you that you had fifteen minutes," she said pleasantly to Shinji, ignoring me. "It's been seventeen. Do you want me to call the police?"

Shinji closed the suitcase and rose, hefting it. "We're going. Come on, Ruth."

As I passed Chitose Kato I ducked my head and said, like a Japanese person, "Sorry for everything."

We took the Yamanote line to Meguro and headed down the station steps into the night. Meguro is an unambitious huddle of pachinko parlors and fast food outlets. The sight of McDonald's reminded me that I hadn't had any supper, but I still wasn't hungry: *There's No There Up There* had killed my appetite. "Where are we going?" I said.

"Please. Just come with me."

We left the station's neon halo and trudged up a broad hill with traffic zooming past us and the Shuto No. 2 Expressway overhead. It strode uphill on concrete legs, walled with fibreglass to keep the noise in. Beneath it, despite the headlights flashing past, we walked in shadow. Weeds ran riot on the sidewalk's verge, garbage lay everywhere, and homeless people had built shacks around the feet of the support pillars. The rolling thunder of the traffic muffled the noise of Shinji's suitcase's wheels as well as our footsteps.

We kept climbing, and the wall on our left tapered down to nothing, exposing an oldfashioned neighborhood of tiny houses built to the limits of tiny plots of land. Narrow streets wriggled away like earthworms when your shovel cuts them in half.

"I'm going to try Dorothy again," I said, taking out my cellphone.

"Wait."

I glanced at him. His face was pale and shining with strain. It had to be hard work hauling that suitcase uphill. I said tiredly, "I was only going to ask if she'd heard from Casey."

"Well, it's none of my business what you ask her."

"But I guess it won't make any difference if I hold off a bit longer."

"Go ahead and call her if you want."

I put my cellphone back into my bag.

We reached the top of the hill and the sidewalk started to descend – into central Tokyo, I thought, but I really had no idea: I was hopelessly disoriented. At the juncture of two little streets stood a house like the Flatiron building in miniature, whose first storey, visible over the slat fence that surrounded it, was done in corrugated chrome, while the second storey looked to be blue or dark grey. Shinji turned off the sidewalk. The space between the fence and the chrome prow of the house barely admitted the bicycles that were leaning there. Shinji fished out a key and opened the door. "I'm home!" He slid his suitcase into the tiny hall, where it came to rest at the foot of a spiral ladder, and stepped out of his sneakers.

I took off my shoes in a daze.

A woman emerged from the room in the prow, which I could see through the door was the kitchen. She might have been the same age as Chitose Kato, but her salt-and-pepper hair, dumpy figure, and defeated expression made her look elderly. I searched her face for surprise, delight, anger, anything – in vain. "Your father's working late. He'll probably be home by midnight or one o'clock. I won't be waiting up for him."

"I will," said Shinji.

"Put the door on the chain, then. I feel uneasy when I have to go to sleep leaving it open."

"Gotcha." Shinji slotted the end of the chain into its runnel, then made for the stairs, saying over his shoulder, "This is my friend I'm taking up with me."

Flustered, I fell back on American manners and extended my hand to her. She didn't even look at it, but only smiled vaguely at me. "It's a pleasure to meet you. What's your name?"

I got out the correct polite phrases.

"Where are you from?"

"She's American, but she lives in Japan now. Careful, Mom, I've left my suitcase in the hall. Don't trip over it."

At the top of the stairs stood three doors at angles to each other. Shinji opened the one that led to the tip or the prow of the house. The room beyond it was a boy's.

"My mother's almost blind," he said, closing the door. "It's a degenerative condition. She can still see shapes in bright sunlight, but according to the doctor, she won't have any sight left in another couple of years."

I collapsed on the bed. Dust rose, tickling my nostrils. The shelves above the wooden desk held high school textbooks; in the narrow point of the room, with windows on both sides, stood an easel with a half-finished painting on it and other canvases stacked up behind it. "'Now that my ladder's gone, I must lie down where all the ladders start,'" I said in English, ""In the foul rag-and-bone shop of the heart.'"

"What?"

I stood up, drew the curtains of one of the windows, and pressed my nose to the glass. I was looking at the Shuto No. 2 Expressway. Not ten metres from the house, the tops of its walls curved in like ribs. I could imagine the shadow it cast on the house during the day. The white noise of the traffic swelled as something large went past.

"Why don't you call Dorothy?" Shinji said.

I said to the window, "Why don't you tell me what she's likely to say?"

"Come here."

I joined him on the bed, keeping my distance.

"She bought that picture from me. But it was… she didn't really *buy* it."

"It was collateral," I said. "She lent you that two hundred grand."

"I was overcome with gratitude. I'd told her I had no money, but I hadn't asked her for a loan, and if I had, I wouldn't have asked for half that much. I offered to give her the picture, but she said, 'No, you hang onto it. I trust you.'"

"So how does it come to pass," I said, "that a couple of thugs have made off with all the *rest* of your pictures?"

"I guess they didn't know which one they were looking for. Or maybe they just couldn't find it."

"I was joking."

"Oh."

"I could strangle Kimura-kun."

"It's my fault, not his. I should have gone over there this morning."

"I'm glad you didn't." I looked at the bandage on his left hand, which was pretty filthy by now.

"That happened the first time I met them. I didn't know who I was dealing with, and I got angry… which turned out to be a mistake."

"It usually is."

"I know… They dropped me off at the emergency room in Shinjuku. I got my hand fixed up and then I walked to your place. Well, that was another mistake. They must have followed me, because when they called me yesterday, they read your address to me over the phone. They threatened to hurt you."

"There are other ways they could have got my address," I said absently. I was thinking about him walking from Shinju-ku to Ikebukuro in the middle of the night, woozy on painkill-ers. I said, "All right, I'm calling Dorothy now."

"Yeah. Ruth."

"Is everything OK?"

"Everything's fine and dandy, far as that goes. Did you find her?"

"No. I think maybe we should call the police."

"Police? Fuck that, girl, we ain't calling no police. I'm sor-ry for her; I tried to help her and all, but there's a limit to my patience." I could hear television commercials backing Doro-thy's voice. Wherever she was, it wasn't Pub Club Paradise. "I'm not going to cry for her, either," she said fiercely. "Aren't there enough tears in the world?"

"Did you know she wasn't really a graduate student?"

"Sure, I knew. I guessed, anyway, and I let her know that I guessed, and she just about admitted I was right. I'll say this for her: she was the best liar I ever met. Would've had me fooled if I hadn't gone to those Mishima meetings with her. Turns out, when I come to talk to the other people there, she don't know much at all about that literary criticism shit. Why she felt like she had to lie about it, you tell me, but it wasn't any of my business to go exposing her – especially to you; you graduated college, you should have figured it out for yourself – so I just let it be. You been talking to Shinji?"

"I'm with him now. It seems like Kaito's bosses, or some subsidiary syndicate of theirs, have made off with all his pictures. Or almost all of them."

""Subsidiary syndicate,'" repeated Dorothy sarcastically. "You don't know what you're talking about. Mind you, I don't know who they are, either. I might be able to find out."

The unspoken corollary came through to me: *Don't ask.* Wincing, I said, "Please ask."

"All right," she said reluctantly. "Hold on."

She covered the mouthpiece of her cell phone. I looked at Shinji, who was on his knees beside the easel, sorting through the old canvases beneath it. I said, "As soon as I finish this call I'm going to get onto the police and report Casey missing."

"Do you think she'd thank you for that?"

There was a knock at the door. Shinji's mother shuffled in, bearing a tray that held two glasses and a dish of snacks. How had she negotiated the stairs? Horrified, I took the tray from her. "Just in case you're hungry," she said. "If you're not, please leave it. I'm going to bed now, so you'll have to wash up after yourselves!" She smiled: it was a joke.

I voiced incoherent thanks. When she'd withdrawn, I said to Shinji, "Why did you move out?"

"Ask my dad," he said.

I took a sip from one of the glasses. It was ginger ale. The dish held individually packaged rice crackers, satsumas, and homemade rice balls with seaweed jackets. I reached for one of these as Dorothy came back on the line. "Yes," I said.

"I can't find out anything right now. It could be they don't know, either. Listen, as a matter of fact, I'm dealing with a situation here. Let me call you back, OK?"

"Dorothy, where are you?"

"Where am I? Well, I'm riding along with Horiuchi san and his boys. Kaito's with us, too. We're cruising the Rainbow Bridge right now, just enjoying the scenery."

I saw in my mind's eye the white Benz rolling across the bridge with its tinted windows shut, its dashboard television fizzing and popping, a man with nine fingers at the steering wheel, and Dorothy riding in back between Horiuchi san, whom I'd never heard of, and a colleague of his in an equally double-breasted suit; and all the traffic signals ahead of them were green.

"We're on our way out to Odaiba," Dorothy said dreamily. "You know they got some nice Christmas lights out there."

"Dorothy, why did you sell Shinji's tab to them? They broke his fingers."

"You ask him if I didn't ask him for the money myself. I asked him – must have been twenty times, and I waited for him to make some money at that exhibition of his. But he ain't made shit, have he? I would have given him as long as he needed, but time got to be short. I made a deal and I got to hold up my end of it. His wasn't the only debt I passed onto them. It was the biggest, though, so I'm not surprised they're chasing it up."

"What kind of a… what kind of a deal?"

"Are you completely fucking blind?" she said. "How you think I got that bonus for Irina and them? How you think I got to hire Vivi instead of another Russkie that Himemiya-san would have been taking all of her money? How you think I been keeping *you* on even though you don't got more than a dozen regulars? I got someone to keep Himemiya-san and Vladimir fucking Ivanovich out of my face! That's how! But they don't come cheap."

"And they aren't ready for a black girl from Texas running her own club in Roppongi," I said.

"Mama-san sure picked the wrong fucking time to drink herself into the hospital," Dorothy agreed. A man spoke to her in Japanese I couldn't catch. "Listen, I really gotta go! You tell Shinji I'm sorry about his pictures, but it was all about the money, and he knew that."

"Dorothy, are you…"

"And tell him don't go and meet them by himself again, or they might break more than his fingers. I'm going, Ruth! I'm cutting this short! Bye."

I covered my face with my hands, unable to stop seeing the Benz's sleek silhouette speeding towards Odaiba and the sea.

Shinji touched my shoulder. "My dad's home. I'm going to go talk to him."

Left alone, I ate a rice ball and a satsuma, washing them down with ginger ale. There was an ashtray on the desk. I lit a cigarette and stood at the window gazing at the expressway. Gradually my thoughts started connecting up again. My dominant one was that I couldn't go back to my apartment – at least, not alone.

A voice, not Shinji's, rose on a note of irritable finality. I put out my cigarette and crept to the top of the stairs.

I could see a little way into the sitting-room. Shinji stood with his back to the door in the insouciant hipshot stance that I disliked. It made me think of a U2 song and gave me a metallic taste in the back of my throat. An older man brushed past him and came out into the hall. I recognized him at the same time as he saw me.

Laughing with shame, I wobbled down the stairs and apologized to him for being in his house.

"I've seen you somewhere before," he said. "Could it have been on television? Or in the movies?" He laughed.

"It was in Roppongi, sir," I whispered.

"Of course! You work at Trinket Box. Or is it Club Perfume?"

"Pub Club Paradise, sir. But not any more."

"Really? Well, that's probably for the best. Change is the spice of life. Never get stuck in a rut! On the other hand, my worthless son here… always chopping and changing. There's such a thing as overdoing it. And now he's in a mess, by the sound of things. I don't suppose you had anything to do with *that?*"

"Actually," I whispered, "it was all my fault."

Shinji's father stared at me in surprise that softened within a heartbeat's time to disappointment. "Never own up," he said, shaking his head. "It's a common failing. Overcome it and you'll be free. But once get into the habit of owning up and you'll find you've spent your life compensating for your mistakes, with not a yen to show for it. Better to put the past behind you."

"He ought to know," said Shinji. "Four failed companies and counting."

"Your manners are as bad as ever. Have you offered the young lady a drink? I didn't think so. Can I interest you in a nightcap… what was your name again? Kathy?"

So we sat around the coffee table in the trapezoidal living-room and I poured their drinks and lit their cigarettes. The whiskey went to my head but didn't touch the chill inside me.

"Can I count on you to tell me the truth about *anything?*" I said to Shinji once we were back upstairs.

"You know it all now," he said, falling on his bed.

"All?"

"All."

"Then I guess there's no more to say. What are we doing here, anyway?"

"I thought he might lend me the money. He says he doesn't have it. I know he does… but whatever. I even asked him to take me on at the cleaning company again. No dice. He's laying people off, not hiring them."

"Well, maybe he'll change his mind, " I said, sitting down on the floor.

"Maybe."

"In the meantime," I said to my feet, "my offer still stands."

"If I take your money, even as a loan, we'll be through, won't we?"

"Yeah."

I heard a faint rumbling in the distance, a change in the timbre of the white noise. At last Shinji said, "I just didn't want to burden you with all my mistakes. I guess that in itself could have been a mistake, but falling in love with you *wasn't* a mistake, and I wanted to keep that… like keeping one good thing for myself when I'd had to give everything else away."

"I felt pretty much the same way about you." I wanted to hug him, but I couldn't bring myself to do it. He was a skeleton in jeans and a sweater. It was strange to remember how nice it had been sleeping with him. "Well, maybe, as your dad said, it's time to put the past behind us, mistakes and all. The question, in that case, would be: what are we going to do now?"

"Commit suicide?"

"Shinji, I'm a Catholic. I know you're not serious, but even if you were…"

"I am serious."

"Oh, go to hell," I said in English, laughing, and stood up just as the house started to shake. It was a juggernaut; it was one big motherfucker of a juggernaut; it wasn't. The ground heaved the house from side to side. The windows rattled and the floor rolled, throwing Shinji to his feet. I clung to him. "Don't panic," he said, "it's all right," but things were falling over. The windows broke. The easel toppled. I heard an earsplitting crunching roar, and the floor dropped out from under our feet like the deck of a ship setting out to sea at last.

THE IMMORTALS

It *was* a pretentious name for a band. We were a cover band, and most of the numbers in our repertoire had already achieved a half-assed kind of immortality, so I could live with it. But I suspected that Jafe Kuklowski, our vocalist, had come up with it in a moment of sheer optimism. He didn't have a very acute sense of irony.

We'd formed in the first place to perform originals (composed, needless to say, by Jafe). Almost a year later, we were still on the pub circuit, and our demo was still out on its grand tour of the labels. Tokyo has more bands per square meter than any other city I know. Jafe adored performing under any conditions, and he made the best of it by sneaking one or two originals into each set, but he made no secret of the fact that he loathed the most popular songs in our repertoire – Stones standards; Oasis; 80s nostalgia numbers.

A few days after the USA invaded Iraq, we got together for our monthly gig at Shakespeare's, a British pub in Ebisu. It was the biggest fixture on our schedule and the only one that paid more than a token fee. One Yamanote stop south of Shibuya, we could draw a good house even on Thursday night. The crowd was about half foreign, and at least one person usually got drunk enough to buy our CD. We kicked off with a pair of Fleetwood Mac rarities, getting people used to the idea that we were there, then eased into "Another Day In Paradise," followed by "Heard It Through The Grapevine." You have to be pretty obvious to start people dancing, but once they're up you've got them. That's one of the lovely things about playing pubs. Forty minutes in, we had them leaping for the ceiling to our version of "Buffalo Soldier." Jafe did a creditable Saint Bob, blue eyes and all, and I harmonized with Aki Shimoda, our guitarist, on the backing vocals. We rounded off the first half of the set with REM's "Imitation Of Life." From my spot on the corner of the stage I could see over the crowd to the door. During the second chorus I saw Makoto come in. He had a girl with him. He'd been saying for ages that he wanted to catch one of our gigs. He hadn't said anything about bringing *her*. I dropped my head and concentrated for the last minute of the song on my fingering.

Jafe wiped his arm across his face. "Tonight we have something important to say to you all; uh huh, thank you, thank you… we want to say we do not support this war. I'm an American citizen but the sh… stuff that's going down right now makes me ashamed of my country. Ashamed, man. For real."

I cringed. I agreed with him, but nice to alienate half our audience. Most expats are more patriotic than they were at home, not less.

"Violence is never the answer!" intoned Jafe. At that there was some clapping. He dropped into his patter: "We are the Immortals and that's Philip back there if you can see him, Aki the master of the Stratocaster, Tamsin on bass…"

I got my very own smattering of applause. There's something to be said for being the only girl in the band, and there's something to be said for *having* a girl in your band. Even in a net income nil, all covers situation, the boys could probably have found a more serious bassist than I was. They probably couldn't have found another bassist willing to go onstage in a halter top. I grabbed my mic, waved a copy of our CD in the air, and said, "*Unholy Communion*. Buy it. Please. Thank you. Yoroshiku onegai shimasu." After the laughter died down, Jafe introduced himself, made another plea for world peace in his broken Japanese, and wandered offstage to socialize with the fans.

He was married. His wife, Midori, was an editorial assistant on a travel magazine. She rarely came to our gigs. Aki theorized that she had a problem with the amount of time and cash that Jafe put into the band. Philip theorized that she moonlighted as a bar hostess to pay the bills, since Jafe was such a rock star that he could never hold down a day job for long. Whatever the truth of the matter was, Jafe did not repine.

Of course, he wasn't the only one.

I leaned my Fender Standard against the nearest amp and went to talk to Makoto.

"This is Lucy. She want to say something to you."

She had short blonde curls and a face like a Raphael cherub's. I self-consciously pushed my long, mousy, sweat-tangled hair out of my face. Makoto, I knew, was a sucker for that Sophie Dahl look, and what's more Lucy had the same nailbiting, hesitant manner he'd found attractive in me when we first met.

"You guys are brilliant," she said sycophantically. "I'd buy the CD, honest I would, if I wasn't a poor skint English teacher."

Small talk, small talk. "How long have you been in Japan?"

"Four months. What about you?"

"Oh," I said, "a while."

Somewhere behind me I could hear Jafe saying, "Nuh uh, not Jeff, *Jafe*. It's short for Japhet. Yeah… Western culture is based on Christianity, you know?"

"So, Lucy, you're from Manchester?"

"Newcastle, actually. Not *quite* the same thing."

I'd got it wrong on purpose, but I felt bad about it when she said humbly, "This is the first time I've been away from home. Well, I was an au pair in Nice one summer but that doesn't really count, does it?"

I could have told her that I'd lived in London for two years – we might have found common ground there – but supposing she'd never been there, either? I excused myself to get a drink. Before I could reach the bar, someone tapped me on the shoulder and offered me a G&T. While I took his request for Billy Idol, I watched Makoto talk at Lucy. I guessed he was telling her all about The Immortals, omitting the fact that this was the first time he'd ever seen us live, and about his long-ago stint as the drummer in a punk outfit – if she hadn't heard about that on their first date. He was making un-Japanese gestures, doing his best to impress her. He'd never introduced one of his girlfriends to me before. I felt sorry for both of them, and just a tiny bit sorry for myself. I wriggled back through the crowd to them. "How did you guys first happen to meet?" I asked, knowing the answer.

"Oh! He was one of my students. And he asked me if I'd give him some extra lessons. Said he'd pay me and everything. So we went for coffee, and I think I was explaining the subjunctive when I looked down and said, 'Aaargh, what's this *thing* on my knee?'" Lucy laughed so infectiously that I had to laugh, too. It *was* funny.

"I persuade her not to lawsuit for sekuhara," said Makoto, his eyes twinkling. He added in Japanese, which I took it Lucy did not speak: "It wasn't that difficult."

"Ooohh Makoto," I said, giving him dead eyes, "you menace, you."

We reassembled on stage. While we waited for the sound tech to turn off the muzak, Philip leaned out from behind his kit. "Oi Tammie, who was that geezer?"

"My husband," I said, tuning my A string up a halfnote.

Aki, overhearing, said, "He's very handsome."

"I know. That's the trouble."

"Not *that* geezer, love." Philip was grinning. "The geezer who bought you a drink."

Fucking Philip. Drop your guard for a minute.

"I almost forgot," I said, "Jafe, can we fit in 'Cradle Of Love'? It's a request. Aki, are you up for it?"

The axework on "Cradle Of Love" is no joke. But Aki just nodded.

"We'll open with it," said Jafe. "Get it out of the way, then back to the set list. Hey, you know, good work, Tammie. Gotta keep the fans happy."

"I saw you keeping that sexy little fan in the white dress happy," said Philip.

"It's all part of the mission, man, you're with me on this, aren't you? To educate, enlighten, and entertain."

And that was *before* the shambles he made of the second half of the gig.

It probably was entertaining, in a way, if you weren't on stage with him.

The spotlights went off at 11 o'clock sharp. I plucked my last chord again and got nothing. They'd pulled the plug on us. The manager came through what was left of the crowd, smiling in the friendly way managers do. Jafe hung an arm around his shoulders and sauntered off with him, still talking a mile a minute. The bartenders ostentatiously wiped counters. Makoto and Lucy had long since evaporated. Philip, Aki, and I looked at each other and dived for our belongings. Two minutes later we were out on the street, hurrying towards Ebisu station, threading our way among the salarymen and office girls who were bowing their goodbyes outside other bars. I couldn't stop laughing. We'd ditched Jafe. We'd *ditched* him.

Aki pulled the elastic band off his ponytail and shook it loose. He was smiling in the way that meant he'd been deeply lacerated by embarrassment.

"Poor bloody punters," said Philip, burying his chin in his muffler. March nights in Tokyo can chill you to the bone. "Never seen a crowd so gobsmacked." He grimaced. He had one of those lumpy, expressive Celtic faces with a permanent shadow of stubble. "It's just another ideology." He used the word like it had four letters. "And it's a fucking dangerous one. It's suicide by any other name." He rounded on Aki for some reason, maybe just because Aki was Japanese. "It'll fucking kill you, mate!"

Aki's smile froze on his face. "I think it is not cool to tell people what they must do."

Philip laughed and slapped him on the shoulder, making him stagger under his gig bag. "That would be my point." He looked at his watch. "You both working tomorrow? Yeah? Me, too. Ah, fuck it. Back to mine?"

He lived in a gaijin house near Shinjuku. We trooped down to the communal kitchen in the basement. It was cold, and there was a smell of stale fat. The Astroturf carpet stuck to my sneakers. Once you get used to taking your shoes off when you go indoors, keeping them on gives you an uneasy waifish sort of feeling. Of course, Sunshine House was waifs-and-strays central. Philip had lived in Japan for six years; he should have been doing better than this. But just a few months ago he'd broken up with his girlfriend and found himself ass out on the block. The irony was that he'd destroyed his relationship by philandering, but now he couldn't pull for shit.

Everything in the communal fridge was labelled with Post-Its. Philip fixed a huge pan of scrambled eggs, using someone else's milk. We carried our plates up to his room and made toast in his illicit toaster oven. Philip sat crosslegged on his bed. Aki and I sat on the floor. All around us towered the boxes of stuff Philip had liberated from his girlfriend's apartment.

Philip blamed me and Aki for letting Jafe wreck the gig. "Didn't you hear… ah, you couldn't not have heard: 'and, uh, history proves that art is for *peace,* man, art is all about —' *ba da da bom bom ba dom dom!*" He battered the air with his chopsticks, reliving his attempt to galvanize us. "Bloody funny I must have looked when the two of you just stood there like wallies!"

I had to admit that Philip had been the only one of us who'd kept his head. Aki and I *had* just stood there – like wallies, doubtless – while Jafe waffled on about the invasion of Iraq, the wrongness in general of war, the intrinsic malevolence of Christianity, and last but far from least, the music industry. My very thin excuse was that I simply hadn't been able to believe what was happening. Aki had probably been paralyzed by mortification. We'd played a total of seven songs during the second half of the set. Two of those had been originals off *Unholy Communion*, and Jafe had introduced each one at excruciating length.

"Where the fuck were you?" howled Philip. *"Bom ba dom dom,* that was your cue, *deeeow de deeow!"*

"Mostly it don't matter, I think," said Aki. "They don't understand what he's saying. They think funny."

"I don't think *either* of you guys is taking it seriously enough," I said.

"Not taking it seriously enough? Tammie, music is my life! It's my fucking soul!" This, from the man who usually referred to The Immortals as 'a laugh.' "That wanker thinks it's his band. It's not, is it? It's *our* band. But if he's lost us the Shakespeare's gig, I'm, fuck, sayonara, mate. I mean it. I take this shit fucking seriously."

I saw the rage on his face and switched tactics. "I didn't even get to do my song," I said sadly.

Most of our sets featured one song with me on lead vocal, usually a Janis Joplin number.

"I was going to dedicate it to *him,"* I mourned.

"Yeah, it's not fair on you, Tammie, is it? It's tough on you, isn't it?"

Aki, as usual, was half a step behind the conversation. He said, "Philip, you are an OK drummer. You know, you're not bad. But Jafe is really talented. He have the voice that he can express suffering. If you quit the band I think you miss out big time. Like Peter Best, you know, drummer who quit the Beatles. You will regret."

I drew breath to head Philip off. But I'd misanticipated him again. It was Aki's turn to be ignored. Giving me a challenging look, Philip reached behind the head of his bed and lifted out his double bongos. He settled them between his knees and started whacking out the intro to my song. I jumped to my feet.

Aki shut his eyes, fingerpicking air. Philip stopped drumming. "Look in the closet... ah, I'll get it." He plunged into his oshiire closet and emerged with a dusty acoustic guitar. Few and far between are the musicians who haven't tried their hands at two or more instruments. Aki tuned the old thing up, and I was ready. I pictured Makoto's face as I howled the words to Janis Joplin's "Move Over."

We were all laughing, and I was hamming it up, relieved to express my tangled feelings, when someone hammered on the door. "We will be told noisy," said Aki excitedly.

"Nah, concrete walls, couldn't hear a fucking gun going off."

"Hey guys, open up! You sound like shit!"

Philip rose and let Jafe in.

"You know, I had a hunch I'd find you guys here. I must be psychic, huh?" Jafe sat down on the end of Philip's bed. "Hey Tammie, I was just kidding, you sounded pretty good. But you gotta cut back on the 'ow, ow, owooo' shit. You're not Janis, so you shouldn't try to be her, you know what I'm saying? You gotta rebirth the song with your own flavor."

"We were just messing around," I said.

Aki was noodling on the acoustic guitar again. I started singing softly, then Jafe took up the song. "It ended up in a shit-filled sandpit..." He closed his eyes and tipped his head back, rotating the cricks out of his neck. "Oh, we gotta do that one next time. One little ballad won't hurt them."

"So there's going to be a next time?" said Philip. "We're still on the schedule at Shakespeare's?"

"Chill, Phil." Jafe chuckled and repeated, "Chill, Phil. You're such a fucking pessimist. As a matter of fact, they offered us Friday instead of Thursday next month." He lighted a Marlboro, reaching for the coffee tin Philip used as an ashtray. "The Young Fogeys' guitarist got himself arrested or some shit, so we get the slot. Are we moving up in the world or what?"

"Is that a fact, now?" Philip said. "Is that God's truth, cross your heart and hope to die? Yeah? Well, then, Jafe, I'll be truthful with you, too. We've been doing a bit of talking here. In fact we were having something of the nature of an emergency summit meeting before you barged in. *Br-rr-rr-bah!*" He riffed theatrically on the bongos. "The focus hasn't been on the music lately. That's a fact, isn't it? The question is, what can we do about it, like. Now Aki and myself, we've always fancied giving it a go as a threepiece…"

I squeaked involuntarily in astonishment.

Jafe laughed, puffing out smoke. "It's cool, Tammie, he's just fucking with your head. We'd never drop you. Would we, guys?"

"Lose the fucking ego, Kuklowski," said Philip. "It's not Tamsin we're dropping. It's you."

I was taking an intermediate conversation class on Tuesday afternoon when my phone rang. "Fuck," I said, making my students giggle. I'd forgotten to transfer the damned thing from my pocket to my locker. As I turned it off I glimpsed Makoto's name on the caller ID screen. My students looked at me expectantly: three girls and one pensioner, all paying the equivalent of $20 an hour. I blushed.

My shift ended at seven o'clock. The staff room was full of teachers, most of them closer to Lucy's age than mine, eating sandwiches and bemoaning their lot. They weren't a bad bunch of kids, but I couldn't be bothered with them. I was not Jafe, sweating the public relations in every area of my life. I grabbed my bag, punched out, and dialed Makoto on my way downstairs.

"Oh, it was nothing special. I was just wondering if you wanted to have dinner. I'm still at work, but I don't have to stay late tonight."

Makoto worked as a certified accountant at a small but vicious trading company in Shinjuku. Most days he worked until midnight or even slept at the office. My school was in Ikebukuro, the northernmost hub on the Yamanote line. This had been convenient when Makoto and I lived together in Omiya. Now that I lived by myself in Eifukucho, out west in Suginami Ward, my commute took an hour and twenty minutes. I would have switched jobs, but I was loth to give up my train pass. The Immortals rehearsed in Ikebukuro, too, and we had semi-regular gigs in Takadanobaba and Shinjuku, which were also on my route to work, so that train pass had been saving me something like $50 a month.

Now, however…

I stood on the landing, feeling dizzy.

"Hello? Tammie? I thought we could go to Jyu in Shibuya," said Makoto. "It's on your way home, so if you're free…"

I tried to breathe deeply. "OK. Can you get there pretty soon? I'm hungry."

Three hours later we were staggering up Shibuya's Dogenzaka hill, laughing and hanging onto each other. Neon twinkled over our heads. As it was Tuesday, all the love hotels had vacancy signs out. Makoto peered at a price board stuck on a pink pebbledashed wall. "Six thousand and up, it doesn't get any cheaper than this."

We took the room that looked the most spacious in the photographs on display in the foyer. It turned out to be tiny, of course, but what can you expect? The bare minimum: a bed, a TV, and a catalog of porn videos. While Makoto showered, I watched the war and drank a tumbler full of the cheap red we'd bought at a convenience store after dinner. I didn't want to sober up. Makoto came out of the bathroom with a towel around his waist. "Lie down," he said, and undressed me, kissing me all over as he went. He was the tenderest guy I'd ever slept with. (So he should have been, too: he got enough practise.) Sometimes, while we were still living together, I'd flattered myself that he put an extra loving spoonful of feeling into sex with me, that he was uniquely fascinated by me, and that that was why he'd married me. But even back then I'd known better, so I'd never let myself fall in love with him.

Our marriage had been founded on the premise that we *weren't* in love. We were great friends; we'd hit it off from day one, when he'd shown up in my classroom just a couple of months after I arrived in Japan. We'd gone to the movies, tried kissing, and realized that we weren't attracted to each other. But we had so much else to offer each other that it didn't matter.

I'd decided as soon as I stepped off the plane that I liked it here and wanted to stay a while. To do that I needed visa security. The easiest way to get visa security was to get married. Makoto volunteered to be my accomplice. We would be getting the better of the authorities, striking a blow for a world without borders; it would be a laugh, he said; and just to make sure the deception took, we could combine our finances and move into a really nice apartment together. His lease was about to expire. The timing was perfect.

So that was what we did, and ten days later we were rolling around naked on our brand new living-room carpet.

I never felt I had the right to tell him off for womanizing. It wasn't as if we'd vowed fidelity or anything. And he swore he always used protection.

But I came to the conclusion that jealousy was some kind of involuntary physical reaction, not an emotional thing at all. I started to loathe him, and I didn't want our friendship to end like that. We talked it over and made an effort to be a proper married couple, but that was the worst period of all. In the end I threw up my hands in despair and moved out.

At almost the same time, my former band split up and I answered the advertisement that Jafe, Philip, and Aki had placed ISO a bassist.

"We're here on a mission, my friends. To educate, enlighten, entertain, and drink Tokyo dry."

That was the first thing I ever heard Jafe say, and he got a laugh for it. The crowd at The Packrat, a small pub in Shinjuku, had been ignoring the band, so he'd started mixing stand-up comedy with the songs. Little by little he was winning them over.

I lurked by the bar as they swung into Santana's "Smooth." I loved Jafe's voice. I didn't love the way he was hacking at his poor bass guitar. This was such a beautiful song, and with the rhythm lacking cohesion, it sounded like it was decomposing in the air.

When they announced a break, I went up and said, "I'm Tamsin Carey." (Not Ikeda; not here; not any more.) "I answered your ad."

Jafe looked me up and down, then grinned and stuck out his hand. "You're hired. Naw, I'm kidding, but... Yo, guys! This is Tamsin! She'll do, huh?"

The drummer lowered his pint of Guinness. "And I was thinking it's another of Jafe's legion of fans."

The guitarist said, "You can play this?" He held out to me the Rogue LX200B Jafe had been playing. "You know some Stones? Can play 'Beast of Burden'?"

So I joined them for a couple of songs after the break. I was mainly concentrating on not messing up. Afterwards, the boys asked me to hang out until the set was over. While Aki and Philip were packing up, Jafe told me the spot was mine if I wanted it.

"Like I said in my mail," he gulped from a glass of flat beer, "we're planning on going into the studio soon. And we don't want to record with some rent-a-rhythm-section. We want someone that plays with us and grooves on our influences. If it works out, you'll be coming with us to the next level, you know what I'm saying?" He surveyed the boisterous Friday night crowd and smiled at someone I couldn't see. "This shit is cool and all, but I can guarantee it's temporary."

"As far as the influences go, I think we're on the same wavelength," I said. "I'd like to hear your stuff, of course."

I was playing it cool. I could, because I hadn't heard Jafe's compositions yet. When I did, I would understand why Philip and Aki were so loyal to him.

"One other thing... don't take this the wrong way, but since you're of the female persuasion and all, would you be into contributing to the band's image? Just for gigs?" Jafe eyed my sweater and baggy pinstripes. "I mean, you're working that funky look, but..."

I laughed and touched him on the arm. "No problem. I was a teenage riot grrrl, but eventually I learned to stop worrying and love the double standard."

I was 28. I figured the guys for around my age. If you're hoping to make it professionally, 28, 29, 30 is the crumbling edge of the precipice.

"Just don't ask me to get a manicure," I said, giving Jafe my left hand so he could see my calluses.

"We are gonna make bee-yoo-tiful music! Check it out, you gotta meet the support system." He beckoned to someone in the corner. I felt my face stiffening when I saw it was a Japanese woman. She slid off her bar stool and came to say hello. She could have been voluptuous or just plump – it was hard to tell what was under her jeans and oversized sweatshirt. She dressed like an American girl, I thought (and was later to discover that she'd done her degree in international studies at MSU). Her untinted shoulder-length hair was pulled back in a barrette. She wore no makeup.

"This is Midori. My better half." Jafe grabbed our hands and made us shake. Hers was limp, and her smile, when it came, had an edge to it that I took for condescension. Her name was homophonous with *green,* but I didn't think there was anything green, in any sense, about her.

When we went into the studio a month later, she stopped by to bring us thermoses of hot tea and homemade onigiri. But over the course of the ten months after that, I met her just a couple more times.

Meanwhile, my attraction to Jafe festered. He flirted with girls at gigs, not as Makoto would have done in his place, with the serious intention of getting them into bed, but just so that they'd buy our CD and maybe pass it on to someone who knew someone. Philip was a much worse slut. Unfortunately, however, he lacked Jafe's rangy good looks. The best he could do was to pull the girls that Jafe left bobbing in his wake. I sometimes felt like telling them that he, Philip, had a girlfriend waiting at home. But in the end, without any help from me, she kicked his ass out. Did he feel hard done by? Or was he telling us the truth when he said he'd never been in love with her? Whatever. It was around this time that I first noticed the friction between him and Jafe, which intensified into occasional quarrels during the months of silence from all the labels we'd sent our CD to.

I'd originally taken Aki for The Immortals' calm center of gravity. He certainly played the role of buffer between Philip and Jafe. But rock guitarists do not tend to be slow 'n' steady types, and Aki was no exception. Behind his mask of composure, he was as nervous as a stray cat. He used to throw up before gigs, whether from stage fright or from the liquor he poured down his throat in an attempt to beat the stage fright. Philip and Jafe teased him about it. I was horrified. A couple of months after I joined the band, Aki and I started busking together on Sundays. My idea was to cure him the natural way, by getting him to play stone cold sober in a park for the love of it. We never made any money out of it (the Japanese don't tip buskers), but it did seem to help a bit... maybe because, unlike Jafe and Philip, who were as hard on Aki as they were on themselves, I never criticized him. When we were on our own we rubbed along together like two fuzzy caterpillars. We were equally weak.

That was how we got drawn by Philip into what by March had become a tacit (and enjoyable) anti-Jafe conspiracy. That was why we were so quick to abandon Jafe after the gig at Shakespeare's. And that was why Aki and I failed to argue with Philip when he said he wasn't getting on another stage with Japhet Kuklowski in this lifetime: not if it was the fucking Grammy Awards.

We both regretted our spinelessness within hours.

I'd never been in a band that made real money, but I'd planned my life around the gamble that music would start to pay off for me someday. When I joined The Immortals I'd thought it might finally be going to happen. Japan is a great place for bands to perform their way into the major leagues. Bowled over by Jafe's compositions, eager to exchange my shambles of a life with Makoto for a better future, I'd moved into an apartment that I couldn't really afford. To pay my rent I'd been running through my savings. I now had about four months before I would have to break my lease and move into a gaijin house like the dump where Philip lived.

To make matters worse, I hadn't dared to register my new address with the ward office. As far as the authorities knew, Mr and Mrs Ikeda were still living in connubial harmony in Omiya. The deception was essential to my visa status, but I couldn't see it succeeding indefinitely. I'd been holding my breath, waiting to be found out, waiting for something to go wrong… and now something had. It just wasn't what I'd been expecting. It never is, is it?

"We tried to discuss the whole thing like civilized adults," I said to Makoto, lying in bed with the lights dimmed to an orange glow. "But it was hopeless."

Makoto liked speaking English, but it took a lot out of him, so by this time of night we'd invariably dropped into Japanese. One of the things I am OK at is languages, and I could now speak Japanese without giving much conscious thought to it. Of course, I still made mistakes, but how to render them in English? I only know what I thought I said, what I meant to say.

"Philip ended up storming out, and we were left sitting in his room staring at each other."

"Why is it such a big deal?" said Makoto. "Why can't the three of you just tell Jafe, hey, we know you feel strongly about the war and all, but you have to wait until you're famous before you can say that kind of stuff on stage?"

"If that was the issue, it *would* be that simple. But we've lost the Shakespeare's gig. You can't screw up that badly and get away with it. Not when there are a dozen bands waiting to take your place. We knew we had to have lost it that night, too, but Jafe lied to us about it. *That's* what really bugs me."

"Has he ever done that before? Spun a story to keep you guys happy?"

"Not that I know of."

Makoto stared up at the mirrors on the ceiling, which reflected his own perfectly proportioned body and my average one. "Come to think of it, that was a pretty stupid lie, too, wasn't it? He must have known you'd find out the truth before long."

"He needs to take lessons from you."

Makoto laughed. "I'm a hopeless liar. You know that."

It was partly true. With regard to his casual liaisons, his triumphs and humiliations at work, and his doubts about the meaning of life, he'd always told me the truth even when I didn't want to hear it. But I knew he was good at the kind of lies that make casual liaisons possible.

"What have you told Lucy? Everything?" I didn't believe it for a minute, even if he had introduced her to me.

He hooked his foot over my leg and tickled the inside of my knee with his toes.

"Quit it!"

He rolled onto his stomach and lit a cigarette. "Have you seen the guys since that night?"

"Only Aki. We sometimes go busking on Sundays, you know, just for fun. Well, this week we packed it in early and went for coffee. He said he's going to work on Philip. He thinks he can talk him around."

"Well, do *you* think he can?"

"It all depends on Jafe. If Aki promises Philip everything's going to be fine, and then Jafe screws up again… we've got a gig on Saturday at The Piper in Takadanobaba. I guess we're not going to cancel it. I guess we'll know for sure then." I felt miserable. If I was as tense on Saturday as I was right now, *I'd* screw us up without any help from Jafe or anybody. I snuggled up to Makoto's side. He'd showered again after we made love, so I had to bury my nose in his shoulder to get the familiar smell of his skin.

He kissed my forehead. "I know you've put a lot of work into this band, but why couldn't the three of you make a go of it without Jafe? You've always wanted to sing, haven't you?"

"But I'm nothing special. Jafe is. He... I wouldn't go so far as to say he's a genius, but he's got so much ability that it's unbelievable he can't get signed."

"Uh huh," sighed Makoto, and laid his forearm across his eyes. "So why are you afraid he's going to screw up again? You don't think he's deliberately sabotaging the band, do you?"

"Well, before Thursday I'd have said he'd never do that. I mean, we've got a CD out and everything. But... oh, Makoto... it was weird..." My Japanese was not good enough to describe the tenor of Jafe's rambling discursions. "It was scary!"

"Easy. Have a cigarette."

"I wanted you to hear us on top form. I didn't want you to hear *that*."

"I'll come to another gig if you want me to. I just can't say when it'll be. My boss has gone on a business trip and he won't be back until Friday, so I'm taking it easy this week, but I know I'll have to work this weekend."

"And we might never have another gig after Saturday," I said despairingly.

"Well, I've got your CD," he reminded me. "I listen to it and think about you."

"Have you played it for Lucy?"

He stubbed out his cigarette and put his arm around me. "I lent it to her, actually. She said she wanted to copy it."

We switched off the lights. I lay in the dark and thought about the multiple trajectories that lead to Hell. Sometimes I could almost feel myself gathering momentum, like a spaceship hurtling away from the sun at hundreds of thousands of kilometres per second – an intergalactic snail's pace, imperceptibly accelerating. My trajectory was all my own, but no better for that.

I sat bolt upright, heart thudding. From my bag on the floor chapel bells were clamoring. I licked my lips. "Moshi moshi."

"Yo, Tammie, what's up?"

"Jafe? For God's sake." I glanced at the audio console on the headboard of the bed and saw that it was ten past three in the morning. Makoto was snoring. I silenced him with a gentle push. "Is everything OK?"

"Sure, everything's fine. Hey, sorry about calling so late. I just wanted to find out if you're free tomorrow. Say around eight? For dinner? And…"

"Dinner? Wh…" *Why?* "Where?"

"Well, this girl who works with Midori has written a book. She's having the release party, or whatever you call it, at Lilight. Ever heard of it? Me neither. But Midori says it's a cool spot, and she wants to support this girl, so I thought we'd all go together. What do you say?"

Relief washed over me. Here, I thought, was proof that Jafe knew he'd made a blunder that had to be fixed. "So the guys are coming? Hey, sure, Jafe, I'll be there!"

"Uh, actually… I haven't asked them. I mean, I know Aki works the closing shift most nights, and Philip usually works late, too, doesn't he? So… remember that guy you invited to Shakespeare's last week?"

"Yeah," I said, looking down at Makoto's sleeping face. "My husband. But Jafe…"

"How about asking *him?* If he can't make it I guess we could get someone else. But Midori – I hope you don't mind that I told her – she thinks it's cool that you're married to a Japanese guy, you know? And she thought it would be cool for the four of us to go out together. I think it would be kinda neat myself. Don't you?"

"It's a great idea, Jafe." I snuggled down beside Makoto, clutching my phone. "I'll ask him. I can't promise anything, but…"

As Jafe effused in my ear, I reached out and curled my fingers around Makoto's penis. It grew in my hand, as reliable as a little machine. At the same time as I got off the phone his eyes opened, glinting with amusement. He rolled on top of me and bit my neck. "So what's this you've committed me to? Mind if I ask Lucy along? Hey, hey, I'm just kidding!"

Lilight turned out to be in Ebisu. It was tiny and smoky and the DJ favored world music. On the walls hung an exhibition of watercolors depicting scenes from a tropical neverland. The skies in the paintings were grey, the palm trees looked sick, and there were fangy things in the water. Gazing at them, I felt grateful to be alive. I just wished I was alive somewhere else.

Everyone seemed to be a regular, including Midori's colleague Junko. Her newly published book was entitled *Moonless Nights: An Erotic Novel in Tanka*. Settling us at a rickety table, she demanded, "Midori, sweet, are you sure you're *up* to this? It wasn't so long ago you had that awful flu. We'd honestly begun to think you were *dead!*"

"I was only away from work for three weeks," Midori said.

"*Five* weeks, sweet, if not *six*."

Junko abandoned us. Makoto ordered a bottle of wine. "When did you have the flu?" I asked Midori in English. Jafe hadn't said anything about it. But now that I looked at her, Midori did look less *present*, somehow, than the last time we'd met. She even seemed to have put on weight. When I'd had the flu I'd lost weight, but the convalescence had been worse than the fever in many ways – and convalescence takes people in different ways.

"Oh, in the middle of winter when everyone has. Our New Year's vacation was completely wrecked, right, honey?"

"Sure was."

"But I'm fine now. I'm returned to normal. I don't look like ill or something, right?" Midori craned around in a vain attempt to get into her husband's field of vision. Uh oh.

Makoto opened a copy of *Moonless Nights* and started quoting from it. It was the sort of thing he found hilarious.

Over our dinner at a Chinese restaurant he'd read out several whole tankas, translating the longer words into English for Jafe's sake.

The lights went off, leaving a flashlight in someone's hand to illuminate the lap of a man seated on a high stool. He had a mic strapped to each thigh. He slapped and tapped them: digital bongos. "I wish Philip was here to see this!" I hissed to Jafe.

"Oh shit," whooped Makoto. I looked at the percussionist again and saw that he was now caressing his mics with an enormous pink dildo. It writhed with a hum that the mics amplified into a throaty drone. The flashlight wavered onto the percussionist's bearded face, he simulated orgasm, and everyone burst out laughing. I glanced back at Makoto. He was practically weeping with laughter. Jafe was staring with his mouth hanging open. Midori wore a smile that was almost spooky in its detachment.

I leaned across the table to get her attention. "I'm starting to like this joint!" I hissed. "Do you come here often? With your coworkers?"

"*Iya*, this is first time I come here in ages. I don't go out so much these days."

The percussionist finished his performance and tossed the dildo into the crowd. The flashlight homed in on Junko, who began to read from *Moonless Nights*. Her facial expressions weren't as good as the percussionist's. Thanks to the poor quality of the PA system and her theatrical intonations, I could only catch a word here and there.

"I'm sorry to say this about your friends, but they're the most bizarre couple I've ever met," Makoto said as we rode the Yamanote line north. "Aren't they getting along?"

I sighed. "It didn't seem like it, did it?"

"Some couples just make you go *hmmm*." Makoto chuckled. "Even dorky Western guys can pull prettier girls than that. I'm not saying she's not nice, but let's face it, she's a dog. And Jafe isn't your average Western guy. He looks like a movie star! He should have married a girl who looks like one, too.

Then again, who knows what Mrs Kuklowski is like behind closed doors?" He laughed again. He'd drunk most of that bottle of wine by himself.

"Shibuya," intoned the conductor. "Next stop Shibuya."

"See you later. Get home safely," I said, and plunged into the bottleneck of passengers at the doors.

All the next day at work I reviewed my impressions of the evening, weighing Makoto's conclusions against my own. I finally decided that if Jafe and Midori *were* having problems, it was all Midori's fault. Inclining me further in Jafe's favor were the assurances I'd teased out of him that he had no intention of letting himself be carried away by his antiwar convictions again. "You know, it's no use trying to talk to people," he'd admitted, looking as noble and misunderstood as the young John Lennon. "They don't listen, do they? They don't fucking listen. So what do you do? You play the goddamned music."

I repeated these words to Aki when he called me on Friday night. He heard me out with less enthusiasm than I'd hoped for and then delivered his own report.

He and Philip had gone for a beer after work at Hub in Kabukicho. With greater cunning than I'd given him credit for, Aki hadn't harped on the fact that Jafe was our last best shot at making it. He'd just reminded Philip that Jafe had always shouldered the lion's share of our expenditures, and when we recorded our CD it had been Jafe who found a friend to produce it for free. At the very least, we owed Jafe a few second chances. Philip had apparently acknowledged the justice of this argument. He might even have been on the point of agreeing to give it another go. But as luck would have it, at that moment a bunch of his English teacher friends had burst into the pub: oi mate, you fuckin' pisshead, you cunt, etc., etc., and there went Aki's hopes of getting any more sense out of our drummer that evening.

"Well, you did your best," I said. I was standing in the middle of my expensive little apartment in Eifukucho. Behind me, Marines were blowing up bridges. "The main thing is, did you get the impression he's going to show up tomorrow?"

"I don't know."

I extended my right leg and rested my foot on the counter that served me as a kitchen. I leaned over my knee, stretching.

"I think maybe we should cancel."

"What?" I lowered my foot to the floor and stood still.

"Maybe we should cancel the gig," said Aki more loudly.

"You mean you think Philip *is* going to ditch."

"I think *I* might ditch."

"Oh, Aki. No."

"I think I might have a stomach bug or something."

"How much did you have to drink tonight?"

"Jafe called me when I was walking back to the station. He wanted me to come over their place. I said no way, man, I don't even know how to get there, and besides, my last train's about to go. Anyway, I'll see you tomorrow, right? And he said, yeah, I guess. Then he cut the telephone."

I didn't know what to make of that, so I stuck to what I'd been going to say. "Aki, you don't have any kind of bug. You're just trying to get out of it. You're never going to make the grade professionally if you can't leave the interpersonal stuff off stage where it belongs." I swallowed. "It hurts that you think you can fool me that easily. But what hurts even more is that you can fool *yourself* that easily."

The silence on his end stretched out until I started wondering if he was still there.

"I don't want to let you down, Tammie," he said at last. "I'll try to make it."

"'Try to make it'? Is that the best you can do?"

"All right! I'll be there. I promise."

Maybe because he was speaking Japanese now, it reminded me of Makoto, who was always promising this, that, and the other. But there was nothing I could do except to accept Aki's promise and tell him I was sorry I'd gotten mad. He said he understood. I wasn't sure if he really did, but I let it go.

I went to sleep at twoish, and was woken in the dark by my phone ringing again. It had vibrated itself right off the counter and hung twisting on the end of its charger cord.

"'Sh mosh'." Flopping back onto my bed, I sank back into my dream, in which men in fatigues marched with their hands on their heads across a sunlit desert towards a black horizon.

"Tammie? Hey, did I wake you up?"

"Uh, yeah Jafe. Not that I'm not happy to hear your voice, but this is getting to be a recurrent motif."

"Sorry. Yo, I'm really sorry."

"'s OK." As my eyes closed again, it occurred to me that I'd slept around the clock and was even now supposed to be sound-checking in Takadanobaba. I panicked and asked Jafe what time it was.

"Well, the trains are running, anyway. I can hear them from here. Uh... I know this is a big favor, but do you think you could come over here?"

As I ummed and ahhed, hoping he'd get the message, I recalled that Aki had received a similar phone call last night. I woke up. My mind whirled and alighted on the only likely explanation: Jafe and Midori had had a fight and broken up. "Jafe! It's not... Midori hasn't... you haven't..."

The silence that followed my words seemed to confirm what I'd been unable to say. I could indeed hear distant trains rumbling on his end. It sounded like he was outside.

"She hasn't exactly *left* me," he said at last with a bitter laugh. "But I guess you could call it that. I mean, shit was building up, and then boom!"

"God, Jafe, how awful for you."

"How'd you know?"

My heart ached for him. "Uh... I guess I got the impression on Wednesday night that... well, actually, we've all been thinking for a while that there was something, uh..."

"Oh. Yeah, when I fucked up at Shakespeare's, huh? Shit's been getting to me. For real, Tammie. And I couldn't tell you guys about it. I just couldn't, you know? But it's over now."

I had the horrible feeling that you get when someone's going through hell and you can't do a thing for them. Except... there was something I *could* do for Jafe. "I'll come over if you want me to. It'll take an hour, maybe a bit more. Is that OK? Can you meet me at the station?"

"Hey, sure! I'll head over there right now! God, Tammie, you're an angel in disguise!" His voice was suddenly full of life: the Jafe I knew and loved, back from hell in the twinkling of an eye. It sounded as if I *could* make a difference to him.

As I showered, dressed, and put on my emergency makeup, I vacillated between nervous anticipation and relief. On the principle that to understand all is to forgive all, I hoped that even Philip would be ready to make allowances when he knew Jafe's "support system" had failed him. Locking my apartment door behind me, I smiled at the reflection that three of the Immortals had now gone through domestic catastrophes. Only Aki remained unscarred – and he, at 29, still lived with his parents, which was another kind of domestic catastrophe.

The sky was turning grey and birds were singing in people's gardens as I hurried towards Eifukucho station. Nearly empty, the train rocked along above the rooftops. At Shibuya I changed to the Yamanote line on the widdershins track. Grimy club kids slept with their heads on each other's shoulders. Salarymen slept with their briefcases on their knees. I stood by the doors, sipping from the cup of coffee I'd bought in Shibuya station. The rising sun struck into my eyes.

Jafe was waiting for me at Osaki station, a vast glassy edifice renovated to match the Gate City complex of office buildings that overshadows it. Among the Saturday salarymen he stood out like an apparition in his long leather coat and stripy muffler. He greeted me with abject gratitude and then started pouring out a flood of reminiscences about Midori. I encouraged him to talk, as I thought it was what he needed right now, but I became confused as I waited to hear about how it had all gone wrong. He seemed to have gone into denial of what he'd admitted on the phone.

We descended to the street, circled the massive foundations of Gate City, and crossed the river. On the far bank the flashy new buildings peter out and you're in among old factories and lumber warehouses. Until I met Jafe, I hadn't known anyone actually lived in Osaki. His apartment was in a building just two storeys high, about fifty years old and only half inhabited, with outdoor staircases and corridors that looked like scaffolding. He and Midori had inherited it from a musician acquaintance who'd liked the industrial character of the place: with no neighbors to speak of, he could party at his pleasure. The Kuklowskis did not give parties, and this was hardly the time anyway, so I was confused to hear a faint thunder emanating from what had to be their apartment.

Jafe had fallen silent at last. I said, "Are you sure it won't be depressing to hang out here? Wouldn't you rather go to… to a park or somewhere? It looks like it's going to be a lovely day."

"No, I want you to come in." He secured my hand and laced his woolly-gloved fingers through my bare ones.

Oh God, I thought.

The sun skimmed the roof of the factory to the east, rode across a parking lot occupied by a fleet of trucks, and flooded the corridor with golden light that made the rust on the railings sparkle like gilt.

Jafe opened the door, closed it again immediately, and stood behind me in the genkan while I took off my shoes. After the sunlight, the darkness seemed total. There was an unpleasant smell that I couldn't place. The music was loud enough for a nightclub, a wailing vocal almost buried under the weight of grinding guitars. I stepped hesitantly up onto the wooden floor. Jafe brushed past me. He still had his shoes on. Straining my eyes, I made out the doorless doorway, darker than the walls, into which he'd vanished. When he came back into the room he was holding something. It was a knife as long as my forearm. I gasped. But he was holding it out *to* me, not pointing it *at* me. He was holding it out to me, and I took it. I said, or rather shouted over the music, "What is this? What are you giving it to me for?"

"Just hang onto it." He headed for the door.

"Jafe! I said, if you want to go out, we can go out. We don't have to mope in here. Just wait until I put my shoes on!"

"Jesus, don't be like that, Tammie! I didn't want it to be you. I called a bunch of people, but none of the fuckers could do me a favor when I needed it, so it has to be you, OK? Just stay here! That's all you gotta do! Just give me a couple of hours!"

"For what? Where are you going?"

He had the door open. He was silhouetted in the sunlight. I put the knife down on the floor and tumbled outside after him in my sock feet. He shook me off. He was breathing noisily. He picked me up and threw me back into the apartment. He was no sumo wrestler, but he heaved me off my feet and *threw* me. I bashed my knees on the lip of the genkan. The door closed. I scrambled to my feet and shook the handle, shaking the door itself in its frame. In a few seconds I realized I was locked in. This was an ancient building. The locks on the doors were ancient, too. They could be locked from outside.

"OK," I muttered, barely able to hear myself over the music. "Priorities. Find the spare key. There must be one. Obvious places. Look in obvious places. And... and get out of here before he comes back."

I had no doubt he *would* be coming back.

A couple of hours, he'd said.

I shuffled across the room to the window and eased the curtains open. Daylight streamed into the room. I saw the navy blue living-room set, the TV, and a round rug littered with bright plastic toys. I also saw the knife I'd put down near the genkan. It was an ordinary kitchen cleaver, not quite clean.

I was going crazy. I had to do something about this music. I tiptoed through the doorway on the far side of the room and found myself in a narrow kitchen with the cooker and sink at one end, twin bathroom doors at the other. Another doorway, this one with a door in it, faced me in the kitchen's opposite wall. The door was almost closed but not quite, and the stereo was beyond it. I pushed it open with my fingertips.

The curtains were still drawn in here, but it was not too dark for me to see Midori lying on the floor. Even before I switched on the lights I saw the lake of blood under her head and upper body. It extended almost to my feet, blocking the doorway.

I used to indulge in morbid speculation as to how I'd react in a situation like this. I'd envisioned myself swooning gracefully away. I did no such thing. I half squatted as if I meant to go to my knees, but there was nowhere to kneel except in the blood, so I straightened up again and slammed my hands together. "Lord have mercy on us," I gabbled, "Hail Mary full of grace blessed art thou among women and blessed is the fruit of thy womb Jesus, holy Mary mother of God forgive us our sins," as if I'd done it myself. It was just the two of us here, and I was alive and she was dead. The implied relationship between us was one of guilt and complicity.

Still praying out loud, I stooped and pushed her shoulder with my knuckles. The flesh under the cotton sweater she was wearing felt heavier and harder than flesh should be. I couldn't see her wound. Had she been rolled over after she was dead? Her hair hid her face, its trailing ends glued to the floor in clumps. Her blood had spread along the grooves between the floorboards. It looked dark and tacky. She must have been dead for several hours. She'd probably been dead when Jafe called Aki last night. He'd called Aki and how many other people? Until he found a sucker: me.

A movement caught my eye. My heart went into spasms. Belatedly, I took in the rest of the bedroom: a double bed, the stereo, and a crib where a baby lay tangled up in blankets, wailing.

I jumped over Midori's body and hit the power button on the stereo. The baby's cries emerged into the silence. It sounded lethargic, as if it had been screaming for hours and no longer had much heart for it. I lifted it out of the crib. It looked to be two or three months old. It wore a weeny pair of white leggings and a woolly sweater, all stained brown, as were its hands and face. It writhed against my shoulder and cried harder. "Stinkypoo," I said. "You want changing. Oh God, you want Mommy, don't you? Oh God, your daddy's framing me for murder, baby, what am I going to do?"

I couldn't take any running leaps with a baby in my arms. There was nothing for it: to get out of the bedroom I had to step in Midori's blood. It was not so dry that I didn't leave tracks on the kitchen floor. I carried the baby into the living-room, laid it down on the rug in front of the TV, pulled off my socks, and threw them into a corner. Now I could see that the substance staining the baby's clothes and skin, even to its mouth, was blood. I felt dizzy. I might really have passed out then if the kid hadn't still been yelling, giving me no peace.

It struck me suddenly that some of the blood on its clothes might be its own. I wiggled all its little limbs, pried its eyes open to check that they were clear, and even placed my fingers on its chest to make sure its heart was beating. When at last I calmed down, although by now I was uttering dry sobs myself, I stripped the baby off, washed its face and bottom in the kitchen sink (finding out, incidentally, that it was a girl), and dressed it, *her,* in a clean set of baby clothes. I had to jump over Midori's body a dozen times in the search for these and for diapers. Priorities. An adult's priorities are different from a baby's. In the end, however, I cottoned onto what the baby must have been trying to tell me all along. In the fridge I found a couple of bottles full of what looked like formula. I heated one of them in the microwave, fifteen seconds at a time until it was warm to the touch, and poked its nipple into the baby's mouth. Magically, she stopped bawling. She drank half of the bottle, then fell asleep on my lap.

As the silence returned, so did my terror.

Sunlight filled the apartment. Cradling the baby in one arm, I reached for my coat, which I'd taken off for Operation Diaper Change. I got my phone out of its pocket and saw that it was just 8:14 am.

My phone.

"Oh God, I'm such an idiot."

I started to tremble again as I speed dialed.

"Mosh' mosh'."

"Oh thank God, Makoto. Have you got a hammer or anything to break down a door with?" I was speaking English, but he interrupted me in Japanese.

"It's the crack of dawn! What on earth's wrong?"

"It may be the crack of dawn as far as you're concerned but I've been up for hours." Speaking Japanese forced me to organize my thoughts. "I need your help. I'm in Osaki. I'm locked in… in someone's apartment. And I've got… someone with me. Please come over and help me break the door down, or else bring a ladder so that we can climb out of the window. We're only on the second floor."

"How many times have I told you to do as I say, not as I do? *Don't* pick up strangers and go home with them! What kind of nutter is this guy? You're not hurt, are you?"

"Wait a minute, Makoto, are *you* at home?"

"Uh… yeah." In the instant's pause that followed I heard a girl's voice – Lucy's voice – asking who that was.

"If you're in Omiya it would take you too long to get here, anyway. Forget it," I said, and stabbed the hangup button. He called right back. I hung up on him and called Philip. He didn't pick up. I left a message on his voicemail and called Aki. He picked up. I said in English, "Hi. To understand all is not to forgive all. I was wrong about that, sorry." As soon as I'd said it, I remembered I hadn't said it to him to begin with. Whatever. I plunged on. "Jafe and Midori have a baby. Yeah, I know. I've got her, I mean the baby, here with me. She's OK. She's asleep. I'm at Jafe's place. But I'm locked in, and Midori's dead. She's on the bedroom floor. I said she's *dead.* There's blood everywhere. Him, I expect. No, he's not here."

"If he comes back, lock yourself and the baby in the bathroom." I couldn't believe how calm Aki sounded. "Have you called the police or do you want me to do it?"

"No! No!" I almost screamed. The baby stirred in the crook of my free arm. I rocked her distractedly. "I'm just hoping Jafe hasn't called the police already. And I'm afraid he *has,* or he's going to as soon as he gets far enough away, and they're going to come and arrest me."

FELICITY SAVAGE

"Arrest *you?*"

I explained about the knife. I figured Jafe had cleaned the handle (though not the blade) before giving it to me, so that my fingerprints and mine alone were now on it, as they were all over the apartment. It could even be said that I'd had a motive for killing Midori: I'd always had a crush on Jafe (as had half the female population of Tokyo) and might have become unhinged with jealousy, mightn't I? The measure of the case against me, I thought, was that Aki said nothing more about calling the police.

"I'll be there in about thirty minutes. I'll borrow my mom's car. What's the address?"

"I don't know." Tears filled my eyes. "Just start out, would you? Philip knows the way, he's been here a couple of times. I'll keep calling him and with luck he'll pick up before you get here."

"I'm on my way." He hung up, and then all I had to do was wait and wonder who'd get to me first: Philip, Aki, or the police.

I no longer thought Jafe was going to come back.

I mean, he'd have had to be crazy.

I set the sleeping baby on the living-room rug and flitted around the apartment, wiping off the things I remembered touching. I smoked a cigarette from the packet of Parliaments I found in the kitchen, then plucked the strings of Jafe's Rogue LX200B. He also had an acoustic guitar. I was getting used to the sight of Midori lying in her blood, but I can't have been as calm as I thought, because I nearly jumped out of my skin when I heard a cry from the living-room.

The baby was awake and grizzling. I sat down beside her with Jafe's guitar. Strumming chords, I sang, "Hush a little baby, don't say a word, Papa's gonna buy you a mocking-bird.

And if that mocking-bird don't sing, Papa's gonna buy you a diamond ring. And if that diamond ring turns to brass…"

Tiny babies supposedly can't focus on anything more than a couple of feet away, but she seemed to be watching me. Her eyes were brown, her feathery hair as fair as her father's. The instant I stopped singing, she scrunched her face up. I took it from the top.

A gust of wind chilled my back. "You're good with her. I should have known you would be."

I dropped the guitar, scooped up the baby, and backed into the corner by the TV. Jafe closed the front door behind him, locked it, and vanished through the kitchen doorway. "Did you get her stuff together? Guess not, huh." His voice came from the bedroom. He must have stepped over his dead wife to get there. "Thanks for changing her, anyway."

"I fed her, too." My voice wobbled. "She was hungry."

"Formula's not the best for them, but what can you do? She's had to get used to it with her mother at work all day."

Between his remarks and mine minutes were passing, so that the conversation felt as fake as it was.

"So you're her… her caregiver?"

"Yeah. She's Daddy's little girl, aren't you, Arisa?"

"Is… is that her name? Arisa?"

"Yeah, it's like you can write it in kanji, or change the 'r' to an 'l' and it's Alisa."

"That's… uh… that was a good idea. To give her a name that works in both languages."

"Yeah. I guess she might not end up being bilingual after all, but at some point she'll probably want to find out about her heritage. So her name will be something she can be proud of." Jafe came back into the living-room with a changing bag over his shoulder. It was pale blue with a Winnie-the-Pooh motif. From his other shoulder hung an Adidas duffel bag, and over his leather coat he'd buckled a pink corduroy baby carrier. "Gotta get going. Thanks, Tammie. I really owe you one."

It was as if he thought I didn't *know* that Midori was lying dead in the bedroom. Did he intend to lock me in again? Good luck to him, if he were encumbered with Arisa as well as two bags. But I couldn't let him take her. I hugged her so tightly that her eyes opened. "She needs her coat, Jafe! And her hat! You can't take her out in this weather without a hat!"

"Got it right here." He touched his pocket and then held out his arms. "Anyway, we won't be out in the cold for long. We're only walking as far as the station."

"And… and after that? Where are you going?"

"Well, I think it's probably better if you don't have that information."

He lowered his voice and met my eyes as he uttered this cliché. My sense of responsibility came blasting back, and this time it wasn't my imagination. I really was going along with him. Alternatively, I could do the right thing. I filled my lungs and screamed, "Help! Please somebody help!"

Arisa burst into wails.

Jafe slapped me in the face.

"Give it a rest, Tammie! Nobody came last night and nobody's coming now."

He slid his arm around Arisa, between her body and mine. We wrestled for possession of her. I realized he was going to hit me again. I let go of Arisa. He started stuffing her into the baby carrier, a task made more difficult by her struggles.

I skittered towards the door and saw the knife still lying where I'd put it down. I picked it up, holding it by my side.

Something crashed into the front door.

I screamed.

Another impact struck the door, and I whirled around as if I might be able to see whatever or whoever was slamming into it. Jafe grabbed me from behind and tried to disarm me. I had strong hands and wrists, but I was still a woman and he a man. While he couldn't pry my fingers off the knife, he could and did turn it upwards, forcing its point towards my throat. The door shivered and echoed again. It was meant to open outwards. It wasn't going to give. The point of the knife danced in front of my face. I could feel Arisa struggling against my back, trapped in her baby carrier between her father and me. The door exploded inwards, rotten old hinges ripping right out of the jamb, and crashed into the genkan with Philip on top of it. He picked himself up and charged at us.

I pushed the knife upwards as hard as I could and simultaneously let myself collapse so that the blade sliced over my head – but only just, catching my hair. I dropped to the floor and rolled out of Philip's way. A high thin shriek mingled with the men's shouts. Aki knelt beside me and crushed my face into his shoulder. I wrenched free. Jafe and Philip were kneeling in the sunlight that flooded in over the broken door, working together at the buckles of the baby carrier on Jafe's chest. Blood stained the pink corduroy and their hands. "Go look in the bedroom," I sobbed.

"Aki, call an ambulance," grunted Philip.

"This is all wrong, man," said Jafe, and stumbled to his feet, dumping Arisa on Philip's knees. He grabbed the knife, which was still right there on the floor, and came at me, calling me a baby-killing bitch. I dodged around the room. He pursued me confidently, like something out of a Hollywood war movie, covered in blood not his own.

As soon as the police finished with me, I went to Makoto's place, and stayed there.

The first two weekends he spent entirely at my side – or under me, or on top of me. On the third weekend he brought Lucy over for dinner. The day after that, I moved back to my own apartment.

Midori's parents organized her funeral, to which half the paparazzi in Japan were apparently invited but Philip, Aki, and I were not. Nor, needless to say, was Jafe. During his absence from the apartment that morning he'd called ANA and reserved a bulkhead seat, complete with cot, on the next flight from Narita to Los Angeles. They put him in Sugamo, the legendary maximum security joint. Philip, when I finally met up with him in early May, told me that he'd gone there twice with

Jafe's parents. The senior Kuklowskis, it seems, had heard so many horror stories about the jails of the Far East that they'd expected to find Jafe mutilated and starving. They'd been reassured on that count, but their attempts to bail him out had been fruitless. The best they'd been able to do was hire him a bilingual defense lawyer. Mr Kuklowski had since returned to the States, but his wife remained in Japan for Arisa's sake.

The knife had almost taken her arm off at the shoulder. The paramedics had arrived in time to save her from bleeding to death, and physical therapy was restoring her use of the arm, but she would carry the scar all her life. It remained in question who, if anyone, could be charged with injuring her. Jafe insisted that I'd done it. Philip and Aki testified that it had been an accident. Maybe because of the xenophobic noise the media was making, the police seemed to want to implicate me, but they also wanted me in the clear so I could testify against Jafe. They couldn't have it both ways, and the detective I saw most of told me it was ten to one they'd end up declaring Arisa's stabbing accidental.

That didn't solve the problem of her future. To all four of her grandparents, the news of her existence had come as almost as much of a shock as the murder. Now they were fighting over her. The tabloids backed the Fujitas. It did make sense (especially in Japan) to think Arisa should go to her mother's parents rather than to the Kuklowskis, whose parenting record was pretty badly stained at this point, but it seemed to me that their case was the stronger. He managed a supermarket in the San Francisco area; she was a high school history teacher. Meanwhile, the Fujitas lived in a village in Hyogo prefecture on his pension from the post office. They were ten years senior to the Kuklowskis, which was the difference between middle and old age. I quailed at the thought of Arisa's childhood in the poky little house that had appeared over and over on the news.

The media used the custody dispute as an excuse to drag the whole thing out interminably. It made a change, I guess, from Iraq. I had to change my phone number, and they would probably have doorstepped me at work if I hadn't already lost my job.

Philip, Aki, and I moaned about the media coverage on the May afternoon when we got together for the first time since it happened. "Fame's not all it's cracked up to be!" Philip said. But we had other things to discuss, too – such as whether we could resurrect The Immortals.

To my astonishment, the boys were dirt keen. They'd been working on some originals of their own behind my back, and they wanted to start hawking a new demo around. "There's no such thing as bad publicity, Tammie. Every exec in Japan knows who we are now," Philip kept saying, and Aki nodded in agreement.

They wanted me to sing.

I almost lost my temper. I could never perform in public again, let alone step into Jafe's shoes. I hadn't touched my Fender since the day the police drove me home... not to Eifukucho, of course, but to the address on my alien registration card. I couldn't admit this to the boys, so I took issue with their budget projections. Who was going to come up with at least ¥200,000 in studio fees?

Wouldn't you know it, Philip had made twice that sum by talking to the tabloids. And they say there's no money in speaking Japanese these days.

We'd been planning to meet some friends and make an old-fashioned Saturday night of it, but I wasn't in the mood any more. I went home to Eifukucho and watched TV. The war was over; chaos had set in. I wondered if Jafe got to watch TV in jail. "Violence is never the answer," I remembered him saying.

My apartment seemed tinier than ever. I switched off the lights and lay in the darkness. When my phone rang, I scrambled for it.

"Let's go to the beach."

"Fuck off, Aki. Tell Philip I don't change my mind that easily."

"What'll it take?"

"If I could turn back time," I sang into the phone.

Aki laughed. I could tell he was drunk. "Well, staying in the realm of possibility, do you want to go to..."

"Not if you're thinking of Enoshima. I hate those crowded beaches."

"How about Wakasu Links?"

I rolled to and fro on my bed and said OK.

I'd assumed he meant the three of us were going, which had surprised me because Philip at the beach made about as much sense as a seagull in a pub, but when Aki picked me up at noon, he was alone in his mother's car. He'd been borrowing it from her more often – a shortcut to growing up. On the back seat was his acoustic guitar in its hard case. Had he been busking on his own these past few weeks? I felt a prickle of jealousy.

Wakasu Links covers half of a landfill island in Tokyo Bay. Unreachable by train and (I assume) unsatisfactory in some way as a golf course, it's usually as close to deserted as anywhere in the metropolitan area. Aki drove to the end of the access road and parked alongside no more than half a dozen other cars. He took his guitar out of the back and we walked down through the rough to the water. The sun shone and the salty breeze snapped. No one except a few anglers could be seen on the skirt of tumbled stones that stretched, straight as a curb, out into the bay. We perched above the lapping waves and ate lunch: onigiri, bottled green tea, and a bag of those chips shaped like edamame pods.

"Why didn't we notice that anything was wrong?" I said. "What could we have picked up on that we didn't pick up on? It's like a math problem where you know the answer but you don't know how they got there."

Aki ate in silence for a couple of minutes. At last he said, "When do you think they planned to tell their parents and everyone that they had a baby?"

"I guess whenever they could face up to it themselves."

"I was watching TV and – you can't get away from it, can you? They were interviewing some famous psychologist. He said he wondered whether Midori hadn't tried to kill Arisa –"

"What?"

" – and Jafe killed Midori in the belief that he was protecting his daughter. I thought he might be onto something. Postnatal depression can alter a woman's personality, you know. They explained about that, too."

I remembered Midori's smile at Lilight. In my memory her eyes were as flat as pennies, as if she were already dead.

"Psychologists have filthy minds," Aki said. "But if I was Jafe's lawyer, that's the defense I'd use."

I stared out to sea, shivering, although it wasn't cold. "Do you think they'll hang him?"

Japan is the other advanced industrial democracy that has the death penalty. And there's no messing around with Jesus juice here. They hang you by the neck until you're dead.

"I don't want to think about it," said Aki. "And I don't really want to talk about it, either."

"I thought you wanted to talk about it." I corrected myself. "I thought you knew I wanted to talk about it."

"I'd rather talk about other things."

"Like what?"

"The band. It has to be you. You're the other Immortal. If we brought in someone new it would ruin the whole vibe."

"I don't understand how you guys can think about going on with the band at all."

Aki looked embarrassed. "You're the one that used to say Jafe was our last best chance at making it. Well, I know it's ironic, but maybe that's exactly what he's given us: our last best chance."

"And do you really think people won't say we're cashing in on a sensational murder?"

"If they did, what would that make us? No better and no worse than anyone else in the industry."

"I'm not hearing this."

"You know you want to give it a shot. *I* know you want to."

"No, Aki, I don't. It's not so much that I object to cashing in. It's that... Jafe loved music as much as anyone I've ever known, and it couldn't save him from going crazy. So what's the point?"

"We've got to get on with our lives."

"Easy for you to say! You weren't locked in that apartment for three hours. You don't have to dream about trying to wash the blood off Arisa's face, trying to make her stop crying, and the knife... the knife... in the dream it keeps on coming at my throat, and I can't wake up in time."

There was a silence. At last Aki said, "You know, I did dream about it once. It was morning and I was driving along the expressway. And when I got there you were dead. I went in the bedroom and found Midori, but when I rolled her over... you didn't see, did you? Her face was all cut up. One of her eyes was... and a piece of her cheek was hanging loose."

"Oh God, Aki!"

"But in my dream it wasn't her. It was you. And I knew Jafe had killed you, and I was going to kill him for it. It was like this moment of total clarity. I understood how a guy could commit murder. That's why I believe that psychologist, because it makes sense. It made perfect sense, and that was when I woke up. I opened my eyes and I was thinking, 'OK, Jafe, it's not such a mystery any more.'"

I stared at my ankles, trembling with frustration. Aki didn't understand what it was that really got to me. Don't get me wrong: I was sorry Midori was dead, but I hadn't known her well or liked her much. There was a limit to the grief I could muster for her. Worse than that, worse even than the nightmares, was the riddle of my own responsibility. Jafe and I had been friends. We'd made bee-yoo-tiful music together. And my affection for him had nearly ended up costing me my life and Arisa hers. I told myself every day that I was alive, and Arisa was alive, and that was what mattered. Jafe had almost killed us, but Philip and Aki had rescued us. End of story. But if it was that simple, why did I feel so responsible? What had I bought with my passive crush on Jafe? One minute I was afraid I knew, and the next minute I was afraid even to wonder.

But maybe, as Aki said, it wasn't really such a mystery after all.

"Why did you bring your guitar if we're not going to jam?" I said.

"Sure." Aki thrust his arms into the air, shaking out his fingers. "Sure!" He climbed off the boulder, took his guitar out of its case and climbed back up to settle it on his knee. "I don't know if I can remember this one," he said in English.

"Try it. Try me."

"OK." He started fingerpicking, then shook his head and started again in a lower key.

I remembered it. Not one of Jafe's, nor one of Aki and Philip's compositions (about which I was dubious), but one of the obscure ballads we had favored when busking in parks. Aki's very acoustic version. He was calling my bluff, and I hated him for it. But I found my note and started singing. "There's no going back, there's no going back, there's no going back this time…"

Sitting on the hood of Aki's mother's car with the sun setting, we made a phone call each.

Aki called Philip and told him that I'd changed my mind. From where I sat I could hear Philip's response: "Tell her she could have had a third if she'd come in straight off, but it's down to twenty-five percent now. The other eight percent'll be our contribution to world peace. We'll give it to fucking UNICEF or something."

After they finished talking, I called Makoto and said, "Let's get divorced."

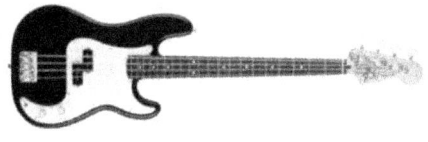

THE SPIRIT OF HARLEM

"Let me get this straight," said my boyfriend. "You think my sister's lying to us."

In Japanese it was "telling lies," which sounded worse to me somehow than the English. But I stuck to my analysis. "I think she's crying out for help."

"Even though she says everything's going fine?"

I said, "Well, can you really imagine her saying, 'By the way, Mom and Dad, I can't cope any more and I'm coming home'? Especially if…" I paused long enough to make the point that I was respecting the family's feelings by naming no names. "Especially if her personal life isn't going well."

"Yeah, well, that would be a blessing." Taka could be very cynical. "It can't last much longer," he said with conviction.

"I don't think it can, either. But supposing it ends, or it *has* ended, would that be an improvement? She's so *vulnerable.*" I used the English word because there was no satisfactory Japanese equivalent. I added, "Maybe that's what she's trying to tell us, but no one understands her."

If Taka had objected again, I would have concluded that he really thought I was talking nonsense, but he said nothing. We walked up Kagurazaka, through clouds of smoke and around floods of water from the kitchen doors of izakayas. We'd just come from dinner at his parents' house. The Kagurazaka neighborhood has been called the Montmartre of Tokyo, and the comparison is ironically valid: in both places the avant-garde has moved on and left its reputation to glam up a maze of twisty little streets that barely made it out of the nineteenth century. Mr and Mrs Nishino lived in a cul-de-sac overgrown with magnolias and bougainvillea. He was an Executive Director; she taught kimono-wearing classes and took calligraphy classes. They both worried about Shizuka, the younger of their two children, in much the same way, it seemed to me, as the Japanese government worried about North Korea. Unpredictable, ungrateful, almost an enemy but impossible to write off: that was Shizuka. She lived in New York, where I used to live myself. It wasn't a startling coincidence. What artistically inclined girl *doesn't* want to live in New York? But Shizuka seemed to be more intent on living out the drama than I'd ever been. She painted pictures full of gore and deformities.

And now she was starving.

"She's got a strong mind. She knows what she wants," said Taka. "And she's never had trouble making herself understood before."

"Yeah," I said. "But has she ever been in love before?"

I glanced sideways in time to see him frown. He wasn't admitting that it qualified as love, and I knew why. I instinctively felt the same way, for all that I was supposed to be the open-minded one. Yet I also felt that nothing short of love could have reduced Shizuka to the thing in the photos we'd seen tonight. She certainly was not short of money.

Friends of the Nishinos had happened to travel to New York a few weeks ago and had looked her up. The photos had been taken in Central Park in the autumn sunlight. In all of them Shizuka was beaming, and in all of them she looked ready to collapse inside her layered sweaters and skirts. I'd graduated from Bryn Mawr; I knew anorexia when I saw it. Except for her smile, Shizuka looked like a junkie interposed by digital wizardry between the Vice President of Marketing and his chunky wife. "She seems to have no plans to come home," had been their comment to the Nishinos, passed on to us by Mrs Nishino tonight as she handed the photos around the coffee table. But that the photos had been taken and given to Shizuka's parents at all was a stronger comment, and that they'd been shown to Taka and me was an even more ominous indicator of prevailing feelings.

As a rule Mr and Mrs Nishino discouraged Taka from worrying about his sister. With his MBA from Stanford, his gruelling job as a management consultant, and me, he was the basket into which they'd transferred all their eggs. I thought they knew him less well than I did.

"If only she'd go back to college," he said after we'd walked another few blocks. "Here, if you drop out you're well and truly fucked, but over there... if she explained that she'd been working on her portfolio... I'm sure they'd let her graduate. She's only short a few credits."

"*Has* she been working on her portfolio?"

"Good question. Actually, I doubt it."

I forced myself to confront what I'd been thinking all along. I hated criticizing him, but this time I felt it was fair. "If you talked to her, Taka, I mean talked to her properly and didn't take no for an answer, she might go back to school... or something." I would have liked to say the same thing to his parents, but I obviously couldn't. I was going out on a limb saying it to him. And I saw immediately that I'd gone too far.

"Me? *Me?*" He laughed unamusedly. "Where would I start? What would I say? It's always been against her principles to take my advice. And I can't really blame her."

He grabbed my arm as I was about to step off the curb into traffic. I swallowed my heart and smiled at him in embarrassment.

That Saturday we went to a show. Taka when he was an undergraduate had played guitar in an outfit influenced by the likes of Black Sabbath and Pantera. Two of his former bandmates were still at it, rehearsing on the weekends and performing at underground clubs in the suburbs, and through them we knew a lot of people on the scene. None of the bands ever seemed to solidify their lineups for long enough to have a chance of breaking out. But Freshpig 10 had achieved a rare gestalt. Varying the standard thrashcore sound with *three* guitarists, they'd toured as far afield as Sapporo in the past year. Now they were back in Tokyo, second from the top of the bill at Milk, a renowned den of rudeboys in otherwise refined Ebisu.

Taka and I sat out the opening acts in the kitchen, three floors below ground, where people dumped their belongings on a steel table big enough for a barracks. His friends rollicked and joshed each other with an air of playacting that seemed very funny after your first gin and lime. Many of them had goatees, dyed hair, piercings, and cargo pants hanging off their butts. In contrast, Taka with his short black hair and unfaded jeans looked like… well… like a management consultant. I probably did, too. It's true that I have, or had, my artsy side (I used to make lamps with handmade paper shades and sell them at flea markets in Soho) but for the last four years I've been teaching corporate English classes, and my employers insist on an even more staid look than Taka's do. A long Diesel skirt with zips up the sides was the ruffest item left in my wardrobe. If the hardcore boys and girls gave me any props, it was for speaking Japanese, not for being cool.

Someone looked at his watch and we filed upstairs. One of my deadly secrets is that I can hardly tell thrashcore from melocore from speedcore, and the music filling the main floor still sounded like pure noise to me. But the crowd had fused into an enthusiastic mass. Taka grabbed me around the waist and hiked me up until my feet dangled. I saw Freshpig 10's mad vocalist flinging himself to and fro across the stage. The guitarist with pink hair was wearing a t-shirt that said 私 ♥ *NY*.

Wriggling to the ground, I kissed Taka near the mouth and rolled my eyes upwards. He shouted into my ear, "Get our stuff and we'll leave as soon as it's over."

We'd been invited to Freshpig 10's afterparty, to be held at an izakaya nearby. It was an honor, but I'd already guessed that Taka didn't want to go. He did enough social drinking in connection with his job. He gladhanded people at shows to make up for not accepting many invitations, and got away with it, he'd told me, because he was a returnee. What this amounted to was that the Nishinos had lived in Singapore for eight years. (Shizuka was born there.) Taka had been sixteen when they came back to Japan, and although he'd been attending a private school with a Japanese curriculum, he'd apparently picked up some outlandish social instincts that were remarked on to this day (as you might remark on the bump in someone's nose) by all his friends. I wasn't very impressed with this analysis, but because it came from Taka himself I couldn't discount it entirely.

I lugged our stuff up to the gallery that overlooked the club floor. Because Freshpig 10 was so popular, there was hardly anyone up here. I got another gin and lime, leaned my elbows on the railing, and watched Taka and his friends working their way towards the mosh pit in front of the stage. When they got there they respectfully looked on for a few minutes and then hurled themselves into the action, kicking out at each other and bodyslamming the human walls of the circle with what looked to me like a joyous disregard for life and limb.

Did Shizuka go to shows like this at CBGB's and the Bowery Ballroom? I had an impression that she was more into female singer-songwriters of the Sarah McLachlan school. But maybe that was just an assumption based on a stereotype. I'd always tended to see her as a younger version of myself, making the same mistakes I had, eventually to suffer the same disillusionment with New York and everything it stood for. Our conversations, spaced out over years, had often made me wince with sympathy. I wanted to put electrodes on her head and download the lessons of my own life into her brain. But now I wondered in a fit of subjectivism whether she might not live in a city I didn't know, even though we called its streets by the same names. That quality of multiplicity is one of the biggest things that differentiates New York from Tokyo, after all. Tokyo is the common property of a whole nation – even faintly scary places like Milk are in the public domain, so to speak – whereas every nook and cranny of New York seems to be someone's private property, jealously guarded, fiercely contested. If Shizuka had succeeded in claiming her very own piece of the mayhem, no matter what it had cost her, she would be capable of thwarting intrusions, even by her own family.

Taka was probably right that talking to her would get him nowhere. Most likely, nothing could be done for her until she got weak enough to be hospitalized.

I felt sorrier for her than ever, and unusually appreciative of my own good luck.

My mood seemed to communicate itself to Taka on the way home. We held hands on the train, stumbled into our apartment wrapped together, and had drunken sex on the sofa. Afterwards we spread out the futon and sprawled on it. I smoked a cigarette. Taka lay half on top of me, sloppily kissing my shoulders and back. "Marry me," he said.

"Nope," I said.

This was a ritual exchange.

He got up, padded into the kitchenette, and came back swigging from a half-litre of Calpis soda. He had a passion for the stuff. He switched on the light and started reading in English from the card in his hand, which he'd pulled off the fridge. "'We miss you as ever, darling, especially on your birthday, and hope you will use the enclosed to buy something you want. Our news isn't much to speak of…'"

"My birthday was last month," I said.

"'Molly…' that's the eldest sister, right? 'came over with the little ones yesterday and Dylan, who I think I told you is taking piano lessons, played something very pretty for us but said our piano needs tuning…'"

The birthday card, desktop-published by my mother, had a drawing by my elder brother Bri on the front. Bri was the creator of a successful comic strip, and for me he'd drawn one of his trademark tots in an uncharacteristic pose, crouching on the edge of a quay labelled Boston Harbor, gazing out at the ocean. Never mind that it was the wrong ocean. I deserved it. I loved my family and I'd deserted them. The analogy of the rats and the sinking ship fit exactly, and I knew how the rats felt. That was why I'd stuck the card on the fridge. But I regretted my masochistic impulse as Taka kept on reading aloud, describing family adventures that he'd shown no interest in when the card first arrived. My mother had typed in one of those fonts that looks like handwriting rather than actually setting pen to paper. Taka didn't stumble over a word even when I jumped up and chased him around the apartment.

I caught him in the other room and pinned him on his back on the carpet. He held the card up in the air. "'… so it will be a rather modest Thanksgiving, but in compensation we should have a full house for Christmas.'"

I lay still on top of him. He had a milk moustache.

"'As always, darling, we would love you to come, and Takao too, although of course it is a long haul for a silly family holiday. But if you intend to come you might look into tickets soon, although they say that flights are still relatively empty due to 9/11…'"

He let his arm fall across my back and gazed up at me. "Well?"

The house is one of the big red brick ones on Brattle Street, and it was full all right. My parents; my grandmother, who was senile and seldom left her own suite of rooms; Bri, his wife, and their small son Nicky, whom Bri credited in interviews with being his inspiration for the strip; my *other* elder brother Paul, an architect, and his wife; my older sister Molly, her editor husband, and their three holy terrors including Dylan the future concert pianist; my *other* elder sister Sadie, a lawyer, divorced, and her small daughter; and my younger sister

Claudia, who was studying for her master's in Comparative Religions at Yale. Molly and family lived in Somerville, so they weren't resident, but it was still a lot of Tarrants. At dinner on Christmas Eve my father said with satisfaction, "We have mustered a concentration this year, haven't we?"

Paul said delightedly, "That's the collective noun for us. A concentration of Tarrants!"

No one laughed louder than Taka. And then everyone rounded on him and started teaching him obscure collective nouns.

This was why I'd refused their invitations to both of us for three years running. I'd even suggested we stay at a hotel this time, but my parents wouldn't hear of it, and Taka himself had told me not to be uptight.

I had worried that he would expose a side of his personality I hadn't seen before and wouldn't like. But my fears seemed to have been baseless. I was relieved but also confused. His braying laughter at dinner sounded both unnatural and weirdly familiar. As I lay sleepless that night in Claudia's room it dawned on me. Taka worked for a company that was more or less the same size as my family. Half his colleagues were foreigners. He was simply acting the way he did at work.

Cambridge looked like hell frozen over: bleak and red under a foot of snow. The panhandlers in Harvard Square were bundled up like Third World peasants, their breath puffing out white. It never gets this cold in Tokyo. I skulked indoors feeling purposeless. Taka, on the other hand, was full of energy, or pretended to be. On Christmas morning he helped my brothers chop and carry in the cedar logs for the fire. Open hearths in Japan are known only from the movies, and ours had startled him into praise. He admired the brass fender, the decorative buckets of pinecones, and the fire-irons on the clawfooted stand that the children were always knocking over. My brothers promptly overreached themselves by trying to start the fire with twists of newspaper. The whole house smelled like a bonfire by the time they gave up and resorted to lighter fluid.

For Christmas dinner my mother had roasted a free-range turkey, Bri's wife Rachel had made cranberry jelly, Paul's wife Angela had made pumpkin and apple pies, Molly had made scalloped potatoes, Sadie had made vegetarian stuffing, Claudia had made a sort of couscous casserole, and I had dumped frozen vegetables into saucepans and boiled them according to the instructions on the packets. As soon as everyone had said everything was delicious, the conversation turned political. The subject matter was a foregone conclusion; the unChristmassy urgency in the voices surprised me. One hallmark of people like my family is that, although they're doing well out of the sociopolitical situation, they're invariably in opposition. I'd often thought this was merely a canny choice of ground: they knew they excelled in criticizing, denouncing, and ridiculing, whereas the lustre would go off their rhetoric if they ever spoke in earnest support of something. But the events of the last three years had exceeded their most pessimistic predictions. They were genuinely disgusted and frightened. Some of them fell back on satire. My father was made of tougher stuff. At the mahogany table, with the angel chimes tinkling among the leftovers, he expatiated on the pathology of what he called the junta, dissected their propaganda, and predicted a war by spring.

I looked out of the window at the big desolate yard. Nothing alive was moving out there.

The children were squirming and complaining and at last we went into the parlor to open the presents. My parents had given eight-year-old Dylan an envelope. It was a card saying that he could collect his very own piano, a Yamaha upright, from Cambridge Soundworks when it opened on Boxing Day. Molly looked stricken. "Where will we put it?"

"We'll get rid of the television," said her husband Arthur, triumphantly. "Charles, Viv, you've done more than you know for these brats."

Dylan and his sisters said that if it was a question of choosing, they wanted to keep the television, and that reminded them, could they and Nicky (Bri's cherubic son, a favorite with the two girls) go watch the Cartoon Network?

When they'd thundered off, we opened a box of liqueur chocolates and made bleak jokes about their future.

My mother, starting to pick up the wrapping paper, found Sadie's daughter Céline hidden under the tree, crying silently. She said she was scared of being "terrored."

"Marry your man," said Arthur to me. He was drunk. "Take out Japanese citizenship, have Japanese babies, and we'll all come and live off you when they start muzzling the intellectuals."

"Don't you think they have already?" I said.

"Speaking of Taka, darling, where is he?" said my mother. "I hope he liked his presents. We weren't sure what to get for him. I hope he wasn't disappointed or… or embarrassed."

They'd given him a Ralph Lauren tie, a leatherbound diary for the upcoming year, and an inscribed copy of my father's most populist book, *The Haunting of America*. My father is a psychologist who's often quoted on the sorry state of society, but all the same I couldn't decide whether giving Taka one of his books had been legitimate or in poor taste. I personally wouldn't have done it, if only because I knew it would be a chore for him to read that much English. He'd given my parents (without consulting me) half a dozen *fuurin* windchimes for the porches we didn't have, but I knew he hadn't expected to receive anything. He'd been so dumbstruck that the family had spotted it and covered up for him. Hence my mother's concern.

I found him in the room where he'd been put, my old one, smoking a cigarette in the dark. He had the window open, and the room was freezing, but it was a wise move because no one else in my family smoked. I kicked off my shoes and knelt beside him on the windowseat. He put his arm around my shoulders. Outside, snow topped the naked branches of the maple trees. The sky was not black but a ghostly orange color. There were no aircraft warning lights blinking in the distance, as there always were in Tokyo. I could hear one of the children bawling downstairs. I couldn't hear a sound from outside.

I started talking, mainly for my own amusement, repeating and explaining things my family had said. Taka listened, grunted, and laughed. With every word I spoke it grew less likely that he would tell me why he'd been sitting alone in the dark. I was proud of myself. I *knew* why, or thought I did, and I didn't want him to feel he had to spell everything out to me as if I was a stranger.

This was Taka's first time on the East Coast. Before we met he'd spent two years in California getting his MBA, but had done no domestic sightseeing. At the height of Alan Greenspan's irrational exuberance, the closest to irrational exuberance that the big dreamers at Stanford Business School had ever come, according to Taka, was smoking a joint or two. He went back to Japan with his degree and could, I suppose, have stepped straight into his current job, but for a while he hung around Tokyo doing nothing. Maybe he'd just run out of steam.

That had also happened to be Shizuka's last summer at home. Their parents had consented to send her to SUNY Buffalo, half a world away from Tokyo. She'd had a difficult time in high school. They'd pushed her to maintain her English, so she was equally at home in both languages, and she was apparently driving herself crazy with the whole returnee / identity crisis thing. (No one seems to have suspected at the time that there was more to it than that.) Buffalo seemed like the cure to fit the malady. There was nothing Taka could have said about it either way. Besides, he had his own preoccupations. I was one of them.

We met that July 20th at Vuenos, one of the clubs on Shibuya's Dogenzaka hill. He was there with a bunch of his flamboyant hardcore friends (so I got the wrong impression at first) and I was there with a Finnish girl from the course I'd been taking in Nagano prefecture. It had been she, not me, who'd wanted to see the band performing that night. I lost touch with her soon afterwards, but I owed her. The domino theory doesn't apply to international relations; it does to private lives. In a matter of months Taka had started at Goldstone Associates, we'd moved in together, and I'd got a job teaching English, not imagining I'd keep it a year, let alone four.

What had I been doing in Japan in the first place? Studying papermaking. *Washi* paper used to be used for lanterns and festal tableaux. Now it's just stationery with snob appeal. In reaction to the excesses that surrounded me in New York, I'd worked up a case for my personal integrity based on my handmade paper lampshades. I could talk with convincing passion about my art, and my friends from college who'd gotten real jobs said that I was being fearlessly original. The lampshades had horns, protrusions, and knobbles; I gave them titles such as "Unholy Light" and "Kindly Light." I got away with it as long as I was in New York, but when I tried to underpin my activities with an ancient tradition of artisanship, the whole show came crashing down around my ears. For me, as for Taka, the summer of 2000 was a breaking point. But he gathered his forces again and carried on, whereas I never went back.

As a prophylactic against our first visit to New York, I'd emailed my best friend from college, Gillian Carter. Like me, Gill had moved to the city after graduation. Now she was a social worker with an MA and student loans to pay off. A year ago she'd become engaged to a graphic designer named Victor Bermudez. I was looking forward to meeting him, and Gill was looking forward, she wrote, to meeting Taka. She promised they would treat us to dinner. I replied that, knowing Taka, it would probably be our treat.

And I wondered if I was factoring Shizuka into our plans heavily enough.

Our plane banked low over Queens; I confirmed for myself that the twin towers were missing from the skyline. We landed at LaGuardia and got a taxi into the city. The driver took the usual route through East Harlem. Nothing seemed to have changed. Maybe there were a few more Duane Reades, KFCs, and CVSes, but the place still looked wrecked. Since long before 9/11 this part of town had appeared to have been bombed and left to grow weeds while the authorities argued in circles about it. What was it that Brecht wrote? I tried to remember the quotation but couldn't. Taka laughed out loud at the sight of a group of tourists, tall and blond and dressed for a wilderness hike, huddling outside a bodega among the intoxicated locals. I said that I admired the tourists' savvy. Why queue for hours at Ground Zero when you could get the complete experience just by taking the 4, 5, and 6 to Lexington Avenue? There were all sorts of ways to save money in the city if you had the courage.

"Yeah, that's what she says." He wasn't looking at me, so he hadn't caught my sarcasm. He was talking about Shizuka, of course. For the last eighteen months – ever since she dropped out of college – she'd been living at 142nd and Edgcombe Avenue in Central Harlem. "$600 a month for three rooms in Manhattan? Not likely, I thought. Someone's being played for a fool. But I get it now."

Taka and I had booked a room at the small hotel often patronized by my parents, the Milburn on 76th and Broadway, instead of at the Holiday Inn or some such. I'd insisted that while Shizuka might think the Milburn stuffy, she would certainly despise the Holiday Inn, and probably us for staying at it. Taka had grumbled but allowed me to make the call. It was a quaint neighborhood, well known to me (I used to live at 101st and Amsterdam), with Christmas trees lying, shedding their needles, outside the brownstones. Snow mounded in the gutters and on the plastic chairs in front of the Greek restaurant on the corner. Taka was quiet as we checked in and dumped our bags. I went out to the nearby Fairway market and bought some provisions. When I got back to our room he said crossly, "What took you so long?"

"You didn't think I'd gotten mugged, did you? I couldn't work out where the mineral water was. There was no one to ask. And a woman made trouble ahead of me in the checkout line. New York, New York!" I broke into song: "If you can make it here you can make it anywhere…"

He eyed the fruit I'd bought: apples, grapes, Navel oranges, and a honeydew melon. "I hope you're planning to eat all that."

The room had a little kitchenette. I put the fruit in the fridge, saying, "So what if I went a bit overboard? It was cheap."

"Oh, just as long as you don't start doing the same thing at home." He went into the vast ensuite bathroom and said over the sound of running water, "I saw the fridge at your parents' house. Old food, new food, so much food you couldn't fit anything else in, and *rotting* food at the back of it all, I should think. And butter and jam and stuff out on the kitchen table all day."

I turned on the TV and sat down on the bed. When he came out of the bathroom, shirtless and towelling off his hair, I held out my hands to him. His expression softened. He picked up my hands, folded them together, and kissed the top one.

"Look," I said, nodding at the TV, where some politician was making up to a crowd of fat, unsmiling elementary school kids. "Malnourished children."

That evening we went our separate ways. Taka was scheduled to meet up with Shizuka for dinner *à deux*. I met Gillian for a drink at one of our old haunts, Jake's Dilemma on Amsterdam and 81st. I ended up meeting Victor, too, because he appeared after two hours to escort Gill home. It seemed prearranged, but he said he'd just left the office. (It was eleven o'clock at night on Boxing Day; the guy worked Tokyo hours.) Since he knew Gill wouldn't be home yet, he'd decided to stop by and clap eyes on her famous friend. That was how he put it, and it took me a few seconds to realize he was talking about those everlasting lampshades. (It seemed like they *would* be everlasting in some cases: Gill had one, and my family must have had a dozen.)

"She's in culture shock," Gill excused me. "She hasn't been home in three… is it? No, four years."

I felt hurt that she'd had to think about it.

"Oh yeah? I was gonna go to Japan one time. These guys wanted me to do some designs for them, and hey, it's a cool country, I woulda went, but it just didn't work out, you know?"

Victor had himself a Rolling Rock, ordered us another round of cocktails, and told me the story in detail. The bar was as fashionably dark as it had always been, but I could see that he was smaller and plumper than he'd looked in the photos Gill had emailed me. He had the enchanting smile of someone who loves the world and assumes that it loves him back. Puerto Rican, born and raised in the Bronx, he was a couple of shades darker than Gill, who was black but far from *black*. They were a touchy-feely couple, he pawing her while he talked, she squeezing his knee and nuzzling his neck. I'd never seen Gill participate in that kind of exhibition before. Her father, a suburban chief of police, espoused Old Testament family values, and she always used to behave as if he could see her. She was the inhibited one and I was the bold one. But now it was me sitting here with a fixed smile, vaguely scandalized. I told myself not to judge on this evidence that Victor was wrong for her. But there was other evidence, too.

We finalized our plans for dinner the next day.

I'd told Gill about Shizuka before Victor showed up, and she'd filled him in briefly. I knew she'd tell him all the rest later, but because she was a devout Christian I trusted her not to make a meal of it. They said Shizuka was welcome to join us. "Bring the whole family. The more the merrier," said Victor. "We can make some extra reservations and then cancel, you know?"

When I got back to the hotel Taka was already there, sprawled on the bed watching CNN with the sound down. The ashtray on the nightstand was overflowing. As I skipped through the icy wind I'd been translating in my head all the things I wanted to tell him about Gill and Victor. Sighing, I junked the script and said, "So where did you end up going?"

"A Japanese place in the forties. We got great service. They're hurting for customers now the tourists aren't coming."

I could hardly believe it. If only he'd asked my advice first! "How did it go?"

"She didn't eat anything." He sat up, swinging his legs off

the bed, and stubbed out his cigarette. "No, actually, that's not quite true. I ordered sashimi – I wanted to see if the fish was fresher than it is in California; it wasn't – and she ate some of the shredded daikon it's served on. Daikon has lots of nutrients, so maybe I should have been pleased, huh? Oh yeah, and she drank her miso soup."

I took off my coat and hung it in the closet. I'd normally have dropped it on a chair, but in this mood he'd have noticed and snapped at me for it. "Did you…" I dared not ask him what they'd talked about. "Did you catch up? Tell her about your promotion, find out how her art's going?"

"Her art, no. I heard plenty about Becky's art, though."

Mr and Mrs Nishino never referred to Becky in my hearing. Taka rarely did, either, and never by name. She was from Iowa or somewhere like that. She purportedly went to NYU, and it was my suspicion that she shared the apartment on 142nd Street with Shizuka.

"Here." Taka picked up an Associated Supermarkets plastic bag and took out a newspaper bundle. "Speaking of Becky's art, here's a example of it."

The bundle was so heavy I almost dropped it. Unwrapping the newspapers, I saw why: it was a stone, an irregular natural pyramid. On its flattest side was painted an Asian girl's face. The girl's pink, purple, and yellow striped hair flowed around the rock and turned into hands that clasped each other. The face was in the anime style, deftly executed. The whole was varnished. For once I could scarcely credit my own suspicions. "Is this… this isn't supposed to be Shizuka?"

"Not in the sense of a portrait. But they do model for each other. It's not badly done, is it?" He took the stone and tossed it into the armchair. "The Christmas presents just keep right on coming this year."

"Becky must be very anxious to make a good impression on you."

"Maybe, but I have a feeling we're not going to be allowed to meet her."

I took a deep breath and went for it. "Did you ask Shizuka

about dinner tomorrow? Gill and her fiancé said to bring her along. They know a great Italian place."

"Italian, Japanese, American, it doesn't matter. It'll go to waste."

"If she doesn't want to eat, she doesn't have to. She can drink water and nibble lettuce."

After an instant's pause, Taka laughed. "True. And who knows, if the food's good enough she might be overcome by temptation!" He looked around for his lighter, spotted the hotel matchbook, and lit another cigarette. He watched me as he exhaled, eyes glinting.

"And don't you think," I said, "we ought to ask Becky, too? After all, as we say in English, *the more the merrier!*"

It served me right for having expected a bull dyke with attitude. Becky Sharman was one of the quietest Americans I'd met in years. Plump and tall, she wore paint-stained jeans and a Fair Isle turtleneck. Her hair was in pigtails fastened with teddybear bobbles. It was dyed black, but judging by her eyebrows its natural color must have been blonde. She spoke in a little girl's voice, and with any degree of unforced volubility only on the topic of herself. My faith that I could win her over ebbed with each new revelation.

I'd been under the impression that she and Shizuka had met after Shizuka moved to the city. I now learned that *both* of them had been at SUNY Buffalo. They'd met at glee club tryouts at the beginning of their sophomore year. "The queer community was totally supportive," Becky recalled, but for some unspecified reason she had begun scheming to escape the place. Her machinations had borne fruit at last in the shape of a transfer to NYU. That shouldn't have been possible even if she was a straight A student. The NYU fine arts people must have detected some quality in her work that had escaped me. I said that I'd like to see her larger pieces. She hesitated, then turned pink and said shyly, "Ask Shizuka to show you her tattoo. I designed it. Actually, she designed mine, too."

I stammered, "Where is yours?"

She smirked into her wineglass.

She wasn't from Iowa or anywhere like that, but a small town upstate with a polysyllabic Indian name I'd already forgotten again.

"There were only six Hispanics at my high school," she said. "No Af... African-Americans and no Asians. But I was always into anime." A reminiscent giggle escaped her. "I was like the first person to see *Ghost In The Shell,* and everyone was like, oh my God, what's that?"

"Wow. Yeah," I said. "I thought I could see an anime influence in the piece you gave Taka."

"I'm majorly influenced by Kazuko Tadano. A lot of people don't get that she's really subversive."

She paused as if waiting for me to prove that I'd heard of the woman, which was impossible as I hadn't.

"I used to be a kind of artist, too," I offered. She gave me a tiny smile. A burst of laughter came from behind me. Her gaze slid past my head. I realized I'd been tactless, and felt angry with myself.

Our antipasti plates were removed and giant dishes of baked ziti bolognese and shrimp luciano appeared on the table. Taka refilled everyone's glass (except Shizuka's, which was still full). We started talking about our favorite hangouts in the city. It seemed that Shizuka and Becky usually chilled in the East Village, where there was a Japanese tapas bar called, wait for it, Japas.

"This isn't really my type of place," confided Becky, looking at Gill. "I mean, you know…"

Intrigued, I had another look around. Tony di Napoli's was on the Upper East Side. It was a bit pricey, but Gill and Victor took the view that eating out was supposed to be pricey. Two or three times a month they dressed up and went out for dinner in the same spirit as Taka and I dressed down and went to a show. This was one of "their" places. And just as well, too, because I knew Taka had made up his mind to pay and would have been irked if we'd insisted on going somewhere cheaper. Shizuka, I thought, was too busy not eating to notice whether she was on the Upper East Side or the dark side of the moon. Did Becky object on principle to the conspicuous consumption all around her?

I told myself not to be too hard on her. Maybe she was identifying with Shizuka. Maybe she couldn't stand seeing Shizuka like this.

Having proclaimed that this wasn't her kind of place, however, she no longer seemed so uncomfortable. She started talking to Gill, asking her nicely about her job and her background. It struck me as funny: Gill, the social worker, coped poorly with such questions directed at herself, and stammered shyly.

Shizuka had hit it off with Victor, and the two of them were teasing each other loudly. Taka was laughing in all the right places, as usual, but I figured he was pretending. To an extent, I figured we were all pretending.

Shizuka had always been a vivacious girl with a falsely confiding manner. On her visits home, she'd usually take a night out of her schedule for dinner with Taka and sometimes me, too. A few hours of her chatter would leave us sated to the point of incuriosity until she was safely out of reach again. I'd thought I was onto her game: appeasement played a part in her campaign for autonomy. But now I had a queasy sense that she'd been several jumps ahead of us all along, developing an escape strategy that was both fiendishly deep and breathtakingly simple. She seemed to have lost a few more pounds since the Central Park photos were taken. Her hair, dyed blonde and cut pixie style the last time she was in Tokyo, had grown out messily. Her cheeks were hollow, her skin the color of vanilla yoghurt. I'd caught strangers staring at her earlier. Whenever for an instant she was not the center of attention, her head would droop and the corners of her mouth sag in a sour way that made her look much older than 21, even though the weight loss made her look bizarrely ageless.

"Well, we're paying $900 for three rooms in Inwood," Gill was telling Becky. "And it's a pretty safe neighborhood. My only problem is my Spanish sucks, so I go in the supermarket and it's like, uh, *como estas?*"

"Hey, it's America," said Victor. "If they can't speak English it's their problem. I tell my mom she better start studying so she can talk to her grandkids!"

Gill smiled and touched his hand as he went for a second helping of ziti. Becky looked offended. I caught Gill's eye and she followed me to the ladies' room. It was in the basement, away from the noise and the flash of cutlery.

"Oh boy!" said Gill, getting her foundation compact out of her purse. "So she says we could save three hundred bucks a month if we moved down to the 145th Street area. Thanks, but no thanks."

"I guess it's gentrifying. Bit by bit," I said doubtfully.

"Well, you'd know better than I would," said Gill with a laugh.

I wasn't in a bantering mood. "I wouldn't bank on it, to be honest. I kind of expected everything to have changed, after 9/11 and all, but nothing has. Maybe it's just me that's changed." But that wasn't evident, even to me, on the face that looked back at me out of the mirror. I said rather hopelessly, "You know what I mean?"

Gill was still smiling. "So I guess you're not planning to hook up with Malik while you're here?"

The last boyfriend I'd had before I left the city, Malik was a reggae vocalist and a committed Afrocentrist. While we were together my lampshades had tended to be red, green, and black. I explained that I was so over that Jah love and ganja shit, I was going out with a management consultant, for God's sake, and we looked at each other in the mirror and laughed, but it didn't feel like happy laughter. I tried again, reminding her that Malik's legal name had been Wesley.

"Wesley! Mek dem say Wesley a de wickedest! Damn, you're making me cry!"

Watching her touch up her mascara, I realized I'd missed my chance to tell her that I had the same bad feeling about Victor she'd had about Malik. But then again, for all I knew, there was more to their relationship than met the eye. For all I knew, they'd talked over each and every issue that stood to divide them and decided that none of it mattered.

For all I knew, it didn't.

I hitched my hip on the counter between the sinks and asked Gill what she thought about Shizuka.

She gave me a serious look. "That girl needs help."

"That's exactly what I told Taka," I said, swinging my foot rapidly. "He, he…"

This seemed to remind Gill that she'd just met Taka, too, and she started congratulating me on what a sweet guy he was. I had a funny feeling that she didn't take my relationship with him seriously. But maybe she was just flipping the script on me. Maybe she'd picked up on my doubts about Victor, even though I'd said only nice things about him.

We got back to the table to find that two more entrées had arrived: eggplant parmigiana and some kind of green spaghetti. It was unclear who'd ordered them. Taka and Victor were apologizing to each other while the waiter hovered, ready to prove that *someone* had. Shizuka was saying brightly, "It doesn't matter! We can get doggie bags! Italian food still tastes really good the next day!" I had a sudden urge to scream at her, and realized I'd had too much to drink. But there was still a bottle of wine to be finished. We couldn't put that in a doggie bag.

The bill came to almost $250. I didn't want to be alone with Taka until he got over it, so when Shizuka announced, "Me and Becks are going to walk home instead of riding the subway! It's such a nice feeling to walk at night, and it's not so cold!" I said I'd go along with them.

In the event we all did, jostling along in a noisy group. We crossed over to Madison Avenue at 86th and trudged uptown under the high brick wall of the park. Needless to say, it was very cold. The snow heaped around the streetlights had frozen solid again, as had the puddles of snowmelt on the cobbles. Gill, who was wearing heels, kept skidding and being caught by Victor. We'd all run out of jovial commentary by now, so her yelps were the only sounds that broke the silence.

At the top of the park we turned left on Cathedral, walked for two long blocks, and then turned uptown again on Adam Clayton Powell. The avenues are broader and emptier north of the park. Occasional gypsy cabs raced along, swerving towards us and then accelerating in disappointment. I remembered how much fun it was to rollerblade on this street: wherever a pothole had been filled in there was a hillock of asphalt that bounced you right off the ground. It felt like flying. No one rollerblades in Tokyo. My exercise there was walking. Like this, in fact, in all weathers, from one part of town to another – although walking in Tokyo often feels like walking on a treadmill: indistinguishable office buildings, temples, pachinko parlors, gas stations, and poky little eateries pop up again and again like video scenery, and the cumulative effect is rather restful.

Adam Clayton Powell is lined with enormous white apartment buildings of antebellum proportions. Despite the cold, in their lighted portals people sat on folding chairs, bundled in coats, talking and drinking. I gazed up at rows of dark windows, remembering long hallways, lino floors checked like draughtsboards, and leprous plaster rosettes in the centers of ceilings too high to jump up and touch. The bodegas on the corners, where they aren't shuttered, have Budweiser, Old English, Kool, and Salem posters plastered all over their windows. Lightbulbs frame the signs above their 24-hour hatches. These contraptions – bulletproof perspex windows with revolving carousels set into them – are unique to Harlem as far as I know. When we passed close to them we could hear the faint strains of Arabic music.

At 125th Street Gill and Victor broke into thanks and goodbyes. They were going to walk west to Broadway and catch the 1 and 9, which ran all the way up to Inwood. Gill hugged me. "It's been so cool seeing you again."

"You, too," I said bleakly.

"I promise I'm going to be better about emailing."

Victor grabbed her hand and said he would remind her of

her promise. They scuffled, kissed each other's noses, and hurried off, waving back at us. "Later," we all called out. "See you later."

The four of us who were left stood in the snow, waiting for the walk light. A white Hummer rolled past, making the street vibrate to the muffled beat from its stereo. It was the first time I'd seen a Hummer in real life, and I stared after it in such awe that I almost didn't hear Becky telling Taka that he and I could catch the 2 and 3 over on Lenox. It would take us back to the Upper West Side in six stops.

"I don't feeling safe for you to walk alone," said Taka.

"Oh God," said Becky in cheerful exasperation. "We live here, you know."

We crossed the street.

"We were actually hoping," said Becky, "that you'd be able to see it isn't a bad neighborhood. I mean, in case Shizuka's... your parents were worrying, you could, like, reassure them."

"They don't worrying," said Taka. I saw the hint of a smile on his face as he lit a cigarette and tossed the spent match into a snowdrift.

The trickledown from the boom of the 1990s that had produced, on 125th, the Harlem USA mall and Starbucks had reached no farther north. We crossed over to Frederick Douglass and filed along sidewalks shattered under the ice, past demolition sites splashed with graffiti, vacant lots full of saplings inside chainlink fences, and terraces of brownstones with hair salons and check cashing joints on the ground floors. Even dilapidated, the brownstones would have had a dignified air, but they were all painted mud brown or red, layer upon peeling layer. Thanks to the weather, the streets were almost deserted. The few people we met stared at us. A group of men pedaling past on kids' bikes hooted derisively. I felt hot all over. Ever since Gill had mentioned Malik, I'd been thinking about him off and on, and now I ignobly wished he was here. With him I'd been able to go about Harlem fearlessly. He might have been stoned out of his skull most of the time, but he never deviated far from first principles. Once, walking uptown to visit him at his place on 137th and Lenox, I'd been followed by catcalls of "Whitey" and suchlike. In the safety of his apartment I'd started crying. He'd put his hands on my shoulders, bowed his head until our faces touched, and said, "You've got more soul than any of them." Remembering that now, I felt like crying for different reasons.

He lived at that time in one of those grand old buildings with moulded ceilings and a mosaic in the lobby where a man was shot one night. Sitting on his fifth floor windowsill was like being on board an ocean liner, watching the flotsam and jetsam drift past. Up here, it was more like floundering through the wreckage of the *Titanic*.

I walked beside Becky in silence. Taka and Shizuka kept up a muttered conversation in Japanese, too far behind for me to overhear.

The devastation was worst of all on the cross streets. 142nd, where the girls lived, appeared to have been systematically vandalized, with the banisters of the brownstones' steps hanging askew, broken windows gaping, and garbage bags torn open on the snow by foraging cats. The V of Edgcombe and Bradhurst Avenues perpendicular to the western end of the street, which should have been graced with a Flatiron-style tenement, had been razed to rubble. The brownstones climbing up the Edgcombe side were windowless and doorless. On the uptown side of 142nd stood a housing project. Those massive buildings, as monstrous as any product of the Stalin era in the USSR, have the dubious quality of indestructibility.

"If I lived in one of those," I said, pointing, as Becky got out her keys, "I'd want to flatten it. But the worst I could do would be to fuck with the elevator. I can't imagine anything more frustrating."

We went into a hall with the familiar checked lino floor and started to climb unlit flights of stairs.

"I'd want a tank," I said. It was something I'd first thought of years ago. "A mortar. A rocket launcher. Heavy artillery. A suitcase full of C4." I laughed as a new thought came to me.

"I'd want a fucking Boeing 747."

I distinctly heard Becky mutter, "Jesus Christ."

"What?" I said.

"I guess it's easier to joke about it if you weren't here at the time."

"Oh," I said, "I wasn't joking."

"Now I'm working on a canvas on the theme," said Shizuka. "Since you're here, you can see."

Their apartment on the fourth floor was unexpectedly welcoming. Swathes of colorful gauze hung in the windows, the tables and chairs were the best of Dumpster salvage, and standing lamps in the corners of the living-room gave a cozy effect. Shizuka put a CD on the minisystem: Underworld's *Everything, Everything*. Taka and I had it, too. "Anyone want coffee?" asked Becky.

They'd installed track lighting on the ceiling of the kitchen. I'd been wondering whether they might have chosen this place for its natural exposure, but evidently not. Halogen floods illuminated the chaos of a studio. The kitchen counter was covered with Becky's stones. In the corner stood a lumpy object about four feet high, shrouded in a dropsheet. On an easel was a 60 by 40 inch canvas so sketchily begun that I couldn't tell what it was going to be of. It turned out to be Shizuka's work on the theme of 9/11. She showed us a number of preliminary drawings and where their elements would appear on the canvas. The twin towers were to be depicted in all their old glory, but from their top floors people would be jumping, and that famous storm of paper would blow all over the canvas, one or two sheets appearing lifesize in the foreground. These last were to be collage items: faxes of corporate asset valuations from South America that a friend of Becky's had picked up off the street (with an eye to this use for them?). Shizuka showed us them in a plastic folder.

Taka said in Japanese, "Be careful you don't get hauled up for unauthorized use of private material."

I said in English, "I think you've got hold of a really good idea." I wasn't flattering her. I loved the fact that there were not to be any airplanes in the picture. "When do you expect to finish it?"

"I don't know," she said with disarming honesty. "Some days I don't want to touch the canvas. Right now I haven't worked recently. But I have to finish before I can start another project."

She was paler than ever. When I gave her back the folder our fingers touched. Hers were ice-cold.

"Milk? Sugar? Amaretto flavored creamer?" said Becky, pouring out from the Mr Coffee that sat atop the gas rings on the stove. I guessed neither of them did much cooking. The sink had nothing in it except a tumbler full of paintbrushes. Over Becky's shoulder I saw inside the fridge: three Granny Smiths, a dozen fat free yoghurts in various flavors, a bowl of bright red Jello covered with foil, and condiments.

Taka sipped his coffee. "What about your new project, Becky?"

"Oh. Well, it's not finished yet, but..." She put her mug down and lifted the dropsheet off the object in the corner. It was a papier mache sculpture of a nude woman, slightly larger than lifesize (if Shizuka had been the model), kneeling in the seiza pose with hands flat to a wooden pedestal that looked like a fruit crate. A sculpted curtain of hair spilled down, almost hiding the lowered face. The effect of abject apology was so powerful that I wanted to rush over and lift the figure to its feet.

"Very moving indeed," said Taka in Japanese. He was looking at Shizuka, who was compulsively picking flakes off the neck of a tube of red gouache. I had a sense of impending disaster.

"It's really impressive. What do you call it?" I asked Becky, just to say something.

"Guess."

"Oh, God. *Still Apologizing After All These Years*?" I moved closer to the sculpture and saw that its back was covered with pencil marks. "*Fantasy Figure*," I tried in Japanese. Taka's and Shizuka's heads snapped around.

Becky said gruffly, "*The Spirit Of Harlem*."

"It's a feminist interpretation," said Shizuka.

"How do you figure that?" said Taka in Japanese.

Starting in English, then dropping into Japanese, Shizuka explained that Becky saw a link between the historical oppression of Japanese women and that of African-Americans, and that the sculpture was intended to place the viewer in the role of the oppressor, the viewing experience creating a space in his or her consciousness for the oppressed groups who were customarily denied such recognition...

I forced myself to smile at Becky and tried for a wry tone – maybe it was time for a bit of American solidarity. "It's all Greek to me, what about you?"

"I speak little Japanese only," she enunciated. Her accent was so poor that it took me a minute to understand what she'd said.

I wandered over and looked at *The Spirit Of Harlem* again. "Are you going to give her tattoos?" I pointed to the sculpture's back.

"Yeah. I haven't decided what yet, though. I could show you my rough drafts." She made it into a question.

"Sure." I followed her through the living-room, into the bedroom. She picked up a sketchpad that had been lying on the bed and showed me her ideas: a snaky dragon such as elderly yakuza have on their arms; a multicultural group of slaves in chains; a crucified man who looked like Tupac Shakur; a 1920s jazz club scene with a large saxophone in it. She didn't seem to be crazy about any of the sketches, so I didn't have to pretend to be, either. I said, "What about a tattoo of a face? It could be angry or defiant or even gloating, whatever her real feelings are."

"But we can't know her real feelings," said Becky. "That's the whole point."

I listened for the voices in the kitchen and caught something over the music about "Mom's friends." I said, "What about Shizuka's real feelings?"

"About what?"

"I don't know, about school. About her art. About you."

Becky stood up. I thought she was going to hit me. She fumbled with the buttons of her jeans and slid them down her thighs. She was wearing black cotton panties. Blonde pubic hair showed at the legholes. She turned half around. Covering her left buttock was a tattoo of a tree, a tree in the old Shizuka style with blood veins for roots and malformed limbs for boughs, each leaf a hand dripping blood from its fingernails. Becky craned over her shoulder and jabbed her finger into her own skin. "Can you see it? It's pretty small." I had to move closer. She smelled faintly musky. At last I saw that on the trunk of the tree was written in a heart, as if carved, *SN + BS 4 EVER*. "She designed it, like I told you." Becky pulled her jeans back up. "So I guess it expresses her real feelings."

I went to the window and moved the purple gauze curtain aside. I was looking into an airshaft. There were lighted windows on the second and third floors, but I couldn't hear a sound from down there. I said, "Shizuka dropped out of school to follow you down to the city, didn't she?"

"She's a big girl. It's pretty dumb of you to think I could influence her, if that's what you're saying."

"It's not a bad thing to have influence over people. If you do have some over her, you might be able to save her life by using it."

"Well, I don't."

Becky's frustration came through as clearly as if she'd started screaming. I turned around. She gave me a frightened look and sat down on the bed.

"I can't make her do anything. I can't even make her eat. I don't even buy any groceries for myself because she'll just binge and get all weirded out and throw up. I read on this website that you're not supposed to enable them, but if I do buy stuff it's like I'm encouraging her to be bulimic, so no matter what I do it's wrong. But I don't know what to do. It's like, why do I have to be the adult around here? Why am I the one that has to be responsible?"

"I... oh my God. Have you thought about talking to her

parents?"

Becky's face darkened, and I knew she was going to tell me why she couldn't. As I racked my brains for some other suggestion to make, I overheard Taka saying in a joking tone I knew of old, "Well, if you're really in love with her then marry her!"

There are no four-letter words in Japanese. That doesn't compromise the language's range of expression. *Fuck* and *shit* and sheer helpless rage were all there in his voice.

We left them with some documentary they wanted to watch just starting on the History Channel. We trudged up the hideous slope of Edgcombe Avenue, turned left on 145th Street, passed a bunch of boys with red eyes shivering in the cold, and descended icy concrete steps into the subway station. Swiping our Metrocards, we pushed through the turnstiles. The walls were tiled in stripes of orange and white. Our footsteps echoed in the concrete vault. On the faces of the other people waiting for the A train, unpleasant emotions showed in a way that struck me as precivilized. My head was aching badly. The world seemed to be rotating like a pulsar, almost too fast to see, showing me now a bright side on which compassion was necessary and now a dark side on which only revulsion was possible.

Before the train came we had to cope with several demands for money, and when it did come a very stinky homeless man sat down across from us. He got off at 125th and Taka and I started talking. We hadn't been shown Shizuka's tattoo, and we speculated as to what it might be of. As to *where*, there seemed little doubt: on her back, of course. Like a yakuza moll. We discussed Gill and Victor and agreed that even if they did get married, it wouldn't last. Victor had said that he thought in Spanish a lot of the time, whereas Gill couldn't even speak it. How was she ever really to understand him? We got off at 59th Street and climbed to the 1 and 9 platform, discussing the dissimilarities of English and Spanish. It was an established habit of ours to scapegoat language for everything that could go wrong between two people. Referring to the setup on 142nd Street, Taka said, "Did you notice there wasn't a single Japanese book or magazine in the place?"

"There was a whole shelf of manga in the bedroom."

"Manga," he said scornfully.

"Probably Becky's," I admitted. I paced the platform and peered into the tunnel. Becky had made us a present of two more stones: one flattish with a geisha-looking nude on it and one, roughly hemispherical, painted to look like a snow globe with Santa Claus on his sleigh inside. I had them in a plastic bag, and this I now started swinging violently.

A yellow garbage train clanked into the station. Taka sighed and said, "Let's take a taxi."

On the seat we found a crumpled $5 bill, which we handed over to the driver. He seemed astonished by our honesty. Having established that we were tourists, he started telling us about his scheme to go back to Cote D'Ivoire and start an import-export business. I made sympathetic noises. Taka stared out the window. While still listening to the driver I tried to remember if we had any aspirin in the hotel room.

We stumbled out onto the corner of 76th. Taka headed for the Milburn's green awning without looking to see if I was following. "I'll be up in a minute," I shouted, and dashed to the Duane Reade on the next block. There was a whole aisle full of painkillers. I dithered for several minutes before buying a box of Tylenol. Running back to the hotel, I realized I didn't have my keycard. I knocked on our door. Silence. "Taka, Taka." After another few minutes I went back to the desk and had them call our number. The call was answered. The clerk put down the phone and told me to go on up. I fell out of the elevator to see Taka standing in the open door of our room, wearing nothing except jeans, his hair dripping wet.

"I was in the shower. I thought you had your keycard."

"Well, I didn't." I went past him, then stopped. The room was dark. He shut the door and it was darker. He touched my waist. I turned, locked my arms around him, and said into his ear, getting my face all wet, "I'm sorry."

"It's OK." He undid my arms and padded back into the bathroom, closing that door, too. No light showed underneath it. He was showering in the dark.

I put on one of the nightstand lamps, took Becky's stones out of their plastic bags, and dumped all three of them on the bed. Then I saw the Duane Reade bag lying on the floor where I'd dropped it. I took three Tylenols with a glass of water. Swallowing, I spotted Taka's Marlboro Mediums on the nightstand, took one, and lit up.

I was on my second one by the time he came out of the bathroom. I stood by the TV on top of which I'd placed the ashtray, watching him search through his suitcase for a clean t-shirt. He didn't find one. Sighing, he put on the plain navy one he'd been wearing and a pair of boxers. "Let's talk about it tomorrow. Let's get some sleep."

"I'm not tired," I protested. It sounded childish, and I would have laughed at myself if he'd so much as smiled, but he didn't. He lit a cigarette, sat down on the bed, and fingered Becky's stones.

"We've got one more day. I figure I'll call her in the morning and arrange to have lunch or something. I'll put it to her then."

"Wait, did I miss something?"

"I'm going to give her an ultimatum. Either she comes home, or I tell our parents the truth and they come here."

I'd been convinced all along that going home would be the best medicine for Shizuka. But now I said, "She's an adult. You can't force her to abandon the lifestyle she's chosen."

"She hasn't chosen any lifestyle." He stood up to reach the ashtray and stayed standing, half turned away from me. "She's chosen to die."

I'd thought he didn't get it, or would never admit to getting it. I gripped my left elbow tightly in my right hand. "What if she tells you she's going to come home after she finishes that painting, or whatever, and then she just doesn't?"

"Then I'll fly back here and try again."

"But your job… what if you can't get time off again?"

"To hell with my job."

"I could come back in your place, if it came to that. I can take vacation time whenever I like as long as I apply in advance."

"That wouldn't work."

"We just have to convince her we care about her," I muttered, but I didn't believe it any longer. He'd taken the wind out of my sails. My eye fell on Becky's stones and I remembered what I'd decided to do with them. I went over to the window and pulled back the curtains. I could see nothing outside the glass, of course, but I remembered that we looked down on a strip of cement backyard with a Dumpster in it. I tried to open the window.

"What are you doing? You've got to lift the catch."

"Oops." Ignoring whatever else he was saying, I lifted the catch, but I still couldn't get the window open. It was stuck, or not made to open at all. I jerked at it and ripped a fingernail to the quick. "Ow, shit, ow!"

"Calm down!"

"I am calm." Blood welled up from under my fingernail. I went back to the bed and picked Becky's stones up, two in my left hand and one in my right. Taka moved towards me. I threw the stone in my right hand, the one with the face that might or might not have been Shizuka's on it, at the window. A crack shrieked the length of the pane, but it held. I darted to where the stone had fallen, scooped it up again, and bashed the window with it. Pieces of glass fell into the room and out into the darkness. I hurled the stone out after them. The moment in which I expected to hear it hit the ground passed in silence, as if there was really nothing down there at all. Taka grabbed me, dragged me over to the bed, and threw me flat on my back. He plunged on top of me and pinned my wrists. I still had a stone in each hand. I threw them up at him: not very forcefully, because I could only move my fingers. One of them hit his shoulder. The other one hit the side of his head as he turned it. I screamed.

He let go of my right wrist and touched his head.

"I'm sorry, Taka! I didn't think it would hurt you!"

"I'm fine." He rolled off me and sat on the edge of the bed with his back to me. He pushed up the sleeve of his t-shirt and squinted at his shoulder.

I recovered the stones, tiptoed to the window, and dropped them out. The room already felt colder.

"Had enough?"

I jumped. He was watching me.

"I thought you'd given up smashing things... oh, *years* ago!"

"I thought so, too. I guess I forgot how much stuff there is to smash."

He shook his head, then winced and touched the place over his ear where the stone had struck. It didn't seem to be bleeding, but it must have hurt.

Suddenly I knew what to do. I darted around the bed and dropped to my knees on the floor in front of him. "I am terribly sorry!" I'd seen this done on TV, but it wouldn't have occurred to me now if not for Becky's *The Spirit Of Harlem*. As I bumped my forehead on the carpet, I felt sick with embarrassment. "I'm sorry! I'm sorry! I'm sorry!"

"Jesus Christ!" shouted Taka in English. He jumped up and seized my shoulders, dragging me to my feet. "You don't have to do this shit! It's not necessary. You didn't hurt me at all." He hugged me. "Jesus Christ, honey..." He carried on speaking the endearments that don't exist in Japanese. Baby, darling, sweetie, angel... the very words made me feel safe.

I had no strength left in my arms, but I wrapped them around him. He kissed my forehead and then my mouth. I kissed him back weakly.

"Thank you," he whispered, incomprehensibly.

I rested my head on his shoulder and felt myself starting to fall asleep. Straightening up, I said with an effort, "Let me see those bruises. If I *have* hurt you I'll never forgive myself."

Sometime in the small hours of the morning the telephone on the nightstand rang. Taka rolled over and grabbed it.

"It's probably about the window," I muttered wretchedly.

"Hello," said Taka in English, and then his face went blank. He sat up and fumbled about with his free hand for his cigarettes. I switched on the bedside light. His cigarettes were on the other nightstand. I held them out to him, but he didn't take them. He got out of bed and pressed his back against the wall, hunching his shoulders, still clamping the receiver to his ear.

A freezing wind bulged the curtains and blew across the bed. I jumped up and started dragging my clothes on.

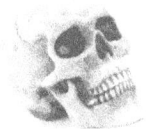

GOING UNDER

The restaurant was a cross between a shoebox and a cave, lit by spitting fluorescent fixtures, open to the plaza in front of the station where people milled and ate and slept on the asphalt with their heads on their bundles. Our last night on the train had been cut short by our arrival in Chongqing. We ate an early breakfast of noodles and sat on with our (probably very disparate) thoughts. At last the sky outside turned grey. My eyes puffy, an unwanted cigarette smouldering in my fingers, I sat up straight. "There they are again."

Tom was tapping on his laptop. He gave me a fake-tolerant smile that said the joke was wearing thin.

"*Look*... no, too late. They're gone now. But it was definitely them."

"Our... minders?"

"Stumpy saw me. They were looking into all the restaurants. I met his eyes for a second."

"Yeah... Fay, you know what? Twenty, thirty years ago, they *did* follow tourists around. Hell, they wouldn't have let us bum around the country by ourselves like this. You had tour guides riding herd on you all the way. But nowadays we could step off the beaten trail and vanish and nobody would even notice. Welcome to the brave new world order, honey. Nobody gives a fuck where we go or what we do."

He sounded so sure of it. I had a guilty conscience, and maybe I *was* letting my imagination run away with me.

Since Tom wasn't going to take me seriously, anyway, I decided to let him think he'd convinced me. "I guess they do all kind of look the same to me," I said humbly.

"*See?* You can't even tell them apart, so how do you know it was the same…" He got bored with his sentence in the middle of it, sighed deeply, and went back to his laptop. He'd been the valedictorian of his high school class in Somerville, MA; had graduated third in our class at Princeton; and after getting his master's in East Asian Studies, he'd soared with the greatest of ease into the Foreign Service. That was back in the nineties when expounding American policy was a job even liberals could get excited about. Did you know that almost all US embassies and consulates general have Public Affairs sections responsible for telling America's story abroad and creating mutual understanding? Nor had I known it until Tom started as a junior officer at the embassy in Bangkok. Two years later he was transferred to Kingston, of all places. The Foreign Service is not known for maximizing its employees' potential, but it recognized Tom's. After just a year in Jamaica he got tenure and was posted to Tokyo as assistant information officer. That was then; this was autumn 2002. Even in friendly Japan there was precious little understanding on offer these days. Tom's job had become an exercise in futility. As an escape from the despair that it occasioned him, he'd branched out into translating contemporary Chinese fiction. For such an intelligent man he was easy to fool – at least if you'd been married to him for the past nine years.

"Why isn't there any coffee in this country?" I said. "No coffee in restaurants. No coffee in cute little cans in vending machines. No coffee *shops*. This is a *huge* opportunity for Starbucks."

He refused to be drawn.

"I can't drink this stuff." I sipped from my bottle of green tea. Only one brand of it was sold in China, as far as I could discover, and they didn't make a sugarless version. "It's too sweet. It's disgusting."

"Agribusiness," said Tom distractedly, meaning that American corn syrup finds its way into everything, even Chinese green tea. He was very strong on that stuff, which made it all the odder that he so resolutely ridiculed any suggestion of dirty dealings in his own vicinity. "Anyway, it'll do you good to kick the caffeine habit."

A mosquito landed on my wrist. A spear of solid golden sunshine slammed into my face. The couple at the next table, who could have been us except that they were Chinese and had suitcases at their feet instead of backpacks, started quarrelling noisily. Or that was what it sounded like – but I couldn't speak Chinese and it *all* sounded like quarrelling to me.

"Buses should be running soon. Might as well get going; it'd be pointless to miss the first one. Zhàngdān!" shouted Tom. The waitress shouted something that I took to mean *Ya pay at the register, buddy!* It turned out to mean just that, and I felt more hopeful. See, I told myself, it's not really that difficult to operate in this country. It's not really that different from Japan when you first moved there –

But it was.

Around the station towered windowless highrises. The economists said Chongqing was booming as fast as Beijing, but the process of obliterating and rebuilding didn't seem to have gotten as far here yet. We boarded a bus that carried us out along a road lined with mossy concrete buildings teetering on precipices above the Yangzi. Tom decided we were going the wrong way, and we got off. After walking for half a mile we found another bus stop and boarded a No. 57 back into the city. By now it was eight o'clock. We were veterans of Tokyo rush hour, but this bus should have been labelled For Advanced Players Only. The flashily dressed workforce of Chongqing had no scruples about shoving. Tom and I were forced apart, hugging our backpacks. The overloaded bus must have been a bitch to handle in the traffic that clogged the hilly city center, but our driver, a dark girl in a tank top, made it look easy while periodically turning around to yell at her passengers. We parted from her at the top of a street that zigzagged downwards in modified hairpin bends. There were many such in Chongqing, and people cooked at outdoor griddles on the staircases that intersected them, as if the whole city was their house.

"Your guess is as good as mine," said Tom shortly when I asked him where we were now.

I cheered up at the reflection that our wanderings must have confused Stumpy and his colleague – *if* they existed.

Tom studied the map and then started downhill without looking at or speaking to me.

With the sun up, the temperature had risen from pleasant to hot. September was supposed to be the best month to visit central China, but this seemed to be a relative statement. The humidity gave the light a gelatinous quality. All the food stalls and the traffic added smoke and steam to the air. Bowed under our backpacks, we trudged up hills and down flights of outdoor stairs until we found the travel agency that Tom had preselected as the right one. He was working from Japanese guidebooks with the aim of dodging what we called "Lonely Planeteers." I thought his precautions unnecessary: in six days I'd seen exactly one other white person, an elderly man wandering across Tiananmen Square at night. But it suited my purposes, too, to avoid other tourists, so I went along with Tom's idea of a good time – not that I could easily have done anything else.

He had two weeks of vacation and he'd figured out that we could fit into them what was left of old Beijing, the doomed splendors of the Three Gorges, and Xi'an, the capital of Shaanxi province. His love affair with Japan had withered in three years of daily contact with Japanese flacks and hacks, but his love affair with China had been going on all this time, and had been publicly consummated with his first book-length translation (*Snowbound Feet,* a novel by Xu Ailing: Simon & Schuster, $24.99). This was his second trip here and he'd intended to make it alone. I'd persuaded him to include me by playing on his insecurities.

Sure, I had my own agenda, but it *would* have looked bad if he'd left me behind. His colleagues and their wives had already given up on us: Tom on account of his literary activities, me on account of speaking Japanese and working as a translator in my own right. I'd majored in East Asian Studies, too, and I hadn't let my time in Tokyo go to waste. Incredible as it seems, this had cost me the goodwill of the older wives whose counterparts' friendship I'd treasured in Thailand and Jamaica. In some ways Foreign Service culture is bizarrely out of date. In other ways it's wired into the news cycle. Tokyo isn't a hardship post, so the sense of community there shouldn't have been too oppressive, but the post-9/11 security measures made up for it, instilling in our neighbors a siege mentality that neither Tom nor I subscribed to. They would have loved to see some evidence that our marriage was on the rocks. I was determined to preserve for Tom for as long as I could whatever was left of our public image, and I was determined not to ruin his career.

As I trailed after him into the travel agency, these thoughts led to others, and I got a lump in my throat from sheer excitement. It was like being six years old and remembering that your birthday was coming up; it was like being nineteen and remembering that you were about to get married without your parents' approval; and it was like preparing for an interview with an editor and going to the doctor and taking amphetamines.

Tom pulled a stool up to the counter and started bargaining in Chinese with the woman behind it. Everyone else in the place gathered around to watch the fun. I sank into an armchair with broken springs. A mirror on the far wall mocked my mood by showing me what I looked like after three days on the train from Beijing. I was oxybenzone white (the alternative to being an unappetizing shade of lobster) and dripping with sweat. My straight brown hair was coming down from its ballerina knot. My mouth, before I rearranged it into a smile, was upside-down with tension. There was a mosquito bite on my neck and I was covered from the sneakers up with beige dust. I'd never felt more alive, but I looked like hell. No wonder Tom had been reluctant to look at me all morning.

But he wasn't the only man in the world – and I knew one man, at least, who loved me whatever I looked like, who saw through my comic turns as a diva and a latterday Sylvia Plath and a helpless bimbo and a firebreathing harpy and all the other roles I played for Tom's benefit. I'd started catering to my husband's prejudices long ago in an attempt to make him feel better about himself. Somewhere along the line I'd realized I was manipulating him, but by then it had become a habit so ingrained that I couldn't stop. To have met, then, a man I *couldn't* manipulate had restored my faith in humanity. Toshitake Mizuno was a professional translator. He had a stammer, which made him very patient but not infinitely so. During the first week of the war on Afghanistan I'd given in and started sleeping with him. I'd been doing it ever since, too.

"They say they'll keep our backpacks for us," said Tom, looking down at me. "We've got the rest of the day to kill, so I want to see Luohan Temple."

Oh God, not another temple.

"They've got hundreds of figures like the Terracotta Warriors, only smaller."

He spoke offhandedly, but I realized that he was trying to tempt me. He knew the Terracotta Warriors were what I was really looking forward to. Undone, I went along with him, asked questions about the temple's history, and did my best to listen to the answers.

After lunch we hit the Carrefour hypermarché in the Chaotianmen district. It was as crowded as the temple had

149

been empty. Hunting for groceries, I stumbled into the live meats section. "Cootchie cootchie. Hello guys," I said faintly, touching the glass of a tank full of frogs. They clambered over each other, scrabbling with their sticky little hands. Tom appeared at my shoulder. I wailed, "I don't know whether I'm in a supermarket or a pet shop!"

"I would venture to say you're the only person who remains unclear on that point, Mrs Lynch. Hey, if you want, we'll buy one and you can set it free."

"But which one? And where? There aren't any parks, and they'd just catch it again." I clutched my head. "Did you find the sandwich makings?"

"Well, I don't know if you're going to like this bread. And I hate to break it to you, but the Chinese are not big on dairy products. The closest we're going to get to cheese is this weird generic Velveeta." Displaying a shrinkwrapped yellow slab to me, he couldn't quite hide a smirk of amusement at my reaction. I'd once seen this very smirk as a sign that I'd succeeded in pleasing him.

After standing in the checkout line for about sixteen hours, we hurried back to the travel agency. Tom was worried we'd be late, but he needn't have been. We were in for another interminable wait. Eventually a dainty little tour guide bustled in and gave us laminated tags to hang around our necks. Dark had fallen by the time our party finally assembled. We straggled downhill and crowded into a cable car that clanked down the face of a rocky cliff. Down at river level, all was dim electric light and yammering crowds. I couldn't see or hear the Yangzi, and I didn't see our ferry until we had already crossed the gangway and the companionways were echoing beneath hundreds of shoes.

We were sharing our cabin with two elderly gentlemen, Mr Hu and Mr Wang, who looked to me like retired apparatchiks. They let us have the top bunks, and I think all four of us believed we were getting the best of the bargain. As the ferry began to move, Mr Hu and Mr Wang took off their shoes and switched on the television.

Tom and I piled up the stairs, laughing uncontrollably, and burst onto the aft deck. There were no benches here, only massive ventilators blowing out stinky fumes, which might explain why we found ourselves alone. The ferry was already out in the middle of the river, chugging downstream. Now that Chongqing was invisible except for its twinkling lights, I thought it was a beautiful city. I took the elastic out of my hair and let it blow loose. Tom leaned on the rail. I stood beside him. There was a thirty-metre drop to the water. Garbage slid through rippling rectangles of light. Craning over the rail, I could see people smoking and chatting on the lower walkways, and voices were coming from the observation deck higher up, but here, secluded behind the ventilators, we had some privacy for the first time in days. I sorted words into sentences in my head.

"I know I was a dickhead today," said Tom, taking me by surprise. "It was getting on the wrong bus this morning. I just hate fucking up like that. It puts me in a shitty mood, but that's no reason…" he trailed off, then added almost inaudibly, "Sorry."

I could have cried. What made it worse was that I hadn't thought he was being much more of a dickhead than usual. I hugged him. "I feel like I'm not being any help at all. I'm just trailing around after you."

"If we were African I'd make you carry all the luggage," he said, laughing. "Aren't you glad we're civilized?"

"That's what civilization leads to," I said edgily, pointing down at the garbage in the water.

He sighed. "You know, there's never any guarantee you'll get your first bid. Even with my language skills… I'm trying not to get too fixated. But we *might* end up living here, so give it a chance, OK?"

I giggled.

"I can't tell him," I'd said to Toshitake a few months ago, when we'd had our Big Talk and I'd promised him I *would* tell him. "I can *leave* him, but I can't *tell* him I'm leaving him!"

151

The voices were descending from the observation deck. On an impulse to camouflage our situation, I pecked Tom on the lips, and he kissed me back with an intensity that got my antennae twitching. He, too, felt guilty about something, and I thought I knew what it was.

We'd been living in Tokyo for three years and five months. A tour lasts four years. You do the math.

Foreign Service Officers can't work two consecutive tours in the same city. Washington knows a thing or two about psychology. Get it? Tom wouldn't have wanted to stay on in Tokyo, anyway: he felt that in that city of 12 million he was carrying the burden of sanity alone. But he knew I'd been happy there. I'd established the foundations of a career of my own and met a lot of interesting people, and in a few months I'd have to leave it all behind to go with him to his next post. He wouldn't have been the man I married if he hadn't felt bad about it. Theoretically, of course, I could be a translator anywhere: I had enough contacts now to get commissions without schmoozing. Actually, of course, my reluctance to leave Japan had little to do with my career. Poor Tom couldn't understand where my spirit of adventure had gone. He tried to get me interested in bidding on our next post, but I didn't want to think about it, and said things like, "Norway, because the fjords are so pretty."

In the event that Tom wasn't posted to China – and it was by no means a sure thing: his lack of seniority cancelled out his language qualification – he didn't care where he went, so Norway had actually made it onto the list as our sixth choice. I lay awake in the grip of agonizing premonitions that by some bureaucratic irony he *would* end up in Oslo… alone.

I'd already decided that wherever he ended up, I wasn't going.

All that remained was for me to work out the logistics of leaving him.

Months later, I was no closer to knowing how to go about it.

When we were at home, he worked long days – long nights, too, if there were visiting dignitaries to be nannied – and devoted most of his free time to his translations from the Chinese. These, I knew, were just what the doctor ordered to keep him from going over the edge. Sex has nothing on philology as a lasting distraction. But if I hadn't been having an affair I would have felt spurned. We seldom spent time together when one of us was not multitasking. Tom had been known to bring his laptop to bed and keep right on typing, simultaneously channel surfing on the bedroom TV, while I curled under the covers, surreptitiously texting Toshitake on my cell phone. On the rocks? Our marriage was on the Great Barrier Reef. But we never actually quarrelled, so how was I to tell him it was over? I couldn't say straight out that I was having an affair. I just *couldn't*. And even if I did, I knew that my mouth would wobble into a smile as I uttered the words, cueing him not to overreact. He would pretend to jump to the conclusion that I was having it off with our ghastly next door neighbor, I would deny it, and the whole thing would get passed off as a joke.

Toshitake had suggested to me, cautiously, that this trip to China would be a perfect opportunity to have it out with Tom. In his hesitation I'd heard the echo of his suspicion that I was *never* going to have it out with Tom and consequently was never going to leave him. Naturally optimistic, Toshitake was starting to get cynical – and it was my fault. Crying, I'd promised him that one way or another, by the time I got back from China, my marriage would be over.

I awoke as the ferry juddered to a halt, feeling more than mildly desperate.

We'd berthed at Fengjie. I couldn't get back to sleep, so when our tour guide rousted us out at seven o'clock I was in no shape to go ashore. Tom went with Mr Hu and Mr Wang to see the White Emperor City. When they got back, he told me about it while our cabinmates settled down to watch television and eat salted melon seeds. They spat the husks directly onto the carpet – indeed, I'd caught Mr Wang *spitting* directly onto the carpet – so that it wasn't safe to walk around the cabin in your stocking feet any more. In the same way, you had to get to the cafeteria on the early side for meals, because a table after a party of Chinese had finished eating there tended to look as if they'd just finished being sick there, with gristly bits scattered far and wide – and if you hung around waiting for someone to clean up, you'd never get to sit down at all.

According to Tom, this indifference to public hygiene was excusable in a people who'd been lectured, taxed, conscripted, denounced, reeducated, and massacred by their rulers for thousands of years. If we'd grown up in a corrupt autocracy, he said, we too would think public littering and noisiness very minor evils. Bearing this in mind, I forgave Mr Hu and Mr Wang for inviting two more retired apparatchiks to our cabin for tea just when I'd climbed into my bunk to take a nap. They had good intentions: they'd given us oranges and told us about their families. I saved my resentment for the television, for the loudspeaker grille in the wall that intermittently blasted light orchestral standards, and for Tom.

Between them they drove me out of the cabin to explore. The Chinese seemed to have mastered the concept of the cruise ship, after a manner of speaking. On B Deck I found a games arcade, a karaoke bar, and a mahjong parlor, all packed out. On C Deck there was a commissionaire's kiosk that sold snacks and souvenirs. Yet in front of it indigent families were camping out in forts of bundles, kiddies squabbling while grannies and uncles slept like the dead on the floor. They, too, were tourists. If Toshitake had been there to say it out loud to, I would have gotten a fatal fit of the giggles. As it was, I went back upstairs and sat on the walkway outside our cabin with my book-for-emergencies, protected by the overhang of the observation deck from the drizzle that had begun to fall.

Whether you called it the Yōsukō, the Chōkō, the Yangtze Kiang, or the Yangzi, it was a godforsaken body of water, milky brown and not very wide. We were moving through a valley, not yet a gorge, with steep barren sides. High up at regular intervals there were billboards that said in red numbers *148.4* – the ultimate water level of the Three Gorges Reservoir, which was scheduled to submerge this whole stretch of river. Now and then we passed landslides of grey scree. These puzzled me until I saw the concrete shelves at river level and the staircases winding uphill from them. Scree? It was rubble, and these were towns flattened to make way for the rising waters. Where had their inhabitants gone? I had an idea where they were going to end up, at any rate. On the treeless crests of the ridges stood apartment blocks so new that the sky was visible through their windows. Bulldozers grazed on the debris around them. They looked like American housing projects, only gray. Contrary to our expectations, we were not out in the country, but inching along the lines of a vast subdevelopment that barely amounted as yet to more than a blueprint. No signs of life (apart from the bulldozers) could be spotted ashore, but when the river curved I saw half a dozen ferries ahead of us. It was like rounding a bend on a railroad and looking out of the window at the leading carriages of your own train… and in fact, now that I thought about it, the river valley bore an uncanny resemblance to a railroad cutting.

I couldn't concentrate on my book (it was *The Brothers Karamazov* – not exactly light entertainment) owing to Tom chatting with Mr Hu and Mr Wang inside the cabin. The sound of him speaking Chinese had started to irritate me. Even though I couldn't understand a word he was saying, I could tell his accent wasn't authentic. He looked out to say he was going to dinner. "Do you want to come?" At the sight of his exalted face, I felt a passionate, weepy desire to be shot of him. I smiled and got to my feet.

After dark we dropped anchor at the mouth of a creek, and at midnight a fleet of small motorboats crowded around to take ashore those who wished to see Baidi Temple.

"Tom," I said, "I think I'll give it a miss. I really have to get some sleep before I'm good for anything."

"But it's Du Fu!" He was understandably disappointed in me. This temple was a shrine to the one Chinese poet whose works I really liked.

155

"You'll just have to take lots of pictures." I hung my head, hoping I looked as wiped out as I felt. "By the way, can I use your laptop?"

"Sure," he said after a scarcely perceptible pause. "Do you want to go online?"

"Yeah."

"OK, well, you know the password, right? Just make sure to unplug it when you're done. I don't trust the generator on this tub." He zipped up his waterproof jacket as he spoke, for it was now raining hard.

With almost everyone off the ferry, a blissful silence descended. I gave them time to get clear, then plugged Tom's laptop into its transformer, plugged the transformer into the television's outlet, and climbed onto my bunk with the laptop. It had a PCMCIA satellite modem card that worked like a roaming cell phone. The per minute charge was something crazy, but Uncle Sam wouldn't flicker an eyelid. I looked at my watch. Half past midnight = half past ten in Tokyo. Better give it a bit longer.

I took stock of Tom's desktop. I wasn't barred from using this computer, but in Tokyo I had my own, so I had no call to mess with Tom's constant companion. I couldn't in fact remember ever sitting down alone with it before. The demarcation between embassy stuff and *his* stuff was pretty clear: the former was 80% in English, 20% in Japanese; the latter was all in Chinese except for his actual manuscripts. I found the novel he was working on, Xu Ailing's second production. It opened with the death of a history professor in a reeducation camp during the Cultural Revolution. Unsure whether I should be looking at it at all, I read the first few pages. Tom's prose was lucid and balanced, allowing the dramatic situation to speak for itself. My nose prickled with tears.

"Oh God." I quit Word and opened Internet Explorer. The modem took awhile to make contact with the satellite. While I waited, I cried and wiped my face with my sleeve.

Conveniently for me, Tom had set MSN.com as his IE homepage. I opened Hotmail and started to enter my screen name, which was my name. As soon as I typed the first letter, a box dropped down to show me a screen name I didn't know: *francis1993*. My heart skipped a beat. Then I understood what I was looking at. I tabbed to the password blank and typed *eleanor1998*.

Francis Lynch Jr., Tom's grandfather, had died in 1993. His widow, Eleanor Lynch, had followed him in 1998. Hardly cryptic if you knew Tom, but all the same I felt like a hacker when I saw that it was working.

Welcome to Hotmail… in Chinese.

"Oh, Tom." I couldn't help laughing, which made tears come to my eyes again. "How unsporting of you."

All of the 258 *(258!!)* emails in his inbox came from the same string of three ideographs. I had a feeling I'd seen them somewhere before, but I could have been imagining it. He had new mail from him/her/it, too. Just for the hell of it, I opened a couple of the older messages and cast my eye over the dense blocks of text. No hacker in American history, I thought, could have deciphered this little lot.

Fay!!! Are you back already?!? Is everything OK?

No and more or less. I'm on a ferry on the Yangzi, getting eaten alive by mosquitoes and missing you.

We were using MSN Messenger, just as we had when Tom and I had gone to visit my parents in Charleston, SC, over Christmas. I typed in English and Toshitake typed in Japanese, which allowed us to "talk" as fast as if we'd been speaking one or the other language over the phone. Faster, perhaps, given Toshitake's stammer.

You've been in my thoughts all the time. I've been dreaming about you, too. I dreamed that you came back and told me you'd decided things were better left as they are. I couldn't get any work done all day after that. What's an artist (ha, ha) to do when his muse is away? I'll end up drinking myself silly at this rate. Oh yeah, by the way, Mimi misses you, too.

Mimi, his beagle, had been my original excuse for seeing so much of Toshitake. I loved dogs, but we weren't allowed to have one at the compound, so I became Mimi's adoptive aunt. It was during one of our walks with her through Inogashira Park that I'd first been seduced by the possibility of a life entirely different from the one I had. Knitting my brows, I typed, *Give her a big hug from me and tell her we'll go for a LOOOONG walk the day I get back!*

So are the Three Gorges as beautiful as they're said to be?

Tom says we haven't reached the best bits yet. Speaking of which, Toshi, you'll never guess what... I wouldn't have snooped into his stuff on purpose, but I found out by accident that he's been writing to someone in Chinese. Wouldn't it be hilarious if it turned out that he's been seeing someone else, too?

I lit a cigarette as I waited to see what effect this would have.

But isn't writing to people in Chinese, like, his hobby?

Ha ha. Yeah, but this isn't about the implied tenses of verbs or the etymology of tones or anything. He's got a secret email address dedicated to her.

That does sound suspicious. But how can you tell it's a her? What's her name?

Something Chinese. But they've written 258 emails to each other! And you know how a lot of the ideographs look enough like Japanese kanji that you can recognize them? Well, at the end of all the emails of hers that I looked at there's 我 [I or we] *followed by something almost exactly like* 愛 [love] *followed by something I can't read, but what do you want to bet it means* you??? Thoroughly carried away, I hit enter.

"Wo ai ni." That's how you say it in Chinese.

I love you?

Yeah.

I love you, Toshi. About to post this, I went on typing thoughtfully. *Do you think I feel angry about this? Do you think it makes me feel differently about wanting to leave him? It doesn't. It's actually a huge relief. I mean, supposing I'm right, it lets me off the hook, doesn't it?*

I bit my nails. After the longest time Toshitake's response came back. *What do you mean?*

Shit. He probably wasn't familiar with the idiom "to let off the hook." I explained, *If Tom's been seeing someone else, even if it's only a virtual affair, it means he's in the wrong, too! So I can leave him any time I feel like it!*

The words blinked onto the screen in my color, pink, and I couldn't believe my stupidity. It was Toshitake's view that committing adultery did not automatically put you in the wrong. In our case, he thought, our compatibility had fully justified him in persisting and me in succumbing. Furthermore, he didn't understand why, if I loved him, I hadn't left Tom already. He didn't understand that I could love him *and* feel guilty about breaking my marriage vows and letting Tom down. This was one of the few really troublesome differences between us. Sometimes I thought it was a cultural thing. Sometimes I thought it was just Toshitake's comparative lack of experience showing. He was a year older than me, but owing to his stammer and his looks, which were homely in the most endearing way, he'd never been seriously involved with anyone before.

There's something I have to tell you, he typed at last.

A pang of fear shot through me. But I wasn't destined to find out what it meant, because the modem chose that moment to go on the blink.

I pummelled the keys in vain. There must have been a host of angels transiting Chinese airspace, jamming all frequencies with their wings. I couldn't get back online. Cursing, I wiped the browser's memory. It would be pointless to have Tom start wondering who I'd been talking to on Messenger – especially if I was going to *tell* him who, and why, the very next chance I got.

No longer relishing the silence as much as before, I smoked another cigarette and tried to think of a positive spin to put on Toshitake's words. He might have been going to tell me he'd found an apartment. Yeah, that had to be it! A spacious yet inexpensive apartment near a park. As nice as his current place was, in the event that we moved in together we'd need at least one more room. Bringing up the topic of real estate was the closest he came, as a rule, to telling me to get on with it.

The templegoers weren't back yet. Now that I'd convinced myself Toshitake still loved me, I started hoping their launch had capsized and they'd been scarfed up by maneating dolphins.

No such luck.

The port of Fengdu had won a stay of demolition on account of Mt. Mingshan, the peak that loomed behind it, and the Ghost City on top of the mountain. Tom and I stumbled uphill from the ferry in the predawn dark, in drizzling rain. Most Chinese towns are built on a grid, like gigantic grey Lego accessorized with lion dogs, but Fengdu seemed to inherit a different tradition. The twisty streets were lined with small houses of ochre stone or brick. On a dry day the streets would have been mostly pothole; now they were mostly puddle. Bedraggled civic pride banners hung across them. From storefront eateries, each with its ceiling fan and television, drifted smells of breakfast. I said that I was hungry. Tom ignored me. Of course, we ended up waiting interminably in a parking lot while everyone around us munched on food that they'd bought en route, and I laughed at him. I was in a slightly hysterical mood.

It turned out that we'd been waiting for a chair lift. The ride was exhilarating, a series of swoops uphill between dripping treetops. It had the effect of making me wobbly on my legs.

The temple grounds on the hilltop were a maze of walled staircases and nesting yards. We jostled through a gauntlet of stone gods who were wrestling dragons, treading on snakes, and slaying each other with monumental zeal. Stylistically they were Italianate: muscles bulging, faces contorted with passion. Under the eaves of the main temple stood braziers full of tapers wafting smoke into the wet morning. I veered wide of the temple doors, repulsed by the noise of half a dozen tour guides lecturing through megaphones. This cacophony was a normal hazard of sightseeing in China, but up here the mob was particularly dense, and the competition among the tour guides to make themselves heard correspondingly stiff. I caught Tom's arm and pulled him away along a path that ran around the outside of the temple, under the trees. I'd thought of something so funny I could hardly stop laughing long enough to get it out. "Ghost City," I choked, *"Ghost City,* Tom, this is less like a ghost city than anywhere I've ever been in my life! They ought to rename it *Grand Central Sichuan!"*

Toshitake would have laughed with me and then asked me to explain the joke. Tom said patiently, "OK, let's go around the other way. I don't care about hearing the spiel, anyway. They've excised all the cool bits about the history of the place. Do you know why it wasn't destroyed during the Cultural Revolution?"

While he told me, we wandered out of earshot of the tour guides. We arrived at a small hall with skylights and glass cases set into its walls like the reptile house at the zoo. There was no one else there. "This used to be the abode of demons," said Tom exuberantly.

"Sounds like it needs exorcising, not excising." I gulped as I peered into the cases. Each one held a tableau of hell. Amidst real rocks, little plaster people with vividly individual faces, ranging from Borrower size up to eighteen inches tall, were being disembowelled, dismembered, burned, boiled, flayed, crushed, whipped, strangled, and blinded by fiends with bright red or blue skin. One little woman in the tatters of a green dress was being made to sit on an iron spike so that she impaled herself. No prizes for guessing what *her* sin had been. The agony on her face was so believable I felt sick. "It's all amazingly realistic, isn't it?" I said faintly. "Making a virtue out of necessity, I guess: combining deterrence with artistic excellence."

"Deterrence," said Tom, "is that what you think it was for? People weren't as easily scared in those days, you know. The Chinese aren't as easily scared as we are even nowadays. No, this was *homage.* Just like they'd cast ninety-foot bronzes of

Buddha to magnify his glory, they'd make shit like this to glorify *him.*"

He pointed into the shadows at the back of the tableau. I squeaked as I saw a man sitting there, knees apart, watching the tortures. He had a kindly mustachioed face beneath his iron crown. The folds of his yellow robe were thick with dust. I looked into the next case. There he was again.

"In O," said Tom. "Also known as Yama, the King of Hell."

"Yama is *mountain* in Japanese."

"I know."

"Yami is *darkness.* Yamai is *sickness.*"

"Yamai wa ki kara," quoted Tom, proving his Japanese was as good as mine. "Sickness starts from the heart."

"It's all in your imagination," I countered, translating the proverb as I had in one of my articles.

"Ki no sei." *You're imagining things.*

"Oh no I'm not," I said softly.

"It's because people have so much imagination that they're so easy to control. That's why they always buy the party line, the product, the big fat lie. It's the same shit that's been going on forever." Tom wandered over to the bulletin board by the door. Everything on it was in Chinese, of course. "You can have tea in the Pavilion of the Gods or pay five yuan to see the Haunted House. I'd kind of like to do that."

"This is enough of a haunted house for me."

"Oh, Fay, would you quit bitching? Would you just do me a favor and try to keep it to yourself? I'm not even asking you to be flexible and accept that some people have different values from yours, because I know that's impossible for you. I'm just asking you to quit ruining everything for *me.*" His face was white with emotion.

"So you think you'd enjoy yourself more without me? I hope you're right. I really hope so, because I know *I* will without *you.* Have fun, Tom," I said. "Knock yourself out. See you on board."

Back in Fengdu, I found myself hurrying for no good reason. A bicycle almost ran me down. I hadn't seen it coming because the hood of my waterproof jacket obscured my peripheral vision. I shoved it back and let the rain drip down my face and neck. I instantly felt more in touch with my surroundings, but it was too late: I'd deviated from the route we'd come by, and now I hadn't a clue where I was.

The charms of Fengdu's twisty streets paled on me as I scurried onwards, taking every turning that seemed to lead downhill. I figured that sooner or later I'd reach the river. What I reached instead was a swathe of demolition. Apparently I'd been wrong about Fengdu being spared the wrecking ball until the last minute. All that was really left was its core, which had become a façade concealing the destruction of its extremities. Nibbled walls towered over rubble heaps. Men and boys, bareheaded in the rain, were further dismantling the ruins by hand, loading salvage into dumptrucks or carrying it away in buckets balanced across their shoulders. Loose chunks of concrete swam in the slurry underfoot. My hiking boots weren't waterproof. I would have been better off in plastic sandals like the laborers had.

Raising my eyes, I saw the lozenge roof of our ferry.

When I got over the rise beyond the devastation I saw that it *wasn't* our ferry. There were no names to tell by, but it had a different silhouette. To my further horror, I saw that it was one of no fewer than a dozen ferries lying at a series of floating docks that stretched as far as the next bend in the river.

I couldn't walk along the shore. It was solid with cargo hoists and dumpsters and coal chutes. I had to go back up over the rise and pick my way through the demolition, attracting some very funny looks from the laborers. One of them, a young man with no front teeth, shouted at me and pointed back the way I'd come. I looked where he was pointing. Magically, pain shot through my temples. Coming along in the distance, *following me*, were the figures of the two men I thought of as Bristlecone, because his bristly head was unmistakably conical, and his wiry little colleague, Stumpy.

The gaptoothed young man seemed to want me to go back and talk to them.

"Sorry, I don't speak Chinese," I screamed, and floundered away. Even from this distance it was plain that Bristlecone and Stumpy, in their nice city shoes, were having difficulties with the mud. I could outdistance them, I thought; and I did.

Bursting into our empty cabin, I climbed onto my bunk and buried my face in my pillow. Then I jumped down again and locked the door.

Ten minutes later the knob turned and turned in vain.

"Hello! Hello!" and a burst of Chinese.

Shamefacedly, I let Mr Hu and Mr Wang into the cabin.

"You all OK?" demanded Mr Hu, who was the better English speaker of the pair. "Where husband?"

I had a bright idea. What if I told them Tom wasn't coming back? They could pass it on to our tour guide and anyone else who might notice he was missing. We'd sail without him, leaving him stuck in Fengdu. Before he could catch up with me I'd be back in Beijing, and I was pretty sure I could talk China Airlines into letting me fly home early. I'd clean my stuff out of our apartment, take my money out of our joint savings account, and that would be that. Talk about a painless separation! Tom had never met Toshitake and knew of him only as one of my contacts. Even if he somehow found out the truth, he'd be so flabbergasted that he wouldn't be able to bring himself to hunt me down and confront me. He'd just call my mother and report the news, "deeply saddened" as he pretended to be when reacting on behalf of our government to Japanese domestic tragedies. Then he'd ship out to God knows where in the world.

I said, "My husband has decided to stay in Fengdu. He'll be fine. He's got his passport and some money. Please don't worry about him."

"Eh? What, what? Wǒ tīng budǒng!" exclaimed Mr Hu, easing off his boots.

I fished my notebook and pen out of my backpack. I could write it in Japanese and they'd be able to work out what I wanted to say. But as I scribbled I realized what a stupid idea it was. Tom would come back, of course – why on earth did I think he might not? Just because *I'd* lost *my* way – and they'd tell him I'd said he *wouldn't,* and then… no, perish the thought. If I wanted him to get left behind, I'd have to make sure he *got* left behind.

I scratched out what I'd written and wrote instead *I think two men have been following me.*

I used the most formal words I could think of because these have less hiragana and more kanji. I also rearranged them. Unlike Japanese, Chinese has the same basic syntax as English.

Mr Wang grabbed the paper. "Rìběnwén!" Giggling with emotion, he revealed an unheralded command of English. "Rìběn rén no good! Too much kill Chinese, now too much moneys!"

"But—"

"China maybe dangerous for you," said Mr Hu severely.

"What's that?" said Tom, walking into the cabin. "For fuck's sake, Fay, I looked everywhere."

"It was them again," I whispered.

He gave me an angry, pitying stare and inclined his head to Mr Hu, who was talking at sixty words a minute, no doubt telling him that he ought to keep his wife stapled to his side to prevent her from wandering off alone and picking up reactionary ideas. I took refuge on the walkway.

"You told them we live in Japan?" hissed Tom a few minutes later, coming out to find me. He'd taken his waterproof jacket off. His shirt was dark around the neck where the rain had gotten into his collar. His hazel eyes shone with a light that was painful to see. "How could you be so… so… I'm going to call a spade a spade, Fay; how could you be so fucking stupid? Have you forgotten everything you learned in college? Don't you know how they feel about Japan, especially the older generation? These guys were kids during the war.

Mr Wang saw his father killed by Japanese soldiers. Now he feels like we've betrayed him, too!"

"Wait a minute, Tom. Where did you tell them we live? Did you *lie* to them?"

"I told them we were American. Was that lying?"

"No, but I guess you conveniently forgot to mention a few pertinent facts." I stared at him in astonishment tinged with admiration. "You've actually got a knack for that, haven't you? And I always used to think you were incurably honest."

"But now I work for the Bush administration," he threw out bitterly. "That cures you of honesty."

"You shouldn't let it get to you so much." My old sense of helplessness revived as I spoke. "It's going to drive you mad, honey. You just *have* to compartmentalize!"

"Yeah, I know."

The ferry strained into motion. I stared at my feet through strings of damp hair. After a few seconds I heard the click of the cabin door as Tom went inside.

He was out most of the day on a motor launch trip to the Three Little Gorges. As an alternative to brooding on happier times, I fretted over the mystery of Bristlecone and Stumpy. I now discounted the possibility that I was imagining things. I'd first spotted them in Beijing when they kept taking the same buses as Tom and I did. Beijing was a long way from here. I likewise discounted the possibility that they were tourists who happened to be going to all the same places as us. In the wrecked part of Fengdu this morning there had been nothing worth seeing. That left me with my original theory that they were following us. They weren't passengers on our ferry, or I would have spotted them before, so they had to be on one of the other ferries with which we were travelling in haphazard convoy. *What* were they? Every time I'd seen them they'd been dressed in dark shirts tucked into neatly belted dark slacks, sans neckties. Bristlecone looked to be in his forties and carried a navy blue nylon holdall. Stumpy was in his early twenties and prowled behind his partner emptyhanded. They looked, in fact, pretty much like what I thought undercover policemen did look like.

As Tom said, the Chinese government had mellowed in some respects. But didn't it still have the world's largest national security apparatus? Didn't it still execute more people per year than the rest of the world's legitimate governments put together? Didn't it still arrest people for criticizing it, and for reminding it of this fact? The key point, I thought, was that Tom worked for Uncle Sam. Not only that, his title was Assistant Information Officer, which *sounded* sketchy, and one of his jobs was writing speeches for the ambassador, which involved a good deal of contact with His Excellency. If you weren't very well informed, you might conclude that Tom was important; if you were paranoid, you might even conclude that he was a spy. This was what differentiated us from other tourists. And this, I thought, might be enough to have convinced some guy behind a desk in the bowels of the Chinese equivalent of the NSA that we were worth keeping an eye on – especially if he could wangle a holiday for two of his agents thereby.

Well, go wild, boys, I thought, enjoy it while you can. It'll all be underwater in a few years.

If Bristlecone and Stumpy only wanted to keep an eye on us, I had nothing to worry about. But I felt like there should be some way I could use them for my own purposes.

If only Tom believed in them!

That afternoon we passed through the Three Gorges, which were notable for having trees on their clifftops. Elsewhere in China I'd seen none. "I suppose these have survived because they're impossible to get at," I said, and was surprised when Tom agreed with me. Maybe he too felt the Gorges were a letdown after all the hype.

As dark fell, the cliffs ended and the riverbanks flattened out. At nine o'clock or thereabouts we reached the Three Gorges Dam itself. Floodlights illuminated cranes perching on the tops of concrete walls jutting out into the river. On the north bank sparkled the lights of a city which, according to Tom, hadn't been here fifteen years ago. It had sprung up to house the tens of thousands of people who came to work on the dam, which hadn't been here fifteen years ago either. But it was a proper city, not a shantytown. As we waited, becalmed between towering concrete reefs, for our turn to enter the lock, I watched the headlights of cars gliding past the feet of tall buildings. It was reassuring to imagine that they belonged to ordinary people driving home from work to eat dinner and watch television with their families.

At last we edged into the lock and its walls began to grow. They loomed over us and kept growing: five, six, seven storeys high. Tom and I stood at the rail of the observation deck, craning our necks. Many of our fellow passengers had joined us, talking quietly among themselves. The water dripping down the walls gave off a rank smell. It grew dark and chilly on deck, as if we were watching an eclipse. I leaned over the rail and looked back along the length of the ferry at the iron doors that were keeping out the whole Yangzi; I looked up at a rectangle of night framed by concrete. At last, with a terrific clanking, the lock opened at the other end. We bobbed out on-to what was now the lower Yangzi and chugged on past the widely spaced streetlights.

Tom had been quiet while we were in the lock, unrespon-sive to my excited speculations about how far we would go on sinking. Now he said, "They've got us beat."

"Who?"

"The Chinese. They're going to overtake us. It may take them another twenty or thirty or fifty years, but they're going to leave us in the dust. This is the writing on the wall. We can't compete. Do you remember looking out of the windows of the train our first night? No, you were asleep, but I remember thinking… town after town, all of them sparkling with neon, all of them electrified and bustling into the small hours of the morning… We've succeeded on the sheer scale of our national resources and our national effort. But China's bigger. We have a population of 270 million; they have a population of 1.3 bil-lion. That's all you really need to know, isn't it? *And* we're overextended and they're hungry; we have universal scruples

– at least in principle – and they don't. Now that they've finally given up shooting themselves in the foot, there'll be no stopping them."

I couldn't tell whether he spoke gloatingly or bitterly. I didn't know which side he was on. Personally, I didn't want to be on either side. The habit of apocalyptic prophecy had spread like the flu during the last couple of years, and the more of it I heard, the more I wanted to opt out of the diplomatic life. Tom was all that stood in my way. I wanted to tell him that I didn't give a fuck who knocked holes in whose hegemony. I dared not say anything of the kind, so I said, "I think it's still up for debate whether they've stopped shooting themselves in the foot. I mean, what about the ecology? You were telling me about all the species that are going to be endangered by the dam. And the air in Beijing and Chongqing: it was terrible."

"You're just not used to it."

"Maybe it's because I smoke," I said humbly. "But it really did bother me."

"Yeah, well, the ecology *is* an issue. We've been bugging them to reduce emissions and stuff, but now that we've gutted our own regulations, we look like worse hypocrites than ever." He shrugged and hooked his arms over the rail, standing on tiptoe as if he were trying to see something in the river. Nothing was visible to my eyes but brown water surging along the ferry's flanks. I studied his profile instead. He looked tense and melancholy. I knew he was pretending not to know that I was watching him.

Everything I'd felt for him in nine years seemed to be repeating on me at once. I pitied him from the bottom of my heart, I wanted to cheer him up, and I wanted him to suffer for being such a goddamn holy fool about everything – but I didn't want him to suffer *too* much, because he'd been the sweet sensitive boy I'd met in senior year, and I was sure that if I really turned on the love I could get him to tell me who he was now. I just couldn't be bothered to try. So he'd turned, presumably, to his Chinese penpal. And no matter what I'd said to Toshitake, I was seething at him for having a secret like that from me. I wanted to have *that* out with him, if nothing else.

But it was too late to have anything out with him. It was too late to do anything except leave him. I decided that as soon as we got off the ferry I was going to implement my bright idea, or a version of it. I couldn't ensure that he got left behind. I could, however, leave *him* behind. I'd just wait until he fell asleep and then slip off, taxi → train → taxi → airplane, leaving him a note so he wouldn't come after me. If I was able to get a flight (a biggish *if*, but life is all about taking risks), I'd have four or five days in Tokyo to complete my vanishing act. He would never see me again, and I would never have to explain anything.

We arrived in Yichang at two o'clock in the morning. I didn't spot Bristlecone or Stumpy in the crush at the ferry terminal. Those of us who had nowhere else to go squeezed onto a minibus and were taken to a hotel that charged 300 yuan as opposed to the 110 we'd paid in Beijing. In the angry scrum that developed at the front desk, I clung to Tom's waist, and when he hiked up his shirt to unzip his money belt, I managed to peek into it without seeming to do so. There were more yuan notes in it than I'd expected there would be at this stage. Behind those was what looked like a wad of US dollars. If they were twenties, he was carrying almost $1,000. If they were fifties or benjamins... well, he'd come provided for emergencies. The sight made me feel more optimistic about my plan. I could borrow from him to insure myself against the risk that I wouldn't be able to use my credit card. It would make me look more underhanded than I felt myself to be, but I could send a check to his parents to cover the sum. This thought pleased me.

Of course, if I really started repaying Tom what I owed him, I'd have been looking at the high six figures. I had, after all, been using his money for years: a perfectly normal arrangement that had always embarrassed me. Since I'd started seeing Toshitake, the very sight of my Citibank card had been able to cause me hot flushes of shame. That didn't stop me using it, though. I'd been struggling to earn more money with my translations, but I still wasn't covering my own expenses.

I lay awake in the dark until Tom was twitching in his dreams. Then I got up. His money belt lay on a chair on top of his folded clothes. I picked it up and put it down again. First things first. I retired to the bathroom to write my note. It had to be cryptic yet definite, with a touch of humor to reassure him that I hadn't taken leave of my wits. I smoked two cigarettes, flushing the butts down the toilet. I made five attempts at the note, ranging from a single sentence to two pages, and flushed those down the toilet, too. Then I climbed back into bed, turned on my face, and cried into my pillow.

I was awakened by the sound of the shower running. Sunlight soaked into the room through the net curtains. I parted them and gazed down in despair on flat grey roofs tasselled with laundry.

Catching sight of my watch, I saw that it was 9:40. We were supposed to check out at ten o'clock, and after two nights on the ferry I *had* to wash my hair. Pulling myself together, I stripped off so that I could pack up everything except my sponge bag and the clothes I was going to put on.

Tom came out of the bathroom to find me wrestling with the catches of my backpack. "Sexy." He slid his arms around me from behind. His damp hair touched my neck, and I shivered as he caressed my breasts.

"Oh, honey. We're running late." I pushed his hands away.

"We're on Chinese Standard Time. Ten o'clock means whenever the cleaning staff gets around to us. Come on. You don't know when we'll get another chance."

Never would have been soon enough for me, but I felt as if I owed it to him, and it ended up being half an hour to remember.

"How many times did you come?" he asked me, ultra-casually, as we waited in the lobby to return our room key. "I lost count back there."

"Enough times," I muttered, blushing so hard it almost hurt. He was smirking, pleased to bits with himself. Of course, he wouldn't have said it if he thought he could be overheard. But how did he *know* that that expensively dressed couple sitting on the couch, for example, couldn't understand English? He didn't know, and he didn't care. It turned him on to talk about our sex life when we were nowhere near a bed, just as it turned him on to make love when there was a risk that the cleaning ladies might walk in on us. It had taken him years to work up the courage to share this quirk with me. I knew it was a measure of his trust in me. But I hated it. We hadn't had sex in so long that I'd forgotten how *much* I hated it. "It was lovely, now let's go catch our bus, OK?"

"We have time for lunch," he said, and while we ate our rice and braised tofu with cabbage, elbow to elbow with a dozen Chinese at a communal table outdoors, wouldn't you know he reverted to the subject? "I'm sorry if I kind of got carried away back there. I mean, I hope you aren't bruised or anything."

"Tom, shut up," I pleaded, my rice turning into inedible lumps of plastic in my mouth.

"You look so sweet when you're all red in the face. My prissy little Southern belle."

"Now you're just teasing me. Stop it."

"That's what you always say, and then you come ten times. You know, most women can't come just from vaginal penetration. You're one of the fortunate few."

I put my chopsticks down. Tom kept eating, speculating about the mechanics of female arousal in between mouthfuls. He was taking it well past the point where he should have relented, and the more I protested, the more he had to smother chuckles. I realized he was doing it on purpose.

We boarded a sleeper bus with bunks instead of seats. Japanese style, you took off your shoes at the door and stashed them in a plastic bag at your feet. There was minimal headroom in the top bunks, so I let Tom have the lower of our pair. It suited me fine to have a view that didn't include him. Nibbling on some roast chestnuts I'd bought from a street vendor,

I watched the outskirts of Yichang give way to flat dusty fields. Each farmhouse had a duckpond and a silage rick weighted down with old tyres, just like in Jamaica, except that here instead of jungle the dominant theme was emptiness. Goats grazed along the verges of the road. Stooks of grain stood tall on the stubble. The atmosphere was thick and the distance milky, so that the setting sun looked like a red football. I reflected with something approaching disappointment that there was no way Bristlecone and Stumpy could still be following us. Theoretically, they might ask at all the bus stations in Yichang to find out where we'd gone... but I didn't think they would go to such lengths.

A tsunami of music crashed through the bus as the video monitor over the driver's head came on. A few of the other passengers propped themselves up to watch the first feature (a collection of Mr Bean episodes). Everyone else went to sleep. I read Dostoevsky until the light went. I could sense rather than hear Tom writing in longhand in the bunk below me, conserving his laptop's battery.

We stopped for dinner at a farmhouse where they served mystery meat in hot sauce for two yuan. You had to stumble out back into a corn field, tripping on clods of dirt, to find the toilet. It was a typical Chinese one: a hole in the ground with a wall around it. This example was overgrown with a vine that resembled, and might have been, kudzu. After peeing I walked out into the part of the corn field that had already been cut. The smell of earth clung to the insides of my nostrils. A low moon floated overhead. I could hear rats, or maybe some other animals, scuffling in a ditch nearby.

The jolting of the bus and the repartee blaring from the video monitor, so irritating at first, had a gradually stupefying effect. When I woke up the next morning, I wasn't sure whether I *had* been asleep or whether I'd successfully wished myself into a different world. We were crawling through craggy mountains that had fields tucked into their pockets, past clusters of stone houses with ropes of corncobs, garlic, and hot peppers hanging beneath their eaves. Trees grew everywhere

here, gnarled and weighted down with persimmons. The people threshing grain with long rakes in front of their houses had bright red cheeks and raw-looking black hair. Toddlers in padded coats and split trousers rode on women's hips. As I gazed out of the window, I felt weirdly heartbroken – an after-effect, perhaps, of Dostoevsky. I dozed to escape the feeling, the sun warm on my face.

At nineish we drew up at a gravelled layby. The snappy cold air neutralized the stink of the toilets. All twenty or so of us stood around the outdoor sinks brushing our teeth. I hadn't spoken a word to anyone, which meant Tom, for almost 24 hours, and he said nothing to me now to make me break my streak. Sharing toothpaste tubes, spitting, gargling, and drinking icy water from the taps, I felt myself to be in harmony not only with him but with all the other passengers. I could go on like this forever, I thought; and then we reached Xi'an.

"... So I let her know we were coming. I mean, it's not every day I'm in this part of the world."

Tom, I'm in love.

"But it's not like I think meeting her in the flesh will cast any new light on her work. It might even screw me up, because I already have my own ideas about…"

He's thirty and a Libra and he hasn't a cruel bone in his body. He has a funny face and a funny sense of honor. He despises hypocrisy and selfishness, but adultery is all right.

"… just for curiosity's sake, basically."

Oh, Tom. Not that I really give a fuck any more, but what would it take to get us back to where we used to be? Nuclear war? The little red and blue men with their bags full of torture instruments?

"… so she'd like to meet you, too. She doesn't speak English, but I can interpret, of course. If you don't think you'd be bored…"

"I'm so bored already I can't get any boreder. Sure, I'll tag along."

"For fuck's sake, Fay! You don't even have to be here!" Just like that, he was white with anger. "You could have stayed at the hotel if you were still feeling sick!"

"And not see the Terracotta Warriors after coming all this way? I'm fine, Tom. Just leave me alone for a bit, OK?" My stomach was tying itself in knots. I wobbled away from him. We were on top of Emperor Qin Shihuang's mausoleum hill, which was the size of the Great Pyramid and planted with sacred persimmon trees. I hung over the wooden railing around the observation area, holding my sleeve to my mouth so I could breathe through it. The hill was an island in a sea of noisome white fog.

"Are you all *right?*"

"I think I'm going to throw up. No, I'm not. I just…"

"It can't have been anything we ate last night, because *I'm* fine. Maybe it was that apple you had for breakfast."

"Nobody gets sick from eating an apple. It's the air."

"Oh God, there's nothing wrong with…"

"It's much worse here than it was in Chongqing or Beijing."

"It's the time of year! They're burning the stubble!"

"Oh, *really?* It says in the guide book that you're supposed to have a spectacular view of the surrounding mountains." I gestured at the haze, which obscured even the parking lot where our excursion bus was. For once, I felt the facts were on my side. "Well? Come to that, why did they build here in the first place? It was supposed to be defensible, wasn't it? You were supposed to be able to see your enemies coming, weren't you? There could be a whole Mongol horde out there and we wouldn't know it until they were on top of us."

"First of all, this isn't a castle. It *wasn't* supposed to be defensible. Second of all, the pollution's no worse here than it is anywhere. The only problem is there's no wind to carry it off. We're in a bowl…"

"A dustbowl!" I giggled. "It may take another twenty or thirty or fifty years, but they're going to turn this country into a dustbowl!"

175

Needless to say, Tom didn't laugh. "I just hope you're feeling better by tomorrow," he said grumpily.

"Why does she give a damn about meeting me? *You're* her translator," I said, and knew immediately I'd gone too far. I was relieved when he turned away without another word and went to read the plaques in the middle of the observation area.

Xu Ailing, the author of *Snowbound Feet,* lived in the city of Tongchuan. I'd known that, and felt as if I knew Tongchuan, since it was the setting of her fiction. But she never located it explicitly, so I hadn't been aware, although Tom had probably told me, that it lay in central Shaanxi province, less than half a day's drive from Xi'an. With that piece of information, everything had fallen into place. Tom could express all the reservations he liked about meeting Xu Ailing in the flesh. I now suspected we had come to Xi'an for no other purpose. It was she, of course, who had written 258 emails to Tom's secret address. I *knew* I'd seen those ideographs somewhere. And no matter how preoccupied I was, I would probably have put two and two together already if I hadn't from the beginning of Tom's involvement with her been under the impression that she was in her late forties.

He'd said nothing yet to contradict that impression, but I was already touching up my mental picture of her (the one that appeared on the dustjacket of *Snowbound Feet*), erasing crow's feet and making the shadow under her chin into youthful plumpness instead of a sagging jawline.

Wo ai ni wo AI ni. It was stuck in my head like a jingle. It went well with the rhythm of our footsteps on the shallow stone stairs leading down the mausoleum hill. People were wandering among the trees, picking the sacred persimmons and leaving behind the baggies that had been tied over them. At this point, most of the trees bore a crop of rainwater and dead insects. We got back on our excursion bus. The driver yelled nonstop into his cell phone; the fields bordering the highway swam in the noisome haze. "Wo ai ni," I whispered without moving my lips. "Tom, are you listening?"

Our next stop was the Terracotta Warriors, aka the Eighth
Wonder of the World. Back in Tokyo I'd thought this sight was
all the excuse a person needed to come to Xi'an. After seeing it,
I still thought so. Buried for 2200 years and they were still
standing, mucky but unbowed, beneath concrete domes,
amidst twinkling cameras. The setup filled me with misgiv-
ings. The longer something lasts, the likelier it is, as a matter of
statistical probability, not to last much longer. As Tom and I
returned to Xi'an and set out for a walk along the top of the
old city wall, it was my turn to indulge in apocalyptic speculation about the future, not of our country but of our species.
Tom pretended to think I was playing devil's advocate, but the
vigor of his responses betrayed the fact that he agreed with me.
While this felt like a little victory, I knew it was a defeat: the
defeat of his faith in humanity. One of the things I'd originally
loved about him was that he'd really believed – in those days
he'd really believed – that we weren't done progressing yet.
He'd seen the rise and rise of the American empire as a chance
for good people, liberal humanists, people like us, to get hold
of the world's steering wheel and spin it out of jeopardy.

We were standing at the battlements of the city wall, looking down at what had been no man's land and was now a
slum. I realized Tom was no longer listening to me. I stopped
talking. He jerked his chin back in the direction we'd come.
"Paranoia is catching," he said with a fake laugh. "Those guys
have been following us for a while. They aren't your friends
from Beijing, are they?"

It wasn't Bristlecone and/or Stumpy. It was two other
men in white shirts, ragged slacks, and plastic sandals. They
were lounging, smoking cigarettes, on one of the benches
along the edges of this cobbled road in the air. "I've never seen
them before," I said, and added disingenuously, "Why should
they be following us?"

"They may think we're easy marks." Tom sounded irritat-
ed by my question, as well he might be. "Xi'an's got something of a reputation for crime. Muggings, theft from hotel

rooms, that kind of thing. I wish we hadn't had to enter our passport numbers in the guest book."

"What's that have to do with it? Anyway, the Hongqiao's a reputable hotel. It's in *Chikyū no Arukikata* and the *Rough Guide*."

"Yeah," he said grimly, "exactly."

"**I**'m sorry, Fay. I g... *guess* you can leave your stuff here for now, b... *but*..."

"But I've left him!" I stared in shock at Toshitake, who was hovering in the front door of his apartment. I was standing in the hall, surrounded by luggage that had been a nightmare to drag over here. "I know it'll be a squeeze, but it'll only be for... I mean, I thought maybe you'd already found an apartment for..."

"Well, I know we were talking ab... *bout* doing that." Toshitake looked desperately unhappy. He was dressed the way that suited him best: jeans, bare feet, and a buttondown shirt hanging loose on his thin frame. "The trouble is, I g... *guess*... a while ago I stopped b... *believing* you were going to leave him. And if you weren't g... *going* to leave him, what was the point of loving you? It hurt too much. So I made myself stop. Loving you. And it's not like flipping a switch. Once you've stopped loving someone you can't start ag... *gain*. So I don't think there'd be much p... *point* in our living together." As he spoke he slid his feet into a pair of plastic sandals that I didn't remember him owning. He came out into the hall and put his arms around me. "Maybe it was b... *bad* timing," he said into my hair. "Or maybe I'm just not the type to b... *be* with someone every day for the rest of our lives."

"In other words," I said, pulling away from him, "I'm up shit creek."

"*Fay*..."

"By the way," I said, "where's Mimi? Why hasn't she come out to say hello?"

"*Fay*..."

I cartwheeled up from the depths of sleep. Muzzily raising myself on one elbow, I couldn't tell if Tom was still asleep or not. He lay on his back with the covers down around his hips, grasping at the air over his chest.

"Fay…"

It wasn't his normal voice: it was hoarse and gravelly. It was how he sounded on the rare occasions when he got extremely drunk. Tonight was not one of those occasions. The room was silent and cold enough that we had two blankets over us. Since we were on the second floor, glimmerings of street light came in through the curtains. Tom clutched at the air, groaned, and turned his head towards me. His eyes were wide open.

My first impulse was to shake him. Before the impulse got as far as my muscles, it occurred to me that to move would be to betray myself to whatever it was that was here with us in the room, whatever it was that Tom could see and I couldn't. I froze, scarcely breathing. I'd been dreaming that I was in deep shit. Now I knew the difference between dream shit and real.

"Get the fuck off me!" It came out as *Gerruck aw me!* Tom moved violently, bucking under the covers. Then he relaxed. Smiling at me with wide, empty eyes, he said, "It's gone. I thought there was something sitting on my chest… but I was just imagining it. G'night."

Within minutes he was breathing deeply.

I couldn't get back to sleep. For hours I stared into the darkness, revising what was left of my plans.

"Tom," I said at breakfast, "do you remember waking up in the middle of the night?"

"What are you talking about?" He spooned down his rice porridge. "This stuff is pretty good. You should try it."

"I guess you were talking in your sleep, then."

That got his attention. "What did I say?"

"Nothing intelligible." *Your eyes were wide open.* "It sounded like you were having a nightmare."

"No recollection. Refer to Political." He grinned, reaching for my hardboiled egg. "You're not going to eat this, are you?"

"Go ahead. I don't feel like eating anything."

"Feeling sick again? Could it be that some air got into our room during the night?"

Oh, he was in a grand mood.

"Go back upstairs and rest for a bit," he commanded me, shelling the egg. "I'll come and get you before I head out to the pagoda."

I clutched my stomach, hoping I looked pitiful. "I don't think I'm up to it. Sorry. You'd better go without me."

"*God*, Fay!" There it was again, the anger, spurting out like steam from a crack in a rock. "Can't you make an effort for once?"

I simply couldn't understand why he was so keen for me to meet Xu Ailing. It made me feel harassed, which gave credibility to my act. "I'm not *up* to it!" I clapped my hands over my mouth as if I were about to vomit. The other people in the dining-room stared curiously as I pushed my chair back from the table and doubled over my knees.

He offered to keep me company for the morning, which was the last thing I wanted. "All I want to do is go back to sleep. I'll be fine," I assured him. "Tell her I'm sorry I couldn't make it."

As soon as the coast was clear, I got dressed again in my last clean set of clothes: black Levis and a stripy t-shirt with long sleeves, loose enough to conceal my money belt. I repacked everything else I'd taken out of my backpack. Tom, of course, was wearing *his* money belt containing his passport and cash stash. He also had both of the tickets we'd purchased in advance for the last leg of our journey, the flight from Xi'an back to Beijing. I probably couldn't have used mine two days early, anyway. I'd just have to pray they took Visa at the airport.

I fixed my hair in a braid down my back and then headed for the bus stops on Jiefang Lu. The sun beat down on the crowds. It was quarter past ten. Tom was due to meet Xu Ail-ing at twelve thirty. I didn't think he would be early. I *hoped* he wouldn't be early, because I was planning to be early myself.

After taking the wrong bus twice, I reached the Little Goose Pagoda just after twelve. I bought a ticket, which left me with a grand total of 120 yuan, and ventured into the park. It was laid out in the same confusing style as the Ghost City at Fengdu, with shadows lying across all possible sightlines like swathes of black cloth. Dragon gates with red pillars and curly gold eaves framed gaps in the walls that cut the place up like a Mondrian painting. Above the roofs of the auxiliary temple buildings the pagoda, a slim cylinder of thirteen storeys, shot up into the chemical blue sky. The temples were more or less empty: a few elderly people knelt on the hassocks before the display cases and a few Western tourists wandered about daz-edly. I imitated their divagations. Apart from the inevitable monumental golden Buddhas, the best thing I saw was a fres-co of dozens of fat little men floating on lilypads picked out in gold, all identical, as if the effect aimed at were that of mass production. The excellence of China's secular art, I thought, was only matched by the boringness of its devotional art, and the case in the West was by and large the opposite.

Rounding a corner, I found myself on the edge of a plaza where people were relaxing at plastic tables shaded by um-brellas and trees. Vending carts sold soft drinks. I bought a bottle of water. Some twenty metres away, she glanced up from her book. Her mouth was composed in the same da Vin-ciesque smile she'd worn in the photograph and her eyes gave the same impression, even from this distance, of being recep-tive to more than just light. Unhurriedly, her gaze traversed the plaza. I didn't breathe until she lowered her head again. I was assuming that she didn't know what I looked like, but she knew there was such a person as me, and I was the only per-son in view right now who fitted the specs. I edged around until I was out of her line of sight. Keeping two trees and a table full of Europeans between us, I sidled closer.

From this angle I couldn't see her face, and her petite build gave no indication of her age, but I thought it unlikely, after all, that she was under forty. Glittering threads ran through the black hair casually fastened in a ponytail. She wore teal green trousers with a white blouse. Instead of the platform sneakers that the younger generation favored, she had on a pair of navy court shoes, and beside her chair sat a small knapsack in royal purple faux crocodile. I swallowed a hysterical giggle. I couldn't wait to see Tom's face.

Twenty to one.

How unlike him.

I hurried away and stood near the public toilets, just out of range of their stench. There were enough trees in front of me to serve as a screen. Soughing in a breeze that was undetectable at ground level, they spilled dapples over my eyes. Tom appeared in an archway on the far side of the plaza. Xu Ailing rose. They hurried towards each other like Hollywood lovers. I almost expected them to embrace. Instead they shook hands – or rather, Tom stuck his hand out, and after a couple of seconds Xu Ailing reciprocated. That one little lapse told me how tense he was. They started walking in my direction, Xu Ailing swinging her knapsack in one hand, Tom gesturing emphatically the way he always did when he spoke Chinese.

I dodged into the toilets and breathed through my mouth. I'd caught only the briefest glimpse of Tom's face, but that had been enough to throw me into confusion. He'd looked excited and stormy and ready to snap, the way I'd seen him a thousand times when he was dealing with a crisis at work. The demands of a PR emergency could temporarily submerge everything except the crazy motherfucker in him. This was the aspect of his character that came out when the chips were down. So why here? Why now?

By a mysterious process of association, I suddenly recalled all that money. Why dollar bills, anyway? He'd deliberately taken the trouble to change Japanese yen into greenbacks. Why?

I followed the sound of his voice through sunlight and shadows, starting to recognize Xu Ailing's voice, too, as she interjected comments. Emerging into the sunlight again, I saw them vanishing into the gate at the foot of the pagoda.

"Sightseeing," I whispered to myself. "Get a grip, Fay. She grew up around here, she's an expert on the history of the region; she can probably tell him all kinds of stuff that's not in the books. He'd love that."

I'd noticed earlier that the pagoda had just this one entrance/exit. I moved into the nearest band of shadow, no longer directly in front of the gate but keeping it in view. I pulled out my Camel Lights and searched my pockets for my lighter. A man came up and offered me a light in his cupped hand. "Thank you," I said, flustered. "Xièxiè."

"Bùxiè."

He smiled down at me before going back to his friend. Both of them were dressed nicely, for Chinese guys, in slacks, sneakers, and clean white shirts. The tall one had a decent haircut, too. He had a complicated camera around his neck, and his friend carried a long black tube that might have contained a tripod. If I could speak Chinese I'd have known by listening in on their conversation whether or not they were natives of Xi'an.

Ten past one. People trickled in and out of the pagoda.

The guy who'd given me a light came over again. "You no climb this… tower? Very beautiful. Very old."

"I'm waiting here for my husband," I said. "But thanks for the recommendation."

"Husband? Where?"

"He's climbing this beautiful old tower, I believe."

The guy stared down at me, his smile slightly altered. A thrill of alarm ran over my skin. It was like the moment when I'd glimpsed Tom's face in the plaza. This wasn't the way that the facts of which I was in possession dictated that people ought to react. Impulsively, I said, "Actually, I've changed my mind. It would be a shame not to check out the main attraction after coming all this way. Y'all take care now."

As I started walking across the cobblestones there was a flicker of movement at my back. I turned over the remaining half of my ticket to the clerk at the gate and hurried past her. Inside the pagoda it was cooler. Tom and Xu Ailing were not among the people peering into the cases of historical artefacts. Did I really want to surprise them like this? No. I started climbing anyway. The second floor held more artefacts. Higher flights of stairs zigzagged upwards through the center of the pagoda, while its diameter narrowed until there was no room on the landings for anything except for people to squeeze past each other. Rowdy young American voices echoed down the stairwell, laughing and complaining. None of them was Tom's. My leg muscles burned and sweat dripped down my ribs. I hauled myself up towards the eighth floor.

Nine. Ten. Take it easy, Fay. Eleven.

The walls were still almost three meters thick. Tunnels pierced them, leading to small windows latticed with bars. Twelve.

Thirteen, and there were no more stairs, only the tunnels leading to four different views of Xi'an: north, south, east, and west. People jostled each other, determined to get their money's worth by having a gape out of each of the windows. My gaze flickered over them all as if they'd been ideographs in a block of text, seeking Tom, the only character I could read. There were the Americans – Lonely Planeteers in shorts and Tevas. "Excuse me," I gasped, "did you see another white guy up here just now? He's about your height, dark blond hair…"

"Naw, sorry."

"Oh. Thanks anyway." I started back down the stairs, my thoughts racing. Tom and Xu Ailing couldn't have gotten out of the pagoda without my seeing them. There'd been that instant when I was talking to the photographer, but surely they couldn't have got past me that quickly? Was there another way out I hadn't seen earlier? If so, where?

Footsteps came down the stairs hard and fast. Someone hurtled past me, knocking me into the wall. By the time I recovered he was at the bottom of the flight, swinging himself around by the banisters, so I only got a glimpse of him, but damned if it wasn't Stumpy. I'd have known him anywhere, I thought, even as I wondered whether it could possibly have been him. There was only one way to find out. I plunged down the stairs after him, barging through the tableaux of confusion created by his passing, jumping over people whom he'd presumably knocked off their feet, and so between the display cases on the second floor, and on down to the first floor where I came face to face with the photographer and his friend, the latter now looking disillusioned with life and gripping his tripod case as if it had been a rocket launcher he was about to fire from the hip. "See that guy just now?" I gasped. "Come on! We've got to get him!"

"You find husband?"

"Oh Christ," I said, and started around them. The photographer caught my arm. I jerked back, resultlessly. He was stronger than he looked. Saying something in a commanding tone, he started to switch his grip as if he was going to grab my other arm, too. I seized the moment to throw my weight sideways. My arm came free but my sleeve stayed in his hand until the ribbed neck of my shirt ripped loose, baring my shoulder. He let go. I darted past him, aware of some confusion in the far corner, raised voices and uncontrolled movements; I burst past the ticket clerk into the sunlight. Looking over my shoulder, I saw a glimmer of white emerging from the pagoda entrance.

I ran flat out, zigzagging through the temples. At the main gates I had to slacken my pace. I concentrated on getting my breath and then on getting my bearings. Holding the torn part of my shirt to my mouth so as to breathe through it, I trotted back down the hill to the street where I'd gotten off the bus. The haze had intensified, limiting visibility to the next traffic light but one. It was like being at the bottom of a dirty aquarium heated to 70 degrees. I reached the bus stop and leaned against a tree, trembling from head to foot.

I stared into the haze, waiting for it to reveal Tom and Xu Ailing; or Stumpy, possibly accompanied by Bristlecone, who couldn't have been far off; or the photographer and his friend, who might just have been trying to help, or... It occurred to me that they might have been the same pair Tom had seen following us yesterday. But on reflection I didn't think so. Those two had had more of a scruffball look.

In the end all that came was my bus.

I sidled cautiously up the steps and through the big glass doors of the Hongqiao. The woman who'd checked us in the day before yesterday was back on duty at the front desk. She had a motherly face and some knowledge of English. I wanted to tell her what had happened, but I was no longer sure *anything* had happened. I took the elevator to the second floor. The weak electric bulbs shone soothingly on the dark red carpet. There was nobody else around. I turned my key in the lock of our door. It didn't open. Huh? I turned the key back the other way.

Oh fuck.

The moment after your worst fears are confirmed is always tinged with unreality. I checked under the bed and in the wardrobe before I had to accept that our backpacks were missing. I let out a shriek and collapsed on the bed, flat on my back, as if I'd just been hit by a truck – which was how I felt. It was monstrously predictable, almost Newtonian. Every action provokes an equal but opposite reaction. Forget to lock your door and you will be robbed. I didn't know which was harder to bear, my negligence or the robbers' undiscriminating cupidity. If they'd ransacked our backpacks they would have found nothing much worth taking. They must have been disappointed, I thought viciously, when they got away and discovered that all they'd scored was clothes, books, toiletries, and...

Oh *fuck.*

I jumped up and searched the room again. I found a t-shirt and a pair of Tom's boxers drying on hangers inside the wardrobe door, one of our Japanese guidebooks, and *The Brothers Karamazov,* which I'd forgotten to pack. Still missing was his laptop, its transformer, and the rest of his paraphernalia including the floppies on which he backed up his files.

I started crying. The laptop itself wasn't the issue. It belonged to Uncle Sam, who would replace it, probably with a newer model (what else were tax dollars for?). It was losing the contents of the hard disk that would kill Tom. All his translations, all his correspondence, all his work files. He'd probably left extra backups in Tokyo. But the loss of two weeks' work – not to mention the notebook he kept in longhand – would hit him as hard, at least to begin with, as if it had been everything.

Recovering enough to string two thoughts together, I realized there was only one constructive thing for me to do. I washed my face – already mourning the loss of my moisturizer, sunscreen, pressed powder, etc., etc. – and left the room, making sure, pointlessly, to lock the door this time.

On the way downstairs it occurred to me that Tom might have removed his stuff himself.

He would have had time to come back after I'd gone out and still, taking all the right buses, been at the Little Goose Pagoda at a quarter to one. (In that case he'd know I'd faked my collapse at breakfast, and I'd have another reason to dread his return.) He'd been emptyhanded when I saw him, but he could have deposited his backpack any number of places: at the train station, at the restaurant where we'd eaten last night and whose proprietor he'd befriended, even with the tickettakers at the main gates of the pagoda.

This idea opened up a whole new line of reasoning, and while I was still trying to decide whether it was plausible, I reached the front desk. "Sorry, I just wanted to let you know that... uh... our room's been robbed. They've taken everything."

If Tom *had* removed his own stuff, I was lying. If not, I deserved to feel ashamed of myself. And I did; I did.

The motherly desk clerk stared at my right shoulder. I'd forgotten my shirt was torn. I pinched the rip closed with my fingers. Almost reluctantly, she returned her gaze to my face. "You say what? Say again!"

"Our stuff… our backpacks."

"You room number?" She hauled the guest book along the counter, flipped it open and spun it around so I could see the entries for the last few days.

"Room 207. Thomas and Fay Lynch."

He'd written our address in ideographs. But it wasn't our address. She started to spin the ledger around again. I held onto it long enough to understand what I was looking at. The first bit was illegible to me, but at the end, where it should have said 日本, it said 美国. The first of these ideographs means *beautiful.* The second one means *country.* I knew only a dozen words of Chinese, but this was one of them: Měiguó.

The first bit, I thought, was probably a phonetic approximation of his parents' address or of mine.

Paranoia was catching, all right.

I despised Tom for pandering to prejudices that probably survived only in his imagination. But I also remembered Mr Hu's passionate reaction to the sight of Japanese script. I remembered the way he and Mr Wang had cooled off on us after that morning. I imagined myself persevering in my attempt to report the robbery – if it *was* a robbery. Sooner or later I'd find myself filling in forms for the police, which would mean giving them our real address. It would conflict with the entry in the guest book, and for all I knew that would make us criminals. For all I knew, in someone's eyes we already were criminals. I remembered thinking that Bristlecone and Stumpy might be policemen. I remembered Stumpy hurtling past me. I could still feel his body glancing brutally off mine. *Why had he been in such a hurry to get downstairs?* My anxiety about Tom started up again, like a loop of aggravating muzak in my head, and this time it was louder. In comparison, the loss of our backpacks hardly seemed worth bothering about. I smiled and backed away from the desk.

"You check out? You go airport today? Last bus six twenty. Six twenty!" She made the numbers with her fingers the Oriental way, which always looks to me as if the person is playing shadow animals.

"Six twenty," I confirmed I'd understood her. "And the first bus tomorrow?"

"Morning! Seven thirty!"

"Well, I don't think we'll be checking out today. I..." I gave up. Her English was obviously more limited than I'd thought. Anyway, there was something else I had to do. I went back upstairs, armed myself with our remaining guidebook, and slipped out to the variety store on the corner. But the useful phrases section turned out to be use*less* for my present needs. *To the Editor,* I thought in frustration, *Please consider including in your next edition a translation of the sentence "Do you sell sewing kits?"* The girl behind the register scowled at me as if I was ruining her day. I gave up again and bought myself some fruit, chocolate, and a bottle of that sweet green tea. I was on the verge of buying Tsingtao instead, but it was slightly more expensive.

I counted up all the notes and coins I had left. 92 yuan = less than $10. Later, I told myself, I could collapse; right now I needed money. The obvious thing to try was a bank, and I tried three of them, slogging along Jiefang Lu in the blistering sun, before giving up yet again. Neither my Citibank cash card nor my Visa card impressed the tellers. An ATM would be more cooperative, I thought, and in hopes of finding one I made a bus trek to the shopping mall at the Bell Tower intersection. Its interior presented a ritzy contrast with the streets smoking under construction outside. Most of the stores were ones that I wasn't used to seeing inside malls – Yves St Laurent, Dior, Lacoste, Chanel, Gucci, Fendi, Aquascutum – and all of them took Visa. Here was some kind of a silver lining, at least. I replaced my skincare products, bought some clean underwear, and splurged on a Prada shoulder satchel to tote it all in. But the sole ATM in the place was a washout. It flashed a screenful of ideographs and spat my cards back at me.

Tom and I were paid up at the Hongqiao through tonight. Another night would cost about thirteen dollars. It might as well have been thirteen hundred for all the difference it made to me. At ten o'clock tomorrow morning I'd have to check out, and after that Tom would no longer know where to find me.

I found it difficult to formulate a plan of action beyond that point because I had a recurring premonition that he was about to walk into the room.

Determined to stay awake until he *did,* aware I had to confront him with all my faculties on line, I nevertheless fell asleep, only to awake in the dark. The wardrobe door stood ajar, and behind it, in the corner of the room where the light from the street didn't reach, hung a motionless shadow. It was a man hanging by the neck from the hook at the top of the wardrobe door.

I sat up in bed, my heart thumping. There was a faint crackling noise, as of a badly tuned radio, that seemed to be coming from somewhere in the room. The shadow moved slightly. It was speaking to me, I realized: this was its voice, thin and extraterrestrial and clogged with static —

My perceptions shifted and I saw that it was Tom's shorts and t-shirt. I laughed – a short bark that didn't sound like laughter – jumped out of bed, and switched on the lights. I could still hear that weird crackling noise, so I switched on the television, too. When I switched it off again to listen, the noise had stopped. Maybe it had been coming from the set itself. It was old and might be malfunctioning.

"Jumpy, jumpy," I said, and my voice still didn't sound like my own. I knew with a certainty equivalent to clairvoyance that I couldn't stay in this room alone any longer. I also knew that Tom wasn't coming back – not tonight, probably not ever. I put on my jeans and sneakers, took the guidebook, and went downstairs. The motherly desk clerk had gone off duty. A scrawny man with a moustache stared at me blankly as I read out, "Wǒ yào dǎ chángtú diànhuà."

He replied with a bark and waved at the telephone in the corner of the lobby.

I fed some of my precious coins into the slot. My first attempt didn't go through. I tried dialing different combinations of zeros and ones before the country code.

Toshi, I'm up shit creek.

The phone was an ancient rotary one that seemed to take forever to dial.

Toshi, I need you to find a home phone number for the Chief Information Officer at the embassy. That would be Gerry Ramirez, Tom's boss. I need you to call me back and give me that number so I can call Gerry and ask him why Tom was carrying a thousand dollars in greenbacks. Actually, if they were hundreds, it would be more like $5,000. That's still a funny amount. I mean, on the one hand, why carry US dollars at all? On the other hand, why not carry more? I mean, what can you buy with US$5,000 these days?

At last the phone started to ring in Tokyo. It rang on… and on… and on. Glancing at my watch, I calculated that it was three in the morning there. Toshitake should have been at home, and even if he was asleep, it shouldn't be taking him this long to wake up. I didn't know what else to do, so I kept the receiver pressed to my ear. There was a heavy click. The phone burped, swallowing my coins. "Moshi moshi! Toshitake, mada Chūgoku ni iru kedo, kikoeru?"

Beep… beep… beep…

I replaced the handset and felt in the chute for my coins. They hadn't been returned. I shuffled back to the desk. "Excuse me. I didn't get through, but the phone's eaten my change. Do you think I could possibly have a refund?"

The moustached clerk snarled at me.

"I wouldn't make an issue of it, but…"

Another snarl, this time with a questioning lilt.

"I'm sorry, I don't speak Chinese…"

Another man came out of the door behind the desk. Heavyset, he had red eyes and tousled hair. He looked first at my shoulder (I was still flashing a bra strap through the ripped neck of my shirt) and then at my face. "What you want? Trouble?"

Cringing, I opened the guidebook and pointed.

"Kéyǐ! OK! Telephone there! Yǒu qián?"

"But…"

The moustached clerk took my guidebook and leafed through it, chuckling mordantly. I suspected he was finding mistakes.

"Why you want telephone?" The heavyset man was being patient with me.

It was none of his business, but sooner or later I was going to have to tell someone. In fact, I'd come downstairs on purpose to tell someone, hadn't I? I said as steadily as I could, "My husband's vanished. He went out this morning and he hasn't come back, and I think maybe I ought to call the police. But I also think that might be a big mistake. What do you think? I mean, are the police… are they… do you *trust* them?"

He stared at my shoulder, appearing to think deeply. At last he nodded. "You wait. OK? Wait."

He went back through the door behind the desk and came out of another door on my side of the desk. Up close his breathing was stertorous. He took hold of my shoulder so gently that I didn't resist, although I tensed up and stared nervously at the hair growing out of his left ear as he fiddled with my shirt. At last he stepped back. "OK! You all fix!"

I touched my shoulder. He'd reattached the neck of my shirt to its body with safety pins.

Fighting back tears, I thanked him effusively. While I spoke I couldn't help looking at the blackness outside the glass doors.

His hand came down on my shoulder again. This time it was closer to my neck and heavier.

I recoiled and fled, apologizing over my shoulder. When I got back to my room (as I'd started to think of it), I locked the door.

As the night wore on, I lost some of my ability to think rationally, but under the circumstances that wasn't a bad thing. I had so few facts to work with that the process of making deductions from them was largely intuitive, anyway.

My first step was to discard any theory that was logical but basically laughable. That included the possibility that Tom had been on some kind of job for Gerry Ramirez or (this had also crossed my mind) for the Cultural Affairs Officer, who was well known to be the chief spook on post. Tom might be devious enough for the role, but it was an intrinsically silly idea, and besides, he didn't love his country or his job enough these days to take that kind of risk for them.

On the other hand, it would be exactly like him to take a risk in the name of some stupid scheme of his own. Joining the Foreign Service had originally been part of just such a scheme – to save the world from financial, ecological, and moral bankruptcy (and would you like fries with that?). For the last few years he'd been subliminating his crusading impulses into his translations, or so I'd thought. But what if his involvement with the China of thirty or forty years ago, as depicted in Xu Ailing's fiction, had developed more than emotional ramifications?

Snowbound Feet dealt with the Cultural Revolution. Told from the point of view of a little girl whose family is subjected to a relentless string of persecutions, it took place between 1967 and 1969. This, of course, was where I'd got my idea that Xu Ailing had to be over forty. I thought the novel was auto-biographical. Its publication in Chinese had been a muted affair. Tom's translation of it, on the other hand, had attracted rave reviews. I remembered him being less thrilled at the time than he should have been, saying the *New York Times* was doing Xu Ailing no favors by stating that she "fearlessly exposed the dark side of China's Communist past." The trouble, of course, was that the Communists were hardly "past" yet. As far as I knew, Xu Ailing hadn't been persecuted for her work – *Snowbound Feet* was, after all, *fiction* – but consequent to its success in America she'd hardly been able to publish a thing in this country; nor had she been awarded any honors or offered any speaking engagements, as successful authors, it appeared, usually were.

Her new novel, judging by the pages I'd read on Tom's now missing laptop, dealt with the same historical period. The scene in the reeducation camp was devastating and could not possibly have been autobiographical. She must have done some research, visited the site in question, talked to survivors…

I sat on the bed with all the lights on and thought about the Internet. Tom had told me, and I'd read in various places, about the CCP's project to enclose Chinese cyberspace with a Great Firewall of filters and censorship. That stuff didn't apply to regular email, clearly. Without possessing any special hacking skills, Tom and Xu Ailing had corresponded both openly and secretly for more than three years. But that didn't mean that some guy behind a desk in the Chinese equivalent of the FBI hadn't been reading every word they wrote.

What *had* they written, anyway?

All those emails.

"I bet she told you to erase them, Tom," I said out loud. "And you didn't. You didn't want to print them out or save them on disc, because I might have found them, but you wanted to keep them so you could reread them sometimes, because you were falling in love with her."

Wo ai ni.

What's fifteen years between soulmates, after all? Especially when you're fifteen hundred miles apart?

Wo ai ni.

What can you buy with US$5,000 these days?

How about a ticket to freedom via Mongolia or some other country with equally shitty immigration controls?

"For fuck's sake, Tom," I whispered. "How about a ticket out of the frying-pan and into the fire?"

But all right. We're all Borrowers, travelling through eternity on the palm of the hand of authority. Suppose Xu Ailing had felt that hand starting to close on her, reminding her what it could do. Writers tend to be fragile creatures. The strain of living in fear might have stifled her creativity, even if she hadn't been in any danger. So she'd decided to defect. And

Tom had withdrawn a chunk of his savings to fund her flight. That would explain the money – in fact, it was the only plausible explanation for the money I could think of.

Unfortunately, I still didn't believe he'd planned to go *with* her. I didn't believe he'd planned to abandon me like this. Maybe I should have believed it, given that I'd been planning to abandon *him* – but I'd intended to break the news to him first. To vanish without so much as leaving a note would have required a degree of narcissistic callousness that, I had discovered, I was incapable of. I believed Tom also to be incapable of it. I might be wrong, of course. But if he *had* planned to take off, wouldn't it have occurred to him that I might panic and call our embassy in Beijing, raising the alarm before he could complete his vanishing act?

For that matter, I *could* call the embassy, couldn't I? My guidebook listed the number for the Japanese embassy, and they would certainly be able to put me onto the Americans. Robbed and victimized, with 81 yuan in my pocket, I wouldn't be accused of overreacting. And no matter what they made of Tom's disappearance, they couldn't blame me for it.

On the other hand, if I held off on calling them until I was back in Tokyo, I *could* be blamed for not having raised the alarm earlier.

So why didn't I call them?

I lit a Camel Light. I only had three left. A tinge of grey showed at the bottom of the curtains: dawn was coming.

My eye fell on the shorts and t-shirt that had given me such a scare. I fingered them. Dry as a bone. As a matter of fact, they'd been dry this morning, too. Had Tom been in such a hurry he'd forgotten to pack them, just as he'd forgotten to lock the door?

"Yeah, *right*," I said aloud. "Tom never forgot to lock a door in his life."

I stubbed out my cigarette and paced the room, twitching with fearful certainty. I could sit here theorizing until the clock struck ten and it wouldn't change what had already happened.

The light creeping over the windowsill had turned clear. I threw the curtains open. Surprise, surprise! It was going to be another beautiful day in historic Xi'an!

Maybe I had plenty of time, but all the same I thought I'd better get a move on. I took a shower, got dressed again, and smiled at my reflection in the bathroom mirror. Having slept for less than three hours, I looked like I'd slept for twelve. My skin bright and clear, my shirt held together by safety-pins, my hair wet from the shower, I looked like the healthier type of Lonely Planeteer. And I no longer had to hump around my own weight in luggage. It was a liberating feeling. I packed up the little that I had in my new satchel, smoked my last cigarette, and headed downstairs.

"Bus go from station!" the motherly desk clerk informed me. It was as if she'd never seen me before. "Don't come hotel! *Next* bus come hotel! Eight thirty!"

"OK. Can I buy a ticket for the seven thirty bus here?"

"No! You buy station! Bus go from *station!*"

"Chill, ma'am," I said. "I was just asking. By the way, it's fifty yuan to the airport, right?"

"Yes! Fifty!"

Had sweeter words ever been spoken in the lobby of the Hongqiao? I gave her a big grin, signed where she told me to, and turned away.

The lobby was bustling with people crossing from the elevator to the doors of the dining-room. My breakfast was paid for, and I probably should have stopped to eat it – God knew when I'd get another meal – but I wasn't hungry. I pushed open the glass doors. The sun hit me in the face. I started down the steps.

He must have seen me before I saw him. He stood staring up at me with one foot on the Hongqiao's steps, as if this was where he'd been heading. Where his camera had hung around his neck, this morning there was nothing. Black smudges of what looked like oil or tar decorated his shirt. The sunlight showed up a strawberry graze on his jaw, and there seemed to be something wrong with his nose. I registered these last details as he lunged towards me, shouting in English, "You! Wait! Please wait!"

I jumped down the other side of the steps and took off running. Away from him was also away from the station. Thanks to the grid system, however, I didn't think I was in any danger of getting lost. I ran, jogged, and ran, with my satchel bumping against my back and people staring at me. At last I stopped to catch my breath. I stepped into the shade of an awning and looked back the way I'd come. The day's haze was already gathering, but at the end of the block I could make out a disturbance moving closer, like wind moving over the troubled water of a lake.

I started to run again.

COMING CLEAN

I knew nothing about Gen Tajitsu, not even that he was called that, until he walked into the Kuroiwas' kitchen behind Joaquin. We all stopped what we were doing, me with my mouth open.

"Je te présente notre chanteuse," drawled Joaquin.

"Salut. Je suis Shanti Hazard," I said, automatically giving my name the French lilt.

"Enchanté de faire votre connaissance. Je m'appelle Gen."

"Voici ma femme," said Joaquin, sliding his arm around Nina's waist.

She'd been chopping potatoes. She'd dried her hands on her skirt as if she meant to shake with the newcomer, but when it came to the point she just bobbed her head. She probably wasn't even conscious of having dried her hands. She and Joaquin had been living in Tokyo for longer than I had. Gen started to tell her he was enchanted to make her acquaintance, too. "Oh God," she said with one of her lovely smiles. "I'm American. Sorry."

"Tu ne parle pas l'anglais?" I asked Gen apprehensively.

"Juste un peu. Only little. Quand je vivais à Paris, j'allais quelques fois à Londres pour assister à des concerts. Mais mon anglais est tellement mauvais que les gens là-bas se moquaient de moi."

"Combien de temps as-tu habité à Paris?"

"Trois ans. Ca fait déjà neuf ans que je suis revenu au Japon. Et toi, tu es Francaise?"

"Elle est Parisienne," Joaquin broke in.

It was awkward. Joaquin, as ever, took pleasure in speaking French in front of Nina, but I felt guilty about leaving her out, while Gen seemed oblivious to her presence. He listened politely as Joaquin explained that I'd been born in Paris and lived there, running wild in the 17th arondissement with my brother, until I was ten. My mother now lived in a farmhouse in St. Nazaire, painting her silly heart out. That part was true, anyway.

Gen lit a cigarette and told us about his years of busking and starving in la Ville Lumière. He was a few inches taller than me, broad-shouldered and lean, wearing jeans and a Serge Gainsbourg t-shirt on top of a longsleeved black one. Over his shoulder peeked a guitar in a nylon gig bag. I couldn't remember when I'd last seen such a striking face: long and sallow with prominent cheekbones, a hooked nose, and eyes like the slits in a Spartan warrior's helmet. He had a crest of loose black curls, short in back and long in front, flopping in his eyes. Only his shy smile saved him from looking entirely the part.

He was the fifth guy Joaquin had auditioned to replace our guitarist, who'd gone home to Hokkaido when his father died suddenly. They were going to be difficult shoes to fill, as Yuki Matsumoto had been one of the original members of Gorot. We were melodic and heavy with a tendency to jam, aiming to sell truckloads without selling out, at present paying to play at tiny clubs in and around Tokyo. Yuki had said he felt terrible about leaving us in the lurch. He'd promised to be back as soon as his family could spare him, but Joaquin had hardly waited for him to pack his bags before posting want ads at all the clubs on the circuit. That was Joaquin for you. Did I mention that his surname was Gorot? By sheer force of personality he'd persuaded the rest of us to name ourselves after him. He was the most ambitious person I'd ever been in a band with, and one of the most screwed-up.

He poked his head through the door that led into the dining-room. "Ou est elle passée?"

"Chiharu?" I shrugged. "Sais pas!"

Chiharu Ota, one of Joaquin's likeliest side projects, was a high school dropout with a remarkable soprano voice. She spent almost as much of her time here as we did. She'd scuttled out of the kitchen when we heard the men at the door. There was a reason she'd dropped out of high school.

"Ce n'est pas grave. Je vais te montrer le studio, Gen."

The men went upstairs, still talking in French. Oh God, I thought. This is going to have to be nipped in the bud.

The lid of a pot on the stove clanked, steam escaping. Nina turned down the gas. We looked at each other and started to giggle. I said, "What did you think of that?"

"Well, I think Jo's made up his mind about him, don't you?" Nina paused, then clapped her hands. "He's your type, isn't he?"

I hugged myself and hopped around the kitchen. "Don't let me do anything rash. Promise. Promise. Nothing ever works out for me when I push it."

What was the point of asking her to protect me from myself when she didn't know what I was asking for, or why? It was just my way of trying to pretend we were closer than we were – as close as we could have been if I'd been able to confide in her properly. She'd laid out carrots, daikon, and pork chops on the chopping board with the potatoes. We were going to have nikujaga, the Japanese version of Irish stew, for dinner. The smell from the pot on the stove made my stomach rumble. I went upstairs.

The house belonged to the father of our bassist, Tad Kuroiwa. It was dilapidated and gloomy, with dark wooden panelling and small windows, but with three rooms downstairs and four upstairs it was a warren by Tokyo standards. I guess Tad had felt oppressed at the thought of being left to rattle around alone here with his father – a taxi driver – only coming home to sleep. Joaquin and Nina lived in the big bedroom at the end of the upstairs hall, paying a nominal rent. Some of the people Joaquin brought home took it for *their* house. The Kuroiwas had left less of an imprint on the place in fifty years than Joaquin and Nina had in one. Passing through the dining-room, you noticed Nina's lesson planning materials spread out over the big oval table, not the sombre family photographs on the walls. And at the top of the stairs, if you hadn't already been hit by a wall of sound, you discovered the studio.

Joaquin and Gen were comparing pickups, rearranging cables, and twiddling knobs. Boys will be boys. Most of the equipment, including the Roland MC909 sequencer and the Apple Powerbook running Pro Tools, belonged to Joaquin. He earned a more or less regular income as a DJ, spinning hard house and trance a couple of nights a week. He got his vinyl, the hot and the rare, from European sources that he guarded fanatically. A couple of weeks' drop on the cult remixes gives you an edge on the trance scene. But Joaquin's first love was rock 'n' roll. With Gorot he was making a long-cogitated assault on the establishment. In his spare time he produced demos for other hopefuls, drawing a distinction between his protegées such as Chiharu, whom he charged beans, and his customers, whom he fleeced. Making money is still a matter of owning the means of production. *Making it,* of course, is a different story.

It was so cold that I could see my breath. I wriggled around the boys and turned on the oil heater. As I dragged it into the middle of the room, a familiar rhythm thumped out of the two main studio amps. Joaquin sequenced our beats on the Roland and recorded them as backing tracks. We still hadn't found a good full-time drummer, but the sequencer could make sounds that were beyond the powers of the standard kit, and it was more reliable, anyway. After four and a half seconds of crash and tickle the bass kicked in, putting flesh on the rhythm's bare bones. Tad wouldn't be home until eight or nine o'clock – he was the only one of us who had a real day job – but we could do without him.

I suspected that Nina was right, anyway. This audition was just for form's sake. Joaquin wouldn't have asked me to be here if he hadn't thought Gen had the right stuff.

I took the lead mic off its stand, coming close enough to touch our busker boy as I did so. "One. Two. Check." We were keeping it quietish. The house stood between a factory and the Keihin Tohoku line, but this was still a residential area. "Check." Gen closed his eyes, strumming the air above his guitar. It was an Ibanez. Not cheap. The absorbed look on his face made something go *pyong* inside me like an out-of-tune string. "Commençons!"

"D'accord." Joaquin started the rhythm tracks over again. The Roland and the Powerbook sat on a table at right angles to his Korg synthesizer, the same setup we used at gigs. He lowered his hands to the black and whites, caressing out of them a tinkly, scary melody. Gen came in right on time with one of Yuki's best hooks. I'd never missed Yuki as much as I did at that moment, and even as I realized that no one could ever replace him, I knew I'd probably never miss him this much again. Gen was playing it straight, note for note. He must have listened to the CD Joaquin gave him backwards and forwards. You'd almost have thought Yuki had made TABs for him. I turned my attention to my own breathing and started singing on the downbeat of the second hook. "Nobody touched me the night that I died. Nobody stopped me from going outside. Up on the rooftop we were all so high…"

Joaquin was the tunesmith. I was responsible for the lyrics. The boys had been impressed when they first found out I could not only sing but write lyrics in English. If only they'd known. This song, "So High," was my private tribute to a guy I'd known in New York City who'd overdosed a week short of his 21st birthday. ("Up on the rooftop" was just for the sound of the words. It had happened at a warehouse rave where everyone had been too happy to notice that he wasn't breathing.) Gen was putting as much feeling into it as if he'd been there, too. Joaquin hit the glissando that took us into the first chorus. He pre-programmed most of his electronic effects on the Powerbook. If he'd wanted to, he could have pre-programmed himself, too, and just stood there with his arms folded.

"How does it feel to be doing well?"

"Prison cell," sang Joaquin, filling in for Tad.

"Coming down always hurt like hell. Taking chances 'cause I'd nothing much to give, nothing special to do but live..." My voice was something of a space oddity. On a bad day I sounded like Janis Joplin, post-overdose. On a good day I sounded like Layne Staley from Alice In Chains.

Tad's recorded ghost went into a holding pattern. Gen took it away. He didn't try too hard to impress us, but I liked the way he used sustain on fragmentary motifs lifted from the fill. Sweat glistened on his bony cheeks. The end of the break caught him by surprise, but he handled it well, dealing out one last arpeggio before locking onto the tempo again. Two more verses, Joaquin's piano solo, one more chorus. "How does it feel to be born again? How does it feel to be born again? How does it feel to walk among the living dead? How does it feel to be born again?"

I put a lot of myself into my lyrics without meaning to. If I wasn't careful I'd give myself away one of these days.

At gigs we usually closed this song out with repeats, giving Yuki another chance to indulge his love of feedback. It was unfair to challenge Gen like that without an audience to impress. I jammed the mic back on the stand and spun in a circle, crossing my arms like an airport ground staffer. "OK, les mecs! Ça va, assez, assez!" Joaquin shut off the backing tracks. I suddenly felt as if I was tumbling off the planet into outer space. I said, "Let's do 'The Hound Of Heaven.'"

Gen stared at me blankly. Joaquin said patiently, for him, "Il ne la connait pas. Elle n'était pas sur le CD que je lui ai donné."

I foresaw long months of speaking French whenever Tad was not around, and perhaps even when he was. "彦さんはまだ聴いていないけど 'The Hound Of Heaven' という曲をやってみたいの," I said. Joaquin could speak Japanese, too. It was one way around the problem.

At our urging, Gen stayed for dinner. Chiharu wasn't there: she must have skedaddled while we were upstairs. Tad got home as I was laying the table. He was an IT guy and could wear whatever he liked to work, so there was no need for him to change before we sat down – although if I'd had anything to do with it, there would have been. His wardrobe ran to leather, velvet, and alarming floral patterns. It was his way of asserting his personality among the geeks and drones he worked with. In no other way was he particularly assertive. He laughed at anything intended as a joke, flattered men and women with equal assiduity, and let other people (especially Joaquin) walk all over him in the name of keeping the peace. Without him Gorot would have fallen apart long before Yuki left. I was anxious to see if he would take to Gen. They ended up seated across from each other but not talking to each other. Tad listened as he ate to Joaquin's account of how he'd happened to hear that a representative of the indie label Skoopagroove might be coming to our next gig. Gen talked in French to me.

After the meal I helped Nina clear up. I thought the boys would want some time to work things out among themselves. But ten minutes later Gen looked into the kitchen to say he was leaving. I made that my cue to leave, too. Nina made kissy lips at me.

Gen and I walked side by side down the narrow street, past the factory (we called it the Armageddon Institute because it made noises during the day as if it were about to blow up). The street was too narrow to have sidewalks. It ran parallel to the Keihin-Tohoku line, close enough that we could hear the trains. Ota ward is the southernmost tip of Tokyo proper. Heading further down the Kanagawa peninsula, you come to Kawasaki, Yokohama, and Yokosuka, where the defense facilities really are. The Kuroiwas lived smack in between Omori and Kamata stations. Even though they had a 20-minute walk to either station, this was real estate to fight for, and not many family homes remained among the blocks of condos with their floodlit flowerbeds. Salarymen glided past us on bicycles. The asphalt gleamed in the headlights of occasional cars. Gen and I fell into single file to round a blind curve overhung with privet.

"Je me rejouis à l'idée de jouer avec vous," he broke the silence from behind me.

"Moi aussi," I said, glad he couldn't see my face. I didn't want him to know that I hadn't been sure until now whether he was hired or not. "Comme Joaquin a dit, nous avons un concert le huit Mars à Haven. Il ne nous reste que deux semaines. Sans toi, nous aurions dû l'annuler."

"Et si le gars de chez Skoopagroove était venu, quel dommage!"

206

I couldn't take it any more. "Gen, I'm not French." I repeated it in Japanese, looking up at the sky. Night skies in Tokyo are usually blue or brown, but tonight, because of the cloud cover, the sky was an interesting shade of pinkish gray. Distant spotlights swung above the roof-tops.

"Mais Joaquin a dit que…"

"Joaquin thinks I'm French. So does Nina. Tad thinks I'm Irish. I met him first, and that's what I told him," I said in Japanese, "but I asked him to keep it to himself after the possibility of my joining Gorot came up. I figured Joaquin would be likelier to hire me if I was French."

"Uh huh." Gen nodded as if he'd already worked that out. He said in Japanese, "But how come you can speak French at all?"

"I lived in Paris for three years when I was a kid. When you learn a language at that age, you never lose it. And my mother does live in St. Nazaire."

"But where are you really from?"

"I'm American."

Now he looked astonished. "No way."

I thought he was going to tell me I didn't look American. I got that a lot. Why? I have no idea, and it used to bother me. How could people tell? Long before I left the States I'd decided that looking foreign was preferable to looking American, anyway. It gave me more to work with. But Gen didn't say one word about my brown hair, greenish eyes, and sadly spotty complexion. He said, "Your name is French, isn't it?"

"It was about four hundred years ago. But now it's not really *Hazar'*, it's *Hazard.*" Frontloaded emphasis, hard consonants, hey presto. *Shanti* means "peace" in

Sanskrit. My mother had been in the throes of Hinduism when I was born. I hadn't yet sunk to using an alias, but if I ever did, I planned to pick something more plausible.

"When I lived in Paris," said Gen, "I used to pass myself off as Chinese sometimes. People just assumed I was Chinese, and I went along with it. I mean, what does it matter, right? Let them think what they like, right?"

"So you understand," I said. I fished my Marlboro Lights out of my bag.

"But I would never have tried to pass myself off as Chinese in front of a genuine Chinese."

"Joaquin is Canadian," I said. "He can't tell I'm not a native French speaker. I try to avoid his French friends, though."

For an instant there was nothing but the sound of our footsteps. Then Gen started laughing. He shook his head and wheezed, "I'm sorry. It's just so funny. I can't believe you've got them fooled like that."

"If you breathe a word to any of them I'll have to kill you."

"Your secret's safe with me." He calmed down and looked me in the eye. "Thank you for telling me the truth."

Now it's your turn, I thought. What's your secret?

I knew he had one, if not several. It was all in the contrast between his personal reserve and the passion that came out when he played the guitar. He gave himself away in the studio more dramatically than I did. Besides, when you live a double if not triple life, you know what to look for: the reticence, the vagueness, the counterattack strategy of evading questions.

I tried the indirect approach. "Where do you live, Gen?"

"Near Yokohama." He hesitated. "Are you ever going to tell the others the truth?"

He'd done it again! I wasn't ready to accept defeat, but I answered his question. "I'm planning to kind of break it to them slowly. I speak English to Nina, to Tad when she's around, and to Joaquin when either or both of them are around. I'm hoping to break Joaquin of speaking French to me altogether. It shouldn't be impossible: after all, he's bilingual. Speaking English is no hardship for him, or it wouldn't be if he weren't such a chauvinist. And as long as we're all speaking English, it won't matter where I come from. I'll be able to start telling people I'm American, and if Joaquin doesn't believe it, he'll think it's a great joke." I paused. "Unfortunately, with you around, I'm back to square one. Not that I'm not happy you're joining us, but…"

Gen was shaking his head. "If it was a bit darker I might think you were Japanese."

"What can I say? I'm good at languages. I didn't graduate from college, but I had straight As in German, Japanese, and Urdu." I was lying again. I had no idea why.

"I didn't graduate from college, either." Gen clicked his lighter to the Gauloise that had appeared in his mouth. The flame illuminated his strange, strong profile. "Actually, I didn't even finish high school."

"Why not? Had you already decided to be a rock star?" I smiled as I said it. He smiled back, but it was more like a wince.

"I went to France on my seventeenth birthday."

"And your parents stood for that?"

"Oh, they didn't mind. I've got an older brother."

"So have I."

We'd crossed a small public park – a rectangle of asphalt with bushes and trees around the edges – and were now walking through the dodgier end of Omori's shopping district. There weren't many shops, but there were a lot of snack bars (read: clip joints), regular bars (sans prostitutes), noodleries, and people. We turned a corner between two enormous pachislot palaces rattling and humming fit to shake themselves to bits. Gen said, "Do you like places like this? I don't. They make me feel like killing myself." We threaded our way through a herd of illegally parked bicycles and scooters, crossed the street, and climbed the outdoor stairs to the JR station entrance. He was going south. I was going north.

"I guess I'll see you at rehearsal," I said. "Have fun learning the rest of our songs."

"It's Saturday at ten o'clock in the morning, right? Do you guys really like getting up that early?"

"Not on principle, but Joaquin's a morning person among his other faults, and Tad and I are in the habit of getting up for work…"

I trailed off as I saw Gen's lips tighten. His train pulled in and I waved goodbye. I figured I'd divined another of his secrets: he didn't have a day job. That meant he had to be still living with his parents. Next day I called Tad and ascertained that this was the case. Tad volunteered the further information that Tajitsu père was a semi-famous jazz guitarist, so presumably not badly off.

Well, there was something Gen and I *didn't* have in common.

Like most foreigners in Japan, I worked as a teacher. I'd started off at a national chain of English schools. It was a McJob: we flipped flashcards instead of burgers. But I'd soon learned Japanese, learned my way around, and found myself a sinecure at Meguro Language Academy, a onehorse school that offered lessons in English, Japanese, French, German, Chinese, Korean, Portuguese, and Spanish (and Amharic and Inuit for all I knew – I'd been working there for a year and a half now, and was still liable to bump into teachers I'd never met before). Joaquin and Nina thought I was a French teacher. It wasn't exactly untrue: the demand for English was greatest, but I sometimes substituted for the French teachers. Even so, I didn't get enough hours to earn a living wage. Nor did my coworkers. What we got out of it was "Specialist In Humanities / International Services" visas and free time, so we could earn our livings in other ways – or be amateur rock singers. Personally, I had no need to supplement my income. I could always wheedle rent money out of my brother.

Alastair was two years older than me. He acted nowadays as if it were ten years. Being a art dealer will do that to you, I guess. He was the assistant manager of Windrose & Sons, a 150-year-old gallery in Boston's Back Bay that sold objets d'art and antiques from all over the world. His significant other, Maisie, was a stage actress; they lived in half of an old wooden house in Somerville with two Weimaraners, a Volvo, and a BMW. Maisie never even noticed that Alastair was slipping me a few hundred dollars a month.

So I could get by, but this was Tokyo. I was spending half my income on rent and utilities. In some parts of the world I could have lived in luxury without having to do a stroke of work. In Thailand, for example. The idea did not appeal.

In the week leading up to our gig at Haven we rehearsed daily. Fitting a new guitarist into a band is a huge challenge. Mercifully, Gen put a lot of hard work into learning our songs. He and Tad didn't seem to be hitting it off on a personal level, but they had a musical chemistry that made Joaquin dance with excitement. Gen played Yuki's looping chord progressions straight rather than dirty. He was good enough that you didn't miss the PA-annihilating effects. Finding himself audible for a change, Tad unleashed a smooth, undulating tone that I'd never heard before. One thing Gen didn't have was Yuki's instinctive grasp of time signatures, and I worried that we were no longer rhythmically tight enough. But I figured we'd be able to pull it together in front of an audience. I suspected Gen was one of those musicians who give of their best on stage, just as certain people in all walks of life perform best in crises, or with permanently elevated levels of nervous tension.

We met up after lunch on the 12th in Shimokitazawa, a funky little city in Shibuya ward that had lots of ethnic boutiques, chic cafés, and approximately three live music venues per resident. Haven was one of the ones people had heard of. It was a big basement room, painted black, with a stage at one end. The bar was a countertop with handwritten price lists stuck up around it. This diveish atmosphere was deceptive: the towers of speakers in the corners were top quality, so you could crank it up to 11 with confidence. The technicians and the manager joked around with Joaquin while ignoring the rest of us. This was par for the course. His Svengali pose endeared him to them: they took to him as one whose support they could count on against the enemy rabble of whiners and strummers.

We'd walked in on a duo, she lisping in Japanese while he scraped on an electric violin. When they vacated the stage we went on and sailed through our soundcheck. We'd played here once before, at five o'clock in the afternoon, to our friends. This time Joaquin had not only gotten us a decent start time but had managed to wangle Chiharu a slot on the bill, too. I couldn't imagine where she'd found the box money.

In New York you play for nothing, for exposure, or for a meager cut of the door. In Tokyo, if you're not a headlining act, you pay to play. Box money at a tiny club in an unfashionable part of town is anything from ¥20,000 to ¥50,000 – in other words, anything up to $500. For this gig we were forking out ¥15,000 *each*. To recoup it we would have had to sell 50 tickets between the four of us. Joaquin, as usual, had disposed of more than his share. Tad and I had each palmed off a dozen on our coworkers and musical friends (although this was something of a mutual backscratching arrangement: we had to buy tickets to *their* gigs when the time came). Gen turned out to have sold a grand total of three tickets. He shamefacedly laid the remainder on the table at McDonald's, where we'd repaired to kill time. Joaquin looked as if he might be reconsidering Gen's suitability for the band.

I said, "Oh God, don't start droning about the bottom line, Joaquin. After all, it's Gen who's out of pocket, not you, and you're so fucking boring when you get onto the subject of money." I punched Gen gently. "Tu as déjà vendu des entrées à ta famille? C'est un bon debut."

Joaquin chortled and let it drop. He loved it when I was feisty. What he thought of as my feistiness, however, was actually irritability – I started getting tense on the

213

morning of a gig, and it got progressively worse until we were on stage. I needed distractions or I would start snapping and snarling.

Luckily, I had a distraction today in the form of Chiharu.

We got back to the venue half an hour before she was scheduled to kick off the festivities. Tad helped Joaquin set up his synthesizer and then joined me and Gen in the very sparse audience. Joaquin remained onstage. He was Chiharu's accompanist as well as her producer. He only wrote a little of her material, though. Our teen prodigy fought hard for creative control. I admired her for it, although I privately thought Joaquin's compositions superior to hers, and liked best of all the ones that I'd written the lyrics for myself. I'd taken on this challenge because I enjoyed the change from writing for Gorot. In keeping with Joaquin's vision of Chiharu as a punk Charlotte Church, I could indulge in romantic clichés that would have sounded absurd coming from me but that sounded sparkly fresh when she delivered them. The joke was that she would probably have balked at them, too, if she'd had more than the vaguest idea what she was singing. She couldn't speak English at all; she memorized it phonetically.

Her drummer, a pimply guy with a mohawk, sauntered out and sat down behind the kit. Chiharu leapt onstage, petite and sweet in three ragged black skirts and an LA Lakers jersey, and launched into a vitriolic little number she'd written for her boyfriend (an elusive character: none of us were sure he actually existed). The set went downhill from there, while the audience swelled with her disreputable friends and a few older people in normal clothes. One woman in particular caught my attention.

Tiny, with a fierce face framed by an auburn bob, she stood near the stage and stared at Chiharu as if she were trying to put her off. I wondered if I was looking at Chiharu's famously abusive mother. There was no family resemblance, if so, and Chiharu didn't appear to notice the woman. She shrieked, whooped, gasped, writhed, and snogged her mic in a transport of ecstasy I'd seen many times before. Her friends cheered.

Tad went to get drinks.

"It's a shame," said Gen angrily. "She has such a beautiful voice, and she'll ruin it before she's twenty-five at this rate. She should have been an opera singer or something."

I agreed with him.

He sighed. "Of course, she's just a kid. It's not too late for her to start taking her career seriously."

"First she'd have to start taking her friends *less* seriously," I said. "She puts on these performances for them; they're all into Slipknot."

To my surprise, Chiharu closed out her set with a hat trick of the songs Joaquin and I had written for her: "Limited Time Offer," "Your Girlfriend," and "This Heart Of Mine." Her friends fell into conversation among themselves. The drummer helped Joaquin lug his synthesiser into the wings. They reappeared through a side door, minus Chiharu, and stood talking to the midgette with the auburn bob.

"I've just realized," I said in anguish. "That's the Skoopagroove rep."

Our set wasn't until nine o'clock. We grabbed dinner at Saizeriya, an Italian chain restaurant. Nina joined us with a couple of her coworkers in tow. I was too strung up to eat much, so I just sipped wine and smoked cigarettes. It seemed to work for the celebrities; it didn't work for me, but I never learned. By the time we got onstage, I was weary, slightly drunk, and giving the boys shit over the set list we'd finalized earlier. I wished I'd gone home and taken a nap instead of staying to support Chiharu. I wished I'd never set eyes on the Skoopagroove rep. I wished I'd never let myself be roped into this insanity. There were now close to a hundred people out front, and I knew most of them.

Two bars into our first number I was OK, and eight bars into it I was enjoying myself. Tad was as solid as ever on the rhythm and the backing vocals. He had a mournful baritone voice that reminded me of David Gahan's. When we harmonized, I felt like it had all been worth it to end up here. Joaquin was impeccable. Gen was spectacular. He churned out solos on "Revisitor" and "It Doesn't Matter (Genocide)" that Yuki couldn't have improved on. We did ten songs: eight originals and two covers – Guns 'n' Roses's "You're Crazy" and "My Cinderella," a hidden track on Cracker's second album. The audience applauded. I yelled at them in English, French, and Japanese. We went offstage, went back, did an encore, plugged our CD, and trooped off again. As soon as the lights went down and the muzak came up, the boys slipped back out through the stage door to recover Joaquin's gadgets. I squatted in a corner of the so-called green room balancing Gen's Les Paul and Tad's Fender against my knees. I was drenched in sweat and I felt like crying – letting go that last bit of control that I had to hold onto while I was singing. There was graffiti in magic marker all over the walls. It smelled like vomit. The headlining act, a visual-kei threepiece, were checking their hair and makeup in the mirror over the dressing-table. "Great show, Shanti," said the frontman. "Your new guy's all right. Too bad about his presentation."

I laughed. I knew he was mentally contrasting Gen with Yuki, who would not uncommonly go onstage in green bodypaint, a sarong, and a dalmatian print fur coat. "Visual extravagance isn't our selling point," I said, "it's yours." My boys piled back in through the stage door, carrying Joaquin's stuff. The visual-kei guys went into a huddle, arms linked, foreheads almost touching, then charged onstage to a welcoming roar of applause.

We packed up to the winding chords of their first song, filed out through the side door, and rounded up our near and dear. We were throwing an afterparty at an iza-kaya near Shimokitazawa station.

As we straggled down the dark street I saw Joaquin and Nina herding along Chiharu, who ditched afterparties given the chance, *and* the Skoopagroove rep. Of course, the rep had no cause to stay for the headliners – they already had a deal – but it still seemed like a good sign.

The people walking with Tad and me were talking about the bands who'd performed in between Chiharu and us, finding more to criticize than to praise. A familiar frown line appeared between Tad's brows. He hated the gossipy, backstabbing aspect of the scene.

As the conversation developed in multiple directions, the two of us found ourselves walking alone. Gen came up between us, dragging a gangly guy in a suit and tie. "This is my brother. Shanti Hazard," he gave my name the French pronunciation, "Tadashi Kuroiwa."

With an air of surprise the brother congratulated us on our performance.

"I guess I'd better tell you before he does," said Gen, laughing. "This is only the second real gig I've ever done.

I still can't believe I didn't dissolve into a puddle of fear out there."

"You're shitting me," said Tad, brightening up. "Where've you been hiding all these years?"

"But you've been in bands before, haven't you, Gen?"

"Oh yeah… but it never really worked out."

"He's had plenty of experience, mind you," said the brother.

"In the studio and on the street." Gen gave a rueful shrug that I recognized as a Gallic mannerism, adopted anew after hanging out with Joaquin for two weeks (the Japanese in their natural state do not shrug). "It took me a long time to get over being scared of failure."

"Funny, I've never had that problem. I take failure for granted," laughed Tad, and I felt embarrassed for Gen. He was probably wishing he hadn't opened his mouth now. Why couldn't he have waited until he and I were alone?

In the tatami room we'd reserved, the tables groaned under pitchers of beer and bottles of cheap wine. I ordered a seafood pizza and ate most of it myself, making up for my abstention earlier. Joaquin appeared to have the Skoopagroove rep well in hand. The party was a success. Shortly after eleven o'clock my mood collapsed. I located the plastic bag that held my shoes, put them on in the hall, wrestled my coat off the loaded hooks, and went outside. It was a cold night. Thanks to the alcohol in my bloodstream, it felt like 30 below. Nothing in sight apart from a Lawson's convenience store was open. I went around the nearest corner, sat down on a doorstep, and cried silently.

"Are you OK?"

Why do people ask you that when you're obviously not? It's just the same in Japanese as in English or French. I looked up, met Gen's eyes, and looked down again. I would have been overjoyed if he'd followed me out immediately, but now I was not fit to be seen. "Tell them I'm fine, Gen."

He sat down beside me. "Joaquin's mad at you."

"Why?"

"You're neglecting your PR duties."

"We know all these people. I'm not going to win us one single new fan by staying in there and smiling until it hurts."

"Cheer up. There's some good news, too. The Skoopagroove rep wanted a copy of our CD."

"We sent it to them when we cut it. We sent it everywhere. They must have lost it. Did Joaquin give her another copy?"

"No. He said we were about to record a new demo, anyway, and he'd prefer to give her that one."

It irked me that Gen had gone in a couple of hours from having stage fright to filling me in on our recording schedule. "I guess that's good news for *you*. Poor Yuki."

"I'm not sure Joaquin meant we were going to record the whole thing over again. I think he just said it as a ploy to get the rep's input. If she tells us what she'd like to hear, that's almost as good as an offer. All we'll have to do then is deliver."

"'All,'" I echoed, and shook my head. "I don't know if I'll ever get used to Japanese business practices."

"She liked Chiharu's stuff, too. Well, not Chiharu's own stuff, but the songs you and Joaquin wrote for her."

"Figures." That made me feel a little better.

The next thing Gen said took me by surprise. "Who do you think about when you write a song?"

"It depends. For Chiharu? Or for Gorot?"

He lit a cigarette before answering. "I was thinking of the second one we did tonight. 'It wasn't me, it wasn't you, the devil told us what to do.'" His English accent was terrible.

"We'll be keeping secrets till we die," I completed the line. I felt half pleased and half frightened that that particular song had piqued his interest. "'You're No Fun.' That one's kind of a mess in terms of who I was thinking about. It's one person in the verses, another person in the chorus."

The chorus went like this: "Hold on, move on, touch me, it's over. Hold on, you're not gone, won't you move over? You drop the gun and you turn around and all the fun is gone." Poetic license notwithstanding, I'd had a job persuading myself I could get away with it.

"My brother," I said, telling half of the truth. "It's mostly about my brother. Childhood stuff, you know. It leaves its mark. You'd like to forget all about it, but you can't."

"I'm sorry. I shouldn't have asked."

"It's OK."

There was a long silence. Gen drew on his cigarette. I reached for it and took a drag. Our fingers touched as I passed it back to him. Some people came out of the izakaya and went down the street towards the station without seeing us. I reflected that the last train would be going soon.

"I…" Gen hesitated as if changing his mind about what he wanted to say. "Don't hate me, Shanti. I couldn't stand it if you hated me."

"Nothing could make me hate you," I said in surprise.

"You don't really know me yet."

"I know that you're a sweet guy and a great guitarist."

He stubbed out his cigarette and rubbed his hands over his face in a childish gesture of embarrassment. "Nobody's said anything like that to me in a long time."

"I'll say it again if you like." I wanted to hug him.

"I don't think I'm a great guitarist. Not at all." He hesitated. "But I have made some recordings of my own."

"Your compositions?"

"Yeah. They're in thirty-two track MIDI format. The quality's not great, but... would you listen to them? If you liked them enough to write lyrics for them, I'd be so honored."

"Sure. Can you copy them onto MD or CD?"

"Well, that's the thing. I don't have the equipment for that. Would you... when's your next day off?"

"Monday," I said, and held my breath.

"OK. Monday's good for me, too. How about coming over to my house?" Unexpectedly, he gave me a cheeky smile. "If you listen to my stuff, I'll fix dinner for you."

"Won't your parents mind?"

"Oh, no. I always cook for myself. Sometimes I cook for my brother, too. My mother says we've had all the family dinners we're ever going to get out of her; she signed up for twenty years, not thirty. She doesn't even do our laundry any more."

"She sounds like a cool lady," I said, giggling.

"Hey guys, we're heading back. You coming or not?" It was Tad's voice, edgy. He walked up to us with his bass slung on his shoulder, carrying another gig bag. Everyone else was spilling out of the izakaya behind him. "Here's your axe, Gen. One of the guys wanted to have a look at that wooden shim you've got under the saddle. He's still here."

Tad was barely taller than me, deepchested and wiry. When he took his shirt off you could see the muscles in his arms, but in his long leather coat he looked like a brown wisp. His skin was the color of rich tea biscuits – he wasn't tanned, just dark for a Japanese – and his hair was usually dyed some shade of red. He had the terrible habit of wearing sunglasses at night, which made it hard to tell what he was thinking. But I didn't need to see his eyes to guess what he was thinking at this juncture.

"Nice of you to worry about me, Tad," I said, standing up. "It's OK. I was just having a fit of artistic temperament."

You can't be betrayed by someone you never trusted. Alastair always said this was a good argument for trusting no one. I tried to live by this rule, too, but it was an effort.

Naturally, each of us made an exception for the other. That is to say, we *had* to trust each other. Our mother was a lost cause, and apart from her, we had nobody. So it was the two of us against the world, just like it always had been, even if we didn't talk for months on end.

Or at least, that's how it had been until Alastair met Maisie.

I figured he trusted her. They were living together; they had dogs, which they fussed over like surrogate babies; they had a mortgage, for Christ's sake. You don't commit yourself to monthly repayments with someone you don't trust. I figured he'd told her everything. How could he *not* have?

And if he could do it, I could, too. Right?

So around the time they moved in together, I'd got serious about looking for *my* "Maisie." I had few hard and fast criteria, but I knew that whoever he was, he'd have to be pretty understanding, because my life was like a Hieronymus Bosch painting: isolate any one grouping of figures and it made more sense at first glance than the whole panorama where the angels stand in judgement and the sinners are stumbling dazedly into Hell.

"I'm not sure I want to be famous," I told Gen. I hoped he realized how great a confidence this was.

"Why not?"

"I don't like the idea of strangers prying into my personal life."

"How about being *moderately* famous? Like my dad?"

I shook my head. "Anyone you've heard of is more famous than I want to be."

We'd listened to Gen's recordings and now we were drinking whisky and water out of tumblers on a Monday evening. No one else was home. The slinky sounds of Morcheeba's second album drifted through Gen's bedroom. He sat in the swivel chair in front of his mixer, which was an ancient woodlook machine the size of a desk. I sat on his bed. The room was spacious, in keeping with the rest of the house (it stood in a surbuban development half an hour south of Yokohama, on a hill), but you could hardly move for the detritus of Gen's life. He'd kept everything from picturebooks to superannuated PC peripherals. There was even an electronic drum kit in the corner. Out of the window we could glimpse, between rooftops, the darkness of Tokyo Bay. It was stretching a point to say that Gen had grown up with the sea, just as I had, but I liked the thought of him as a child gazing out of this very window, plotting his escape. And after he came back from France? Had he looked at the sea differently since then?

"If you don't want to be famous, Shanti, why are you a singer? Most people become singers because they want to be famous."

"I wasn't a singer to begin with," I said. "I started off playing the bass in a friend's band, when I was in college, because they couldn't find anyone else. Then the vocalist dropped out, so I took her place. That was when I started writing songs, too. I do write melodies sometimes, not just lyrics. I came up with the chorus on 'Let's Talk About You,' for example, and I wrote all of '100% Brand New' and 'Propaganda.' Joaquin did the arrangements, of course. I don't know if I'll ever be able to do that, but what I'd like to do is write one good song. Just one song so good that everyone remembers it and other bands cover it and you hear it on the radio forty years later, and people say, 'This takes me back!' and sing along with the chorus. If I could write one song like that I'd quit music the next day."

Gen started laughing. "In other words, you aspire to be a one-hit wonder."

"Something like that." I laughed, too.

"I wanted to be famous when I was a teenager," he said. "But I thought there was no point in being famous in Japan. So off I went to chase my dream."

His ironic detachment made me cringe. Yet I knew how he felt. "Why France? I've been wondering."

He shifted in his chair. "Serge Gainsbourg."

When I could speak without laughing, I said, "I guess you didn't start listening to Britrock until later."

"Oh, that started when I got to France and found that no one there listened to anything French."

"You're telling me," I said. "I remember when I was a kid Michael Jackson was all over the radio." I was starting to feel comfortable with him. "So when you came back from France, had you given up the idea of being famous?"

He was staring at me strangely. His eyes were so black and level under his brows that I had an impression of stern, almost priestly scrutiny. I wanted to hold his gaze but I couldn't. I slid off the bed and stood beside the desk. I was facing the window, but what I saw was the collection of dinosaur stickers on one corner of the windowsill and the dust on the dials at the top of the mixer. All the recordings he'd played for me had been old ones. He'd made them during sporadic creative bursts in his early twenties. In the last five years he'd scarcely done any composing at all. Why? Because the lessons he'd learned in Paris had finally sunk in, I thought. Why had I asked him such a silly question? All my Parisian memories were childhood ones, and I no longer felt much sympathy with my former self – dirty fighter, boy hater, bonbon guzzler, expert shoplifter – but when I was on stage, swearing at the audience and throwing my hair around, I was that horrible little girl again, la petite americaine. I knew what Paris had done to me at eight years old. I could only imagine what it must have done to a sheltered Japanese boy of seventeen.

Gen's hand touched my wrist. It was as if my pity for him had telepathically reached him. He pulled me backwards, wrapped his arms around my waist, and sort of pushed his head under my arm. He was still sitting in the swivel chair. I wriggled free, put out my cigarette, and dropped to my knees in front of him, placing my hands on his thighs. He lowered his head and rested it on top of mine. I was already starting to sense that something was wrong when he pulled back, spinning the chair away.

"I'm sorry, Shanti. Don't hate me."

"I sense a theme here, but I'm not getting it," I said. "For your information, I'm farther from hating you than I ever was."

"But I know you will in the end," he said sadly.

Over the music, I heard a car pull into the garage. Someone in his family had great timing.

We had no rehearsal that weekend. The next weekend we did, but I had to work and then go to two gigs in different parts of Tokyo, supporting assorted friends who I couldn't put off any longer. It would have sufficed at a pinch to buy the tickets and skip the gigs, but that does nothing for a band's reputation. Money isn't the only thing that counts. It's your ability to pull the people that determines whether you graduate from sixth-floor living-rooms to soundproofed basements. So I went and did my bit for the cause, and Chiharu filled in for me at rehearsal. I asked Tad how it had gone. He said she'd been amazingly well-behaved: not a yelp, not a shriek, not an ad lib.

"Joaquin's in a good mood, too. He waltzed my old man around the kitchen last night. I think he's got a touch of spring fever," said Tad.

Spring was here, all right. Just before March turned into April, the blossom front reached Tokyo. All the parks and avenues foamed up pinkish white, as if the cherry trees had been lathered by a giant hairstylist. I had to go blossom viewing with my coworkers and selected students (i.e. those who paid their activities fee), and there went another weekend. I'd asked the boys to move rehearsal to Sunday, but it seemed that on Sunday Gen had to go blossom viewing with his grandparents and Tad had to go with the geeks from his company.

"We've only got two and a bit weeks until our next gig," I said.

We were headlining at Club Goya, a tiny space in Higashi-Koenji, on the third Thursday in April. We'd already started selling the tickets.

"I don't want to have to pack a month's worth of rehearsals into one week again," I said.

"Soyez calme," said Joaquin. "Nous n'avons aucunes nouvelles chansons, alors faudra qu'on joue le même répertoire qu'à Haven. On n'aura pas besoin de se casser le cul. Un ou deux répétitions suffiront."

"And whose fault is it that we don't have any new songs?" I said, but in a whisper, because it was my fault, too. For all my boasting to Gen, I hadn't been very creative lately. And why was that? Because I'd been so preoccupied with *him* – or rather, with his inexplicable reluctance to get any closer to me than he had on that Monday evening. We'd met several times for dinner and drinks, and we'd talked about everything under the sun except *us*, and we'd kissed only as the French do, once on each cheek at parting.

Nina said Gen was intimidated by me. Jobless at twenty-nine, he was a loser in the eyes of a materialistic society; as the new boy he was at the bottom of the Gorot pecking order, too. There was also the nationality thing to contend with. I was the sexy French girl he hadn't been able to pull when he was actually in France. (This aspect of Nina's analysis worried me. But surely Gen wasn't so shallow as to like me less for being American?) Frustrating as it was, I had to allow him to take the lead, she said, or the whole thing would fizzle out.

I usually took her advice on guys with a pinch of salt. She preached empowerment, yet her own marriage was a feudal arrangement. But I knew she was right this time. I had to let Gen operate at his own pace.

Joaquin, on the other hand, I could annoy with impunity. I pressed him for a rehearsal date.

"Bon! le weekend prochain: exclus! Samedi, je fais le DJ au club Core, et le dimanche on va se piquer le tube sous les cerisiers, non?"

It had slipped my mind. "J'en ai ras le bol des cerisiers en fleur," I complained.

"Hé, mais ma vieille, on en a jamais assez des cerisiers," said Joaquin with an evil snigger. He dropped into English. "It'll be a bonding thing. I'm getting everyone to come. The whole Cold Coeur Family." This meant Chiharu and all the other wannabes who he produced.

"Are you charging them?"

He chuckled. "It's bring your own bottle. Tu viens, non?"

"Oui, mais j'éspère qu'il pleuvera," I said, which made him laugh more.

Unfortunately, Sunday dawned bright and breezy. Tad camped out in the park and secured us a spot under a tethered cloud of flowers. By the time the rest of us got there at eleven o'clock, there was hardly room to walk between the tarpaulins and blankets on which half the population of Tokyo was drinking itself into a stupor. I plopped myself down in the middle of Coralie, a trio of pretty girls whom Joaquin was trying to teach to play their instruments. Joaquin made a comedy skit out of opening the 3 liter bottle of saké he'd brought. At last everyone had a cup: 乾杯, cheers, ooh this is lovely, à votre santé, いい天気だね, etc., etc. Most of the food was storebought – regional delicacies from your local supermarket, a slight improvement on the potato chips and gyoza we'd had at the MLA party – but Nina had brought a lacquered box full of homemade onigiri, and a bearded guy I'd never met before had brought a campstove on which to reheat something in a big pot. I never found out what it was. When he lit the campstove, Coralie uttered a triple-throated scream and he flinched, spilling the pot's contents on the flame.

Gen was on the far side of the circle, drinking beer and talking riffs (I could tell from his gestures) with one of Joaquin's French connections. Philippe sold little white pills in addition to playing the guitar, off and on, in bands that never gelled. I didn't think Gen knew this. I wasn't even sure Philippe's girlfriend knew it. She was an earnest creature, a professional translator. Taking in the rest of the faces, I saw I'd been right to doubt Joaquin's motives in bringing us here. If this had really been a gathering of friends, the French contingent would have been represented by the likes of trance event promoters Yves and Rashid, not Philippe. The other members of Tad and Joaquin's former band, Dufek Intrusion, would have been here, too. *These* were the odds and sods, and we had a part to play in propitiating them. Nina was kneeling in the midst of the food, cutting slices of pâté with her blonde hair tucked behind her ears. Chiharu sprawled on her tummy beside Joaquin, sulking. The bearded guy asked me if I'd ever climbed Mount Fuji. I went and sat next to Tad and complained that the afternoon would more profitably have been spent in the studio.

He gave me a strange look from behind his sunglasses. "You'd better talk to Joaquin."

"Tad…" I reached out and pushed the sunglasses up on his head so I could see his face better. "Is something up with the Club Goya gig? Joaquin said it wouldn't matter if we missed a few rehearsals. He said we were going to do more or less the same set as last time. But he hates doing that. He thinks it's slacking. Is there something I'm not being told?"

"It's nothing to do with me." Tad looked down, swirling his beer in its plastic cup. "Actually, I'm not sure what's going on, either. All I can tell you is that he's totally wrapped up in the Skoopagroove deal right now."

"*What* Skoopagroove deal? I thought it was just talk. Have they made us an offer?"

"I knew you wouldn't like it. Gen said you wouldn't mind, but *I* knew…"

"Gen said what?"

"He told us…"

"What?"

"It wasn't my idea. I don't like it, either."

"*What* wasn't your idea, Tad?"

He mumbled something inaudible. I stared at him in confusion. I didn't know if we were talking about some atrocious coup de main of Joaquin's or about a conversation that Tad had taken too seriously because of its potential to upset me. You couldn't always count on Tad's sense of proportion. Better to ask Joaquin himself. But when I stood up, the world swam around me, and I realized that a) I was drunk and b) I had to use the bathroom.

Joaquin was deep in conversation. Gen was missing from his place. I put on my sneakers and slipped off among the picnic parties on a zigzag course, stepping over radios and carrycots, passing downwind of hibachis and breathing smoke while petals fell, singly and in flurries, onto everything. Some of them caught in my hair.

The queue outside the log cabin on the ring path was about sixty women long. I joined it and crossed my legs.

Gen told us…

What?

What?

I racked my brain to recall everything I'd told him about myself. Trivial stuff, most of it. Anecdotes. I'd easily resisted the urge to tell him about the crucial period of my life from age ten to thirteen. The only real dirt he had on me was that I was American. And he *couldn't* have told them that. He'd promised!

Besides, even if he *had* betrayed my trust (I realized now, too late, that I'd begun to trust him), would it really have made such a big difference to Joaquin? Gorot had existed for almost a year now. We had oodles of songs at various stages of completion. Joaquin and I understood each other's strengths and weaknesses, and we'd worked out a division of labor we could live with. He would have had to search far and wide before he found another vocalist as useful as me who *wasn't* a high-maintenance diva. Surely it would take more than the exposure of my silly lie about my nationality to make him start leaving me out of the band's plans?

The only way I could see it happening was if he let his pride get the better of his common sense. No one ever fooled Joaquin, so I didn't know how he would react when he found out he *had* been fooled, but I had an idea it would not be pretty. The sheer improbability of my deception might make it harder instead of easier to take. A certain complexity of background is the prerequisite for pretending to three or four different nationalities. If Joaquin found out I was that much more complex than he'd known, he might well decide he could never trust me again.

And he would be within his rights.

But Gen *hadn't* told him. He *couldn't* have.

I shuffled along one step at a time.

So what *had* Gen told him? I couldn't imagine.

The infectious beat of a Little Richard song penetrated my thoughts. I looked up. Near the log cabin a laborers' union was picnicking with mucho saké and a banging sound system. They'd been there all along, of course, but the ambient noise level was such that I hadn't registered on this source of it until the DJ put on an ultrafamiliar song. While the younger laborers slept off their lunch, their toothless elders were dancing, twirling imaginary partners and doffing imaginary hats. A womp bomp a doo bomp! Why is it that old people always seem to have the most fun? Why, come to that, was the music of their generation about living life to the fullest, while ours is all about murder and suicide?

My breath caught in my throat as I spotted Gen. He was talking to someone leaning against the log cabin's corner. I couldn't see her face: he had one hand flat on the wall above her shoulder, boxing her in with his arm.

As I watched, he moved in closer, using his height advantage the way men do when they're fresh out of verbal tactics. Then he stepped sideways and bent his head to light a cigarette. He still hadn't seen me. But I could see the exasperated scowl on his face – an expression I'd never seen there before – and I could also see the girl leaning against the wall with a matching scowl on *her* face. It was Chiharu.

The darkness inside the log cabin smelled awful. I washed my hands, thought for a minute, and then whipped my comb out of my jeans pocket and scraped my hair into a high twist, fastening it with a couple of the elastics that live on my wrist. My hair was waist-length, so the updo instantly altered my silhouette. I'd seen that both Gen and Chiharu had their coats and knapsacks. I hurried back to the picnic site and collected my own belongings. The odds and sods who hadn't passed out yet asked me where I was going. "Personal obligations," I snarled. Tad watched me worriedly. I plucked his sunglasses off his head. He made a belated grab for them. "I'll give them back to you later," I said, and chased the strains of Little Richard back to the toilets through a world sunk into reddish twilight.

Chiharu and Gen were still where they had been, still arguing, if that was what they were doing. I joined the queue again. Provided you're not queueing up yourself, people in queues are invisible: they're just obstacles. To be doubly sure, I'd turned my coat inside out. It was a reversible one, perfect for these 007 moments. This morning it had been lavender, now it was khaki. At last Chiharu and Gen got their asses in gear. Just as I'd thought, they weren't going back to the picnic site. They wandered off in the direction of the park's main gates. I trailed them.

No matter what I did to my appearance, short of slipping into a Disney character costume, I was not ideally equipped to trail anyone in Tokyo. But it could have been worse. At 5'4" I could hide in crowds, and Yoyogi Park on a cherry blossom Sunday is *crowded*. We're talking not a square meter of grass left in sight. You could pass your best friend without knowing it on the path among the pedestrians, bikers, trikers, baby buggies, skateboarders, rollerbladers, kids in Heelies, and stray badminton players.

The lines at the ticket machines in Harajuku station, just outside the park, were ten deep. Hurray for prepaid passcards. I hung back with my Suica in my hand until Chiharu and Gen passed through the wickets. He took her hand to lead her down the stairs, but dropped it again when they reached the platform. They stood staring at their shoes, not talking. I lurked behind a gaggle of cosplayers dressed as vampire parlourmaids.

The Yamanote line train charged in along the outside track. Gen and Chiharu got on. I got on, too, and fought towards the back of the train until I was close enough to see, through the windows in the doors between the carriages, that they'd found one seat and Chiharu was in it. Gen was straphanging in front of her. Their knees touched; more than that; he was almost straddling her lap. The train was crowded, but Gen had enough room to move back if he'd wanted to.

Chiharu's head nodded. She'd dozed off.

They got off at Takadanobaba, the second station north of Shinjuku, and I knew where they were going.

'Baba until now had had only pleasant associations for me: gigs at Hot House and the Fiddler; afterparties at cheerful little bars that were always overflowing with students from Waseda University. I knew that henceforth I wouldn't be able to come here without remembering this: hanging out at the station, drinking takeout coffee, smoking cigarettes, fending off lechs, and reading all the billboards on the buildings until my eyes were drawn to the few kanji I *couldn't* read like fingernails to scabs. For hours I vacillated between coldly reasoning rage and the sinking feeling that I might as well go home.

It was growing dark when Gen came across the street alone. I stayed put, my hip hitched on one of the steel crowd control barriers jumbled against the station's exterior wall. He stood in front of me and gazed at me with the black ecclesiastical sadness I remembered from that Monday evening in his bedroom. I said, "What did you tell Joaquin about me?"

"Are those Tad's sunglasses?"

I'd pushed them into my hair and forgotten about them. "Yeah. Is that Chiharu's lipstick?"

"Where?"

"On your neck. Here," I said, and reached out. He flinched. I caught him and tried to wipe it off with my finger. But it wouldn't come off. It was a little pink hickey.

"Chiharu told me you were looking for a guitarist. She'd been after me for ages to get involved in music again. I'd been practising, but I was terrified that first day. I felt so rusty."

"You said you'd seen one of Joaquin's want ads."

"Chiharu thought Joaquin would be biased against me if he knew I was her…"

"Boyfriend?"

Gen shook his head. He looked as tired and stressed out as I felt. His cheeks were hollow, his complexion pale yellow, and there were flakes of dead skin on his lips. We'd walked from Takadanobaba to the south side of Shinjuku, almost all the way back to Yoyogi Park, before we sat down in a bar and started talking. "We're in a relationship," he said at last, "but I don't think of her as my girlfriend. She's more like my pet. Or, no, she's like a stray cat. I feed her and take care of her. Sometimes she scratches, sometimes she purrs. Sometimes she disappears on me, and I think she's gone forever, but every time she shows up again I forgive her."

He smiled; not because he was happy, certainly. I thought he was trying to make fun of himself.

"But you implied that she's the one pushing you musically. Even though she's ten… no, eleven years younger than you are."

"It could be that she pushes me *because* she's so young. But I push her, too. In vain, mostly."

"How long have you known each other?"

"About two years. All her friends are older than she is, you know. When I first met her, I thought she was at least twenty."

"Yeah, everyone does, so they expect her to be more mature than she really is."

"I need her." He spoke with the beguiling simplicity that made him seem defenceless. He moved his glass of draft beer from one place to another on the table between us. "Well, maybe I don't need *her,* but I need someone to look after. Someone to worry about."

I took a sip of my G&T. It's not a good idea to get drunk twice in one day, but right now it was the best idea I could come up with. "Chiharu seems to be fairly good at looking after herself," I said.

Gen laughed. "She's thrown away her one and only chance of an education; now she's throwing away her future. I feel like I'm watching myself screw up all over again. And she's got a better chance of making it professionally than I ever did. Actually, we had a big fight today. About that, among other things."

236

"And you came away honorably scarred." I reached across the table and touched the raspberry mark on his neck again. He didn't seem to notice.

"Have you ever been to her place? Well, you can't call it *her* place. Jiro's place."

"The squat," I said in English, there being no equivalent Japanese or French word.

"Whatever, yeah."

"Once. Taking her home drunk."

"It's hell, isn't it? Yeah, it's cheap, but can you imagine never having a moment to yourself? A dozen people partying in the next room while you're trying to get some sleep? And the *cockroaches!* When she's got a perfectly good home in Saitama prefecture."

"I don't know that it's a perfectly good home. Her mother's supposed to have abused her."

"Oh, well, they have their issues, I guess." He tried to cover up his slip. "But family is family."

Holy shit. I'd picked the wrong guy to confide in, hadn't I? Thank God I'd hadn't told him anything that *really* mattered.

"I'd like to be her savior." There was that simplicity again. "But I don't have the… the qualifications. If anyone does, it's Joaquin. He's the best thing that's happened to her since she came to Tokyo. I sometimes feel like kissing that guy's feet."

"He wouldn't mind," I said. Gen didn't seem to hear.

"He genuinely wants her to make it. And his melodies are so much better suited to her voice than anything she writes for herself. If we get this deal with Skoopagroove it could be a turning point for her. She's worried about performing with the band, but I know she'll do fine. After all, she's already used to singing in English." He looked up at me. I had the impression that he'd forgotten for a minute who he was talking to. "I admire you, Shanti. Honestly. I admire you for giving her this chance. There's so much ambition and jealousy in this business, but you're different. You care more about the music than about making money or making a name for yourself. You want your songs to find an audience even if it's someone else who sings them."

I definitely didn't remember saying *that*.

"Before I met you, I never knew there were Americans like you."

I'd been wrong and he'd been right all along: I might yet end up hating him.

"**C**hiharu and I have completely different vocal registers." I stood in the middle of the Kuroiwas' kitchen, facing Joaquin and Tad. It was Tuesday evening. I'd had time to think about what I was going to say. "It's not going to be like changing cartridges on a Playstation."

"It would be a pain in the ass if she's a mezzo or an alto, but because she's a soprano we can kick the vocal line up one whole octave. This is very easy. We don't have to change the key. For the most part I leave the entire song as it is. Sometimes it's better to kick the bass line up, too, but Tad can record again. Oh yeah, and on 'The Hound Of Heaven' I'm playing around with the synth to make a counter-melody line with her top notes. It sounds fucking revolutionary."

I hadn't realized until just now that speaking English was Joaquin's way of being chilly to me, distancing himself from the combative friendliness of our relationship in French.

"She's already laid down vocals for 'The Solution' and 'Dreamstomper.' I finished remixing the tracks today. I'll play them for you; you'll understand what I'm talking about." He started moving towards the door, as if he expected me or all of us to follow him.

"But Shanti's voice is part of the Gorot sound," said Nina. She stood beside me, clutching a mug of peppermint tea. "Chiharu's vocals sound good, but they don't sound the *same.* Isn't that what you were saying, Tad?"

Joaquin turned around again. "It doesn't matter who sounds better. For myself, Shanti, I'm crazy about your vocals. You've got a gritty feeling in the bottom of the register. When you're on stage and people are staring with the eyes popping out because they can't believe this little girl is singing like a man, my God, I don't want to trade you for a fucking soprano. And we have a creative relationship; that's important to me, too. But the Skoopagroove team have different priorities. They say a more feminine voice is generally appealing. Also, they're thinking about the band's image. Chiharu is very cute." He shrugged. "It's commercially good sense."

"It's discrimination," muttered Tad.

"You are too fucking idealistic," said Joaquin, predictably. It was what he said whenever Tad ventured to disagree with him. "Listen, we're performing now on the small scale and our audiences, whatever one may say, are comparatively sophisticated. They see that fifty percent of this band is gaijin, they're cool with it, and if maybe they stay for our performance out of mere curiosity, it's still a good thing for us, no? Suppose we sign with a fringe label, like ZK or Captain Trip. They will promote us like any other band, but we stay on the fringe. Skoopagroove is different. They have distribution deals with

239

Disk Union and Tsutaya. They will not refuse a buyout offer, I think. They want to be much bigger. On this point I agree with them." Joaquin chuckled. "If we're trying to get a deal in Europe or America they don't care if we are purple with green hair, but over there we don't have the opportunity, either. This scene is very healthy. Nowhere else in the world have we such a chance to develop naturally while performing. So for now we stay in Tokyo and we sign with Skoopagroove. Or maybe we don't. First they want to hear us live with Chiharu on vocals. We give it a try at Club Goya. If it goes well, bon! we have a deal. If we can't capture the Gorot feeling with her, tant pis! we abandon this stupid experiment. Nothing is decided yet, Shanti, so don't give me any more headaches."

He went out of the kitchen. I followed him. The others trailed after me. He sat down at the dining-room table, which was invisible beneath a sea of documents, receipts, and bank draft foils.

"I must do my taxes. The date of filing returns is coming up."

"I can't stop you from doing as you like with the band, Joaquin. But I think I deserved to be consulted. As you said, we have a creative relationship, and I wrote the lyrics that Chiharu is going to be singing." I spoke in English. I was still hoping for support from Tad and Nina. "If you'd asked me I would have told you that her inflections are going to be a problem. She's great at memorizing strings of syllables, but no one's ever going to take her for a native English speaker. It makes songs like 'Your Girlfriend' sound fresh, like she's just landed from Mars and found love for the first time. Our songs are more subtle. They need more… more soul."

Joaquin shrugged. "You're not a native English speaker, either."

Oh God. I didn't dare look at Tad. If he was feeling sorry for me, I didn't want to know it.

"But Shanti has hardly any accent at all. She *sounds* like a native English speaker," said Nina.

"It's unimportant. They like our lyrics because English is fucking fashionable, not because we give a pronunciation lesson."

"C'est pas juste. C'est *mes* chansons."

"But you don't want to be famous." Joaquin glanced up from his documents, and there was no mistaking the anger on his face. "You'd quit the band if we ever arrived. It would have been good of you to tell us this shit in the beginning, Shanti, instead of misleading us to make us think you're more serious about the music than in fact you are. I don't like having to learn the truth from someone else, some guy we've known for only a few weeks – some guy *you've* known for only a few weeks, and yet you can tell him things we're not important enough to hear."

Heat flooded my face. I said, "Je te comprends, mais je vais vous dire une bonne chose: vous n'arriverez à rien sans moi."

Joaquin sprawled in his chair, grinning.

I turned and left.

I didn't get the last word, though. Tad did. He followed me to the door and watched me putting on my shoes. "Where are you going?"

"Home."

"Shanti, don't… don't leave Japan without telling me. OK?"

I laughed. "Leave Japan? Not planning on it. Where would I go?"

His face took on the sullen look that meant he knew he was screwing up, but didn't know how to get back on track. "Home?"

Oh, Ireland. "Well, Tad, next time I plan a trip to the auld country I promise I'll inform you. But the closest I expect to get to Ireland in the near future is the ceilidh night at O'Carolan's."

"I was supposed to be the one to break it to you. I just couldn't. I kept hoping Joaquin would change his mind. I'm sorry."

One step forward, two steps back. Contentment ages you; misery takes that expensive veneer right off. I spent the next couple of weeks acting like the crazy teenager I'd once been. I moped at work and cried myself to sleep. I accepted every invitation to go drinking that came my way, and ended up fooling around in dark nightclubs with two guys I barely knew on two successive weekends. I wanted to reassure myself that a) I wasn't repulsive, and b) I was still capable of the old juggling act. I'd also wanted to have my mind taken off Gen. But afterwards I felt like I'd betrayed him. I was more thoroughly obsessed with him than any past experience had led me to think possible. I walked around only half aware of my surroundings, reliving key conversations with him and scripting future ones that I would probably never get a chance to initiate.

I expected Joaquin to get in touch after the Club Goya gig. But he didn't.

I was still talking to Nina, of course. She wasn't so much under Joaquin's thumb that she would let him break us up, too. When I got over my bout of adolescence, we met up for Sunday brunch at T.G.I. Friday's.

It felt weird to be hanging out with her in Shibuya. I could count on the fingers of one hand the times we'd gone out to eat together. Our friendship had never been completely intimate. Joaquin had always been off limits for dissection (as insufferable as he could be, that was between Nina and her soul, and if she'd ever talked to me about him in any but the most jocular terms I would have known their marriage was in trouble); now the other Gorotties were off limits, too. It was a question for Nina of balancing her loyalty to Joaquin with her desire to stand by me. I couldn't make it harder for her than it was. So, while she might have told me all kinds of stuff, I didn't ask her to. There was also an element of cowardice in my restraint. Anything she told me about Gen would have been edited to make me think I still had a chance. I knew I didn't, and false hopes would have been worse than no hopes at all.

She brought me up to date on the band's activities. The Club Goya gig had gone OK, and they were planning to go ahead with the two gigs we'd booked for May. The Skoopagroove negotiations seemed to have stalled. According to Nina, Joaquin was going around saying that he'd submitted the new demo in too much of a hurry: he should have organized everyone to record the tracks over again instead of just remixing them with Chiharu's vocals.

"I know why he didn't, though," I said. "He likes the original recordings with Yuki on guitar. Gen…" Damn it.

"I love Gen's solos," said Nina.

"They're all planned out to the last note. He can't *jam* like Yuki. At least, maybe he can, but not to my knowledge. He's scared to cut loose, so he never reaches the threshold of pure noise." I tried to be objective. "He's technically deft. His attack is nice and clean. But he's too much of a purist to use distortion, and that makes his sound less attention-getting. He also has a nasty tendency to drag, and if you aren't playing with a live drummer, you have to be rock-solid rhythmically."

Nina gazed at me with wide blue eyes. "If you say so."

I sipped my coffee and felt so bored all of a sudden that I wanted to scream. If I lost Nina I would lose my last connection to Gorot. And now that I thought about it, she probably wouldn't have been happy to be released from her sense of obligation to me, either. She didn't make friends easily. But what did we have left to talk about?

Ourselves?

She tried to draw me out on the subject of my recent "romantic" encounters. I answered monosyllabically. I could see that my reticence bothered her, but what right did she have to complain? It wasn't as if she ever had adventures to report to *me.* She was faithful to Joaquin in a blinkered, passionate way that I admired but that I instinctively associated with women less attractive and intelligent than Nina. I suspected that her poise concealed a mass of insecurities, but I'd abandoned hope of ever getting her to talk about them.

Naturally blonde, as thin and tall as a runway model, she looked like she should be languishing in an Ingmar Bergman film. She was actually a New Yorker. She'd got her degree in art history from Sarah Lawrence and then, as we used to say, she'd busted out. With job offers not perhaps abounding but not far to seek, she went to Paris, married Joaquin the crazy Quebeçois DJ, and travelled with him for several years around Europe, hanging out in all the major capitals, learning none of the languages, and living for one long stretch in a bus. It wasn't until Joaquin hit Tokyo that he started making money. That was why he was such a passionate advocate of the scene here. Nina was earning a decent salary, too, but of all the cities she'd lived in, I suspected she found Tokyo the most challenging... and no wonder. You can get by here without speaking Japanese; you just can't have very much fun.

She licked her lips and said, "My father molested me."

Oh. My. God.

"It went on for years, from when I was in first grade until my twelfth birthday. He used to say he did it because he loved me, and for years I couldn't understand what he meant, but now I do. As far as he was concerned it was *true,* you know?"

It took her two hours to tell me about the fondling, the kissing, and the "games," displaying no greater signs of emotion than an occasionally tremulous lip.

It took me one and a half seconds to tell her that I was American, and another two hours to explain.

It wasn't like I thought this was a dark enough secret to match hers. I mean, come on. But I had to repay her somehow for confiding in me. And in order to show her the sympathy that her confession warranted, I had to let her know who she'd made it to: not a French girl who spoke fluent English, but an American who'd spent long enough in that country to understand the iconic status of the sexually abused child, the ubiquitous threat of therapy, and the silencing effect it had had on Nina. I tried to emphasise the aspects of my own story that made it seem as if I, too, had been helpless in the hands of the grownups. I felt ashamed, in the face of Nina's stoicism, of having been so much in control of my own fate and having been at times so whimsical about it.

"I was born in America. We moved to the west of Ireland when I was a month old. When I was seven we moved to France. When I was ten we moved back to Ireland. When I was thirteen we moved to Thailand. That only lasted a few months. When I was fourteen we moved to Philadelphia, where my uncle lives. When I was seventeen my mother went back to France, but my brother and I stayed behind. He was at Amherst, and I wanted to finish high school. I went to college in New York… well, that part you know," I told her. "And the rest's pretty much like I told you already. I dropped out of school, hung around Manhattan for another four years, and finally came here."

Now that it no longer mattered what Joaquin thought of me, I didn't feel it was such a big deal to make these revelations. I expected Nina would take them as they were meant – FYI. After all, she'd done her share of globetrotting, too. But she was flabbergasted. She asked questions, and I reluctantly filled in some more details, improvising half of them. Enough was enough: she'd had all the truth she was getting out of me for one day.

She didn't think so. The *whole* truth probably wouldn't have satisfied her.

"But why didn't you tell us in the first place?" she kept saying.

I felt like saying: You *know* why. I thought Gorot sounded like a project that was going somewhere, and I wanted to make sure I got the fucking job. Besides, I thought it would be a hoot if I could get away with it. Tad thought so, too. I don't know if he does any more. But can't you see, "Can't you see," I said, "why I thought to begin with that it would be as funny as hell?"

Nina's face told me that she did see but would never admit it. I'd run up against her primary loyalty. My deception pointed like a road sign to Joaquin's biggest blind spot: his anti-Americanism.

"You *have* got an accent, though," she protested. "I'm not imagining it!"

I think she would have been relieved to find out that I was French after all.

"I have an accent but it's not a French one," I said regretfully. "It's traces of Irish mixed with traces of British English. Most of the people we knew in Ireland the second time around were Brits. And… uh… I've sort of gotten into the habit of those French vowels."

I'd said this in a flat transatlantic accent. Nina stared at me. She looked frightened. "It's…no, it's *not* a joke. You can't convince me you meant it as a joke. It's *pathological,* Shanti. No normal person does anything like that."

That, of course, was exactly what I told myself in my moments, which were not few lately, of remorse and terror. The table in front of me seemed to melt into an abyss that exerted its own vertiginious attraction, sucking away my hopes of a new and deeper friendship with Nina, swallowing everything I pretended to be on a daily basis, making me dizzy. I concentrated on not swaying in my chair and muttered, "It's all true, but I didn't mean it to have this effect on you. I'm sorry, Nina, I'm sorry. I only wanted…" I buried my face in my hands. It sounded so stupid now. "I only wanted to make you feel better."

"About?"

"About… about having been molested."

She laughed. "Well, you obviously took my mind off it, didn't you? Know what? I told you about the abuse because I thought it wasn't fair that I'd known you so long without telling you. I mean, no one else knows except Jo and my friends in New York. But after you stopped coming over, I guess I realized that I really do value you as a friend. So I wanted you to know this… this important thing about me."

"Oh, I'm so glad that's how you feel," I exclaimed. "I mean, I value your friendship, too," but at that moment what I wanted was never to see her again.

The next day Tad called me. I didn't pick up. Obviously, Nina had gone home and blurted out everything I'd told her. I couldn't face Tad, even over the telephone. Not that he would confront me with my lies. He was very Japanese in that way. He would just ask me trivial questions about how things were going, and tell me trivial stuff about his job, and the silences in between these exchanges would attenuate indefinitely until, unable to bear it another minute, I broached the subject myself. To brazen it out would have required armor-plated nerves, and right now my armor was corroded all to hell. So I just let the phone ring. The next day he called again, and the day after that. I started leaving my phone in manner mode so I wouldn't hear it.

On Thursday he changed his tactics and texted me. "Free on Saturday? Go's playing at Oasis in Aoyama."

Go was the vocalist of Pragueberry, a band whose gigs Tad and I always went to. I wavered.

But before I could make up my mind and text him back, who should call me but Yuki? He'd got back into town yesterday. He'd been over to the Kuroiwas' and found out about Joaquin's treacheries (so maybe I'd been wrong about Tad's motive for calling me yesterday, but that didn't account for Monday or Tuesday) and now he wanted to catch up with me, too. "Any gigs worth going to this weekend?"

"As a matter of fact, yeah," I said. "Pragueberry's playing at Oasis."

So we met for the first time in four months in a smoky vault decorated with inflatable palm trees.

Yuki revealed almost immediately that he wasn't back in town for long.

"I'm just here to pack up my stuff and cancel my lease."

Pragueberry piled onto the stage. They were a saxophone, a trumpet, a double bass, a synthesiser, drums, and our little buddy Go, who was dressed tonight in a ragged pink leather miniskirt, a silver paratrooper's helmet, and his tattoos. Pragueberry gigs invariably brought out of hiding a bunch of people, more artsy than musical, who you never met anywhere else. As we talked, Yuki kept interrupting himself to greet people who were unaware he'd left Tokyo in the first place. I wondered how many people besides me he knew well enough to say goodbye to. Maybe not as many as I'd thought. He shouted in my ear, "My mom's health wasn't the greatest even before this! Now she's all alone! My sister lives in Sapporo. She's got two little kids; *she's* not going anywhere! Mom says I should stay here, but I have to go back. It's the only thing to do!"

I thought so, too, but I tried halfheartedly to persuade him to stay in Tokyo. It had been enough of a shock for him to find out he'd been replaced as Gorot's guitarist. The more he felt wanted by his friends here, the better he'd be able to feel about choosing his family over us. I also wanted to provoke him into saying something about how sorry he would be to leave *me*. I'd often reflected that he and I were in the same lifestyle crunch: pushing thirty, unattached, playing our lives by ear. And now we'd both been jettisoned by Joaquin. I had hopes of some bittersweet mutual commiseration.

"Hakodate is a cool town!" he shouted, putting a brave face on it. "One of my buddies from high school is in a punk outfit. He's a crazy guy! As a matter of fact, I know a lot of crazy people up there. It's something to do with those long, freezing cold winters! We're on the sea, so we don't get that much snow! But all the same, you stick around in Hakodate and you end up banging your head on the walls!"

"But what about your job, Yuki?"

He'd worked at a boutique in Daikanyama, selling unwearable garments to trendsetters. It was exactly the right job for a fashion victim like Yuki. Tonight, perhaps in honor of Pragueberry, he was even more eyecatching than usual in a pair of yellow, green, and black striped flares and a sleeveless green t-shirt that had probably cost about ¥10,000. A broad blue headband, almost a turban, held back his longish black hair. His platform shoes made him fully six and a half feet tall. He turned away from me, lit a cigarette, and answered my question just as I was about to ask it again. "Well, I couldn't ask them to hold it for me without any guarantee that I'd be back, could I?"

"Oh, Yuki!"

"I could get another job in five minutes if I wanted one. It would be the same kind of thing, too: working on commission for a bunch of humorless tightwads!"

"I guess that's Tokyo," I sympathized.

"This is Tokyo!" Yuki nodded in the direction of Pragueberry. Go had taken off his helmet and was getting ready to toss it to someone in the crowd. The saxophone screamed. Yuki excused himself to get another beer. When he came back to where I was standing, he said, "How long are you planning to stay in Japan, anyway, Shanti?"

"I might be here for the rest of my life. Who knows? Or I might leave tomorrow."

"Well, if you ever find yourself in Hakodate, get in touch, OK?"

"Do you think you'll ever come back to Tokyo?"

He smiled. It was a mere contraction of the lips. "Oh yeah! I expect I'll be back at some point."

"Hey, guys! I figured I'd find you here! They're really on form tonight, aren't they?"

Tad pushed through the crowd, alone, holding high a plastic cup of beer. My discomfort must have been palpable. I suspected Yuki also harbored a grudge against Tad for having failed to stand up for him in his absence. At any rate, conversation faltered. We watched Pragueberry and exchanged pleasantries at the top of our lungs with people who seemed to think it rather sweet that we were hanging out together. The band that plays together stays together? I twitched in agony. Even in this chaotic setting Tad was managing to make me feel bad. It was the way he stood: slightly hunched, gripping the crook of his drink arm with his free hand, glowering at the stage. And Yuki was reinforcing his effect by saying nothing. Their silence trumped Pragueberry's earsplitting onslaught. My misplaced faith in the social conventions disintegrated into fragments of humiliating insight. I made it my priority to keep up appearances. I was a very good liar. But of what use was that when no one else was saying a word, nor acting as if he even wanted to say anything? I felt as if I'd been displaced into a deeper level of Japanese society, a place of scalding and unpredictably shifting pressures.

The progression from nervous paralysis to exhilaration was a swift one. I knew it well enough to experience it as inexorable. My lips parted in a smile. I was ready to take the world on again.

Tad shook my shoulder and shouted, "Remember when we played here last year? Remember how Yuki tied those balloons to his amp, and they *melted?*"

I let drop the invitation to reminisce. Tad was so obvious.

Certain bands exist principally to justify their own afterparties. Pragueberry was one of them. As soon as the gig was over, the band and the entire audience relocated to Raku, an upscale izakaya not far from the venue on Miyamasu Hill. I bagged a zabuton between Yuki and the saxophonist, leaving Tad to fend for himself at another table. All went well for an hour or so, but I hadn't counted on Yuki's having arranged to meet up with the guys and girls from his (now former) job and hang out with them for the second half of the evening at Frames, a trendy lounge bar. I didn't know his Daikanyama crowd. It was impossible for me to leave with him, and when I got up to leave by myself twenty minutes later – inconspicuously, I hoped, slipping the saxophonist a ¥5000 note to avoid the palaver of working out how much I owed – Tad took out his wallet and did the same thing.

I was friendly to him as we walked down the hill into Shibuya. I'd drunk enough wine by now to make this relatively easy.

"I've been trying to get in touch with you all week."

This unTaddish directness surprised me. Either he was angrier with me than he had any right to be, or he had some other motive for pursuing me apart from his own hurt feelings. "So what's up?" I said, smiling.

"Joaquin wants you to come back. He never meant to give you the impression that he was ditching you."

I opened my mouth, closed it again, and thought about it. If it was true, why hadn't Joaquin been in touch with me himself? "I certainly got the impression that I'd been ditched, whether or not that's what he meant. What made him change his mind?"

"It's not working out with Chiharu," said Tad flatly.

"Really? Has the Skoopagroove deal fallen through?"

"Not exactly. But you know how she is. Arrange a rehearsal and she shows up late or not at all; tell her to sing it like this and she sings it like that…"

The implication was that Joaquin wanted me back because I was comparatively biddable. I laughed and said, "Gen must be tearing his hair out." In a certain sense it served him right – he, of all people, should have known that Chiharu was liable to buckle under pressure – but I felt angry with her on his behalf. How could she let him down like that?

"Joaquin's tearing his hair out, too," said Tad. "We've got a gig on Wednesday, and she's AWOL. We don't even know if she's learned all the songs. A couple of days ago Joaquin said, 'How I miss Shanti!' Those were his words."

I knew then that there'd been no concrete offer of reconciliation. It was just wishful thinking on Tad's part. Maybe he thought that if he could trick me into making the first approach, something could be worked out. And maybe he was right. But I had my pride. "Tell Joaquin that if he wants me back he'll have to put it to me himself." I rounded on Tad and gave him a gentle push. "What were you thinking, Tad? What are you? His message boy?"

Tad's face set into a sullen expression. "I wanted to talk to you, anyway."

Oh God, I thought, here it comes.

But for the next few minutes nothing came. I let the silence ride. This, too, was easier on three glasses of wine. We walked into the heart of Shibuya, through clusters of bellowing salarymen, around gangs of college boys giving each other the bumps. It was a warm muggy May evening. Traffic jammed the streets and people jammed the sidewalks. Savory smoke puffed from takoyaki stands and kebab vans. Taxis crawled, limousines idled, derelicts in sandwich boards cadged cigarettes from African touts, masseuses and hostesses accosted drunks, smart couples circumnavigated curbside refuse tips, foreigners searched desperately for bars, and music crackled from a hundred concealed loudspeakers, dominated by the big screens that overlooked the fiveways crossing in front of the station. Oh, how I wished Tad was Gen! So sharp that it took my breath away, this pang of longing had the effect of causing me to lose my grasp for an instant on the strategic realities of my situation. I made a pointless comment about the weather.

"We'll be into the rainy season in no time at all." Tad cleared his throat. "Actually, Joaquin didn't get in touch with you himself because… Do you want to know what he said?"

"Yeah, tell me what he said."

"He said," Tad dropped into English, "'I don't know if I should speak French to her now or English. It fucking de… something… me.' What was that word? De…"

"Deranges," I hazarded.

"Yeah, that was it."

"Ça me derange." I thought about it. "Or maybe he *meant* to say 'deranges.'" Either way, I understood how he felt: it deranged me, too, just thinking about it. All at once I felt terribly depressed. This was a problem I hadn't foreseen, but of course it was the only pertinent one. "I can't talk to him in English," I said, thinking out loud. I'd told Gen I wanted to institute English as Gorot's official language, but the scene at the Kuroiwas' had made me realize that that might be a change for the worse. "And yet I can't go on talking to him in French, either. Can I? No. It would be too fatuous for words."

"Does it *matter* what language you speak as long as you *talk* to him?"

For a minute I thought Tad had a point. Then I shook my head. "It makes all the difference in the world."

"I don't understand why. I mean, what makes one language better or more appropriate than another? I was born and raised in Tokyo, but I don't give a damn what language we speak. Look at the two of us: it makes no difference whether we speak English or Japanese, does it? You're still you, and I'm still me."

His face was flushed, although it was hard to tell in the changeable light, and it could have been from drinking. Anyway, he obviously believed what he was saying. I forbore to remind him that although his English was good, his experience of using it overseas was limited to backpacking trips in between engineering jobs, and therefore he'd never developed a secondary personality in it. To me, speaking English with him was unrewarding for this reason. I felt even sadder as I reflected that he wasn't being honest with himself: a large part of the reason he was willing to make so many allowances for Joaquin, and come to that for me, was that we were foreigners. His ethics did not sufficiently inform his conduct. I said almost despairingly, "Tad, don't you care that I lied to you? I lied to you and then enlisted you to lie for me to Joaquin. Doesn't that bother you at all?"

We were crossing the plaza in front of the station. Tad was momentarily separated from me in the crowd; then he said with an awful grimace, "I didn't want to believe it was true. But it is, isn't it?"

"What I told Nina? Yeah. Roughly."

"Roughly?"

Oh, what the hell? "I told her that my father still lives in Ireland. I told you the same thing, if you recall. *That's* not true."

"Your father. Of course. Well, if he doesn't live in Ireland, where does he live?" Tad spoke with an air of patience. We were standing in front of the row of public phone booths, next to an overflowing garbage bin.

"He doesn't. That is, he killed himself about ten years ago."

Tad looked shocked, and I felt guilty. I'd had no intention of fishing for sympathy. I mean, I'd barely known my father. It was nothing to me whether he really had hanged himself from the rafters of his house in Phuket, or had just upped sticks and moved on again, this time untraceably. Hazard was our mother's name, not his. Alastair and I suspected that they were actually married. Our mother always denied it. But while she'd almost got married several times while we were kids, she'd abandoned the man each time at the last minute for unconvincing reasons. A move had invariably ensued. It had been fun while it lasted. I said to Tad, "When we first met, you asked me, 'Where are you from?' What was I supposed to say? 'Do you have the next couple of hours free, because that's how long it's going to take me to explain?'"

"I guess it must have been tough on you."

"Tough?" I said. "No! Not at all." If anything, it had been too easy. As easy as a dream that makes sense while you're dreaming, but is revealed when you awake to have been riddled with suspect logic and jump cuts.

We trailed into the station. Both of us were taking the Yamanote line on the inside or widdershins track. I stared glazedly at the TV screens over the doors. I was so tired of Tad's company that even a commercial for *Mamma Mia!* was comparatively interesting.

"I guess I'll see you around," I said as we pulled into Gotanda station.

"Yeah," said Tad, listlessly.

He hung out with foreigners and punk rockers. He was used to people vanishing. And yet he was so easy to hurt.

The only person I'd ever really loved was Alastair. Although I was all of twenty-eight, my idea of an intimate relationship was still the quarrelsome complicity he and I had shared once upon a time. But now *he'd* found something different. I'd seen him at home in Somerville when Maisie was due back from an evening performance, bustling around to straighten up for her, putting on coffee and her favorite Schubert album, and spraying Lemon Fresh in the air to kill the smell of my cigarettes. If he'd been a dog he would have met her at the door and jumped up to slobber all over her. It was as if she'd summoned into being an Alastair I didn't know – a *nice* Alastair. I'd done my best to embarrass him about it at the time, but now I was starting to get it.

When I met Gen, I'd discerned the possibility of a relationship that wouldn't revolve around being bad together, but would instead make me a better human being. Gen's simplicity, his tortured but essentially delicate sense of tact, his passion for music (so much purer than mine, untainted by social aspirations), his efforts to share with me the valuable part, as he saw it, of his Buddhist heritage (this had occasioned our most fruitful disagreements), even his partisanship of Chiharu: there was a lot there for me to emulate. I felt that by following him I could have found my way out of the maze of cover stories I lived in. He'd gone to France, come back, fallen apart, put himself back together in his room at home, and now he knew who he was, while I was still having panic attacks. A loser he might be; he was a better loser than I'd ever been.

Maybe it wasn't surprising that I'd made so little impact on him. What did I have to offer *him*, after all? What could I have taught him? How to be a good liar?

Usually, I was aware of lacking only one thing in my life, and that was the intimacy I'd wanted to establish with him. But sometimes, as May turned into June, I felt dispossessed in a different way. Drops of water as big as pennies fell here and there continually from heavy dirty clouds, and the very air felt sticky. I hated these saturated days. I wanted Irish sunshine and showers. I wanted mud and sand under my toes; the pebbled gray sea lapping at the end of the pier; hedges full of meadowsweet and, if you looked hard enough, wild strawberries. Jesus, I wanted to go *home.* I could usually expunge this mood by singing. But now I had no one to sing with. I intended to start looking around for another band ISO a female vocalist, but I hadn't done anything about it yet. So I called Derek Feeney, a guy I used to work with, and arranged to perform with him at the ceilidh night that O'Carolan's in Harajuku held every Thursday.

Derek came from County Clare and had brought with him on the long road to Japan a bodhran which he could play skilfully. He thought no more of this talent than most people think of being able to ride a bicycle. Without prodding, he would never have touched the drum except when he was drunk, for his own amusement. Derek was a drifter. He was still working at the chain of English schools where I'd gotten to know him, but nowadays he was restless and ripe for prodding.

You didn't have to pay box money to join the ceilidh – it was strictly for the craic. The owner, Rob, knew us and gave us a slot at ten o'clock. I told Derek nine o'clock. He showed up, as I'd known he would, at quarter past, and swore at me. I bought him a Guinness. Rob fixed me a vodka tonic on the house, and we sat and listened to a trio consisting of uilleann pipes, acoustic guitar, and obese male vocalist. Derek made fun of them so wittily that I choked on my drink. The place filled up. It was steamy and smoky. When the trio called off the torture, Derek and I freshened our drinks and took them with us to the corner where mics and chairs had been placed.

I sang "I dream of a land that lies bleeding"; I sang, "There was a man who lived in our town, who had a young and handsome daughter"; I sang, "What put the blood on your right shoulder?"; I sang, "There came three gypsies unto our door." The bodhran commanded attention, and people started watching us. I picked up the tin whistle I'd borrowed from Rob and accompanied Derek, who had just one song that he liked to sing.

"And it's oh, the prickly bush, it pierces my heart full sore, and if ever I get away from that bush I'll never get caught any more!"

I had a companion piece to "The Prickly Bush." I sang, putting on the thickest brogue I was capable of, "I am a rambling hackling man that loves the shamrock shore. My name is Patrick McDonald and my age is eighty-four."

We tried to avoid the clichéd songs of exile, but a lot of the best Irish music is about exile. So I sang "Spancil Hill," changing *California* in the last line to *Harajuku,* and I sang, "I know where I'm going to and I know who's coming with me. I know who I love, but the dear knows who I'll marry."

I opened my eyes and saw Gen.

"**I** want us to be friends again. I want us to be able to talk about things again. You made me think new thoughts, look at things in new ways… I want us to play together again."

"Well, that's up to Joaquin, isn't it?" I said.

Gen looked past me. I turned to follow his gaze. At the far end of the bar, Derek was getting noisily drunk with the uilleann piper and a couple of other guys. With their accents in my ears, I almost felt as if I *had* come home – as if Gen had followed me all the way around the world, just to say he wanted to be friends.

"Derek's a great guy. Thank you for introducing him to me. You know, I've met so many people since I started hanging out with you and the others. But no one's as interesting to talk to as you. I've really missed our conversations."

Kill me while you're at it, why don't you? I thought. Just plunge your thumbs into my eyes. Scramble my brain. Stop me from feeling like this.

"I've missed you, too," I said, deliberately phrasing it like that (in Japanese it came out as "I've been lonely without you," which was equally true) to see how he would react. His mouth tightened, and he actually moved his elbow a bit farther away from mine on the edge of the bar. Then he smiled, but he was obviously forcing it.

"These guys can't compare to you and Derek," he said, presumably referring to the duo (acoustic guitar and vocals) now performing in the corner. "I wish I'd come in time to hear you from the beginning. You sounded great."

"Thanks. I haven't been singing at all recently. Maybe taking a break did my voice good."

"You haven't? That's criminal!" He hit me playfully on the arm.

I told him about my intention to look for another band; I told him in fact that I'd already made some phone calls. "I might be going out to Hachioji on Saturday for an audition," I finished. This was pure fantasy. Uneasily, I observed that he didn't seem to be listening. Did he know

I was lying? Did my feelings for him make me transparent to him? God help me, wasn't that what I'd wanted? "I want to start writing songs again," I said. "I've got a lot of new material."

"Shall we get going?" Gen stubbed out his cigarette, drained his Guinness, and slid off his bar stool.

"Where to?"

"Can you spare me some more time tonight?"

"Yeah, but…"

"There's someone I want you to talk to. It's not far. And it shouldn't take very long."

We walked to Harajuku station (shades of that terrible Sunday, although now the platform was comparatively deserted) and took the Yamanote line to Takadanobaba. As we turned off Waseda Avenue, Gen made a phone call. He spoke so softly, rapidly, and briefly, with his free hand cupping his mouth, that I couldn't distinguish a word he said.

Jiro's squat was a large apartment on the second floor of a modest white building. As Gen and I climbed the stairs I smelled curry, and light spilled out into the hall ahead of us. They had the door ajar to let out the heat and the odors. Shoes overflowed from the genkan into the hall, aligned in pairs. We took off our own shoes and entered the living-room, where three men and two girls sat cross-legged around a low table heaped with paperback mangas, travel guides, 500ml cans of beer, and frosted plastic glasses. The Red Hot Chili Peppers emanated at low volume from a boombox. One of the men was the bearded guy who'd come to Joaquin's picnic. One of the girls was Chiharu, deshabillée in a t-shirt and cutoff sweatpants. Gen introduced me to the others. They said we'd met before. One of the advantages of being a foreigner is that people remember you; on the other hand, I was fairly sure I'd never met the guy seated beside Chiharu in my life. He was probably mixing me up with some other white girl. We sat down, but Gen immediately jumped up again and gathered up the empty glasses. I followed him into the kitchen, where Jiro was stirring his curry and rocking along with his Discman.

I felt uncomfortable in this, by Japanese standards extremely irregular, establishment. All the squatters had jobs, and they had no access to hard drugs, but their nonconformism still made them seem forlorn to me – maybe *because* the chaos here was so mild compared to the worst of what I'd seen in New York. Jiro was in his early forties and looked older, but the idea of him as their chaperon was a joke. He was variously spoken of as a rapacious skinflint and a soft touch. Short and fat, he paddled around barefoot in all weathers on horny bluish feet. Belatedly noticing that Gen and I were visitors, he smiled at us. I could hear a tinny crash, crash, crash from his ears.

Next to the pedal bin on the floor sagged a transparent bag full of noncombustible garbage (in Japan you have to separate it or they won't take it away) that smelled almost as strong as the curry. I spotted something moving in the bottom of it. It was a cockroach as long as my thumb.

"Je comprends, oui, je comprends bien pourquoi Chiharu passe tellement de temps chez Kuroiwa," I muttered.

Gen, washing glasses at the overflowing sink, looked at me over his shoulder. "Mais elle n'y est pas allée pendant plusieurs semaines. Tu ne le savais pas?"

"Non!" As I spoke I remembered what Tad had said on the night we went to see Pragueberry. Maybe he hadn't been exaggerating as much as I'd thought. "Pour-quoi?"

"Ca, demande lui toi-même!"

We took the clean glasses back into the living-room and poured out for those who wanted it the hock we'd brought with us. Thanks to Jiro's cooking and the rainy season humidity, the room was unpleasantly hot, and drinking made it worse. Sweat trickled down my back and collected in the creases of my knees. The guy I didn't know had taken off his shirt. Gen did the same, revealing a scattering of black hairs around his nipples. The squatters were talking about Eastern Europe. Everyone had a story to tell about his or her travels there – including Gen, who'd made various excursions from Paris for the dual purpose of seeing the rest of Europe and renewing his French visa (that was in the days before you could cross European borders without formalities). The only people who had nothing to contribute were Chiharu and me. Finally the conversation turned to the British Isles: characteristics of, similarities of Japan to. I had a lot to say on this topic, so now Chiharu was the only one left out. I looked around and saw that she was gone. Gen's eyes conveyed a plea to me. I rose and slipped behind the curtain that hung across the sliding doors at the end of the room, through them, into the bedroom. It was dark. I felt immediately cooler.

Chiharu knelt on the far side of a sea of futons with her elbows on a hardshell suitcase that stood on its wheels. She was gazing out of the glass doors that led to the balcony. The doors were open as wide as they would go, but there was nothing to see out there except laundry and the neighboring apartment building. The bedroom was eight mats big: it could sleep everyone who actually lived here, at a squeeze. The futons were permanently out on the floor, wrinkled and probably grubby. With the balcony taken up by laundry, there was nowhere to air them, and with the oshiire closets full of people's stuff, there was probably nowhere to store them, either. I almost tripped over a bulge in one of them. It was a person with only a few wisps of hair sticking out. Chiharu looked around. "That's Miyuki. She isn't feeling well. She had a fever of 38.5 earlier."

"Is anyone looking after her?"

"I checked her temperature a few minutes ago. It's gone down a bit."

I knelt beside Chiharu and shook a cigarette out of my packet of Marlboro Lights. I wondered what, if anything, Gen had told her about our encounters. I reminded myself that we used to get along quite well. "So how's it going, Chiharu?" I said inspiredly.

"All right, I suppose. I'm looking forward to getting out of here."

"You're moving?" I exhaled smoke.

"No one stays here very long. I've been here longer than anyone else who's here right now."

"So…" Her small triangular face was taut, unsmiling. I ventured a guess. "Are you going home? I mean, to your mother's house?"

"No." She turned to look at me. Half her face was in shadow, but some trick of the light made that eye, too, glitter fiercely. "That's, like, *completely* out of the question."

"Then I suppose you've found a place of your own?" That would make it much easier for her and Gen to spend time together. It occurred to me that the two of them might even be moving in together. "Congratulations."

"It's not exactly my own place. But I'd be lonely on my own, anyway. I'm going to be sharing with a couple of other girls."

It sounded like hostessing, which was not in Chiharu's line. I frowned at her.

"I'm going to be a waitress." She grinned. "In Sendai."

"Sendai?" I wasn't sure I'd heard right. Sendai, capital of Miyagi prefecture? Sendai, which could be dropped into Tokyo and lost a dozen times over? Then again... Sendai, mecca of hardcore headbangers, the Des Moines of the Far East. "Do you know someone there, Chiharu?"

"Sure. Lots of people." Her face lit up the way it sometimes did when she was singing. "The deal is that this one guy – I've known him for years – is opening a new club. There's going to be a live music venue in the basement and a lounge bar on the first floor. It's not going to be a dive with people being sick in the toilets. It's going to be *cool*. There's going to be a VJ on the first floor every night. And we'll be able to wear whatever we like as long as it's black. I'm thinking about those baggy pants I have, the ones with all the zippers, and a nice black bra under that fishnet top that only has one sleeve. And I'll put black silk flowers in my hair. Can you picture it? Won't I look *too* cool? It'll be like going on stage five nights a week. I'm thinking about getting a tattoo, too. One of the girls I'll be bunking with has a zillion tattoos. She knows the best guy to go to. Most of his clients are hard boys, but he can do modern designs, too, like flower fairies and stuff."

Was this what Gen had meant by Chiharu's throwing away her career? I wondered. Or was this scheme a comparatively new one? Was it her response to the pressures of singing with Gorot?

"Chiharu, you're not old enough to drink," I said. The legal drinking age in Japan is 20 – not that it's taken very seriously. "Isn't it a bit irresponsible of this friend of yours to hire you as a waitress? I assume you're going to be tending bar, too?"

"He's making an exception for me. Besides, just because I mix drinks doesn't mean I have to drink them myself."

"True. But what about your career? You won't very well be able to come back to Tokyo for rehearsals."

"Doesn't anyone want me to be happy?" Her voice gained intensity without rising in pitch. "Doesn't anyone understand that I have the right to make my own decisions? I don't like saying mean things about people, but Gen's the *worst:* he's such a hypocrite, wearing me out with good advice when all he means is *stay here*; and Joaquin, telling me I *have* to do this and I *have* to do that because *he* knows best; and now you're telling me what to do, too! I thought you'd support me even if no one else did! I love music, but…" She pinched one of my cigarettes and lit it with an aggrieved flourish. "I'm young, as everyone keeps reminding me. I've got years and years to have a singing career if I want one!"

I just knew I'd heard these words before somewhere.

"Besides, I'm going to perform at the club sometimes. My friend is in a band, too – he's the drummer – and he said it would be cool if I sang with them now and then."

I sighed. "Chiharu, I'm the last person who ought to hold you back. Logically, I ought to be encouraging you to chase your dream all the way to Sendai. And so, for that very reason, I have to have a shot at holding you back. Get it?"

She gazed at me for a long minute, head on one side, and then smiled faintly. "You know, I didn't even think about that. It didn't even occur to me."

The girl named Miyuki stirred and moaned. Chiharu went to her and brushed a clot of hair off her forehead.

"You're OK, aren't you, Mi-chan? How are you feeling?"

A pale hand crept out of the futon and closed on a Volvic bottle that stood amid the fluffy hillocks. It was empty.

"I'll get her some more water," I said, taking the bottle from the limp fingers.

"Anyway, Shanti, consider your duty done," Chiharu called after me. "You tried to talk me out of it. That's all anyone can do."

We assembled in the studio at the Kuroiwas' house. Joaquin had committed the band to a gig on Friday the 20th. We had three days to get our shit together.

Joaquin was hunkered down behind his table with studio headphones on, pressing buttons on the Roland and cursing in French. Tad sat on one of the amps, changing a string. Shingo, our newly hired drummer, was fooling around with the electronic drum kit that Gen had contributed to the studio, trying ultracasually to show us what he could do. The thing was switched off, so his blurring sticks produced only faint thumps. Gen had eyes for nothing except his guitar. He was practising a riff over and over, changing his fingering every time, trying to introduce a dissonance without slipping out of the key of G major. Even at minimal volume it was starting to get on my nerves. He dragged a pack of tissues out of his pocket and blotted his left fingertips. The tissue came away with red spots on it. He caught me looking and smiled guiltily.

I faced an imaginary audience and started singing scales. "Do re mi fa so la ti do," I sang in English, "Do re mi fa so la si do," in French, "どれみふぁそらちど," in Japanese.

"Cette foutue machine a bousillé les carillons," said Joaquin, tearing off his headphones.

"Oh, who gives a fuck?" I said. "We've got the real thing now. 信悟さん, 宜しくお願いします. Why don't we run through a couple of numbers without the special effects just to see how it goes?"

"Elle essaie de faire de nous un putain de groupe acoustique," said Joaquin, laughing nastily.

"Ne te mets pas dans cet état là. Ça m'est égal. But if you can't fix it, what can we do but make the best of it?" I looked at Shingo, who was an advertising salesman in real life. With his shambling frame folded up on a chair, he looked too serious to have much of that oldtime rock 'n' roll fervour. "We've done all the explaining we can, I think, Shingo; we might as well just turn on the juice and hit it."

With special thanks to Emmanuel Pourchet.

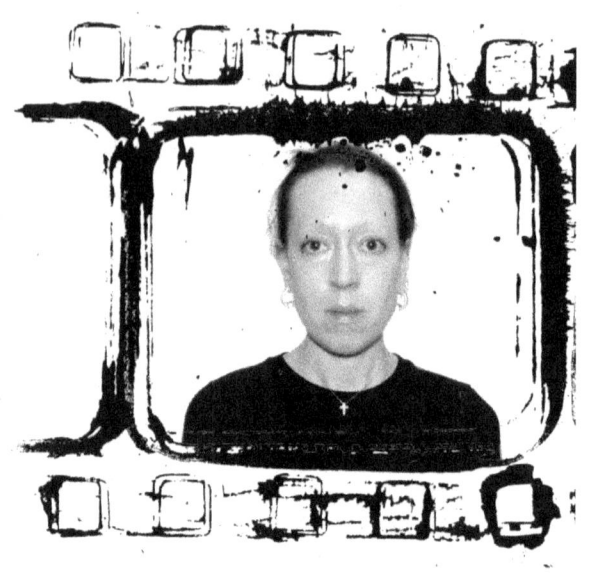

About The Author

Felicity Savage is an American fantasy author. Born in South Carolina, Savage lived until the age of two in rural France, and then in the west of Ireland. At six, she moved with her family to the island of North Uist in the Outer Hebrides, where she joined the Girl Guides and appeared in productions of Robin Hood and Peter Pan at the RAF base on Benbecula. Her first novel, *Humility Garden,* and its sequel *Delta City* were published by Penguin ROC in 1994 and 1995, while she was still at Columbia University. Her *Ever* trilogy was published by HarperCollins in 1995, 1996, and 1997. Savage was a finalist for the John W. Campbell Award for Best New Writer in 1995 and 1996. She currently lives in Tokyo, Japan, with her husband, daughter, and two cats (one fat and one insane). When not writing, she works as a Japanese translator, sings Gregorian chant, and moonlights as a serial houseplant killer.

More information is available at http://felicitysavage.com/

Author's Afterword

I moved to Japan in 2000 because I was in love. Not with anyone in particular, but with Japan itself. This was a relationship fated to end catastrophically. Love affairs with abstractions usually do, as history ought to prove to anyone with half a brain. But when we're in our twenties, we never think history applies to us, do we?

9/11 and the events that followed convinced me that history did apply to me. Suddenly, my American passport was no longer a status symbol. It was a problem. I got so fed up of answering for our government's wackier policies that I started doing a Pontius Pilate on my country: "Love it or leave it, they say – and so I did," I would twerpishly proclaim – as if I hadn't left it *before* 9/11, fleeing across the Pacific to a cooler place.

Love in Japan: Coming Clean and Four More Ways of F**king Up grew out of the contradiction between my love affair with Japan and my politically biased estrangement from the United States. Superficially, it should have been easy to embrace the one and leave the other, like moving on to a new guy when you get tired of your boyfriend – but of course it wasn't easy. It still isn't. It's a problem that has no easy solution, not for me or for the girls who narrate the novellas in this book.

The personal is not political. But the political is personal. The truck doesn't notice the bug; the bug damn sure notices the windshield.

So – what? Do you resign yourself to getting squashed? Do you give up and go home again, like Dylan Thomas's fisherman "with his long-legged heart in his hand"?

Or do you try to make a choice that'll be your own, even if it's not perfect? Do you try to be more than a bug drifting over the summer highway of love – to be somebody, or at least *something?*

Each of the girls in *Love in Japan* tries in her own way to make that choice that'll mean something. For some of them it works out better than others. Fay in *Going Under* and Shanti in *Coming Clean* make the error of taking themselves a bit too seriously. Ruth in *Good Money* takes her faith seriously, but nothing else – also an error, perhaps. Tamsin in *The Immortals* may be my favorite of these girls, for her wry irreverence and her big heart, but I'm also very fond of the nameless narrator of *The Spirit of Harlem*... oh hell, I'm nuts about each and every one of them. Writers are serial monogamists, but we never really move on.

I hope you enjoyed reading these stories as much as I enjoyed writing them.

As for me? Well, as for me, I made my mind up back in Chelsea ... ahem. I still live in Japan. And since my amazing husband and my lovely daughter are Japanese, I'll probably be here for a while. We're looking at houses in South Carolina, though.

Manufacturer's disclaimer: *Good Money* is a sort of prequel to my vampire novel, *Vampire Democracy*. I planned to write a prequel, but it turned into something else – I guess you could call it an alternate-universe prequel. It shares some of the characters from *Vampire Democracy,* but they don't all have the same names. If you spotted the other big difference, come here and let me give you a sloppy kiss... oh, sorry, did I get blood on you?

Disclaimer, part two: I am, of course, primarily a fantasy writer. I think you can see the shadows of magic creeping in around the edges of *Love in Japan,* like the shadow of an uninvited guest falling across the threshold. After all, the supernatural doesn't go away just because we decide not to mention it.

In form and function, however, the book in your hands is what the smart kids call literary fiction. That startles me as much as anyone else. It startled me so much, in fact, to have written these stories at all, that I held off on publishing them for a while. In the meantime, however... Oops, I did it again! The narrator of *Coming Clean,* the wretched would-be rock star and compulsive liar Shanti Hazard, got her claws into me so deep that I had to write a whole novel about her continuing adventures.

So turn the page for a preview of *Music to Die By,* a suspense novel starring the most messed-up American girl ever to wield a mic on a ten-feet-by-ten live house stage in Tokyo...

Music to Die By

a suspense novel by

Felicity Savage

A singer in Tokyo's scuzzy indie rock scene, Shanti Hazard buried her past long ago. But when childhood friend Ned turns up in the audience at one of her band's shows, he threatens to reveal the ugly secret he and Shanti share.

Determined to protect her friends and bandmates, Shanti plots to outwit Ned while the band tours snowbound Japan, sleeping on couches. A botched cover-up leads to murder and a tightening web of deception, as the band clashes with the merciless Japanese legal system.

Ultimately, to defeat her past, Shanti will have to confront it... and Ned... before someone else dies.

Music to Die By plunges the reader into the gritty world of the Japanese indie rock scene, building to a shocking climax. The first suspense novel from acclaimed fantasy author Felicity Savage, *Music to Die By* is now available from Knights Hill Publishing in print and ebook editions.

Excerpt follows...

Music to Die By

Part I: Unfair Game

"Let's talk about you," I snarled. "It must've been the first time. So did it excite you?"

Gen stood on my left, hunched over his Ibanez as if he were trying to protect it from the crowd. He wore his uniform of jeans and a plain black t-shirt. Sweat fell sparkling from his curls. When I tore into the chorus, he raised his head and bellowed the harmony into his own mic. He had the best voice of any of the boys, a raspy tenor that harmonized nicely with my own voice. I was more of a shouter than a singer, and inevitably got Janis Joplin comparisons, although I preferred to think of myself as the female Layne Staley, without the heroin problem. I had enough problems as it was.

Our faithful supporters swayed an arm's length in front of me, chaotically out of step. About three-quarters of our guest list had showed up by the time we went on stage. It does mean something to be headlining. And it didn't hurt, either, that Ace's High was so small that this modest crowd was a capacity one. We couldn't take all the credit: Dew Over, Bloodthirsty Fakers, and Vanilla Camp had left a residue of punters who were determined to get full value for money, curious about a band with two gaijins in it, or simply willing to give us a try. Some of them had trickled away during our first number, but others lingered. They even clapped.

Unlike Gen, I didn't just stand there. I covered the whole stage – which wasn't difficult: I could only take two paces before I bumped into Gen or Tad, our bassist. I struck poses, touched myself, danced with the mic stand, and interacted with the boys. My bottle-green top hat shadowed my face in the hot, shifting spotlights. When I finally doffed it, applause went up. I mugged, did a clownish shuffle, then hooked the hat on my mic stand and started dancing in earnest. I wore my cowboy boots, my lucky talismans, harness brown with turquoise, gold, and white flames. Their heels made me tall enough to see four or five deep into the crowd.

"Let's talk about you," I ranted, "and the little places you call home."

Tad planted his left foot on a wedge speaker and banged his head as he churned out the bass solo. A pair of black cat ears poked out of his flying hair. At home he also had floppy white bunny ears, tall grey donkey ears, and a magician's hat with stars and moons on it. He liked to wear that one with a gold kimono.

"It was the only thing you've ever done! I hope, oh yeah, I hope it was a good one."

I extended the end of the phrase into a melodic scream, jammed my mic onto the stand, and let my head fall forward as Gen took over for the outro. Through the curtain of hair that slid in front of my face, I saw constellations of cigarette ends explode in the outer darkness as the technique freaks applauded. I straightened up and gestured broadly, helping the spotlight on Gen to make its point.

Joaquin crashed both hands down on the keyboard of his Korg. An instant of silence, and then the applause kicked in. I stepped back to the mic and thanked the crowd.

"For those of you that we haven't got to know yet, Joaquin's the tunesmith." In his place behind the Korg, Joaquin bowed. "I write the lyrics. They let me do that because I can't play an instrument."

Tad grabbed my mic and said, "I've got an idea, Shanti. You can have my job and I'll have yours."

I grinned and said over the catcalls, "Shut up, Tad, I'm busy showing off my Japanese."

This got a huge laugh, as usual. To the extent I spoke Japanese, I spoke it like a native. For that I could thank my sense of pitch, but more to the point, as Joaquin could have explained, once you have a second language, it's no big deal to acquire a third one. As a kid in Paris, I'd gone from zero to fluent in French in a year, and as an adult in Tokyo, it had taken me only slightly longer than that to learn Japanese. I still had plenty of holes in my vocabulary, but they didn't show onstage.

"Now guess what, you lucky people, we're going to do a song off the new album. U-Turn Day, out next Saturday from Cold Coeur Records. Available from your local clued-up independent music store, or buy it on our website, where we're streaming select tracks for your listening pleasure. Now here's another dirty little sample." I leaned into the mic. "When I first started writing lyrics for Gorot, I didn't want to write about the same old thing. You know. Lurrrve."

Nina, Joaquin's wife and our recording angel, dodged across the Bermuda Crescent in front of the stage with her digital camera. Our Shimokitazawa gigs rarely got rowdy enough for the crowd to venture into that buffer zone between us and them. Even when they did, they retreated when the music stopped.

"But I've learned a lot since I've been in this band," I said. "I've realized that I have more to say about life in general than I ever knew."

277

I saw him.

His blond hair shone in the dark. He was leaning against the wall about three people behind Nina. At this distance I couldn't see his eyes.

"A lot to say," I repeated. "A lot to say."

I had nothing to say to Ned Gallant, now or ever.

But maybe it wasn't him. Maybe it was just some coworker of Nina's who hadn't been on the guest list, or one of the European drifters Joaquin collected.

Tad glanced sharply at me. I couldn't tell if he was alarmed, or just trying to prompt me, but it reminded me why I was here, why I'd written the song I was currently supposed to be introducing, and how I'd felt while I was writing it, in my tiny studio apartment with my headphones on, pushing rewind over and over again on the rough mix: as far from Ireland as I would ever get.

"Recently," I said, "I realized that I even have something to say about love. And this is it. 'Heartbreak.'"

I signaled to Joaquin with one hand behind my back. The silence lengthened: one, two, three, and the first plaintive piano notes floated out over Tad's bass line. Shingo tapped on the rim of the snare, a sinister rhythm like a clock ticking. Until its closing seconds, this song required no more of Gen than filler duties. "Heartbreak" was that rare thing in our repertoire, a slow burner designed to prove that I could actually sing, and that was appropriate, because it was my song of liberation.

"Struck dumb by a closing door," I sang, cupping my mic in both hands for a bit of distortion, "face down on the bathroom floor. Here's a dirty little sample, better keep it to yourself. I've lived, I've been, I've seen…"

Joaquin's line swelled, surging towards maximum volume.

"I've sunk, I've swum, I've fallen in between…"

Someone whistled deafeningly.

"And you, you think that you'll remain in my memory like a stain, but you'll fade like everyone! You were never here!"

Sweet, languid Jonathan had been the lead guitarist of the

first band I was ever in, back in New York, and I'd thought he was the love of my life, until he turned out to be a cheater and a liar. When he cheated on me, I hadn't just dumped him, I'd left the country. Top that, asshole. I'd won, but it had taken me another four years to write him, literally, out of my heart.

And in the meantime, I'd discovered something strange and surprising, better than sex and almost as good as music.

Friendship.

I'd once had a boyfriend. Now I had four boy friends who meant more to me than Jonathan ever had.

I'd written "Heartbreak" for them, and if the lyrics didn't really reflect that... well, my lyrics always turned out kind of dark.

I couldn't lose them. I couldn't, but my own words sounded like a dire prophecy as I sobbed, "Stupid enough to not quite see the temporary nature of everything behind your eyes!"

It was Gen's moment. Unexpectedly, he launched a gargoyle of a riff that climbed on the back of Joaquin's piano line and reached for the stratosphere. We'd heard this variation in rehearsal, but never live. I signaled to Tad and went for a repeat of the chorus. Gen's riff toyed with my voice, then folded up and flatlined into a distorted hum that grew louder and louder until it swallowed Joaquin's last notes.

After that, our last number was an anticlimax. I thrashed around the stage, but I couldn't stop looking at that spot over by the wall. In a montage of underexposed stills, I saw him draining a can of beer, taking off his knit cap, and putting two fingers in his mouth and whistling. So it had been him.

"Encore! Encore!"

For once I wished our supporters weren't quite so faithful.

"Encore!"

I bowed for the third time. Behind me, Joaquin hissed, "What are you waiting for?"

"No encore," I said through my smile.

"Fuck off. What's wrong?"

With the show officially over, we could take a minute to

confer. I went back to Joaquin, mic in hand. His face was scarlet and his hands hovered on the keyboard. "OK," I told him, "I'll do an encore. But not 'You're No Fun.'"

"Don't give me this shit. If you don't want to do it, why did you want it on the set list?"

"Joaquin, I can't fucking do it!"

Joaquin's jaw tightened. He seized the mic from my hand and plunged around the Korg, shaking the cord clear. "OK, we'll do another track from Xenophobia," he said out of the side of his mouth. "They've heard the whole album many times, but what the hell."

He arrived at the front of the stage in a single stride with his smile on full. A storm of clapping greeted him. Everyone knew he was the brains of the band, and although he seldom took a producer's bow, they felt he deserved it. He thanked them in English, Japanese, and French, and waited for the applause to subside. I hovered at his side, trying to look supportive rather than apprehensive. He said in Japanese, "We are delighted that you come all the way to Shimokitazawa to see us. I mean, it's the middle of nowhere, eh?"

Laughter.

"We hope you will come all the way to Hokkaido to see us, too! We can't reimburse you for the airfare, but we think it will be worth it. They say that Sapporo is a beautiful city. Myself, I've never been there, but I'm looking forward to it. Yes, ladies and gentlemen, Gorot is going on tour!"

I did what I had to do, which was lead the applause. When we were debating whether to tour for U-Turn Day, I'd been anti. I didn't know why I even bothered, since Joaquin always got his way in the end.

"Some of you are familiar with Kinderbox," continued Joaquin, naming another of the acts he produced for our label, Cold Coeur Records, which he also owned. "We tour together. We will look for you next week in Sapporo! Hakodate! Aomori! Morioka! Yamagata! Sendai! Fukushima! And Utsunomiya! But if we don't see you there, we hope to meet on Tuesday the twelfth of March at Oasis in Shinjuku, where we plan a party for our homecoming. It is also the release party for U-Turn Day! Yoroshiku onegai shimasu. Also," Joaquin added rapidly, "we have gigs upcoming throughout March, please check out the information on the flyers. We're running late, but we will do one more song for you tonight. 'Dreamstomper.'" Throwing me a look of triumph mixed with a challenge, he hopped back behind the Korg.

Numbly, I waited for the piano loop to roll out of the speakers. In the interval of rustling silence I cleared my throat. "This one's for everyone who got lost along the way," I said, wishing Ned Gallant had.

Backstage, Nina handed out bottles of Crystal Geyser. Joaquin upended his over his head, splashing everyone. "To Cold Coeur Family Volume I!" This, unbelievably, was what our tour had come to be called. Infected by his mood, the other boys slavishly acted like they'd all been excited about it from the start. The manager played along, too, opining that it would be just the ticket to launch us into the big time. Joaquin followed him into his office to sort out our cut of the door. After retrieving our kit from the stage, Gen, Tad, and Shingo piled into the cruddy little restroom down the hall and jostled for access to the tap.

I gulped water. As soon as Joaquin squared the manager, we were due to join up with our faithful supporters and head to an izakaya. Ned might turn out to be someone else, and it wouldn't be the first time. My fight-or-flight reflex often went off at the sight of a blond head and a pair of blue eyes. But if it had been him...

Pushing a hand through my damp, tangled hair, I went out the side door and said hello to my friends. There were about two dozen people left in the house, and I didn't know all their faces, let alone their names. Back in Gorot's early days, the same people had come to all our gigs and we'd gone to all their gigs; now we had friends and fans, and it was getting harder to tell which were which. I clocked the blond guy hovering near the exit.

I went back through the grey room, past the manager's office and the restroom, looking for another way out. There was an emergency exit, but it was padlocked.

I retrieved my shoulderbag, threw on my coat, and ducked back through the side door. I didn't have a plan. All I knew was that I had to keep Ned away from the band. I couldn't be sure that he wouldn't approach me in front of them, and I was even less sure of my own ability to deny to his face that we'd ever met. I wasn't even sure that would be the best line to take. He might react unpredictably.

"Shanti, you're not skipping out?" Nina said in astonishment.

"You're on PR duty, gorgeous," I said. "Oh, I left my hatbox back there. Could you take it home with you? I'll come over and pick it up tomorrow or sometime."

I beelined to the exit, calling goodnight to the technicians who were shutting down the equipment onstage. As I passed the blond guy, he took an abortive step towards me. I pushed through the door into February. His footsteps echoed mine on the stairs. Out on the street, the rest of our supporters were hanging around in groups, smoking and chatting. I shouted to them that I had an early start tomorrow and inconsistently turned left, away from the station. He caught up with me. I kept walking. At the 7-11 on the corner I turned again. He matched my strides. A cold, dusty wind blew around us.

"Fuck, this feels weird." His voice was deep. I'd subconsciously been expecting him to sound like a child. "But it feels kind of natural, too, doesn't it?"

"Well, it's been a while," I said, head ringing.

"A while?" He laughed. He looked like none of the men I'd mistaken for him over the years. He was still blond, and his eyes were still that eerie blue – but he was no longer small or pale or skinny. His skin had seen a lot of sun, and he hulked over me with shoulders as broad as the axle of a small car. He'd turned out as big as Nigel. But his accent no longer sounded like Nigel's. It had softened dramatically. "I guess you've added the art of understatement to your repertoire. It's

been half our lives. No, more. I was twelve, and your birthday
is before mine, so you'd have been thirteen."

He spoke as if he didn't remember exactly. This confused
me.

"So how's Alastair doing these days?"

We were turning corners at random, and although I
couldn't remember crossing the railway tracks, we must have
done, because we were now descending the gentle hill on the
far side of Shimokitazawa station. Shuttered boutiques lined
the narrow street. Here and there, golden light from the windows of a restaurant shone through a screen of trees. The wind
numbed my face; it seemed to have penetrated to my bones
and slowed down my brain. Ned and I were talking. How had
this happened?

"Alastair lives in the States," I said. My brother had spent
his early twenties trying to be an artist; now he was the assistant manager of Windrose & Sons, a 150-year-old gallery in
Boston's Back Bay that sold objets d'art and antiques from all
over the world, true to its origins as a clearing-house for plun-
der from the Orient. He and his girlfriend Maisie lived together in Somerville with her second-hand Volvo, his BMW 6-
series, and two Weimaraners, and he seemed happy. "He's
doing OK, I guess."

"Figures. He was bound to land on his feet. And June? Still
painting, is she?"

"She moved back to France years ago," I said. Our mother
had nothing to do with it. Ned would have no reason to track
her down, nor could he learn anything from her he didn't already know. "She lives near Bordeaux now. It's la France pro-
fonde, the true France. She keeps chickens and goats. And
yeah, she's still painting her heart out."

Ned laughed. "You know something funny? All this time I
thought your family was still in Thailand."

"You're kidding! We only stayed there for six months."

I remembered promising Ned that he could come with us.
Promising it would be all right. But I was only thirteen and it

wasn't my decision to make.

Ned would probably have hated Thailand, though. We did. After Ireland, it had been so hot that I felt like I'd stepped onto another planet. I remembered the energy draining from my thirteen-year-old body, the sunlight so bright that my eyes hurt, and a hundred and one permutations of boredom and anxiety. That was nothing to how June must have felt. She'd dragged us halfway around the world to the one man who had to take us in: our father. Malcolm Ogilvie had settled in Phuket. He was a poet – we'd owned an actual book of poetry by him at one point – but he subsisted on the generosity of hotel and bar managers who gave him odd jobs. From his point of view, having the three of us descend on him must have been the worst trip of his life, especially since he had a live-in Thai girlfriend.

Somehow, we all managed to cohabit in his disgusting bungalow for five or six months. That was how long it took June to accept that she'd made a mistake. She fell back on her brother Red, my corporate lawyer uncle in Philadelphia. And just like that, as if the first thirteen years of my life had been a dream, I'd suddenly had the life of a privileged American teenager.

Not for long, though. Unlike Alastair, I hadn't been able to keep it up.

"As for our father," I said, "he's dead."

It was Ned's turn to exclaim, "You're kidding!" And in his smile I saw a hint of schadenfreude that chilled me to the bone.

"He hanged himself about ten years ago," according to the letter that the Thai girlfriend had sent June. It had been wrapped around a small teak box that contained Malcolm's ashes. "He left a typical, self-pitying note. Saying he'd failed everyone and he was sorry. Talk about wasted sentiments. *We* weren't."

Ned hissed between his teeth. I thought I'd succeeded in shocking him. But he said in the same easy tone as before, "Funny thing is, *I* live in Thailand now. On Koh Samui. I go across to Phuket all the time, and I used to ask around for you, but no one's ever heard of you or your father."

Shit.

"Ned, how on earth did you end up in Thailand?"

"I'm an architect," he said, and went on expansively, in the strange nonaccent he'd acquired. "Koh Samui is booming. The tsunami created a lot of opportunities. New regulations, new land up for sale. I've got my own business, building villas. Referrals from all over. The clients appreciate having someone on the ground to see their projects through to completion: they don't want to deal with the Thais themselves. They're racist fuckers, as a rule. But I believe in doing the best work possible."

"Wow."

"I'm building my own house, too. It's still under construction. I've been working on it on and off for the last four years. But it's going to be fucking stunning. I can show you some photos if you're interested."

Laughter bubbled up in my chest. Ned was a *builder*. I didn't know why this struck me as so funny. I said, "Cool. Did you study architecture at school?" I wanted to find out where he'd spent the twelve years that were still unaccounted for. Why couldn't I just ask?

"Sure, I learned on the job. That's the best way. Hands-on experience. You've got to be focused, though. Thailand is full of Westerners who just drift from beach to beach…" Ned shook his head.

"Oh, we've got them here, too, except they don't come for the beaches. They come for the jobs."

"Still, I can't criticize that lifestyle. I lived on Bali for a while. Bummed around Indonesia, Malaysia, India." We reached the level crossing at the bottom of the hill. The barrier was down, the warning bell pinging. "I guess I was looking for something, but I didn't know what it was," Ned shouted as a train rushed past. "Maybe it was just a decent living," he added, laughing.

"Look," I said, pointing to a record shop on a side street. "They sell our albums. We've got our own label, and we're hooked up with an independent distributor."

"Oh yeah? Way to go!"

"Jesus, Ned, what *has* happened to your accent? You sound almost American."

"You sound fairly American yourself, Shanti."

"Well, I went to school on the East Coast. High school in Philly, and then NYU." No need to mention that I hadn't graduated, committing myself to rock 'n' roll instead of to the library.

"Get a load of you. I didn't go to university at all. After you left, my grandmother showed up and took me back to Denmark with her."

"Denmark!" That was it, of course. He didn't sound American. He sounded ever so slightly Scandinavian. The legend came back to me all at once: the mother who did a runner when Ned was three, leaving Nigel to raise him whilst making a go of his business, Allihies Ceramics. I even remembered Ned telling me where she'd come from. Somewhere like Norway, but without the funky mythic associations. *Denmark.* "I didn't know you even *had* a grandmother!" I said.

"Neither did I, until she walked in and told me to pack my stuff. I had a terrible time adjusting in Copenhagen. Couldn't get my tongue around the language. I used to think about you and Alastair jabbering away to each other in French. How did you do it? I picked up enough Danish in the end to get by, but as soon as I got out of school I buggered off. I used to go back as often as possible to see my grandmother, though. I owed her, didn't I?"

"She must be an amazing lady," to have put up with you, I added to myself.

"She was. She died last year."

"Oh Ned, I'm so sorry."

I caught his flickering glance of contempt. He didn't believe I was sorry, although when I said it, I *had* been.

We rounded the corner onto the plaza. I veered towards the station entrance and started up the stairs. Ned climbed beside me. He was explaining how it was that he could jaunt off to Japan at his pleasure, with zero hardship or sacrifice, but

I wasn't really listening, because I knew it was just a bunch of excuses. I was wondering if I could lose him in Tokyo's fiendishly complicated rail system. "Have you got a ticket?"

"I need to buy one, do I? Where to?"

I thought quickly. "To Shibuya, but the tickets are priced by distance. It's a hundred and twenty yen."

I watched him shoulder through the milling crowd to the ticket machines, scoop change out of his pocket, and examine every coin before putting one into the slot. I had a prepaid Passnet card. I thought about dashing through the wickets while his back was turned. But there was only one platform. I'd have much better odds of losing him in Shibuya, where the JR, Tokyu, and Keio Inogashira train lines and the Ginza, Hanzomon, and Denentoshi subway lines all looped around each other in a multistorey knot.

As we came out of the wickets at Shibuya, I plunged ahead of Ned into the horde pouring down into the Mark City building. He seized the shoulder strap of my bag. "You don't mind if I hang onto you? This is fucking mad. I've never seen anything like it in my life. Feel like I'm about to be swept off my feet."

"Yeah, it's crazy, isn't it," I said, teeth gritted in frustration.

But then again, if I'd cut and run I would have looked guilty. And he'd just turn up again at our next gig, wouldn't he? My only hope was to brazen it out and get rid of him by some means as yet beyond the reach of my imagination. Leave him as completely as possible in the dark.

Yet every minute he was finding out more about my new life. I showed him how to buy a JR ticket and we rode the Yamanote line south, squashed shoulder to shoulder between drowsy drunks and noisy ones. At Gotanda I got off. He got off. We left the station and walked along a dark street, embroidered on one side with snack bar signs, which led back along the foot of the Yamanote line embankment. There was no traffic. Gotanda was an undercover town, buttoned up during the day and sleazy by night, with the highest concentration of love hotels south of Shibuya. You never bumped into anyone you knew here, which was why it suited me.

Among the office buildings on this side of the station towered a few elderly apartment blocks. I came to the dinged elevator doors at the foot of my building and turned to face Ned, feeling panicky. "Well, now you know where I live."

"Pretty ritzy." He craned his neck to look up at eight floors of concrete balconies.

"At least it's supposed to be earthquake-proof," I said.

"Oh sure, that would be a concern in this country."

We stood between the morgue-like walls of mailboxes. Was he waiting for me to invite him in? Did he plan on crashing *at my place?* No. No. No. This was not happening.

"Whereabouts are you staying, Ned?" I said bluntly.

"I've a couple of mates living in the city." He looked away from me. There was a trace of anger in his voice. "They came to Japan to work and save money, and they're spending it as fast as they make it, but they're good lads. I'll introduce you at some point. Mike's got a job in the public school system; Gavin works for one of these English conversation schools, same as you. They're raking it in. So they've a house, not just a crappy little apartment, in Nakano. You know where that is?"

Five minutes west on the Chuo line from Shinjuku. A goodly haul from here. But nowhere would be far enough.

"I can stay with them as long as I want. It's party central, but I'm not fussy. You've no need to worry about me on that score!" Ned chuckled, an unamused masculine sound that reminded me of Nigel.

"Ned, how did you find me?" I blurted. Immediately, I had a sensation of having taken a misstep. "I've often thought about *you,* but I had no way of knowing where you were."

He looked at me for a long minute. I concentrated on not letting a muscle of my face twitch. At last he said, "I searched for your name on the internet. Googled you, and up you popped. Your band's website. Pictures and everything."

I'd known it. I'd *known* it.

"So I knew it was you. Of course, it had to be you; there

can't be two people in the world named Shanti Hazard."

Oh God. To hell with staying true to myself. I should have changed my name.

"That was about eighteen months ago."

So I'd been living in jeopardy, my illusion of safety hanging by a thread, for more than a year.

But how could I have talked the boys out of putting up a website? How could I have forced them to leave me off it? I was the face of Gorot, literally – Tad had used a picture of me for our logo, and they were always pushing for more pictures: pictures of me walking on the beach, drinking coffee, laughing out loud – pictures that would make me seem like someone you knew. I vetoed all but the blurriest live shots. That had made me feel better about the website, as did the fact that not much of the information on it was in English. But what difference did that make when my *name* was out there?

"I thought about getting in touch there and then, but you know how it is. Life gets in the way. By the time I finally got around to it, I thought I might as well just pop over and see you. So I got a Japanese mate to translate the squiggly bits for me, and here I am!"

"And how do you like it so far?" I keened softly through my chattering teeth.

"Well, I'll tell you. It's bloody confusing and it's bloody cold." Ned lowered his voice conspiratorially. "And do you get the feeling that these people don't know how to relax? This is according to my Japanese mate at home, but the culture here is fucking totalitarian. The level of social control is such that the people can't make their own choices. If they could, maybe they'd choose to be a bit more free!"

"I like it here because I fit in," I said, provoking a cry of disbelief from him. I explained, though it felt futile: "I didn't do very well as an American. It's much easier to be a foreigner."

"Well, in that case, then, I know what you mean! It was a nightmare living in Denmark, as I said. Looking like them but not speaking their language, not knowing their TV shows or their songs, not knowing shit about their fucking history and not caring. But when you're a Westerner out East, no one cares where you supposedly come from. No one asks why you've got a funny accent. You don't have to pretend to be something you're not. You can be yourself, can't you?"

Ned's face lit up as the words tumbled out. I didn't want to agree with him about anything, so I said nothing.

"Shanti, this is the kind of conversation I want to have with you! It's not everyone who understands, is it? But you're on my wavelength. You've had the same life experiences. You were *there.*"

Feeling dizzy, I steadied myself on the mailboxes.

"I just want to talk. No games, no bullshit." He looked eagerly into my face. "I just want us to be open with each other."

"Yeah, OK," I said faintly, "but can we do it some other time? I'm dead on my feet, and if I don't get indoors, I'm going to die of hypothermia."

"Oh well, then, I won't keep you," he said, drawing back with unsettling rapidity. "We couldn't have *that,* could we?"

END OF EXCERPT

Music to Die By is now available for purchase from your preferred online book retailer in print and ebook editions. Learn more about the book and the author at http://felicitysavage.com/

www.ingramcontent.com/pod-product-compliance
Lightning Source LLC
Chambersburg PA
CBHW071258170626
46809CB00001B/271